THE FALL OF DEADWORLD OMNIBUS

An Abaddon Books™ Publication
www.abaddonbooks.com
abaddon@rebellion.co.uk

First published in 2020 by Abaddon Books™,
Rebellion Publishing Limited, Riverside House,
Osney Mead, Oxford, OX2 0ES, UK.

10 9 8 7 6 5 4 3 2 1

Creative Director and CEO: Jason Kingsley
Chief Technical Officer: Chris Kingsley
Head of Books and Comics Publishing: Beth Lewis
Editors: David Thomas Moore,
Michael Rowley and Kate Coe
Marketing and PR: Hanna Waigh
Design: Sam Gretton, Oz Osborne and Gemma Sheldrake
Cover: Clint Langley

Based on characters created by John Wagner and Carlos Ezquerra.

ISBN: 978-1-78108-835-7

Printed in Denmark

THE FALL OF DEADWORLD OMNIBUS

MATTHEW SMITH

ABADDON
BOOKS

For Evie and Joe

*And with thanks to John Wagner, Alan Grant,
Brian Bolland, Kek-W and Dave Kendall,
whose nightmares I freely borrowed
in the writing of these stories.*

INTRODUCTION

What is it about Judge Death's popularity that endures so? When he first entered the *Judge Dredd* strip—four decades ago this year, no less—John Wagner and Brian Bolland's superb design for this mirror image of Ol' Stoney-Face himself made him an instantly iconic addition to the series. If Dredd was the ultimate authority, capable of dispensing summary justice without need for trial or juries, then here was the twisted extension of that idea: a Grim Reaper figure believing that since all crime is committed by the living, life itself must therefore be crime. Dredd's robes of office—the eagle, the shoulderpad, the visor, the badge—all become warped with gothic iconography (bones, skulls, a portcullis), and his no-nonsense grimace is replaced by a terrifying rictus grin. Death was a dark reflection of Dredd, no less driven by his adherence to his version of the law, and the readers lapped it up, especially when he was joined by his lieutenants Fear, Fire and Mortis—they were the perfect villains, pure in motivation and horrifyingly ruthless.

Yet, compared to other comic-book arch-nemeses—the Joker in *Batman*, say, or Lex Luthor in *Superman*, or Dr Doom in the *Fantastic Four*—the Dark Judges have appeared relatively few times in the history of the *Dredd* strip, not much more than a dozen stories featuring them across both *2000 AD* and the *Judge Dredd Megazine*. Despite the characters' credo of overkill, keeping the audience wanting more clearly generates anticipation. When they do appear, they make an impact, and any mention of Death and his murderous cousins on social media yields hundreds of likes and replies. The entity formerly known as Sidney has a following, and is guaranteed to provoke a reaction. He's the supernatural being we love to hate—a Dracula, a Freddy Krueger—that sends chills down the spine even as he entertains. A Halloween costume come to life.

Given Death's fanbase, it was felt that maybe there was potential in a series of novels surrounding him, as had proved successful with Dredd and Anderson. But where to set them? Current continuity has the superfiend off-world and decimating a deep-space colony, and that felt to me to limit your storytelling options. More satisfying would be to embed the tales within *The Fall of Deadworld*, the *2000 AD* prequel series by Kek-W and Dave Kendall that showed how the Dark Judges rose to power and began butchering their planet. End-of-the-world fiction has never felt more prescient, and in Deadworld we had all kinds of creatures going about the bloody business of global annihilation.

I borrowed elements from Kek and Dave's gallery of grotesques so it cleaved fairly closely to the strip—the grey Judges, Justice Department's hideously mutated attack dogs, the Psi-Div freaks, the blazing funeral pyres, the general air of despondent gloom—but created my own protagonists, seeing society around them crumble. For the first book, *Red Mosquito*, I had a hankering to write a lowlife crime story, inspired by novelists like Joe R. Lansdale and Carl Hiaasen and films such as *I Don't Feel at Home in This World Anymore*, where our dim-bulb hero Jackson McGill finds himself ensnared in events he doesn't fully understand (the idea of it opening with him beating up the wrong guy, and thus kicking off the plot, was sparked by a Soulwax lyric). Jackson's criminal adventure, however, is of course set within an ongoing apocalypse, and it's seeing Sidney's coup from the street level; we hear there's trouble in the Grand Hall, but it's not until the second and third books, *Bone White Seeds* and *Grey Flesh Flies*—what I call my '*trois couleurs bleurrgh*' trilogy—that we encounter Death and co properly.

Adding flashes of personality to the likes of Sidney and the Sisters of Death, Phobia and Nausea, fleshing them out, so to speak, with their own agendas and character quirks is great fun, as is coming up with the horrible fates that await the poor sods whose world is being destroyed. It may not seem like a barrel of laughs to read about a planet being hurried towards its extinction, and the fact that ultimately their destiny is unavoidable, since we've seen what becomes of Deadworld, but I've tried to add grace notes of hope and the indomitable human spirit in the face of overwhelming odds, because in our worst moments that's when people often shine best. Plus, y'know, zombies, cannibalism, locusts, all the good stuff.

Without further ado: '*Let the dead fluidssss floowwwww...*'

Matthew Smith
Oxford, February 2020

PART ONE

RED MOSQUITO

CHAPTER ONE

I WAS NEVER a believer in predestination. Hell, if pushed I'd struggle to spell it. It seemed an unlikely state of affairs, your life attached to these rails that lead to one inevitable conclusion. It's a comforting school of thought, I have to admit, to consider that every shitty choice you ever made was fated to happen, that every bum deal you were handed you were never going to escape. Kinda takes the sting out of the guilt. *Que sera sera*, and all that—whatever will be will be, so fuck it, there's nothing I could've done to change it.

But I can't avoid accepting the responsibility, however attractive that sounds at the time. The trains I take are mine alone to board, and where they take me is a journey of my own making. I am the master of my own destiny, even if that destiny is to be a washed-up asshole with no prospects. I got myself to here through every bad decision and crummy situation I found myself in, and no matter how much I'd like to drink that knowledge into oblivion, the fact is that it's no less true. Nothing is fated; the future is yours to mould and shape as you see fit. Your life is in your hands, not the mysterious whim of the cosmos. Sure, I could blame a lot on the arbitrary roll of the dice, and the fact that Lady Luck's been mainly smacking me in the face lately rather than softly nibbling the nape of my neck, but I feel it's better to own your screw-ups rather than rant about outside forces you've got no control over. No one likes a whiner, after all.

So, yeah, I'm well aware of who's at fault for putting me in my current predicament, and I'm cool with it—in the sense that I'm not bitter as opposed to unwilling to change it, because I would be quite happy for the chance to climb out of this pit. But that would require commitment, sobriety and drive—attributes that I don't necessarily possess in abundance; and money too, and it's the lack of folding that's possibly the root of everything. Does my pursuit of the green get me into these scrapes? Probably. Does it plunge me further into debt, in an ever-tightening downward spiral of self-loathing, thereby necessitating me to take jobs that I would otherwise baulk at? Oh, most definitely.

Anyway—predestination. Not a believer. Or I wasn't. But sometimes I guess a moment comes along where you feel it's a turning point; it's setting your life on a path that you're not going to be getting off. It's got nothing to do with choice; the event's been handed to you as a *fait accompli*. Or what's that other Frenchie phrase? *Force majeure*. This is the universe taking that big old junction lever with both hands and giving it a wrench, tugging you onto a whole other set of tracks entirely, and you get no say in the matter: you just have to respond accordingly, which is mostly by barrelling along head first towards the new end-point. Now, you may disagree—you might reckon I could've done things differently at any time; taken a way out, a side exit, picked another route. But I suppose we'll have to not see eye to eye on that, 'cause as far as I'm concerned I'm sure—sure as eggs are cluckers—that my future was mapped out that night. Fate took a guiding hand, and swept me along a road I couldn't turn back on.

Fact is, the bottom crapped out of the world the evening I beat up the wrong guy. I mean on a global scale, not just in some localised woe-is-me way: the whole actual planet went down the shitter. I'm not naïve enough to think that what I did was the catalyst—I'm sure this stuff had been building for a while, and I only became aware of it in the slow, dim, dawning realisation of a man who's just been alerted to the fact that he's on fire—but it felt like a through-the-looking-glass episode. Everything was changed, both within and without.

Now, I don't make a habit of beating up guys, wrong or not. Or at least I don't do it for pleasure. But unfortunately it's something my somewhat sorry state of affairs has dragged me to, and efficient acts of moderate violence are one of the few skills I can legitimately lay claim to. Thirty years ago I was a boxer of reasonable standing—welterweight, semi-pro—and had the potential to make a name for myself in the ring. I was fit—frighteningly fit—and had ambition to burn; I used to spar with Thad Dewberry, if you remember him? This was before he became four times national champion, naturally. Knocked him on his ass on more than one occasion too. Freddy, my trainer, said I had raw, natural talent, and at the risk of blowing my own trumpet, I *knew* I was good: I was fast, nimble, with enough aggression to power a decent right hook, and an obstinate streak that meant I never knew when to quit. So, of course, I took all that aptitude and ability and threw it all out the window in exchange for a serious gambling addiction. Cards, dice, roulette: I was a sucker for everything, and the more it took hold, the bigger my debts grew, and the faster that physical discipline drained right out of me. All I could think about was the next game, and where I could secure the funds to enable it, and with that my concentration was shot.

Organised crime circles the sport like sharks round a stricken dinghy, and outliers on the fringes of the Mob were more than willing to lend me the cash with an interest rate scarier than some head injuries I've received. I took a dive a few times, I'm ashamed to admit, and ploughed the payoffs I got from those straight into my next poker session. I did some bare-knuckle fights—cracked my eye socket, was hospitalised for a spell with bleeding on the brain (which may or may not have had more of a permanent effect than the quacks let on). I backed out of those pretty quick. By this point I was in my mid thirties and starting to feel gravity's sag. I wasn't the dancer on the canvas any more; I was lumbering, and threatening to do myself wheelchair-worthy damage.

I retired from the ring while I could still see and speak without a slur, and got a job at an automobile plant. Picked up a nice little alcohol problem too, which made sure the ship sailed on the last of my fitness: pants got that much tighter, breath got a shade shorter, heart palpitated more times than I cared for. But I... Listen, I don't know why I'm telling you this, or why I think you would want to have all this personal info frontloaded onto my tale. Like, you didn't ask my life story, right? I guess the point I was making was that I wasn't always a bum, and that current fiscal circumstances are the reason I agreed to rough up a complete stranger. Once I abandoned the boxing, my income plummeted, but unfortunately my love affair with the cards didn't lose any of its ardour. Next thing I know, I'm being informed that my debts that I'd spread around town had been consolidated into one big chunk of change that I owed a guy who called himself the Bushman.

I'd never met this dude, and still haven't; the reasons for his moniker are as shrouded in mystery as his facial features. I didn't know anything about him, but he sure as shit knew plenty about me. His intermediaries informed me of his preferred repayment plan, but made sure to point out that if I was willing to do him what they called 'favours', then he would see about shaving off a few kay. This sounded voluntary, but I never considered refusal was ever an option, and frankly a couple thousand off my tab looked better on the balance sheet than the inevitable broken limbs that were heading my way if I didn't start returning my loans. The Bushman was well aware of my former sporting prowess, and figured to exploit it, even though it had been a good half decade since the last time the old Jackson McGill piledriver had been called into use. It was still there, that jab, even if time had not been kind to the body that it was an extension of.

So I became de facto Mob-boss muscle, directed as required. I threw up after the first time I beat someone to a pulp, disgusted with what I'd become, and haunted by the look of fear on their faces just before I slammed my fist into them. They were squirrelly little saps for the most part—losers like me who thought they could take the money and run—and nothing like my opponents in the ring, who had come out of their corners snarling with the intention of delivering equal amounts of hurt. These submissive pricks, on the other hand, snivelled and blew snot-bubbles and apologised profusely, and sometimes I hit them more than was necessary just to get them to shut up. I didn't need to hear it—my own head was filled with doubts and regrets and broken glass, and I didn't want it to get too crowded in there. Block it all out, I told myself. Give the bozo some bruises to remember the Bushman by, and skedaddle. The drinking came into its own there, I have to admit; it was great for blurring memories. I embraced the bottle even more.

I know how all this sounds, and I'm not expecting you to like me. As I say, how I got here is through my own choices, and no one else's. If I was smart, if I truly wanted to get out of this life, then I'd knock the gambling on the head, stop racking up the debts. But I'm well aware that's not going to happen any time soon—and most pertinently, so does the Bushman. He's got no desire to lose me, I'm too much of an asset. Thus, here I find myself, trapped in a role of my own making.

I got the call just after five on my way home from work. I live a little outside of town in a two-storey shitpile on the edge of a derelict street just before the suburbs give way to scrubland and the woods, and it's a good half-hour drive past the factory stacks and abandoned car lots. I saw my cell chirrup on the passenger seat of my Pontiac as I edged it through the rush-hour traffic, rain splodging the windscreen. I knew who it'd be—they always texted from the same number and at the same time. I found a public call box and pulled over, hitching my jacket collar up and ducking through the fat, warm drops to the kiosk.

I don't know if this is the benefit of hindsight colouring my recollection, but something felt off even then: more people seemed to be out in the weather than you'd expect, and they appeared agitated, restless. Sirens blared several blocks over. The radio said something about tailbacks across the river. There was an edgy vibe, as if tensions were going to spill over any second, but I didn't know for what reason. A guy slammed his palm against the call box window and shouted something indecipherable, then tried to yank open the door; I told him to fuck off and he took the hint, but his eyes told me he was barely aware of what was going on. A few more just like him stomped past, and I remember pausing to watch them, this herd of crazies surging down the street, demented in their terror. That should've been the first sign, I guess, but I must've passed it off as random loons—the city wasn't short of them. Even the Judges weren't exactly stable, at the best of times.

I punched in the number and got the message: gimp staying at the RestEazy motel on Rothman, near the airport. He'd booked himself onto the 7.30 flight to Hugersfield, way up north. I was to stop him getting on that plane and gently remind him that he owed fifty kay in unpaid debts, a commitment he was freely welching on. Don't cripple him, they said, just make him piss blood for a week. They gave me a brief description, and I could picture him instantly, since he was virtually identical to every other sadsack that I'd put the frightners on—tubby middle-management drone drowning in a wretched coke habit, and not even embezzlement to the tune of a quarter of a mil could keep him supplied in snow and ensure his girlfriend was happy and sufficiently far enough away from his wife. Dabney Krinkle was his name, like it mattered—I whale on one of them, I've whaled on them all.

I had to book if I was to make it to the RestEazy before he checked out, so I ran and slid back into the car, burning rubber towards the freeway. The news broadcasts weren't kidding about the traffic; the filter lanes were rammed nose to tail, and several of the drivers had given up entirely, abandoning their vehicles and fleeing along the hard shoulder. I still didn't have a clear idea what had put a bug up so many people's asses, and the pundits on the radio weren't clarifying anything—I heard the word 'coup' several times, and listening between the lines, it sounded like some kind of military takeover at the heart of Justice Department. A damn quiet one if it was, since there hadn't been any suggestion of small arms' fire from what I'd seen... but who knew what was going on in the Grand Hall? Something was certainly scaring the locals, unless it was mass hysteria: I'd seen pack mentality in action before. If I'd had the time, I could've stopped someone and asked if they knew what the hell they were running from, but I suspected I would've got little sense in reply.

Madness, I thought. I assumed it'd blow itself out by morning.

I got off the freeway first chance I could and tore down the back roads instead. The newsreader was now listing areas of the city that were either off-limits or impassable, and it seemed like they were radiating out from the centre, sectors being shut down systematically. No wonder so many cits were bolting; they were being forced out towards the edges. Static crackled from the speakers, and before I could retune the radio, it went dead. Nothing was audible on any station other than a low hiss. That was disconcerting. Even the twenty-four-hour evangelist guy had been silenced, and not even the revelations about him and the fifteen-year-old had managed that. The car felt uncomfortably quiet and empty, and darkness was falling fast beyond the glass.

I was driving parallel to the airport, I realised, but on the other side of the chainlink fence, nothing was stirring. No planes taking off or landing, no lights, no signs of life. It occurred to me that maybe all flights had been cancelled—grounding the aircraft sounded like the first sort of thing the military would do in the event of a governmental overthrow—and that I wouldn't have to worry about catching the mark before he departed. The counter-argument in my head reasoned that Dabney possibly wouldn't know that, and could still try to scurry away. I spotted the RestEazy and swung in to the kerb opposite the entrance, turned off the engine and leaned forward in my seat, arms on the wheel, confident I had a decent enough view.

A family were throwing their suitcases in the back of a taxi while the dad was shouting at the harassed-looking driver. They eventually drove off in a cloud of exhaust fumes, destination who-knew-where. Beyond the doors, I could see further consternation in the lobby as arm-waving dweebs berated the receptionist, luggage piled around them. It seemed like everyone was getting the shit out of Dodge; or at least they wanted to and were being frustrated by the lack of transport options. I looked up at the motel façade and saw a few lights on in the windows, indicating some residents at least were staying put, then thumbed the number for the place into my cell, gleaned from the buzzing neon sign hanging off the corner. It took several unanswered calls and a couple of redials before a female voice finally responded with a barked expletive.

I asked to be connected to Dabney's room and the line hummed, then rang. I remained optimistic: she hadn't said he'd checked out. The receiver was picked up after the sixth ring, though no one offered a greeting other than short, quiet breathing. I listened for a moment, waiting.

"Dabney Krinkle?" I asked.

No confirmation or denial, other than the breaths hitching up a notch. Then the line went dead. I scanned the front of the building again, watching the few illuminated squares that were the occupied rooms, and sure enough one blinked out seconds later. The spooked Mr Krinkle was on the move. I pocketed the cell and resumed my study of the main entrance, running his distinguishing characteristics through my head as I awaited his appearance.

People were threading out now into the street, bags gripped tightly in fists, glancing around, wondering where the hell they were going to go. A trickle became a crowd and I sat up, worried I was going to miss him. My eyes roved over the sweaty, concerned faces, trying to zero in on my target. Seconds later I spotted him—tubby, white balding dweeb, glasses perched on his conk, *snap!*—and I wrenched open the car door, tracking him as he stumble-tripped along the sidewalk, away from the bulk of the others, briefcase clutched to chest, head turning left and right as if hoping to catch sight of another cab. I followed discreetly, the others paying me no heed, more important things evidently playing on their minds.

I picked my moment just as he was well separated from the throng and crossing the shadowy junction with the RestEazy's underground car park. I closed the distance in a matter of seconds, wrapped my arm around his neck, and pulled him further into the gloom; he was surprisingly light, and shock meant he offered little resistance. I pushed him up against a wall, satisfied we were alone, and hit him hard on the bridge of the nose, just enough to make the stars dance before his eyes. I always lead with a good pop to the face, gets them disorientated. He gasped, glasses went flying, and his legs buckled. I caught him and propped him back up. He didn't let go of his briefcase though, I noticed. I gave him a couple of quick slaps to get him to focus.

Now I had his attention, I could go to work.

CHAPTER TWO

CHAPTER TWO

SLACK SUBSERVIENCE I kinda expected; nine times out of ten they lose all bravado the moment that first punch connects. The weeping... yeah, it goes with the territory. You always get your snot-noses, who think an attack of contrition is going to make you go soft on them. Usually the opposite in my case—I tend to get less sympathetic the more they blub. But this Krinkle dweeb, man, it was like he was on another planet; like he was barely there. I figured it for drugs at first, and wondered if anything I did was going to pierce whatever chemical haze he was hiding behind. Couldn't have been coke—maybe he'd graduated to smack.

"Do you know who sent me?" I said, his collar bunched in my right fist. He was looking at his feet, still clutching that damn briefcase, trembling slightly. I slammed him against the wall, gave him a backhand with the left. "You know why I'm here?"

He was eerily quiet. Tears formed in the corners of his eyes, but he didn't make a sound. It was starting to creep me out a little bit, and today had been weird enough as it was. I gave him a couple of solid hits to the stomach that left him doubled over and retching, then a flathand to the ear that I knew would sting.

"Answer me!" I snarled, losing my temper a tad, and got

no response. I didn't want to prolong this—like I say, I get no pleasure from strongarm work, and I wanted him to acknowledge that his actions were the reason why I was doing what I was doing. I glanced at the case and grabbed the handle, pulling it away from him. That got a reaction: he grunted in panic and tried to yank it back, an unsettling squeal issuing from his throat. I tugged harder, wrenching it free, then swung it upwards so the corner cracked against his temple. He staggered, then planted himself on the ground ass-first. Blood trickled from a cut below his eyebrow, which he made no attempt to stem.

"Please... give that back..." he breathed. "You don't... understand..."

"I understand that the Bushman wants his money, Dabney," I replied, throwing the case down to one side. It was one of those sturdy plastic-shell jobs, but weighed next to nothing. It couldn't have contained all of the several thou that he was owing. "You spent it all, is that it?"

"What...?" Krinkle murmured, and met my gaze for the first time. There was confusion in his red-rimmed eyes, the first genuine hint of emotion that wasn't passive compliance.

"The Bushman—the gent that bankrolled your snort habit. He ain't happy that you seem reluctant to repay your debt, and sent me as a reminder. What, you were hoping you could skip town and he wouldn't notice?"

He shook his head timidly and reached out towards the case, started crawling towards it. I tutted and put my foot on it, sweeping it along the ground out of his reach. He gave another wheedling cry of exasperation and screwed his eyes up tight, face turned towards the cold concrete. He was starting to do my head in, so I gently placed my boot on his still-outstretched hand and pressed down; he hissed in pain and started to struggle. I applied a little more pressure, and his cries rose in volume.

"Listen to me," I said evenly, making sure I had his attention. "Are you listening to me?" I ground my heel into his palm for a second to punctuate the question, then I leaned forward. "Pay the Bushman back. Pay him what you owe, you get me? 'Cause he'll find you if you don't, and he'll send others that will make sure you never walk again—or worse, throw you off Ankrelli Point and leave you to the gulls." I removed my foot and he snatched his hand back, cradling it in the other. I swiftly toed him in the ribs. "Pay him."

He was whimpering and shaking his head repeatedly, as if trying to deny that I existed. His lips moved slightly, but no recognisable words could be discerned. I had to admit it was a hell of a performance to get out of paying your due. Normally, they gabbled how sorry they were the moment you even threatened violence, and were all but reaching for their chequebooks before you'd so much as bloodied their noses. Not this fruitloop.

"Dabney," I sighed, lighting a cigarette. "Don't do this to yourself. It'll only get worse from here."

He continued to mewl like an animal caught in a trap. Nothing was getting through to him, and his decidedly odd behaviour was starting to piss me off. I stomped over to where the case lay and picked it up, shaking it as if it was an enticing Christmas box. He got more agitated when he saw me holding it, so I persisted. Something was inside—it rattled loosely—but the thing was combination-locked and wasn't going to be opened easily. He shook his head harder as I turned the case over in my hands.

"What *is* this, buddy?" I asked. "Huh? All that's left of your stash?" The guy didn't take his eyes off it as I tossed it from left to right. "Christ, how much of a habit do you have? You think maybe it's time to quit?" For emphasis, I smashed it against the corner of the wall behind me. He shrieked so I did it again, and again. Noticing the catch buckling, I bounced it for a fourth time off the concrete, and the lid twisted up. A blister pack of vials came flying out onto the dirt. He scrambled for them, and I had to tear them from his grip to get a better look; they appeared lab-issue.

An *oh shit* light blinked on at the back of my skull as I sucked hard on the cigarette, peering at them. The tip glowed in the darkness, illuminating a series of ten-digit product numbers stamped on the otherwise blank packaging. Krinkle was meant to be some no-mark furniture-store manager—where the fuck had these come from, and what was he doing with them? No way had he picked these up from a chemist.

Trying to get an answer out of him was pointless, so I flicked the cigarette away and reached into the jerk's jacket, fumbling for the inside pocket. He didn't resist. I found his wallet and yanked it out, stepping away. I had a bad feeling about the situation. I kept half an eye on the guy still lying prone on the sidewalk—though he was making no attempt to move now; instead, he was simply watching me—and flipped it open. Inside was a modest amount of cash, and tucked near the front was his ID: a goofy photobooth pic glared back, next to which was the name Martin Stender.

Crapsticks.

I felt a bit woozy myself. I dropped the wallet, brain whirring. I'd got the wrong dude. Where the hell was Krinkle? Still back at the motel? Or had he vamoosed in the opposite direction while I'd been following *this* poor innocent sucker? I couldn't understand how Stender matched the description I was given... but then I thought about how all these dingleberries look alike after a time, how they're a certain type. This guy unfortunately fell into that certain physiological bracket, and was unlucky enough to be in the wrong place at the wrong time. The stars aligned briefly, and put me on collision course with him.

Shit. *Shit.* I felt like I was losing it. Sickness churned in my guts like gravel. I'd never needed a drink quite as badly as I wanted one then. Never mind that I'd just violently assaulted a blameless bystander, the Bushman was also going to want to know whether Krinkle got his message, and right then I had no idea where he was—which was going to put *me* in the firing line. I'd screwed this up royally.

"Ah. Look, man, I'm... I'm sorry," I said. "I've really fucked up. I thought you were... well, it doesn't matter who I thought you were. I was mistaken." I moved towards him. "Let me help you up."

Stender made no attempt to clasp the hand that I'd proffered, so I had to get my forearms under his pits to haul him upright. He jittered, uneasy on his feet, and I laid a palm on the small of his back to steady him. I saw his specs lying in the dirt, so picked them up, gave them a rub-down and handed them back. He was making a babyish breathing noise, so I passed him back the vials too, which he snatched out of my fingers and clutched to his chest.

"I feel truly awful about this, I really do," I said. "I got the wrong guy. It was dark, you kinda matched the description I was given... I probably should've made sure beforehand." I glanced at him to see whether he was taking any of this in, and he looked as spaced out as ever. Any further apologies were going to be falling on deaf ears. "Can I... Can I get you home? Least I can do in the circumstances. You wanna go back to the motel, or I can drive you somewhere? All sortsa crazy out here right now, dunno if you noticed. Getting indoors might be the best place to be."

I genuinely felt bad for the sap. Poor ding-dong was clearly not all there, and I'd come along and beaten the tar out of him. This foul-up was on me, and now I felt responsible for keeping him safe. I doubted he was badly hurt—any bruising was going to be superficial—but nevertheless he'd feel better if he was off the streets.

I asked him again where he was going when he left the motel, but he simply staggered forward, mouth opening and closing a fraction but nothing issuing forth. He fondled the vial pack like it was rosary beads. I went back to the battered briefcase, and shook out was left inside—another half dozen of the packs tumbled out, identical to the first, which I stuffed in my waistband and covered with my shirt before kicking the case into the shadows. Figured they were important to him, if no one else.

I put my arm around his shoulders and had started to guide him forward when the whoop of a siren caught both our attention and we froze. I squinted at the headlights that were pinning us, their beams harsh in the dark. Two Justice Department Lawriders rolled up beside us, the Judges astride them for the moment just silhouettes etched out of the blackness.

Fuck. Tonight just got better and better. I patted my jacket pocket, made sure my piece was hidden away from view, and stepped sideways from Stender. I had no intention of tangoing with the law.

"Help you, officers?" I called out, exuding non-confrontational co-operation. It didn't pay, in my experience, to antagonise the jays—they had a taste for brutality that they weren't slow to indulge in. Litterers could find themselves with broken legs, thieves a crushed skull. They maintained order through fear and the ever-present threat of applied violence. Needless to say, the ranks were rotten to the core, and corruption was rife. I knew for a fact that the Bushman had several in his pocket, and were routinely employed to exterminate rival dealers and loan sharks.

The Judges swung themselves off their bikes and approached. Something struck me as off even before they got close enough for me to see them clearly: they moved stiffly, and a little jerkily, like they were relearning how to walk. A pungent stench preceded them. I felt my throat go dry and my balls constrict as unease rippled through me. I immediately wished I was holding the gun.

They came into view and queasy details coalesced. They were both helmeted but the skin that was visible between the collar of the uniform and visor looked rancid; open sores stippled their necks and lips, and the nose of one had been shorn off entirely, in its place a pair of black holes oozing mucus. When their mouths creased into sneers, their teeth and tongue were furred with green mould. An involuntary gasp caught in my chest, and I heard Stender whimper beside me. For a moment I was paralysed, rooted under the eyeless gaze of the two figures. I remember thinking I hoped to Christ they didn't remove their helmets; I didn't want to see what lay beneath.

"That's a look," I said before I could stop myself. "Halloween come early this year, officers?"

The smiles grew wider, cheeks splitting in unison, red rawness gleaming beneath grey, papery flesh. "Change," the first replied, his voice thin and scratchy like the soft flutter of moth wings. "We accepted change. Ssoon the world will too."

"From one sstate to another we asscend," the other whispered. "We drank the Fluidss to purify uss of our ssinss."

"Drank the Kool-Aid, more like," I murmured. "Is that what all this madness is about? Some cult thing?" I'd heard of religious mania sweeping through tinpot dictatorships in foreign lands, of shamanistic leaders encouraging people to rise up in the name of some bogus cause. Doomsday freaks, mainly, believing the End Times were here. Mass suicides encouraging the Rapture to pluck them all up to heaven. Rational thought poisoned by rabid fanaticism. But this was the capital—where had *this* sprung from? How had it taken hold so quickly?

More importantly, what was the deal with these two pus-heads? This was not just some weirdo ideology they were spouting—this was a physical transformation. The fuckers were *corpses*, for God's sake.

"The living will be judged," Judge Nasal Cavity said. "The guilty will be ssentenced."

"Come forward to receive punisshment, ssinner," his pal hissed and reached forward, grabbing hold of my shirt and yanking me towards him. I instinctively resisted and took hold of his wrist to tear myself free. That was a mistake: the body was cold beneath the uniform, and softer than it should have been. My fingers clamped down on liquescent tissue, and my stomach did a roll in silent disgust. Nevertheless, the jay still had some strength at his disposal and wouldn't relinquish me.

"Don't let them touch you," Stender blurted, suddenly the

most animated he'd been all evening. "Don't let them get any closer."

The badge that had a hold of me stopped momentarily and did this awful neck-swivel, as if he had lost all his vertebrae. He slid his attention from me to Stender in one slow, fluid motion and studied the man before jerking his head and indicating that his no-nose friend take care of him. No-Nose unsheathed his spiked billy-club and stalked forward, repeating mantra-like that life itself was a crime and the sentence was death. My one turned his attention back to me and tightened his grip, my shirt bunched up in his surprisingly solid fist.

The vial packs that I'd tucked into my waistband came loose and tumbled onto the sidewalk between us. They caught the Judge's attention, and it paused. Stender had seen them rattle onto the ground too, and panicked, trying to barge forward and retrieve them, but he was effectively blocked. "Don't let him get those!" he shouted to me.

"What... are you doing with thesse?" the lawman whispered, and relaxed his hold on me slightly in order to bend down and pick one up. I seized the chance, and brought my knee into the Judge's face just as he was starting to stoop—it crunched into his visor and I could feel bone and cartilage separating. He let go, and I followed up with a powerhouse punch to the side of the neck, the jay crumpling before me.

I snatched up his daystick from his belt before he could recover and pirouetted on the spot, driving the business end into the side of the other cop's head. The helmet didn't offer much protection and caved spectacularly, the spikes embedding themselves deeply into his skull. The jay barely made a sound, just a short sigh, and turned awkwardly in my direction, the billy-club now lodged at a right-angle in his head. He took a step forward, and I pulled the gun from my pocket and shot him point-blank in the face. His putrescent features vaporised, and he dropped to the ground instantly. I turned and put a bullet in the back of the other one's head, just as he was starting to rise. It blew a sticky mass of dark matter out the front of the visor and onto the sidewalk, and he collapsed face down into it. Both were now motionless, lying in spreading pools of ichor, the daystick next to them, blown out by the force of the bullet.

I breathed out, only then realising that I'd been holding it, aware of my heart thudding against my ribs. I met Stender's gaze and he looked equally shellshocked, but he moved before I did—he crouched down and gathered up the vials, holding them to his chest.

"We have to go," he said. "More will be coming."

I nodded and grabbed his arm, pulling him towards my car, the gun still gripped in my right. The Pontiac was where I left it opposite the motel entrance, which was something, at least. The building was all in darkness now, even the foyer, and one of the main doors was streaked with blood. Yeah, we weren't going back in there. I manoeuvred Stender towards the passenger side and unlocked it, indicating that he get in. Pockets of weirdies scampered past, an unhealthy glint in their eyes; I lifted the automatic and exuded enough of a 'don't-fuck-with-me' vibe that kept them at bay. Something major was on fire a block away, the heavy clouds stained orange by the leaping flames. Glass shattered in the distance. Screams. I was starting to wonder if *anywhere* was safe.

"Let's get out of here," I answered numbly, getting behind the wheel.

We peeled away, and drove at speed out of the city.

CHAPTER THREE

The guy didn't say a word in the car, just curled up on the passenger seat like a kid past his bedtime, still clutching those damned vials. His head was turned to the window so he was facing away from me, but I could tell from the reflection whenever I glanced over that he wasn't paying much attention to what was beyond the glass. There wasn't much to see outside anyway, now that darkness had stolen across the sky and we'd threaded our way out of the city. I'd purposefully chosen the back ways and minor roads to avoid the congested areas, and that meant we skirted the vast, flat Badlands, emptier than a church collection plate on a Saturday night. There was no light out there save the twin beams of the Pontiac's headlamps illuminating the tarmac and the sulphur-glow of the moon above.

With no conversation forthcoming, I was left to ruminate on what I'd just seen and done, not that it made a whole pack of sense. Ashamed as I am to admit, those weren't the first men I'd killed, if you could call them men (and I'm assuming they started out normal at some point). I'd been responsible for the deaths of three others over the years—two boxing related, and one in a drunken brawl in a bar, my Mob contacts getting me out of the legal predicaments of all of them—but the pair of worm-sacks that I'd put down tonight were the first that I'd ever shot. I'd pulled my gun plenty of times in the interests of self-defence, knocked a handful of squirrels out of trees when sitting in my backyard, but never popped an honest-to-God human being with one, having never had any desire or reason to. Having done it, it felt kind of removed, like I'd played only a small part in it. I guessed that was why guns were so popular: they took the hard work out of killing.

These weren't just everyday knuckleheads, though. This was a couple of Judges, the murder of which under regular circumstances was an offence punishable by summary execution. What I'd done was a pretty big deal. But these weren't regular circumstances—that was becoming painfully clear—and whatever those lawmen had been, they'd crossed over into something else before I'd blown their oily black brains out. Some takeover had happened at Grand Hall, and the cops had ingested something, been exposed to something, that had turned them. They'd looked half dead; rotting creatures that had crawled out of a grave. One of them had mentioned fluids—it sounded like a zombie ritual.

Christ knew what horrorshow was going on at the top, but the madness was evidently spreading. Swinging the car into my driveway, I was gladder than ever for my relative isolation; few visitors ever came out this way, and that was just the way I liked it. That situation probably wouldn't last if the crazies were on the march, but for now the street was deserted. I climbed out, jogged round and opened the door for Stender. He initially didn't move.

"Come on," I encouraged. "We'll be safer inside."

I put an arm round his shoulder and he didn't resist as I guided him out of the passenger seat, up the porch steps and across the threshold. Flipping on the lights, I was faintly surprised to find the power still working. I directed him towards the kitchen at the rear of the house, and eased him into one of the three rickety chairs that lined the pine table.

"Be better if we didn't let anyone know we're here," he murmured, gazing at his hands cupped together on the tabletop.

"Huh?"

He flicked his head towards the bare bulb blazing from the ceiling. "Keep the signs of life to a minimum."

"Oh. Right." I could see the sense in that. I dug around in a cupboard and found an old oil lamp, which I lit and placed on the table, before clicking the lights back off. The lamp just gave off a weak orange aurora that threw most of the room into shadow. I grabbed a bottle of whiskey from a shelf, took a slug straight from the neck, then plucked a pair of tumblers out of the sink and set them down between me and Stender.

He shook his head and held up a hand. I poured us both a couple of fingers each anyway, knocking back mine in one gulp before refilling my glass. I pushed his towards him. "Take a drink."

"I don't need it."

"It's good for shock, believe me. Settles the nerves. You'll feel better for it."

He took a long look at the glass, then picked it up and downed the contents. He grimaced and coughed, shivered a little, but slid his empty tumbler across the tabletop towards me and I did the honours, splashing some more into it. I could feel an alcoholic buzz setting up residence at the base of my skull, and was content to sit in silence for a moment, eyes closed, letting it mellow me out.

"You think they'll come looking for us?" I asked finally.

He let loose a bitter, exasperated laugh. "They'll come after *everyone* eventually." His voice was hoarse, throat seared by the whiskey. He spoke in a strange monotone, like he was explaining himself to a dim-witted six-year-old. It irritated me, but I was glad he was talking as I wanted some answers. I figured the booze had loosened his tongue. "If we stay here, it'll only be a matter of time. We should be all right for now, as long as we don't draw attention to ourselves. They may be looking for me once they discover I'm gone, but there's no reason for them to know I'm with you."

"The two jays I... I shot. Is that gonna bring down some heat—?"

He shook his head as he took a sip. "They got bigger fish to fry. Soon that's going to be just a drop in the ocean."

"They..." I spat the word into my drink and fixed him with a glare. "So why are *they* going to be looking for you? You know anything about what's going on? It's like the fuckin' end of the world out there."

"Not yet," he answered slowly. "But it's the start."

"Who *are* you, Stender?"

"Not the fool that owes your boss money, I think we've established that." He prodded at some bruising above his right eye for theatrical effect.

I downed the whiskey in one fiery swallow. "Yeah, man, I said I was sorry. Mistaken identity. You were just in the wrong place at the wrong time."

"You some kind of hitman?"

I snorted back a chuckle, swinging back my arms to indicate the state of the room we were sitting in. "Yeah, 'cause this is how professional hitmen live. You should see my second home in Aruba; it makes this place look like a dump, hard as that may be to believe." I poured my third, draining the bottle. "No, I ain't a hitman," I said, slapping the cap back on. "I'm a... an errand boy. I do what I'm told, go where I'm told, menace who I'm told, so I don't end up with my own balls in a vice."

"How's that working out for you?"

"Peachy. Half a dozen more broken legs and I get my own parking space." I could feel a sour mood coming on. "I seem to recall I was asking about you. Why might they be after you?" He didn't reply, dropping his gaze back to his glass, and my patience was running out. I slammed down the empty bottle on the tabletop and got to my feet, striding round to his side, pulling one of the vial packs off his lap before he could react. I brandished it before him, snatching it away when he reached for it. "What's the deal with these things—what are they?"

"They're dangerous, is what they are. Give that back—"

"They're dangerous? You've seen me before I've had a drink, and I put you in the fuckin' dirt in a heartbeat, pal. How much control you think *I'm* going to have when I'm fully wasted? So if you don't want to find out, start answering my questions right now."

He shifted uneasily in his seat. "They're biological."

I studied one, gave it a shake. From what I could see, they contained nothing more than a couple of millilitres of clear fluid each. "It's... what, an agent? A toxin?"

"Of a sort."

"Where'd they come from?"

"The Grand Hall."

My attention shifted from the vials back to Stender. "You a Judge?"

He shook his head quickly. "No, an auxiliary. I work—worked—in Tek-Division. R&D. One of the back-room lab guys, you know? The white coats."

"Did you make this?"

"Not directly. I worked on part of it—there were lots of us, designing different elements. None of us knew the full ramifications of what we were putting together."

"Which are?"

He looked away, and downed his own glass, gripping it tightly. His eyes moistened, and he wiped something off his cheek with the back of his hand.

"Tell me," I persisted, rattling the pack. "What *is* this?"

"You don't understand." His voice took on a reedy quality. "The order came from the Chief Judge, we had no choice—"

I pushed the table away from him suddenly, which made him visibly jump. The table legs protested against the tiled floor, and the bottle rolled off and smashed. I kicked his chair back, and he yelped, struggling not to topple over. *"Tell me."*

"It's called Red Mosquito," he yelled, panicky. The colour had drained from his face, his lashes gleaming with tears. "T-that's its codename. That was what the project was referred to as."

"What is it? What does it do?"

Stender swallowed. "The plan... the plan was to release it into the food chain. It's an inhibitor—it kills off cells, stops them from regenerating. The life form would be dead within four hours of first contact. Seeded into the water table, it would wipe out vast swathes of animal life in a matter of days."

"What...? Why? Why would you think that was a good idea?"

"We *didn't* know, that's the point. We were working on different parts. Orders, you see? I thought I was engineering an antibacterial agent that strengthened white blood cells. I never... I never had any idea what they were using my research for."

"They... This is the Chief Judge? What's his name—Drabbon?"

"There's been a change at the top. There's a new guy in charge; he has his own underlings. It's like a cult. They're ultra-hardcore—they want control by any means. I think... I think they're attempting some kind of genocide to strengthen their position."

"Christ." My legs went a little wobbly, and I had to support myself against the table. "So you got out?"

"Gathered up as much of the prototype as I could before they came for me. Rumour had it that those that refused to co-operate were being dispensed with. I thought if I could get a plane out of the country, I could show some foreign authorities what was happening here—might get them to intervene. The Mosquito was my proof. But all the flights were cancelled; the Judges grounded everything. They don't want anyone getting out."

"This isn't everything?" I held up the pack. "They have more?"

He nodded. "Yes. The... the new head of Tek, he took charge of it all. He... I'm not sure he's human. He doesn't look right."

"Not human?"

"He calls himself Mortis." Stender ran trembling hands over his face. "Dear God, they want to kill us all."

* * *

I ALLOWED THE lamp to burn low, let the dark flood the kitchen. We sat in silence, exhausted, scared and a little bit drunk, and I needed a moment to process what I was being told. Stender quietly muttered to himself as he nodded off, the words indistinct; it sounded like a repeated apology, intoned under his breath, which dissolved into a soft, steady snore. Elbow on the table, one hand under his chin propped him up, his head lolling forward every now and then and threatening to drop face-first onto the hard wooden surface. I contemplated doing nothing, an angry part of me feeling he kind of deserved it, but decided I was being an asshole unnecessarily and went and got a ratty-looking cushion from the living room and placed it under him.

My own eyes felt heavy and gritty, but I couldn't offer myself up to sleep, my head churning with too many thoughts. I stood by the window, my forehead against the cold glass, and listened to the world descending into chaos. As far removed as my house was, I could still hear the crackle of gunfire and the muffled explosion of a building going up in flames deep in the heart of the capital. A Justice Department vehicle rumbled overhead, searchlights roving amongst the clouds, and I instinctively ducked behind the curtain. I didn't know who was on the side of law and order any more, who was the enemy. Surely there had to be those within the Grand Hall that were opposing this coup; that were fighting this madness? Was what I was hearing the sounds of a resistance pushing back against the monsters that had taken root at the highest level? Or it being swept aside?

Ironic, I thought, that I should be caring about who the good guys were any more, when my own relationship with the Judges had always decidedly been one of supreme ambivalence. Economics generally drove my sense of morality rather than any abiding belief in right and wrong. I wished it was otherwise, but a distinct lack of folding has always been my primary motivator, not the greater good. I liked to think I wasn't malicious or overtly criminal, just had a flexible approach to the law, especially if I could benefit financially. And now... now it felt disconcerting to have the Judges' authority upended, like the centre of gravity had shifted. Who was coming to anyone's aid? Were we on our own, left to fend for ourselves as everything collapsed into anarchy? Someone like the Bushman would no doubt be revelling in the power vacuum that this was creating, and the opportunities complete social breakdown would offer for exploitation. He was probably already planning what deals he could make with the new regime, one that was a bit more lax on the whole justice/punishment side of things. Having seen its foot soldiers first-hand, I sincerely hoped he'd underestimated the true nature of whatever was in the process of overthrowing the Grand Hall, and was about to discover that there's *always* a bigger predator. Fucker deserved to be eaten alive.

Watching the flickering orange thread on the horizon as the city burned, I was struck by the fact that this could mean change for me, too; that I wasn't necessarily beholden to the debts of the past. My history, my obligations, could equally be put to the torch. I was on a new path, directed towards a different fate by tonight's events. I didn't have to be the same Jackson McGill; I didn't need to conform to what was previously expected of me, or what I expected of myself. I could step up.

I glanced back at the slumped figure at the table—this stranger into whose path I'd stumbled through my own dumb luck and ineptitude—and the vials that lay scattered around him. I felt some kind of key was being offered here, one I had no choice but to accept. What was the alternative, when it came down to it—to sit here and wait to die? To try to flee amongst all that mania, when they were closing off every way out? I didn't want to be caught and exterminated like vermin.

I moved from the window and nudged Stender awake. He snuffled and opened bleary eyes, groaning as he rubbed his temple.

"Christ, what rotgut did you serve me?" he mumbled, pulling himself upright in his chair.

"It's the antifreeze that gives it its kick," I said. "Listen, we need to get moving. I'm not sticking around until they come for us. If the world's going to shit, then nowhere's going to be safe."

He sobered up pretty quick. "What are you thinking?"

"The thing you said was heading up Tek Division..."

"Mortis."

"Yeah. It was in charge of this Red Mosquito project—you said it had the rest of toxin. Enough to do serious damage?"

"Oh my God, yes. Just what I got here"—he motioned towards the packs—"would be enough to eradicate an entire species. It's got a vault-load—they've probably manufactured more since the prototype tests."

"Does it work?"

"I've seen a lab full of dead bovines that says so."

"Another three cheers for science. Makes you proud."

"That's when I got out," Stender snapped. "When I saw its applications, I got the hell out of there." He grimaced. "Can I grab some water? I don't feel too good."

"Be my guest." I nodded to the sink, and watched as he stumbled to his feet and crossed to the taps with his tumbler, washing it out before filling it and taking a swig. He stifled a belch, and filled the glass again, though this time he paused before it reached his lips. He held it out in front of him, then quickly crossed to the light switch and snapped it on. I squinted at the sudden brightness.

"I thought you said no lights—" I started.

"Look at this." Stender wafted the glass under my nose.

"What?"

"Look."

I peered closer. At first, I saw nothing out of the ordinary, just the cloudy murk that passes for tap water around here (it's never been what you could call inviting; that's why I've sworn off the stuff and drink my poison neat), but something caught my attention: a tiny white flicker that was gone almost instantly. A moment later, I glimpsed it again, twisting with the swirl of the liquid and its own motion.

"There's something in the water," I said, shaking the tumbler and watching the motes eddy. I saw one curl and flex. "Jesus Christ, what *is* that? Is something alive in there...?"

Stender didn't reply, simply spun and bent over the sink, sticking two fingers down his throat without hesitation. He retched, then vomited copiously, spinning the tap with his left hand to wash the bile away. I stepped back from the reek of sour alcohol. He coughed and spat, taking deep raspy breaths, arms hunched on the draining board, face still hovering over the sink.

"You got any bottled water?" he said finally without turning round.

"Fuck no."

He sighed, and his head dropped lower in resignation. "You got *anything* that isn't forty-eight per cent proof?"

"There's some juice in the fridge. Might be on the turn."

He pushed himself away and yanked open the refrigerator door, retrieving then taking a gulp from the OJ carton. He replaced it and wiped his mouth.

"You okay?" I asked, realising I was still holding the glass of contaminated water. "What's in this?"

"Micro-organisms. They've already got into the water supply."

"Like a virus?"

"I don't know." He took the glass from me, gazed at its contents. "Could be a parasite. Either way, they'll have gone for the most efficient mortality rate, one that could wipe out vast swathes of the population. Multiple organ failure, lung damage, that kind of thing. Maybe even something that attacks the nervous system."

"Something that would send the people mad?" I asked, thinking of the crazies that I'd seen running rampant in the streets earlier that evening.

"A variation on a neurodegenerative, sure. If you want to murder the population, why not get them to do half the work for you?"

"Christ, man, are you going to be all right?"

"Guess we'll have to see. Hopefully, I didn't consume enough. But don't touch the water from now on unless you know the source." He tipped the tumbler down the plughole.

"Consider me warned."

"You said about getting out of here."

"I've been thinking… I gotta friend—Loxley. We should talk to her about what we can do to stop this Red Mosquito."

"You'd help me?"

"Right now I don't see there's any other choice."

"I don't think you've told me your name."

"Jackson McGill." I stuck out my hand, which he shook firmly.

Fate sealed, path taken—far as I was concerned, there was no turning back now.

CHAPTER FOUR

We departed the house at speed. I left the front door hanging open, unconcerned as to who might use it as a home now. I wasn't coming back, and there was nothing of any worth anyway, no keepsakes that had any sentimental value. I barely gave it a backwards glance: I had no emotional ties, it belonged to an old life.

A searchlight swept up the road and caught us in its beam before we could climb into the car—an H-Wagon was banking overhead. Both of us paused and stupidly watched it circling, arms shielding our eyes from the glare, transfixed for a moment. When I realised it was getting lower, I had the gumption to get moving, and indicated Stender should do the same. The backwash of the craft's engines as it descended was blowing the dirt in my front yard in a circular dance.

"They coming for you?" I shouted over the roar of the wagon's thrusters as I pulled the driver's door shut and cranked the engine.

"Could be they've tracked me already," he replied, peering anxiously through the windshield. "Might just be a coincidence."

A bolt lanced out of the sky and carved a gouge in the earth a foot or so away from the Pontiac's hood. We both jumped. I put my foot down on the accelerator and twisted the wheel, the tyres spinning on the grass and mud, and shot away, the back-end fishtailing wildly. I fought to keep it under control as it screeched onto tarmac.

"Figure that's not a coincidence," I said, looking in my mirror. Bright light painted the road behind in sharp monochrome. The wagon was somewhere above us. "I reckon they've been keeping tabs on you ever since you went AWOL. Wouldn't be surprised if those two jays we encountered were on their way to pick you up. Just your good fortune you happened upon me first."

"Yeah, I'm still counting my blessings about that one."

"Funny man." I slalomed past some abandoned vehicles, their occupants long since departed. "I bet a little light GBH seems pretty fucking preferable now. Hold on." I threw the car round a hairpin bend, barely easing up on the gas. Stender gripped his seatbelt nervously. We were passing through woodland now, thickly clumped conifers on either side. "They still with us?"

"Think so. Looks like they've gone higher. Too much foliage around here for them to stay too tight on our tail. Are we heading away from the city?"

"Yeah. Loxley's out in the sticks. I don't wanna lead these goons to her, though. We gotta lose them somehow."

We hit a clearing, the ground flattening out and the tree canopy becoming sparser, and almost instantly another laser blast seared through the night air and impaled the trunk, the Pontiac shuddering from the impact. I wrestled with the wheel, the undercarriage now scraping along the road. The car was careering into the bushes at the edges, and I stomped on the brake, swearing loudly, trying to arrest its spin.

"Oh Christ," Stender murmured, glancing round. I followed his gaze in the mirror and saw flames licking the paintwork around the rear window. Beyond it, the car had been demolished, nothing more than a crumpled knot of glowing metal. It squealed against the tarmac.

"Spark could send the whole fuel tank up," I said. "Car's a write-off. We'll have to bail."

I let the Pontiac slide off the road, and it tumbled onto its side as it hit a ditch and rolled, a second before a third beam fired from the H-Wagon lit up the dark and ignited the brush where the vehicle had been moments before. The car travelled several feet on its roof, then came to rest against a tree trunk. I was already unbuckling and kicking open the shattered windscreen before it had even come fully to rest, and gave Stender a hand to free himself from his seat. We flopped backwards off the hood and scrambled deeper into the woods, putting as much distance between us and the burning vehicle as possible. We stopped to catch our breath in the undergrowth, hearing minutes later a soft *wumph* as the Pontiac finally went up in flames.

We sat back against a moss-covered log and didn't speak, simply listening to the distant crackling of the flames and breathing in the stink of burning gasoline. I realised that's all I could hear: it was nearing dawn but there was no birdsong, and nothing fluttered amongst the leaves. It was as cold and quiet as a mausoleum.

"No birds," I remarked, my voice sounding strangely dislocated.

Stender glanced up. "Mass migration. They've seen the way the wind is blowing."

"Abandoning us to our own extinction, huh?"

"You can't blame them for not sticking around. It's a natural instinct to fly from species annihilation."

I let a hollow laugh escape. "Then what are *we* doing?" My immediate reaction should've been to run as far away as I could once all this kicked off, to hole up somewhere remote and wait for the end of the world to pass me by. Instead, here I was sprinting towards it, actively trying to do something about stopping it—or at least lessening its effects. This was most definitely a new path for me.

"Guess you can't fly if you've got nowhere to fly to," he answered.

There was a moment's pause, then I said: "Talking of flying, can you hear anything else?"

"What do you mean?"

"The H-Wagon. Has it skipped out?"

Stender frowned, cocked his head to one side. "No, can't hear it. Maybe they think we're dead."

"Thing was, I didn't get the impression that they were trying to take us out. They had every chance to blow the hell out of the car, and instead they went for shots that incapacitated. I think they were trying to disable us, with a view to capture. Most specifically, you."

"I'd imagine they want me dead as much as everyone else."

"Maybe, maybe not." I turned to look at him. "Me, they don't give a shit about—I'm collateral damage. But you—I'm starting to think perhaps they still need you. The packs you took, I figure they got plenty of their own—you said yourself they could manufacture Red Mosquito in multiple quantities by now—so they wouldn't be after those. It's *you* they want. Your services are still required."

"But I was just one of many who worked on it—"

"And maybe they've got all the others back at HQ, and you're the last one they need. Or maybe all the others are dead, and you're their final chance."

"Final chance?"

"Perhaps they can't get it to work."

"But I saw the test results. The thing was lethal, and extremely efficient—"

"I don't know, I'm not a boffin. Could be they can't get it to work on the scale they'd hoped for—fine for lab specimens, but a failure when it comes to spreading among the animal population. They want you to go back to your research and fix it." I shook my head. "This is all guesswork. I have no fuckin' clue as to their motivations. But if they want you alive, it's a fair bet it's because they need you for something."

"I would never—"

"As far as they're concerned, you don't have a choice, pal. They could probably pull what they need straight out of your head, like those creepy-assed psi-pigs Justice Department wheels out when they want to question someone." People I'd known who'd experienced the interrogation cubes at their local sector house had spoken of having their minds read by psychic cops. It wasn't, by all accounts, a pleasant sensation to endure. It sounded to me like the creepiest shit imaginable, to have someone leafing through your brain, seeking out your guilty secrets. "This Mortis creep—you said he wasn't human."

Stender was quiet for a moment. "No," he said finally. "He was a normal man once, I think. But he's changing... physically. His skin, his bones... He's becoming something else. Something not living."

"Like those maggoty fucks I put a bullet in earlier?"

"Yeah. What you've got to understand is that I think there's a greater power at play here. An entity is responsible for the new CJ, Mortis and the rest, making them what they are. A... a higher level of intelligence."

"Are we talking God... or the devil? This does feel kind of biblical. An end-of-days vibe."

"Neither. More like alien. A being from outside our perception, our universe, is directing them, intent on wiping out all life. Its foot-soldiers are doing the dirty work on its behalf."

"Jesus," I breathed. "Can we really stop it? I mean, do we have *any* kind of chance?"

"I don't know. It's doubtful. It feels so powerful, so... remorseless."

Something rustled amongst the bracken. Both of us froze, glanced at each other, then slowly eased ourselves to our feet. I peered into the green but could see no sign of life. Stender started to whisper a question, but I shushed him quiet, held up a hand, and took a step forward, trying to look past the low-lying branches. The dry leaves crackled again as if a small creature was snuffling through the roots. I reeled through all the likely possibilities in my head—rodent, wild pig, deer—and kept waiting for it to pop its head up above the scrub, but it stayed out of sight, the tremor of a bush several metres ahead the only indication that there was anything there.

I swallowed, my mouth suddenly dry. The events of the last twelve hours had me jumping at shadows. I had run countless times through these woods in my fitter days and would've normally paid no attention to whatever wildlife was crashing about in the undergrowth; plenty of adders and rabbits had slithered and leapt into my path. At any other time, the area would be teeming with fauna. But the pervasive silence had unnerved me, and now every twitch of every blade of grass raised my hackles. I retreated to where Stender was standing.

He looked at me enquiringly. "We should go," I mouthed.

"What is it?" he murmured.

I shook my head and pointed in the direction we ought to edge away to. He frowned.

"Could be nothing," I said as quietly as I could. "But I don't want to take the chance." I sounded paranoid. I had to admit, the panicky jitters were beginning to make themselves known, and I wondered if some kind of delayed shock was settling in. I would start seeing monsters everywhere. Just because you don't know what's out there doesn't mean—

The thing came leaping out of the foliage like a trapdoor spider striking. I didn't have time to register what it was before I felt its weight collide with me and knock me onto my ass. I smelt it first: a putrid cocktail of rotting flesh and disease that seared my nostrils. Then my eyes focused as it pinned me to the soft mossy earth: it was a dog's body, ostensibly, though all fur had long been shorn away and what was left was pale, puckered skin through which veins and bone were visible. Its paws weren't those of a canine, however; it had talons—wicked hooked claws that right now were biting through my jacket and pressing into the meat of my shoulder. Needle-sharp pain travelled down my arms and chest, and I could feel the blood beading at the puncture points.

It was the head that I couldn't stop staring at, however—affixed to the dog's torso was what appeared to be a child's skull, snapping and growling. But the eye-sockets were empty, coal-black pits in which nothing stirred, and the bone was boiled clean of hair and fat. The skull had no muscles, no tendons, controlling it, and yet it freely swivelled on its neck, teeth champing as it lunged forward and tried to tear a chunk out of my cheek. I had both hands under its chin—ensuring I couldn't reach around for my gun—and it was taking all my strength just to keep it up and away from biting off the tip of my nose. It snarled and wrestled, its body shifting in my grip, and any initial squeamishness about handling such a grave-born thing was soon put aside as I struggled to fend it off. For all its half-decayed state, there was power in its assault, and it renewed each attack with hungry, angry venom.

The reek of it got into my throat, and I struggled not to retch. I tried quickly releasing my right hand and punching the side of its head, but it just glanced off the naked skull, the thing barely seeming to notice. Its teeth chattered, opening and clamping shut, attempting to catch my fingers between them, issuing forth a hideous bark as each time it was denied a meal. Its talon-paws scrabbled on my jacket, the material sliced open, my chest now stinging and raw.

"Little help?" I shouted, twisting my head round to see where Stender was. He'd seemingly disappeared. I yelled his name, fuelled mostly out of fear. This thing was like something that had been pulled from the depths of childhood nightmares, and hysteria was starting to inform my attempts to keep it at bay. *This wasn't right, this couldn't be right,* echoed a voice in my head. *This can't be real, this can't be real.* However, the pain, and the weight and physicality of the creature attacking me disabused that notion. This was no hallucination, no matter how much I willed it to be.

The skull-dog succeeded in twisting its head round, and bit down hard between my thumb and forefinger. I yelled in agony, unable to tear my hand free; its teeth were embedded in the meat of my palm, and blood was streaming down my wrist. Fire swept up my arm, but I used it to galvanise me, drawing on a reserve of strength to kick out at the creature and topple it onto its side; I put a foot on its belly and tried to lever myself up, but still it wouldn't relinquish its hold on my hand, the limb now sheathed in crimson.

I sensed movement beside me, and glanced round in time to see Stender step forward and bring a three-foot log down on the thing's neck with a swift, two-handed action. It caused its head to snap back, and my hand went with it. I bellowed, swearing repeatedly, the wrench making starbursts pop before my eyes.

"Get your foot on its skull," Stender said.

I moved my boot from its midriff to its cheekbone and pinned it down. Its clawed feet scrabbled furiously. Stender hit it again on the neck, and again, and I fell back as the head finally detached from the body. That immediately got up on its feet and started running in circles before Stender rammed the end of the log into the stump with a well-timed thrust. It sank forward and lay motionless, propped up like a discarded dog-shaped freezi-pop on a stick.

He staggered over to me, peering down at the skull irremovable from my hand, the teeth impaled in the skin. I felt nauseous and light-headed.

"The gun... Get the gun," I hissed. "Waistband, under my jacket."

He nodded, and quickly retrieved it. I motioned where he should place the barrel—just to the side of the crown—and turned my face away as he pulled the trigger. The retort was deafening in the silence of the wooded glade as the bone exploded, and I felt a shard slice my earlobe as it whistled past. I shook my hand and splinters fell away, pattering onto the leafy ground; the teeth were still firmly embedded, nevertheless.

"You're going to need medical attention for that," he said superfluously, frowning at the mess my right hand had become. The skin was purpling around the wound, the tips of my fingers scarily white. It was limp and unresponsive.

"No shit," I replied. "I was thinking of keeping them as a

memento, too." I turned my hand over, counting half a dozen teeth forming a semi-circle in the flesh like standing stones. I pulled at them but there was no way they were going to release their dead dog grip. Stender helped me tear a strip of material from my shirt—already shredded by the fucker's claws—and wrapped that around the worst of it. He passed me back the gun, which I now held in my left, down by my side, and glanced back at the remains of the horror that he'd run through.

"You seen anything like that before?" I asked, slightly wheezy.

He didn't answer for a moment. "I heard about experiments," he replied finally, not looking back at me. "Vivisection. I thought they were looking into organ regeneration, transplants. I don't know what *that* is." He nodded towards the body. "That's not science. That... shouldn't exist."

"Somebody's pet project. Like some kind of kid's custom-built mutant freakshow." I scanned the edge of the clearing. "What's it doing running wild out here?"

"It smellsss the guilty," came a sibilant voice, and both Stender and I spun as another pair of rotten, grey Judges emerged from the foliage. One—female, barely out of the Academy—held a leash upon which another skull-headed monstrosity strained. It was sleeker in shape than its partner, with human-like hands—I queasily realised on closer inspection that they'd been stitched on—but the same snapping bone-face shook and snarled. "It can track thossse that have not ssubmitted to Death'ss mercy."

I didn't hesitate. I took aim and fired just as the jay unhooked the leash, and the creature had barely taken a step before the bullet entered its right eye socket and exploded out the other side. With half its head missing, it didn't know what to do; it whimpered and sat down on its haunches, exploring its exit wound with those unnerving fingers. The jays advanced, undeterred. I switched targets, and pumped the rest of the clip into their chests. They staggered, but they didn't go down.

"Fuck." I tossed the gun to Stender, then fished in my back pocket for the replacement clip, which I passed over too. "Reload for me. I can't do shit with my hand like this."

"We want you alive for now," the Judge nearest Stender said to him. "We have insstructionss to bring you back to the Hall of Injusstice." It leered, and hefted its spiked club. "That can be in piecesss, if necessary."

Stender worked the automatic's slide and—ignoring my outstretched hand, asking for the gun back—shot the jay in the face, blowing it wide open like a clamshell.

"Don't make thisss difficult," it said impossibly, its mouth now rent asunder. Stender fired again, and a section of its helmet flew apart.

The other badge had a Lawgiver, which it brought to bear on Stender. I dived forward and knocked the weapon down, the round drilling into the ground inches from his foot. The jay caught me with a good backhand—powerful, considering its skeletal frame—and I ducked and rolled just as the automatic barked and the lower half of its jaw pebble-dashed a nearby tree trunk. It didn't drop but seemed taken aback.

"Headshots seem the most effective," Stender said, slapping the gun butt into my hand. Eyes rolling up in the sockets, the two Judges were as dozily confused as their attack-dog as to where their missing skull fragments were. "I suggest we make a move."

"Not yet," I muttered, and slammed the gun into what was left of the Judge's face, pistol-whipping it to the ground and not stopping until nothing was left but greasy residue. Then I did the same with the other one, before putting down the dog-thing for good.

I stood, sweating, out of breath. "Now we go."

CHAPTER FIVE

I TOLD STENDER I had an idea of where to head for, and instructed him to follow. Running cautiously through the woods, ears and eyes open, neither of us had any idea if there were more of those zombie assholes out looking for us, but we stayed alert and ready to act should one cross our path. The silence was all-enveloping—our footsteps crunching as we jogged between the trees was the only sound to be heard—and there remained no sign of the H-Wagon. Nevertheless, I found myself scrutinising every shadow for movement, aware that at any moment some fresh atrocity could come staggering towards us. My mind needed little help in imagining these new horrors; it was cycling through the worst my head could conjure up on a permanent loop.

But I had a destination, and for now it seemed we were going to make it there unhindered. On the fringes of the woodland sat a camping park I was familiar with, mostly used by holidaymakers as a place to set down their caravans, but also home to several residents. I was banking on there still being some vehicles, and as we emerged from the treeline, I issued a quiet word of thanks to whichever non-existent deity was watching over us, for a couple of cars had been left unattended. We edged between the mobile homes, all of which were in darkness and seemingly empty, alive to the slightest disturbance. Had the people taken off for a safer haven, or were they sheltering inside, staying as quiet and still as they possibly could, hoping no one would come looking for them? I was tempted to peer inside, but decided that wouldn't be a good idea—better to be in and out with the minimum of interaction with anyone else. I caught a glimpse of a smear of blood on a window, what looked like words painted in grue—*I'M SORRY*—and shuddered.

Morning had broken by now, and a silvery mist hung over the ground, the grass wet with dew. Stender spotted a four-by-four tucked behind an admin building, and I gave him the nod. We made a dash towards it, and I left him to the business of getting it started while I kept watch; I lent him my gun to smash the driver's window, he leant in and unlocked it, then disappeared under the ignition. Seems like it paid to have a Tek-guy at your disposal, I thought, impressed with the speed and efficiency with which he hotwired the motor. He slid over to the passenger side as I climbed in.

"Shouldn't we see if there's anything worth salvaging?" he said, jerking a thumb towards the building. "Food supplies, batteries, that kind of thing?"

"Not here," I replied, a flash of that red message on the glass appearing unbidden in my head. "I don't think it's a good idea to hang around. Let's get going."

I pulled out slowly, found the main road and headed steadily north, keeping to an unassuming 50mph, one hand on the wheel, glad that it wasn't a stick-shift. Half an eye was almost constantly glued to the mirror, watching for the H-Wagon to return, but the bright, sharp dawn was devoid of any life. It was like the world outside the car had been paused and muted.

Stender noticed my repeated glances towards the sky. "Guess it must've been called back to the Grand Hall."

"For now, maybe. But they sure were keen to take you with them. Those two freaks with the skinned puppies were sent in to check you were still alive after my ride went up in flames.

They weren't taking any chances—you're too important to them."

"Which means Red Mosquito must've stalled."

"Seems so. That buys us some time. But they're going to keep coming after you if they can't get it going on their own, so we can't afford to dawdle."

Stender peered out at the surrounding countryside. We were leaving the highway and taking increasingly narrow roads that circuited farmland and dense forested areas. Some sheep carcasses lay piled up in a field and a huge black cloud of flies swirled into the air as we sped past, both of us putting a hand to our mouths when the stench permeated the vehicle's interior. "Who's this Loxley woman we're going to see again?"

"Old colleague. I've been pally with her since way back. Likes her privacy, though, and not exactly a people person so don't go expecting much of a warm welcome."

"How's she going to help?"

"She's the best thief I know."

ANY OTHER TIME, staring down the barrels of a shotgun would, to say the least, give me pause for concern; on this occasion, however, it came as something of a relief. Firstly, it showed that Loxley was most definitely still here and hadn't tried to hightail it to a desert island somewhere (not that I seriously anticipated that she would, but I had been taking a chance on her having stuck around), and secondly it proved she hadn't gone total nutzoid like a lot of the population. If she hadn't emerged from her cabin wielding some kind of boomstick, then I would've been worried. Yet here she was, waving a pump-action under our noses and warning us to back the hell off. Stender looked perturbed, but I shot him a glance that told him to chill.

"Hey, Loxley," I called, holding up my hands. "It's McGill. Been a while."

"There's a reason for that, I seem to remember," she said, not lowering the weapon. She was standing in her doorway, aiming down at us from the top of the slight incline the cabin sat on. We waited beside the car parked at the foot of a dozen wooden steps built into the rise, so she couldn't fail to have the drop on us. I had no intention of approaching her other than on her own terms so was content to ride this out until we gained her trust. "Who's the gimp?"

I shook my head slightly at Stender, discouraging him from replying. "He's all right, he's with me. Boffin I've managed to acquire. You know how I've always wanted one."

"He looks Department."

Damn, nothing got past her, I thought. Okay, no point trying to sell her a bogie. "Yeah, he's HoJ—"

"What the fuck, McGill...?"

"—but he's a civvie. Lab spod. He got out just before it all went to shit."

"So what in the name of quivering Christ are you doing bringing him here?"

"'Cause we need your help, Loxley. You must have some idea of what's going on in the capital?"

She shrugged. "Radio cut out twelve hours ago. Last I heard it said there'd been an uprising, that a new Chief Fucknut had got himself installed. Then there was all this talk of riots on the streets."

"They're murderin' everyone. It's genocide."

"And I can do anything about it because...?"

"C'mon, Loxley, can we talk about this inside? My arms are getting tired."

She motioned with the shotgun. "What happened to your hand?"

I cast an eye over it. It felt very tight and heavy. "The new regime is what happened. They don't come brandishing flowers and chocolates, I can tell you that much."

"And you do?"

I smiled sheepishly. "Stores were closed. Sorry."

She dropped the gun, and beckoned for us to enter. We climbed the steps and squeezed past her into the functional open-plan dining/living area that took up the majority of the cabin's floorspace, with a wood-burning stove at one end and a pail near the door to visit the well out back. Loxley had never been one for mod cons, despite all the years she'd been cooped up here; she seemed to like the fact that she didn't have to rely on anyone for anything, and would quite happily trade luxury for independence. She made a mint in the two decades that I'd known her; her skills didn't come cheap (and she didn't hire them out to just anyone), and I was always curious as to what she planned to do with her savings, 'cause she sure as shit didn't spend anything on herself.

She shut and bolted the door behind her and indicated that we sit while she remained where she was. "You armed?" she asked.

I nodded and pulled out my automatic, laying it on the table. "On my last clip."

"What about laughing boy here?"

Stender shook his head nervously and wilted under her glare until she seemed satisfied he posed no threat.

"So what do I owe the pleasure, McGill? Last time I saw you, you were part of the Bushman's crew, trying to convince me to help rip off that heroin shipment. Got pretty heated, I seem to recall."

"Nothing personal, you know that, right? I'm at the B-man's beck and call—or I was. He just asked me to make you an offer you couldn't refuse."

"Which I refused."

"Well, yeah."

"And which he wasn't happy about."

"He lost half a dozen guys on that job in the end. He figured if you'd engineered the raid like he asked, no one would've got so much as a scratch."

"I don't work for that human leech, and never will. Pretty much don't want to associate with those that do, either. I told you all this when I was throwing you out."

"True. But like I say, situation's changed. The Bushman's no longer an ongoing concern. He's been... superseded."

"By these end-of-the-world limp-dicks."

I nodded, and winced. A throb, deep and hard, pulsed within my injured hand, and I cradled it, hissing through gritted teeth as fingers touched inflamed skin. The flesh was blackening around the knuckles, and blisters clustered on my palm. The material that had been bound around the wound was stained with fresh seepage, and while I wanted to remove it to clean and re-dress the injury I was reluctant to attempt it. Loxley noticed my visible distress and wandered across, propping the shotgun down by the door, screwing up her face when she saw the extent of the damage done.

"What happened to you?" she asked, taking my ruined hand in hers. Her tone softened, and despite the distracting pain a little knot of yearning pulled tight in stomach at the sound of it. I'd always had a thing for Lox, though I never told her since I doubted the feeling was reciprocated; she always gave the impression she had no need of a man, or indeed anyone else. She was a fine-looking woman—strong and athletic, with bobbed blonde hair and a hearty laugh, the few times she let you hear it—and it got to the point where being around her was making me feel down, so I made a point of wallowing in self-pity on my own instead. Her skills as a burglar were second to none, and she was always in demand, so the idea of her having much time for a numbskull like me seemed unlikely in retrospect.

"I was bitten," I replied, watching as she peeled away the scrap of shirt, sticky patches of blood not giving up their claim on it easily, and exposed the crescent-shaped mark. The teeth were still fused to the meat of my hand where they wouldn't be separated, the small nubs of bone now brown and rotten. The skin around them had turned a mottled grey.

Loxley took a sharp intake of breath. "Holy crap," she murmured. "You need to see a doctor. This is all infected to Sunday and back."

"I think the docs are going have more than enough on their hands." I glanced at the wound and raised my eyebrows. "So to speak. Plus we need to stay out of the populated areas, the city centres. You haven't seen what it's like out there—there're crazies everywhere."

"Well, you're going to lose that limb to gangrene if it's not treated. Is that..." She squinted closer. "Are those *human* teeth?"

"Probably."

"But they're too small to be adult—"

"I know."

She stared at me, almost angrily, as if I was challenging her perception of reality. "Okay, you're starting to freak me out now. What the fuck did this?"

"Wish I could tell you," I replied. "I don't know myself."

"The world's changing," Stender said morosely, and both me and Lox turned to look at him, suddenly reminded that he was with us too. "Or it's being changed. What we think we know, what we understand, is no longer relevant."

"Great," Loxley muttered, and side-eyed me. "Does he do kids' parties as well?" She spun and stomped off to an adjoining room, where we heard the clatter of a cabinet being rifled through, before she emerged with her arms full of disinfectant, bandages, towels and a bowl half filled with steaming water. "Regardless," she continued, laying them on the table, "we need to do something about that. You got any medical expertise?" She addressed the question to Stender, hands on hips.

"He's Tek," I said.

"Well, he can still hold stuff. Give me some help here." She pushed the bowl towards him, and got to work. "I'll do my best," she said, brandishing a pair of tweezers. "I only know the basics. Hold still, this is probably going to hurt. In fact, you might want to take a couple of these first. They're strong." She passed me a tube of pills, two of which I necked.

She started to tease out the first of the teeth, and the pain hit me like an electric shock. I gripped the edge of the tabletop, my whole frame shaking, my eyes tightly shut, feet kicking against the bare wooden floorboards. I could feel blood trickling between my knuckles, and hear Loxley swearing under her breath. Something wrenched free, and white-hot agony blossomed in my head like fireworks.

"Jesus," I heard her say. "How is that...? Look, it was sending out little roots. It was growing *into* him..."

"Get it out of me," I rasped, voice trembling.

"Yeah, yeah. Only another five to go. Show a little backbone, will ya?"

She dug into my hand for the second time, and I passed out, surfing a Valium-induced haze. For some reason, the sensation of hitting the canvas as I took a dive beneath the bright lights of an auditorium sprang into my mind, and then darkness rushed in.

I AWOKE TO the testy back and forth of raised voices, and what sounded like gravel being thrown repeatedly at the cabin's windows. It took me a moment to re-orientate myself, the unfamiliar surroundings and thick, druggy tendrils of sleep still clinging to me both fogging my senses. The tight ache in my hand finally grabbed my attention and pulled me into full consciousness. I rose slowly from where I'd been passed out on a bed—*Loxley's bed*, I dimly realised—and studied my tightly wrapped palm, the wound having been efficiently dressed with clean white bandages. For the moment, I appeared to still have all my limbs, which I considered a minor victory.

There came another shout and a bang against the door. I struggled to my feet, feeling like I could do with a drink, and staggered out into the main living area, where I saw Loxley crouching beneath the window, shotgun clasped in both hands. Stender was in the opposite position on the other side of the door, on his hands and knees. It was gloomy, little light spilling through from outside, though no one had lit any lamps.

"How long have I been asleep?" I asked, confused. It had been early morning when we'd arrived; surely I couldn't have been passed out for most of the day.

"About three hours," Loxley said, then indicated that I should join them on the floor.

I felt drunkenly sluggish, my head taking a while to process information. I didn't move, but instead turned my attention to the window and the shifting blackness beyond. "Why's it so dark?"

"McGill," she snapped. "Get down."

The pane rattled again as multiple hard objects spattered against the glass. I ignored Loxley's entreaty and took a few steps towards it. "Is that rain? What the hell's making that noise…?" I peered out just as the door shuddered, and I caught a glimpse of what was darkening the cabin's exterior.

"Jesus Christ." My head snapped back as the creature scuttled centimetres away from my face and crawled over its brethren, the swarm teeming in their thousands: what I had mistook for twilight was in fact their brown, fifteen-centimetre bodies coating every surface of the cabin outside. The things were winged, and a swirling tornado of them besieged the building, hitting the walls and glass with considerable force. They were of a size I'd never seen in an insect before, and they oozed malevolence, their huge compound eyes seemingly regarding me as I watched them. Antennae twitching, mandibles chittering, their barbed legs traced the window and frame as if testing its durability.

A hand tugged my shirt and pulled me down, and I dropped next to Lox. "Fuckin' giant bugs," I somewhat stupidly announced as if I was offering my expert opinion.

"You noticed."

"Locusts," Stender piped up. "Or an aggressive new strain, at least."

"But… they're *huge*—"

"Genetic mutation," he replied. "Weaponised wildlife."

"It's a goddamn plague, is what it is," Loxley muttered.

"Amounts to the same thing," he said. "Destruction on a massive scale."

"Can they get in?" I asked. "Lox, what about your chimney?"

She shook her head. "Wire cap. I had birds nesting in it. Looks like these things are too big to fit through, fortunately."

"Guess we should be thankful for small mercies," I said, and from the expression on Loxley's face, it seemed we'd been handed a pretty fucking small mercy indeed.

"Do these things follow you around?" she asked angrily. "Have they tracked you here?"

"This can't be localised," Stender said, easing himself off the floor to take a peek through the window. "We must just be in their path. They've probably been bred to swarm down the farmbelt—"

"Move away from there," Loxley yelled just as a roiling mass detached itself from one corner of the roof and threw their hard carapaces at the glass where Stender's flabby head had just emerged. Either the glass had become weakened or they hit it at just the right angle, for it spiderwebbed and small shards tinkled onto the sill.

I had the time to mouth an expletive before the first of the insects burst through like a bullet. It hung in the air for a second, hovering, the buzz of its wings filling the room, before it zeroed on Stender. He yelped and scooted backwards, the locust following, dive-bombing his face, which he tried to cover with his hands.

"Stender, watch out," Lox shouted as she stepped past me and raised the shotgun to her shoulder. She waited until the creature was on the ascent before pulling the trigger, blowing it against the wall in an eruption of sticky green gore. A further half-dozen were through the breach by this point and doing a circuit of the ceiling. She switched targets without hesitation and nailed a further two, punching a hole in the plaster.

One dropped onto the back of my head and I could feel its limbs in my hair, hooks on its feet scratching my scalp. I tried to remove it, pain lancing through my neck as it bit me hard under the jaw. I made for the table and retrieved my automatic, attempting to shake it off; when it wouldn't budge, I used my bandaged hand to curl around its squirming body and plucked it free, slamming it on the tabletop then putting a bullet through it for good measure.

"McGill!" Lox bellowed. The roar of the things' wings was deafening now. "Back into the bedroom! Quickly!"

More flying terrors squeezed their way in as we ran for the rear room, Loxley slamming shut the door behind us. It shuddered with each new impact. She marched across to the far wall, perched on a nightstand and unhooked a narrow skylight. "They're concentrated on the front of the cabin," she said. "We can scoot through here onto the roof, then drop down next to the garage at the back. My truck's inside; key's in the ignition."

"Fuck, Lox, where are we gonna go?" I said, a little desperately. Another safe haven had been compromised.

"Gotta be somewhere better than here," she answered, legs already dangling through the skylight as she pulled herself up.

"*Is* there?"

She didn't reply; I could hear her feet sliding on the rooftiles. I motioned wearily to Stender to follow her as I glanced around the room at the remnants of a life abandoned. Inch by inch the world was being eaten away, and the ground was disappearing beneath our feet. What choice did we have but to retreat, and keep retreating until the darkness eventually swallowed us up? But I was getting tired of running.

I wanted to start punching back.

CHAPTER SIX

"I'M SORRY, LOX."

We were sitting in the cab of her flatbed, parked some distance down the road and looking back at the eddying spiral of locusts that were still swarming over her house. I wondered if they were going to take the whole building apart, beam by beam, reduce it to sawdust, but figured we wouldn't stick around to see it happen, in any case. Clouds of them were starting to break away in search of more to consume, be it animal or vegetable. Loxley quietly regarded her home one last time, then put the truck into gear and pulled away, eyes not flicking to the mirror even for a second. I couldn't help myself and cast a final glance over my shoulder before it was lost to the treeline.

"I shouldn't have brought this to your door," I said.

"It's going to be at everyone's door, sooner or later," she replied, "if that's any indication." She jerked her thumb behind her.

"All the same, I feel bad for getting you involved."

"Right now, I'm not entirely sure *what* I'm involved in. You didn't get so far as to tell me what you wanted from me. The professor here explained to me about... What did you call it?"

"Red Mosquito," Stender muttered.

"Yeah, that. He filled me in on what the sick bastards have got planned while you were dead to the world." She shot me a look. "He also told me how you two met and became unlikely partners. Never were the brains of the outfit, were you, McGill?"

"Believe it or not, I have apologised already."

She snorted back that damn irresistible laugh. "I'll bet. Serendipity, I suppose you could call it. If you two had never crossed paths, you'd probably still be back in that hovel you used to slum around in, Jackson, scratching your balls and wondering why all the TV channels were down. Now, you're the motherfucking saviour of the world."

"I wouldn't go that far—"

"But you *do* have a plan?"

"Well..." I glanced at Stender. "More of a last-ditch opportunity, really."

"So naturally you thought of me."

"You're my number-one go-to saboteur, Lox. I thought you'd be flattered."

She stomped on the brake and we screeched to a stop. I had to put my good hand out on the dashboard to stop my forehead connecting with the windscreen. Loxley shifted in her seat to regard us both, elbow up on the wheel. "Let's get this straight before I go any further with you jokers. I facilitate the procurement of things through unlawful means; that's my talent. I'm a B&E expert, I steal to order. You don't need me for common vandalism, if that's what you're after."

"No, no, that's not what I meant," I said quickly. "I still need you at your thievery best. It's just that, in this case, we're not stealing anything of value—not to us, at least. More like we're putting a spoke in these fuckers' plans. But you'll be our way in, Lox. We won't be able to do this without you."

She smiled thinly. "Not sure if it goes against my principles, taking something of no worth."

"Have to say, anyone's rep is gonna be worth shit if the whole world dies. Won't matter what we were, or what we did or didn't do, we'll just be ash and bones. Who's gonna be left to care?"

She turned and gazed out the windscreen. "That's true," she said. She leaned forward as if something beyond the truck had caught her eye. "Oh, my God," she breathed, then wrenched open the door and clambered out, walking ahead up the road for a few metres before stepping off into the woodland. I called after her, but she didn't look back.

"Where's she going?" Stender asked.

"You got me," I answered, sliding across the seat. "Stay here. Lock the doors. Hit the horn if any more Creatures from the Black Lagoon turn up."

I jogged to catch up with her, pushing aside branches as I followed her path. She hadn't entered very far, and was standing at the edge of a glade, only part of which she must've glimpsed from the vehicle. I joined her at her side, though she didn't acknowledge I was there at first, and simply silently regarded the figures before us.

"Did *they* do this?" she whispered finally, eyes roving over the scene. "The things you say are now in charge?"

"I don't think so. Doesn't seem like their style. I think these people made their own choice."

We were looking at a body orchard: there must've been close to a couple of hundred of them, hanging from the branches, bedecking the beeches and conifers like Christmas ornaments. They turned slowly in the breeze, limbs slack, the creak of the ropes around their necks audible in the unnatural quiet. Ages ranged from infants to pensioners, and there was no unifying element to suggest that this had been a cult or commune that had decided to commit mass suicide; rather, it looked like the cross-section of an average town—suited businessmen swung side by side with hooded youths and farmers still with mud crusting their boots. It was as if a random selection of citizens had made the joint decision to hasten their demise rather than wait for the Justice Department demons to find them. Clearly, the younger ones had had little say in the matter, but the manner in which parents and siblings dangled alongside them suggested that the act had been one of perceived mercy. The sight was both peaceful and heart-breaking; grotesque in the widespread loss of life and chilling in its clear-sighted, fatalistic practicality.

"This must be nearly half of Hadley," Loxley said.

"Did you know them?"

"I recognise a few. The town's a few miles down the road. Used to talk to Tommy Jaffrey there when I'd pick up my groceries." She nodded in one of the dead's direction, but I wasn't entirely sure which one she meant. "It had a little market. There's some faces I'd see around... God."

Her voice cracked, and it was the most vulnerable I'd ever heard her sound. I put a tentative hand on her shoulder in comfort, and she didn't shrug it off.

"They were just regular folk. Was this some... collective madness? What compelled them to all come here and... and end themselves?"

"They lost hope, I guess. Thought this was the easy way out."

"But there's so many. They *all* thought this was the best solution?"

I picked out the black-shrouded figure of a priest hanging amongst his flock and wondered if there'd been some encouragement from the Holy Book, despite the Church's traditional dislike of self-destruction. Maybe Purgatory held no fear, now they believed Hell was here. "Despair can be a powerful thing," I said, somewhat lamely. "If you can see no future, if you feel at a loss, then this is the one thing left you have control over—the decision to stamp your own ticket."

She looked at me. "That the voice of experience?"

I gave her a lopsided smile. "I've had my low points over the years."

She put her hand over mine. "I never knew. Always figured you were too dumb to have feelings." She paused, then asked: "Why did you choose not to, if you don't mind me asking?"

"You sound disappointed at the outcome."

"God, no. I just wondered if you knew what it was that kept you going."

"Cowardice, mainly. I didn't have their willpower." I nodded towards the dead displayed before us.

"No, don't do yourself a disservice, Jackson. You're a scrapper."

"Once, maybe."

"And you still are. You've taken your punches, but you refuse to let it break you." She glanced back towards where her truck was waiting. "What we're doing here, it's not the actions of people giving up. You and me, we don't owe this world anything—Justice Department, government, they haven't done shit for us. We've always been on the outside. Why should we risk our lives on some foolhardy and damn-near-certain-to-fail attempt to stop this thing?"

"'We'?"

"You don't think I'll let you walk into this alone?"

I smiled again, buoyed by having her next to me. "Thanks, Lox. But like you said, this isn't your fight."

"It isn't yours, either. But it's for the sake of everyone." She turned her head back to the hanged. "Every innocent life we'll die trying to save." She stood there for a moment in contemplation, then added softly: "'Cause we're not going to put our heads in the noose. You hear me? Not while we can give it our best shot."

She patted my hand, removed it, and started to walk away. I watched her go, lingering with Hadley's lost souls, beset suddenly by a crushing sadness: of a future stolen, of bright, effervescent lives snuffed out. A wave of inky-black sickness threatened to roll over me and I could feel tears pricking at the corners of my eyes, so I quickly followed Loxley back to the truck, wiping them away before she could see. She was up on the running board, arms over the open driver's door, waiting for me to emerge.

"So c'mon, then, McGill—what's the grand plan?"

* * *

STENDER FILLED HER in as we resumed our journey. "Standard procedure for any biological weaponry is for it to be stored in the Center for Disease Research, based outside of Rennick. From what I saw, the Red Mosquito supplies were shipped there."

"Not the Grand Hall?" Loxley asked.

He shook his head. "Too dangerous, should there be an outbreak. Can't afford for anything to escape the Tek-labs, so better it's contained off-site, where it can do minimal damage should the worst happen."

"Sucks to be one of the poor saps in Rennick, though. Do they know what they've got on their doorstep?"

"It's... not well advertised, no." Stender shifted in his seat, looking uncomfortable.

"I'll bet." Lox, on the other hand, appeared to be enjoying herself, revelling in the spod's unease. "The Judges make a lot of stuff like this—this kind of bacterial warfare? Before the current dickmunches in charge came on board, I mean."

"Experimentation is—*was*—going on all the time—"

"With a view to deploying them against citizens?"

"No! Well, not practically. Theoretical models were floated at the ideas stage, but that's—"

"Standard procedure."

Stender didn't respond and glared sulkily out of the window. Lox caught my eye and bit down on a smirk. She'd never been much of a fan of the jays at the best of times; none of us were, given our circle of acquaintances, but Loxley had a history of pro-Dem sympathies. Rumour had it she ran with that crowd when she was younger and did some weeks in juvie for leafleting. Ironically, it was her subsequent professional life of crime as an ace thief that saved her from receiving the inevitable Lawgiver bullet to the back of the head as an amateur, not-very-effective seditionist.

"So this Center for Disease Research," she continued, "which totally isn't Grand Hall's chemical weapons lab, is where they're storing Red Mosquito—and you want me to help get you in? To... what, destroy the stuff?"

"That's about the size of it," I said.

"If it doesn't work already, as you suspect, why bother? They can't use it."

"Because that's not to say they won't be able to at some point," Stender explained. "We can't afford to leave them the opportunity."

"Sounds to me," Loxley mused, "that we'd be better off blitzing the place entirely. Wire the building with C4 and blow it into orbit."

"That *is* an option," I conceded. "You know where to get your hands on explosives?"

Lox pulled a face like I'd asked if she could crack a safe in under four minutes. "Well, *duh*."

"Too risky," Stender interjected. "Considering what's in there, we could be releasing something even worse."

"Aaaand we come back to why you jaybird shitsticks are the biggest assholes on the planet. Honestly, who needs an army of fuckin' zombie cops to wipe us out when our own law enforcement have the means to instead?"

"I keep telling you, I'm *not* a Judge—"

"You fucking worked for the HoJ, same difference. Your fingerprints are all over that crap in the facility: this Mosquito thing, and lots more besides, probably. You're instrumental in allowing Justice Department to develop stuff specifically made to murder its own citizens."

"That's not fair—"

"Yeah, yeah, you didn't know what you were working on. But your bosses sure did, didn't they?" Loxley slammed the palm of her hand against the wheel in frustration, causing the truck to wobble a little across the lane. "Goddammit, this new Chief Judge, this creature that's instigated this slaughter—it's not like he came from nowhere, right? What's the betting that he was one of you—a badge and a uniform that's just gone up a level. I mean, you fascists wanted this all along, didn't you? Dispose of all the undesirables permanently. Kill the world. Cleanse it." Her voice dropped. "We should've expected it. This was always gonna come as long as you fucks were in power. *You* opened the door for this, and now everyone's going to pay."

Silence descended in the cab. Despite myself, I felt bad for Stender, so I broke the ice after a couple of minutes had passed. "Pretty sure no one wanted this, Lox. This is a madman's coup, powered by god-knows-what."

"It's not like this world was all sweetness and light beforehand," she muttered, eyes on the road. "Summary executions. A president in the pocket of the cartels. TV news was a rolling shitstorm of misery. You know *anyone* that was happy? Christ, they even deregulated dentists a few years back, did you see that? Talk about a sick society in its death throes already. No, this was written in the stars. This was fated to happen eventually."

I glanced at her. "Predestination," I murmured.

She raised her eyebrows. "That's a pretty big word for you, McGill."

"Just don't ask me to spell it."

Rennick was to the south, on the other side of the capital, and as we left the deserted countryside and headed further back towards the more densely populated areas, so the signs of chaos became more apparent. Bodies littered the tarmac, some of them having been dragged from their cars, which were now slung across both lanes and we had to slalom around them. Doors were still wide open where the vehicles' occupants lay slumped, half in and half out. All bore the marks of frenzied violence. Blood was smeared across the asphalt in wide arcs like someone had taken a huge brush dipped in gore and signed this atrocity. I thought of the crazies from the previous evening, and imagined this could've well been a full night's butchery. They may have *all* been infected as far as I knew, and slaughtered each other, lost in their derangement—who killed who mattered little to the architects of this madness, as long as the graves were filled.

"Jesus," Loxley whispered, eyes wide as she eased the truck through the carnage, gaze moving from windscreen to side window as she tried to process the scale of what she was seeing. "This is genocide."

"They got something into the water supply," I told her. "We think it's been sending the population insane."

"Another of *your* genius projects?" Loxley wanted to know, addressing Stender.

He shook his head. "I never saw anything like this virus before."

"We all seem to have avoided picking it up," she said.

"You got your water direct from your well, right?" I replied. She nodded. "I kinda take my refreshments neat, if you know what I mean. And Stender… well, he came close."

"Really?"

"The Grand Hall has its own closed system," he said. "Just to avoid this kind of contaminant. I would've detected the organisms that the water's been seeded with if it had been present. From what I can see, this has been directed at the population at large."

"So they don't want to kill everybody."

"Not just yet. Not those that are still useful to them," I said. "Like I told you, they still want him. It's us scumballs that are the first to be wiped out."

"Thank you for including me," Loxley answered.

"My pleasure."

"The spread of infection must be radiating out from the source," Stender murmured. "I'm fairly sure counties outside the immediate area haven't been affected yet. It's still the early stages. Chances are the speed and intensity of the mania too are burning up a lot of energy."

"You mean the carriers are killing each other at a rate of knots."

"Which would explain why we're seeing a lot of bodies, but few still alive. Efficient in the short term, but not viable for sustained worldwide species extinction."

"Jesus," Loxley groaned, "I can't believe we're talking in these terms so matter-of-factly."

"You'd rather we panicked and ran around like headless chickens because the sky is falling in?" Stender said acidly.

"I'd rather you fuckers hadn't put us in this position in the first place," she snapped back.

"Okay, okay," I interjected. "Let's not get into that again." I turned to Stender. "What do you think their next move will be?"

"A wider means to an end. Red Mosquito is meant to shut down the food supply. They're weaponising the insect kingdom..." He paused then cocked his head to one side, peering out the passenger window. "The weather, maybe."

"The weather?"

"Hacking into Weather Control would give them a far greater reach—even an ability to spread their contagion overseas. If they're going for sheer quantity, which they evidently are, then they're not going to stop until the whole world is theirs. See that?" He pointed up.

"What am I looking at?" I asked, squinting.

"That silver speck, directly above. See it? It's a drone. They use them for cloud-farming."

"Uh, now you come to mention it," Loxley said, "does that sky look right to you?" She nodded towards the horizon on her left, where a thick bank of purplish-pink clouds was roiling in like a thunderhead. What had started out as a bright morning had become steadily overcast, the sun little more than a hazy disc struggling to penetrate the grey canopy. There was a gloomy, rainwater light that cast a pall over everything. Seeing that vast churning mass roll across the heavens towards us was terrifying in its sheer scale.

"*Drive*, Lox," I said, watching it unfold. "We don't want to be outside when that breaks."

She needed little encouragement and stepped on the accelerator, swerving to the best of her ability to avoid the vehicles and corpses littering the highway, but finesse had to be abandoned in favour of speed. Wheels losing traction for a second as they slipped on a wide puddle of viscera, the truck skidded and caught the rear end of a station wagon lying on its side. The bodywork squealed, and all three of us juddered with the impact, but Loxley managed to get it back under control, grunting an apology.

"Hold on," she warned as we approached two more cars blocking the road and slammed directly between them, slewing them aside. We heard the headlamps shatter and the hood buckled, but it kept going. "The old gal ain't built for this kind of treatment."

"The road's getting worse as we're nearing the capital," Stender said. The thoroughfare was choked with wrecks—some blackened and still smouldering—and cadavers in various states of dismemberment piled up against the crash barriers. "It's going to be near impossible to get much further. Can we take an exit?"

"We want to be circuiting the city anyway," I said. "No way should we drive willingly into that horrorshow." If this road to hell had been any indication of what lay within its environs, I didn't want to bear witness to the horrors, had been perpetrated within the capital.

"The 55 is coming up," Loxley shouted over the racket the engine was now making. "It'll be a loop, but it'll get onto the I9 going south." She pulled hard on the wheel and veered the truck down the off-ramp doing a solid eighty, clattering towards the intersection, sparks dancing as it bounced once off the low wall that edged the slope.

"Ah shit." She hit the brakes and the tyres screeched as the vehicle slid to a halt, the air filled with the sharp tang of burning rubber.

Loxley turned to me and Stender, and we wordlessly looked out at the half dozen grey Judges manning the barricade that stretched across the highway. They gazed back at us, then slowly began to advance.

CHAPTER SEVEN

LOXLEY STUCK THE truck in reverse and hit the gas but the engine whinnied and died. Smoke was starting to waft from beneath the hood. She twisted the key in the ignition and tried again but this time it didn't even splutter. She sat back in her seat and slammed the heel of her hand against the dash. Even though we weren't going anywhere, one of the advancing deadfucks raised a Lawgiver and put a round in each of the front tyres. The vehicle lurched forward like it was getting ready to pray.

"I've got a shotgun in the back," she muttered, glancing at me. "You still got your piece?"

"Yep."

"How do you want to play this?"

"Could do with evening the odds some, and right now they've got us cold."

"They want *me*, remember?" Stender said. "They'll be under orders to bring me in alive. Don't do anything rash for the moment."

"If they get their hands on you, this is all over," I replied.

"We haven't got any option but to go along with them right now. It'll buy us some time."

"All right, keep 'em talking," Loxley said. "'Til I can at least get access to the truck bed. Once I've got my shotgun, we're gonna have to move fast."

"Not sure they're big on conversation, Lox," I said, looking out at the jaybirds as they now surrounded the vehicle. They were as rancid as the pair I'd encountered the previous night—skin the colour of six-month-old offal, and it wasn't easy to see where their uniforms ended and the creature inside began. The black leather seemed to be growing into the liquescent flesh—or vice versa—and melding into a similar consistency; they were no longer officers donning the regalia of justice but entities entirely indivisible from their function. They were the law, moulded by the new regime and whatever the hell these fluids they'd all been encouraged to drink—personifications of an ideal. Their badges may have well been stitched straight onto their chests, their helmets carved from their skulls. This was the change the thing had talked about last night: the sloughing off of humanity and embracing a darker, more primal existence.

One rapped on the passenger window with a bony knuckle, leaving a residue smeared across the glass. It leered in, lips peeled back from blackened teeth; a beetle, I noticed, scuttled from under the Judge's bloated tongue, carapace gleaming in the wetness. My scalp prickled. I didn't want to leave the safety of the truck—I didn't want these monsters anywhere near me. It must've sensed my reluctance, for it didn't wait long for a response; instead, it brought up a spiked daystick, lightly scraped the sharpened points against the frame, then drove the head against the window. It spiderwebbed instantly, and the Judge followed up with another powerful thrust and the glass shattered. I yelped and shrank back, but a hand was inside, fumbling for the lock and yanking the door open. A second later, I was pulled from the cab and deposited ass-first onto the road.

"Out," one rasped to the others, and Stender unfolded himself from the passenger seat, arms raised in surrender. Loxley followed, scooting across to climb out the same side, and reached down and offered me a hand, helping me to my feet, glaring at the grey things as she did so. Three of them had their Lawgivers trained on us.

"Been looking for you, Ssstender," the jay nearest the Tek-guy said in a gravelly gurgle. His name was just about still visible on his grime-encrusted badge: Kernick. "Had psssis trying to find you. Too much interference hid you from usss, alasss."

"The sssweet sssounds of the guilty being punissshed," another commented. "Ssso loud. Ssso... invigorating."

Kernick nodded at this. "Ssidney told uss the ssong of jussstice would be a cressecendo at first. The sscreams of the sssinnersss would be deafening as millionsss faced judgement. But sssoon a lawful peace will ssettle."

"I'll come with you," Stender said. "I won't cause any trouble. There's no need to hurt my friends."

It was a vain plea, even I was aware of that. Kernick looked at me and Loxley and then back at Stender as if struggling to understand what was being asked of him. "But they are lawbreakersss, are they not? They breathe, therefore they are criminalsss dessserving of ssentencing. All living beingsss mussst be judged. And the ssentence is death."

"Mortis needs me, right? Well, I won't co-operate if they're harmed in any way."

Kernick chuckled, and it rippled out through the other uniforms as well. "You're in no posssition to bargain. If necesssary, we'll take the relevant bitsss of you and Judge Mortisss will fashion a... proxy. But either way, you are coming with usss." He turned his helmeted head to speak over its shoulder in a disarmingly casual manner. "Execute."

Thunder rumbled overhead. The clouds were blackening as the churning bank rolled in. I shot a look at Lox and indicated with my eyes that she get behind me; she stepped back just as I pulled my automatic from my waistband and held it to Stender's temple. He twisted in shock when the cold barrel pressed against his skin.

"Back off," I said. "Back off or you lose your asset. Figure it's the brain you need most. Not going to be any good to you scattered to the winds."

"You are not going to kill him."

"I will if it prevents him falling into your hands. He means nothing to me." I pulled Stender with me as I slowly edged backwards. Lox was doing the same. I hoped her shotgun was within easy reach; she was parallel with the flatbed now, and her hand was trailing over the side. I could only stall them for so long.

"You're bluffing, and you have nowhere to go," the thing rasped. "End thisss charade now."

"I wouldn't want to be in your boots, pal, when you report back to... Sidney, was it? Tell him that you lost the guy you were after, that was instrumental in your plans, 'cause you made the wrong judgement call."

The mention of the big cheese made Kernick pause. It was impossible to gauge whether anything resembling second thoughts was crossing its fetid brain, but clearly there was something even undead pigs feared and that was the new chief. Christ, he was called Sidney, how fearsome could he be? Nevertheless, he was the one calling the shots, and evidently, it didn't do to displease him.

Fat, warm drops of rain started to fall, drumming a rhythm on the truck's bodywork. I could feel them trickling down my neck. It had grown ominously dark, and the downpour started to increase in ferocity. Zombies being zombies, they barely noticed, but me, Lox and Stender were getting drenched, hair plastered to our foreheads, eyes streaming. The gun was slick in my hand.

"Mow him down," Kernick said finally. "Ssstender too, if you have to. We don't need anything below the neck."

I pushed Stender to one side and shot the Judge in the face, which vaporised in a grey-green deflation, leaving him standing upright and headless. The other jays returned fire instantly, and I caught a bullet in the back of the leg as I scrambled round the back of the truck for cover. I rolled, hissing in pain, and blood swirled in the rivulets coursing across the rain-sodden asphalt. Stender scampered under the vehicle. Loxley was up and armed in a flash, cutting loose with both barrels and blowing another jaybird in half with a wet smacking noise. I had to admit they did come apart easy when you hit them with enough force.

The remaining four Lawgivers all barked in unison, and forced Lox to retreat. She ducked down, leaning against the tailgate and reloading. I was lying next to her like a freshly landed fish on a riverbank, using my bandaged—and what felt like increasingly paralysed—hand to apply pressure to the leaking hole just below my kneecap. The other hand was locked, rain-frozen, around the gun butt.

"So you reckon the odds are evened up now?" she asked.

"Wanted to give them... at least a fighting chance," I said, smiling.

She rolled her eyes and ducked round the other side of the vehicle, standing when she was level with the driver's door and aimed her gun through the window. A grey was stalking past on the opposite side and she fired through the cab, exploding the glass nearest her and severing the thing's non gun-arm at the shoulder. It stumbled but seemingly shrugged it off, turning and firing in response. Lox squatted again, then bent low beneath the vehicle; Stender saw the shotgun barrels emerge and scrabbled away before she shot the jay's foot out from under him. That took him down, and his helmeted head hit the road like a watermelon, facing her. Black orbs stared back at her behind the cracked visor. She fired again, obliterating it.

I'd worked myself into a seated position and peered round the edge of the truck. The remaining three greys had ceased firing and were stepping back as one, still facing the vehicle. I didn't like where this was going. "Stender!" I roared over the incessant downpour. "Get out of there. Lox, move away from the flatbed, quickly." I shuffled back as rapidly as I could, grunting with pain as my injured leg scraped along the road.

Stender rolled out just as one of the Judges hit the fuel tank with a high-explosive bullet and the truck went up in a fireball that immediately ballooned into a huge cloud of steam as it met the chill rain. I caught sight of Lox and Stender being thrown to one side, and I shielded my face from the super-heated blast. My eyes felt cooked inside my skull, my skin boiling. I lay still for a moment and let the rainwater cool me, the breath seared out of my lungs. It was getting quiet inside my head, the drumming of the raindrops diminishing, the aches flattening out.

"McGill!" I heard Loxley's voice and consciousness filtered back. So did the pain as a patchwork of complaints all registered their presence the instant I opened my eyes. I blearily registered Lox crawling towards me like a drowned corpse pulling itself out of the seabed. Everything seemed in black and white and moving in a jerky zoetrope flicker, such was the effect of the storm. I heard her say my name again, and the background sounds rushed in. I lifted my head and saw the undead cops standing over me, Lawgivers raised. I knew I had the automatic in my hand, but it might as well have weighed a ton for all the strength I had to lift it; I was glued to the ground, immobile.

You're done, Jackson, I thought. *Your fight's finally, thankfully over. Wait for the ref to count you out. Let the canvas be your friend: take comfort in its embrace. You're not getting up from this one...*

I heard a rumble I took to be a peal of thunder, but it seemed to be growing in volume. It distracted the greys from pulling the trigger and they looked around for the source. Suddenly, a shape tore over mine and Lox's heads and clattered into the Judges, knocking them apart like bowling pins. It screeched on the slick asphalt, a blur of white and chrome, its thick tyres grinding a jay's head to a pulp. Then it skidded round, and let rip a chattering burst of cannon fire—the other two deadfucks disintegrated.

"What...?" I croaked.

"Lawrider," Loxley said. "It's a Judge. A live one."

"Oh shit," I muttered, watching as the bike circled the remains of the truck, then came back towards us, the engine purring to a halt and the helmeted rider booting the kickstand into place. "That's all we need."

"HOW LONG'S IT been raining now?" I asked, watching the black sheets lance down relentlessly from where I lay in the doorway, head resting on the frame. The sky was a boiling cauldron of clouds through which the sun was no longer visible, imbuing the light with an end-of-days unreality. Everything felt weird and dreamlike, but that partly might have been the effects of the rapi-heal pack that the Judge had wrapped my gunshot wound in, plus some painkilling salve that had been applied to my burnt face. I didn't know how much morphine was in this stuff, but it wasn't long before I was pretty much numb all over. I kept teetering between a blissed-out reverie that I wanted to sink into and a guilt that I was getting high as the world burned, which stopped me from nodding out entirely.

"Good six hours," the Judge, Hawkins, said without turning round. She was on the far side of the barn, running a diagnostic on her bike. Lox was slumped against a huge abandoned tractor tyre, lost in her own thoughts, clothes soaked and steaming. Stender paced the straw floor, growing increasingly antsy. The interior was otherwise empty save for some unrecognisable engine parts heaped in a corner.

I whistled. The deluge was biblical in its ferocity—the streets were being turned into surging rivers, ground washed away up in the hills. In our battle through the storm to this secluded safe haven—me riding pillion behind the Judge because of my leg, the others being led by Hawkins as she drove at a walking pace, high-power beams piercing the murk—we'd seen cropfields submerged and buildings destroyed by falling trees. Lightning would crackle occasionally on the horizon, illuminating a shattered landscape. The jay said, not unreasonably, that it would be impossible to continue in the current conditions, and directed us to the barn that sat just off the interstate, up on a raised concrete foundation, where we could wait out the weather. The way things were looking, we could be here for another forty days, if the creeps behind this were going the whole hog. Locusts, floods—it was the apocalypse playbook.

"We're losing time, being stranded here," Stender whined, pausing by the open door to look out at the tumult before resuming his anxious circuit. "Every minute we waste, they could be developing their genocidal plans further."

"Let me check if I packed my hovercraft," I said, making a meal of patting my jacket pockets.

He was unamused. "This is what they want—to starve us out, drive us into these rat traps. This is only the beginning."

"You're right," Hawkins said, standing up and wiping her hands on a rag, turning back to us. "This is only the start. They're doing all the broad strokes stuff first. All this"—she motioned outside—"is trying to wipe out as many of us as possible. Once the majority's dealt with, they can start to refine it—get in and personal, whittle us down by hand. They're still finding their feet."

"Finding their feet?" Loxley exclaimed, incredulous. "Jesus fucking Christ, they're monsters—"

"But they weren't always," the Judge replied in a measured tone. "They were once men—evil, sick men, but men nevertheless—who have been handed certain... powers. I wasn't at the Grand Hall when it fell, I probably wouldn't still be here if I was, but I heard the reports—of this kid Sidney De'Ath, this psychopathic cadet, who led the coup. There are forces at work guiding him, and the others, but it's tasked them with destroying an entire world—you think that's something you can just launch straight into without a little trial and error?"

Lox snorted and turned her head away. I could tell she was struggling to control her disdain ever since the Judge had turned up. "These forces... what are they?" I asked.

"I don't know. Some creepy-assed black-magic shit. De'Ath's done some kind of deal with the devil. Or *a* devil, at least."

"The Sisters," Stender interjected. "That's what I was told Mortis had referred to once—that he was doing the Sisters' bidding."

"Whatever mumbo-jumbo it sounds like, it's real and it's happening. They've now got half the Justice Department ranks on their side."

"Those grey zombie bastards," I said, then added: "No offence intended if they were pals of yours."

"They're not Judges any more," Hawkins answered resolutely. "Hell, they're not human any more. I won't hesitate to waste them when it comes to it. They're just tools De'Ath's using to increase the body count."

"Ones I encountered last night talked about fluids..."

"Yeah, the Dead Fluids. Christ knows what's in that, but the uniforms were being ordered to drink it, changing them into these freaks. Word is it's getting out into the civilian population now, sector houses shipping it out through the drug gangs. Ding-dongs are smoking it like it's the crack of doom."

"Why would anyone...?"

"If it gets them high, they don't give a fuck what they turn into."

"So what are you jaybirds doing about it?" Loxley demanded. "I mean, the half that aren't walking pusbags. What are doing to protect us? Are there, like, designated safezones that cits are being shepherded towards?"

Hawkins laughed and threw the rag on the floor. "You're kidding me, right? Infrastructure fell apart the moment that creepy fucking kid tore Chief Drabbon's heart out. We fought back as best we could, but they were slaughtering us. People were goin' mad, runnin' rampant... it became clear there was no control any more. It was every man and woman for themselves."

"So you ran," Lox said.

"Guess I did, sister. There was nothin' left to police. The smart move was getting the hell out of Dodge."

"Don't you have a moral code or something?"

Hawkins jerked a thumb at Lox and looked at me. "What's her beef?"

"She's not a big fan of Justice Department, but I guess she was hoping there was someone in authority actively tackling the situation," I said.

"Good luck with that. De'Ath and his creatures are the authority now. How long you stay alive now depends on how far you're willing to flee."

"So where are *you* going?" I asked.

"The coast. Figure my best bet is to find a boat that'll drop me off at the furthest desert island possible."

"Look, man, we've got a real chance of stopping this thing," I said. "In that guy"—I nodded at Stender—"we got a trump card. He knows what's being developed out at Rennick."

"The disease centre, huh?"

"You said yourself that they're trying to find ways to kill as many of us as possible. If they get Red Mosquito out into the food chain, it'll be—"

"Long-term mass extinction," Stender finished, reaching into his coat and pulling one of the vials free. He tossed it to Hawkins, who shuck off her helmet for the first time—revealing herself to be a thirty-year-old black woman with close-cropped hair and a prominent scar running under her left ear and down her neck—so she could take a closer look. "It'll corrupt and eliminate every food source on the planet. No one will survive."

"Red Mosquito?"

"That's what they're calling it."

Hawkins shook the vial, tipped it upside down, fascinated by the contents. "You're crazy."

"Look, we get it," I said, "you just want to escape, live out what's left of your days on a beach somewhere. We don't need you to come in with us. But if you can help us get there, help us avoid the patrols... well, maybe that'll go a bit easier on your conscience when you're lying there with sand between your toes idly wondering whatever happened to the rest of us."

"What makes you think I got one?" she said, passing the vial back to Stender. "A conscience, I mean."

"True. But I see you haven't taken off your badge, so that's still gotta mean something, right? 'Cause right now you're still a Judge. And when you first zipped up that uniform all those years ago, you must've believed in *something*."

Hawkins locked stares with me, then slipped the helmet back on, adjusted her gloves, and replied: "You can't motivate for shit, you know that?"

CHAPTER EIGHT

Hawkins was kind of a dick—then again, I'd never met a badge that wasn't—but her access to the Judgecloud proved invaluable. Sidney and his goon squad were still using the same system that Hawkins' Lawrider bike was connected to, and she was able to map where H-Wagon units were being directed. All had been grounded when the storm broke, but now the rain was easing off some twelve hours later, she flagged several taking to the skies.

"They'll be looking for survivors," she murmured, watching the radar pings and plotting a route that would take us outside the H-Wagons' search vectors. "Surveying the wreckage."

"If you can track them, won't they be able to do the same to you?" Loxley asked, peering over the jay's shoulder.

"Nope. First thing I did when I got the chance was disable the bike's transponder."

"The greys told us that psychics were trying to get a bead on Stender," I said. "Apparently, all that dying on a massive scale had so far crowded him out."

"Yeah, Psi-Div's a bitch if you're trying to keep something on the downlow. They got ranks of sensitives scanning the ether, combing through people's thoughts. I'm not surprised there was a psychic whiteout the moment all that initial craziness kicked off. But we should get moving—they'll find it easier to locate him now there's a few less minds to worry about."

"We'll need transport," I said. "How far's Rennick from here?"

"About another forty miles," Stender replied.

"I got an idea about that," Hawkins said. "Leave it with me."

She was as good as her word. Using a Justice Department secure channel, she radioed in a request for backup, claiming that she was taking fire from the resistance. She kept details deliberately vague, playing on atmospheric conditions for interrupting her broadcast and blaming a damaged Lawrider for an unresponsive transponder signal, but made sure Control picked up her coordinates. She then pushed her bike out onto the interstate, now a couple of feet under standing water, calling over her shoulder to us to stay out of sight.

The three of us leaned against the barn wall and peered out at this grave new world that was being formed around us. It was just after dawn on the third day, and the sky was the colour of bruises—green fading to violet—and genuinely looked like it had been damaged. The clouds had dispersed a little, but there was no blue beyond them, just glimpses of a starry black emptiness as if something irreplaceable had been torn up there. It felt alien now; *other*. That our world was not just being flattened and scoured of life, but also remoulded in tribute to whatever powers Sidney was in league with. Hour by hour it was no longer ours but was being irreversibly corrupted and dismantled, shaped into a planet-sized tombstone. The persistent rainfall gave the air the smell of decay, of everything organic being reduced to putrefying matter.

Within minutes a Justice Department cruiser came speeding along the highway, blue lights flashing silently, dividing the floodwater before it. It pulled up alongside Hawkins, who shielded herself from their gaze by remaining propped on the far side of the bike, head down, appearing injured and unresponsive, cloaked in a waterproof duster. The two greys inside clambered out and circled round in front of the Lawrider, just as Hawkins mouthed an order to the onboard computer, and the cannons opened up automatically—the Judges were instantly bisected, body parts scattered in the now pink and churning water. She got to her feet and beckoned us out.

"Your carriage awaits," she said, motioning to the cruiser. "I'll be able to stay in contact by radio on a narrow-cast frequency, which the Grand Hall won't be able to pick up. You should be able to travel under their radar in that, as long as you keep your heads down and don't attract attention to yourselves."

"In that case, *I'm* driving," Loxley said, already opening the car door, hand on the wheel before I'd had a chance to disagree.

WITH HAWKINS LEADING the way on her Lawrider, we followed, me up front next to Lox, Stender on the back seat behind a wire mesh intended to protect the cops from their prisoner. He complained about the smell initially, shifting about and squeaking that there were troubling stains on the upholstery that he didn't want to sit on, but a look from Loxley shot at him via the rear-view mirror quickly shut him up. She muttered that she had to concentrate, her eyes glued to what little she could see of the road ahead through the spray the tyres were kicking up, and we made steady if slow progress. I sympathised to a degree with Stender—there were gross smears that I could see on the dashboard and doorframe as if whatever these things touched they left a residue, a part of themselves, behind, and the stink was truly noxious as if a trapped animal had slowly rotted in the trunk—but it was getting to the point that squeamishness was redundant now. We were all being tainted by the grotesqueries of this butchered planet, all made to crawl through the shit and filth, and civilities maybe belonged to the old order. We would have to get used to death's sickly sweet stench, for that would now be the norm, and become accustomed to the crunch of bones beneath our feet. We would be like insects scuttling across a vast carcass that was their world entire, for it was all they had ever known. I wondered if memories would eventually fade and no one would remember what their home used to be like before life and civilisation were washed away. All accomplishments, every evolutionary leap and breakthrough, would be lost to a history that no one would ever read, and all that would remain would be a blasted, lifeless rock hanging in space solely defined by its very lack of existence. A dead world.

I stayed defiantly uncheered by the view from my window. On either side of the road, sluiced up against half-submerged vehicles and buildings, was a logjam of bodies, some floating face down, others collecting like flotsam against a storm drain, piled on top each other as they bobbed with the movement of the current. There were hundreds of them, bleached limbs askew, clothes torn from their skin, to the point where they looked like amorphous entities attaching themselves limpet-like to whatever upright object had survived the tempest. It was impossible to discern where one corpse ended and another began; hair and fingers trailed like fronds on the water's surface, but to what person they were attached was not easy to say. Presumably, the elements would conspire to meld them even closer together over time—who was going to be clearing them away, after all? From now on the dead would lie where they dropped—until they became a skeletonised mass, a community fused in calcium and marrow. Carrion-eating birds hopped from body to body, piecemeal offerings in their beaks, though they resembled no species of vulture that I'd ever seen before. They were ugly, sparsely feathered, deformed things that watched us pass with an unnerving intelligence behind their beady black eyes.

I saw something else move in one of the deeper stretches of floodwater that wasn't simply a cadaver working its way loose of the wormfood flotilla; an elongated shape cut through the throng, a good nine feet long, with plated ridges along its back. I strained to get a better look, but it dived, leaving a stream of bubbles in its wake. The bodies swayed with the sudden motion.

"Uh, Lox?" I said. "Don't want to be a back-seat driver an' all, but make sure you stay on the road, okay?"

"I've seen them," she replied, staring straight ahead. "Trying to forget they're there, to be honest."

"Not the bodies. There's something else... something predatory in the water. Over there."

"Jesus, McGill, this is hard enough as it is without you shitting me up even further. Over where—?"

A spume of brownish water suddenly geysered up on her left, sprinkling the side of the cruiser with droplets, and everyone in the car cut loose with an expletive simultaneously. The vehicle wavered as Lox tugged too hard on the wheel in reaction, and there was a momentary loss of control before she righted it again. She flipped on the wipers, the windscreen misting with condensation, and peered ahead.

"Is Hawkins still in front?"

"Yeah," I answered, rubbing my sleeve against my side of the windscreen. "I can see her tail light."

The radio receiver burst into life with a surge of static. I heard the Judge's voice hailing us so picked up the mic and responded. "You guys all right?" she asked. "Looked like you got into difficulties."

"There's, um, something following us. Seems kinda hungry."

"Your momma never warned you about the gators?"

"Not this far inland, surely?"

"New rules apply, I guess. Environment's changing."

"That's a hell of a gator."

"Christ knows *what* they're turning into. Look, just keep going straight, and obviously don't get out of the car. You should be safe—"

There was a wrench as something heavy collided with

the rear wing of the cruiser, and the vehicle wobbled again. I looked anxiously in the mirror, trying to catch sight of it. "Why aren't I reassured?"

"Just don't stop," she reiterated. "It's testing the limits of your defences."

"It's the limits of my sanity I'm worried about," I murmured, watching the roiling water for what lay beneath. "Seriously, I've about reached my personal quota of fucked-up shit right about now—"

It was then, of course, that Stender started spazzing out. He gripped the wire mesh and began to shake his head back and forth, muttering a series of refusals as he did so, before throwing himself back in the seat violently enough to make the whole vehicle shake. He arched his back, rocking to and fro with increasing speed.

"What the hell's got into him?" Loxley asked, casting a quick glance over her shoulder.

"Christ knows," I said, turning far enough around so I could address him. "Stender? What's wrong?"

The Tek man lurched forward to the mesh again and smacked his forehead against it, which made me flinch instinctively; several red marks were imprinted on his skin when he pulled his face away. His eyes were rolled upwards in their sockets, and he was emitting a keening noise, like he was taking a big lungful of air.

"Stender?"

He rubbed his knuckles against his temples, and gritted his teeth. His veins seemingly throbbed, as if something was exerting pressure from within, and he sobbed the word "no" repeatedly, snot and tears now wiped across his nose and mouth. He threw off his glasses, clawed at his eyes. I felt helpless, unable to reach out to him because of the metal divide.

"Stender, talk to me. What is it?"

There was another thump from beneath the car, and the engine roared a little as if the exhaust pipe had been damaged.

Was this thing keeping pace with us? Lox wasn't going fast by any means—the depth of water was pushing back against us—but even so it has some speed on it. It clearly hadn't lost interest.

"*Get ouuuuutttt...*" Stender intoned mournfully.

"What's he saying?" Lox demanded.

"*Get ouuuuttttt of my... heeeeaddd!*" The guy was screaming now. "*Get ouuuuuttttt! Get ouuuuuutttt!*" He started to slam his shoulder against the passenger door, ripping angrily at the handle, yanking on it, but it wouldn't budge. He lifted his feet up and kicked out at the glass, each impact sending the cruiser rocking. The car slid, but Loxley prevented it from fishtailing completely.

"Jesus, Martin," I shouted, slamming my good palm against the mesh. "Calm down. We can't afford to stop here."

"What the fuck's going on?" Hawkins voice spat out of the radio receiver.

"Stender's gone crazy," I said. "He's having some kind of fit. Keeps saying something's in his head."

There was a pause. "Psi-Division's found him," the Judge finally answered flatly. "They've got inside his mind. They know where he is."

"Oh Christ. What can we do?"

"Nothing we *can* do. They'll be remote-tracking him, and units will be dispatched to collect. We need to pick up the pace, get to Rennick before they catch up with us. Let's go, c'mon."

I glanced at Loxley, who nodded glumly and eased down on the accelerator. Water sloshed over the hood, and the car felt even more unsteady as it swayed with the increased motion. A scrape from below told us that our gator friend was still showing no signs of giving up.

"How far we got to go, do you think?" I asked.

"I reckon another ten miles."

"Shitsticks. We're not going to make it."

"We'll make it."

There was further grunting from the back seat, interspersed with hacking sobs. *"I don't wanna see I don't wanna see..."* were the only words that could be discerned. I shuddered to imagine what loathsome visions were being force-fed into his skull by the Psi-Div creatures. He resumed slamming his arm against the door frame until there was a resounding crack, and a scream. I thought at first that the glass had finally splintered under his relentless assault, but when I turned, I saw that it was his right forearm that had fractured, the bone dividing the flesh at the wrist. Blood fountained across the roof of the car as well as the back window. Despite the very real pain he must've been in, Stender continued to screw up his eyes and shake his head, his face pale with shock.

"Aw fuck, he's gonna bleed out if we don't staunch that," I said. "Stop the car."

"You're not serious? You heard what Hawkins said—we gotta go," Lox answered.

"There's no way I can get to him without going in from the outside." I slammed my palm against the mesh to emphasise the point. "We need him alive as much as they do."

"You know what's out there."

"Only too well." I rummaged around under the seat, and came up trumps with a med-kit. "I'll have to be fast, and once I'm in the back, get going again. It'll be a matter of seconds, hopefully."

"I can't believe you're doing this."

"He's gonna die before we hit Rennick. Believe me, I'm not wild about the idea myself, but I can't see we've got a choice." I looked back at Stender; his eyes were fluttering, his breathing erratic. I could smell the coppery aroma of his blood.

"Yo, McGill," Hawkins's crackly voice interjected. "We've got trouble."

A near-hysterical laugh bubbled up my throat and out of my mouth in response. "No shit?"

"Just picked up radio chatter. An aerial unit is on its way. They've zeroed in on your lab guy."

I closed my eyelids for a second, trying to damp down the panic. "How long have we got?"

"Probably a few minutes before it's in visual range. Loxley has gotta put her foot to the floor, man."

"Right." I clicked off the mic, and tucked the med-kit under my arm. "Piece of cake. Stop the car, Lox."

Shaking her head, she braked gently. I quietly counted to five, then popped the lock and slipped out, shutting the door behind me. The water was up to my knees, the cold instantly penetrating my jeans, and I waded as speedily as I could round to the rear door, aware that anything could be hiding in the murk below. The road was firm enough beneath my feet, but the swirling current pushed and pulled at me. Cadavers just a few metres away rocked gently with the little wavelets that I was creating. I grabbed hold of the door handle and pulled, just as Stender tried to barge his way out, knocking us both back into the water. I struggled to maintain my footing, and the med-kit went flying from my hand. Stender fell forward with a splash, his injured arm hanging limply at his side.

"Get out, have to get out," he repeated, his expression and demeanour telling me he was more or less no longer in control of his actions. He was trying to rise and head back in the direction we'd come.

"Martin," I said, reaching for his shoulder. "Get back in the car. It's not safe to be out here."

He resisted, pushing my hand away, and I noted the crimson threads in the water around us where his wound was leaking. I got my arm around his neck and forcibly pulled him back towards the cruiser. He kicked and tried to dig his heels in, growling something inaudible, but he was off-balance, and I made progress dragging him the few metres that separated us from the car's back seat.

Then I saw the suggestion of a plated spine crest the water half a second before I felt a force below the surface tug him down hard. Stender was momentarily plucked from my grip, disappearing up to his waist, and he yelled, face contorting in agony. Fresh crimson clouds blossomed in the water around him. I swore and tried pull him upright, but the gator had a good firm grip on him and wasn't going to relinquish him easy. I changed tactic and let go, drawing my gun from my belt instead, and aimed to the side of him, blindly taking three successive shots. The creature thrashed, whipping Stender with it as he was slammed against the car's trunk. Christ knew if I'd done any damage—what little I'd seen of the thing suggested it had a thick hide—but I just wanted to distract it enough to release the man from its jaws.

Stender was holding on the vehicle's bodywork, trying to stand, when he was yanked from below again. He wailed, long and piteously. I sighted my gun once more at the water's surface, then decided against it and thumped hard on the window, catching Lox's attention.

"Reverse," I called out. "Right now."

The cruiser lurched as it suddenly jerked backwards, hit an unseen obstacle, then rose up a good foot from the road as it rolled over what I assumed was the rear part of the gator. The water frothed and churned manically as the creature curled back in pain, mouth opening instinctively, allowing Stender to tumble free. I grabbed him and heaved him away, trying to get him back into the car, but he was borderline unconscious by this point and a dead weight, his clothes heavily saturated with blood and water.

Loxley pulled forward, and I had a hand on the passenger door handle when the gator snapped with lightning speed and sank its teeth into Stender's thigh. He slipped back down, now on all fours, and I toppled with him, unbalanced. I held his arms, and he raised his head, eyes seeing through me.

A swish in the air above us made me glance up, and I saw the H-Wagon that Hawkins had warned was on its way banking as it descended.

"Aw fuck," I muttered, feeling the warmth of its jets against my cheeks and forehead the closer it got. I turned back to Stender but his eyes were now shut.

A laser bolt lanced out of the underside of the craft and into the water, causing a red fountain to erupt several feet high. The gator had taken a direct hit. It keeled over and Stender almost went with it, head dipping below the surface. The H-Wagon fired again and the beast's skull flew apart, its riven body now floating upside down in a stew of its own innards.

I kept hold of Stender and pulled him towards me. "C'mon, Martin, stay with me. Can you stand?" With my back to the car as leverage, I hoisted him up, and discovered his legs ended just below the groin, the stumps raw and gleaming.

"Martin?" I got my good hand free from under his arm and slapped his cheek. He was cold and still.

He was gone.

Numbly, I let go of him, his body sliding into the water, then turned my attention to the H-Wagon hovering before me, the blast of its engines rippling the surface.

CHAPTER NINE

THERE WAS KIND of a moment where I felt it wouldn't be so bad to be vaporised where I stood—with those H-Wagon guns trained on me, the sense of resignation that swept briefly through was liberating. It was so damn hard, this struggle to survive, scrabbling to cling on to life when everything's doing its damnedest to put you in the ground. To be reduced to ashes and scattered on the wind seemed in that instance to accept your place in the universe, to find some form of peace.

I never quit when I was in the ring, I told myself. Not in the early days, when I was still driven and hungry. I never gave up when there was fight still left in me. But that was so long ago, another voice countered, and all the knocks I took, all the punches that I steadfastly refused to allow to put me down, what good did it do, in the end? Every piledriver I soaked up, every right hook that I rode out—it was all damage. What did my stubbornness achieve in the end other than to punish myself? Years later, I paid the physical price for my obstinacy. It was never grit; I was just too dumb to know when I was beaten.

Suffering never got me anywhere other than in a shit-ton of debt concurrent with a spiralling alcohol problem. Why prolong it? What are you still fighting for when you know you don't have a chance? Why take the smacks and tell yourself that they don't hurt? 'Cause it'll just keep coming: more blows, more horror, more knockdowns. They won't stop—accept that. They won't stop until you're dead; isn't it time to finally give them what they want, and end this brutal, pathetic charade?

Like I say, I had a moment. But it was just a moment.

I barely heard the slamming on the car window next to me above the whine of the H-Wagon's engines, but I glanced over to see Lox banging her fist against the glass and yelling. I was aware of the water sloshing around my knees, then the sound of something else approaching from the opposite direction. I turned in time to see Hawkins powering towards us, bike surging through the flood, Lawgiver raised a fraction above my head.

"High explosive," she roared, and the gun barked. The wagon banked in response to avoid the bullet, but it caught the wing and exploded, causing the craft to veer wildly. Black smoke poured from the burning fuselage as it managed to arrest its list and come back firing, cannons chopping up the water. I yanked open the cruiser's door and dived inside, covering my head, just as the wagon's rounds found the Lawrider and shredded the tyres. It somersaulted and Hawkins rolled to the side, avoiding her ride coming crashing back down again. She got to her feet, looked at me and Loxley, wide-eyed on the other side of the window, and made a sweeping movement with her arm.

"Go!" she shouted. "Get out of here!"

Lox put her foot down. The H-Wagon curved round for another pass and the Judge fired off a second shot, tearing away a section of the cabin. It seemed destined to plough straight into the floodwaters but it managed to pull up, cutting low across the surface, throwing up backwash from its lifters as it aimed itself directly at Hawkins. I watched the rapidly diminishing scene in the mirror as we sped away, the Judge a tiny figure kneeling before the blazing craft that was bearing down on it. Then came the explosion and the sky lighted up in a tangerine flash.

"Fuck," Lox breathed, smoke shrouding the horizon behind her. "Hawkins...?"

"Can't see her," I said.

"You think we should go back?"

I shook my head. "She wanted to buy us some time. We shouldn't squander it."

"But if she made it—"

"And if another H-Wagon comes along, we'll have lost the lead we had. We have to keep going."

We rode in silence for another fifteen minutes. The road began to incline, and the water level dropped away significantly, allowing us to gain some traction. We crested a hill, and slowed—there, nestling below, was the town of Rennick, looking as battered by the elements as everywhere else.

Visible beyond it, looming over the smaller buildings like some sleeping beast, was the glass and steel edifice of the Center for Disease Research.

"CAN WE STILL do this?" I asked.

"We can't turn around now."

"Stender was our expert—he knew what the hell this Red Mosquito stuff was. Without him... I'm kinda lost as to what we can achieve."

"We don't necessarily need the man who helped make something to tear it down." Loxley grabbed my arm and made me face her. "You wanted my help to get you in there—the pair of you were going to destroy all the samples. I don't see how that's changed. We get in, we blitz the place. We make sure that nothing survives."

I was quiet for a moment.

"The vials that he stole—you still have them?" she asked.

I shook my head. "He had them on him. They've been lost to the floods."

"Better they don't fall into the wrong hands, I guess. Okay, we'll have to adapt our plan. I'm still in favour of scorched earth—we level everything that's inside. Burn it all down."

"Stender didn't seem to think that was a good idea."

"With all due respect to the guy, he's dead, and we're out of options. Look, McGill, these creatures, what they're doing; we have to stop them by any means. It doesn't require finesse or a degree from Stanlake to drive a wrecking ball through their scheme. Just takes guts. You with me?"

I nodded. She studied me, clearly not convinced, her gaze piercing mine. "Are you okay?"

"Not really. My head feels messed up. Shock, I think, and a sort of... helpless frustration. I had a wobble, back there, where for a split-second I wondered how peaceful it would be to be atomised by the H-Wagon, to just succumb to the inevitability of it all. Losing Stender after all we've been through knocked the fight out of me, I suppose."

"But we're still here, right? And we can't give up. It's too important to bail out on. I mean, the whole world's at stake here, Jackson—and I can remember how much you used to like high stakes. Well, we're going all in. You wouldn't want to be known as the man that, faced with the responsibility, folded at the last minute."

"I know. I've known from the beginning all paths would lead here. You don't fuck with fate."

"What's that?"

"Never mind. Game faces on, yeah?"

Rennick looked like the site of a natural disaster (which to a degree it had been, if brought about by unnatural means); in the aftermath of something like this, you'd expect to see a relief effort on TV reports combing the debris for survivors, local people pulling together to claw through rubble to find those trapped beneath. But there was nothing—a silence hung over the wrecked streets, where the rising water levels had disintegrated foundations and collapsed apartment blocks, and vehicles had been washed into the side of buildings where they hung, discarded. It hadn't been a big town—one of those communities that had sprung up around a single industry; in this case some kind of textile factory, which sat to the east near the Chapperneam river, and was probably now a crumbling ruin once the banks had burst—and had been evidently quite poor, judging by how much of it had fallen apart. The cheap tenements and trailer parks hadn't stood a chance, roofs torn off and exposing private belongings to the world. Bodies were everywhere, several feet deep in places, as if they'd been shovelled to the side like piles of dead leaves, and the stench was ripe: you could feel it gluing itself to your tongue.

Lox had to drive carefully, picking her way through the destruction, aware that at any moment the thoroughfares might become impassable. A squeal lanced through the stillness when she misjudged the space between two concrete blocks and the edge of one scraped along the wing; the noise disturbed more of those carrion-bird creatures perched nearby, who lazily flapped their large leathery wings and watched us pass. They didn't make a sound in response; just all turned their black, turkey-like heads to study the car. Ahead, the Justice Department institution rose above the town's peaks, the lane leading out to it terminated by a high wire fence. She brought the cruiser to a stop some distance away.

"Is that going to be guarded?" I asked.

"It's likely. If it's not, it'll be alarmed." She tapped her bottom lip with her forefinger as she ran her gaze over the facility. "Haven't got time to go under it," she said quietly as if she was talking to herself. "Gonna have to go *over* it." She turned to the small onboard computer that jutted out from the dash between the driver's and passenger's seats and started tapping at the keyboard.

"What are you doing?"

"Something Hawkins mentioned. She said the greys and the rest of De'Ath's damned followers were still using the Judgecloud. As far as the pusbags back at Grand Hall are concerned, this vehicle hasn't been stolen. They've got no reason to suspect it." She hit enter and looked up from the screen. "I've just included this sector in the nearest H-Wagon's patrol circuit."

"You've asked one to come here?"

She nodded. "They'll get a flag notifying them that this is an area of interest. They'll most definitely be able to pinpoint the unit that the hail came from. I've left it active." She drummed her fingers on the steering wheel. "I reckon they'll be dropping by within the next hour."

"And then?"

"And then, McGill, we'll be hitching a lift."

Lox deduced which was the nearest building tall enough for an H-Wagon to set down upon, and motioned for me to follow. We left the car and waded our way through the wreckage of what had once been the town's main drag, the water around our shins. Looking down at myself as I picked a route through debris and smashed human remains, I realised how filthy I must be, my clothes sodden and grime-encrusted. I hadn't had a shower or change of duds in three days, a small portion of Hawkins' bike rations was the last thing I'd eaten, and the painkiller-induced sleep at Loxley's place was the last time I'd closed my eyes in rest. With that in mind, I glanced at the hand that she'd strapped up, and prodded it: it was worryingly free of sensation. I'd been so distracted and hopped up on adrenaline that I'd given it scant regard, but now it felt as if it had calcified. The clean, sterile environment of a hospital where a doc could treat it seemed like a fantasy now—would there going to be anywhere that wasn't permeated with the reek of death and decay? The air was probably already teeming with bacteria as all these cadavers broke down; infection surely wasn't going to be far away. Plague, madness... the world was being reduced to a twelfth-century charnel pit.

I stuck close to Lox as she headed through the doors of an office complex and climbed the stairs, not risking the safety of the elevator. It was only four storeys, but structurally had survived the onslaught and was therefore the highest in the district; within its walls, however, it was a mess of abandonment as workers had fled in panic. Desks were strewn all over the place, crumpled documents scattered across the linoleum floor. One door stated the occupants were lawyers—pretty low-rent, judging by the décor—but it was in an equal state of disarray, records and files dropped and forgotten. The place was deserted, although a ratchety noise was enough to make me draw my gun in readiness; it turned out to be an electric fan sitting on a windowsill still plugged in and operating, cooling an empty room.

Lox reached the maintenance door that led out onto the roof and shoulder-charged it open. She indicated we crouch down behind some heating pipes, and wait. Sure enough, forty minutes later, the unmistakable sound of the craft's descent advertised its arrival. We hunkered down lower as it circled the area, and I could hear her whispering to herself, willing it to land; finally, after an agonisingly long patrol of the neighbourhood, it hovered above the wide, flat stretch of asphalt that was the office block's roof and extended its landing gear. It touched down but left its engine cycling as two greys disembarked from a ramp and lurched towards the edge of the building, peering over.

Lox tapped me on the arm and nodded. She jogged round the back of the H-Wagon and hoisted herself up on to one of the legs, climbing into the section where the gear folded back into the undercarriage. She reached down and gave me a hand up as I joined her. Despite the rumble of the lifters, we could hear one of the Judges talking into its comm as they both surveyed the ruins—in particular the cruiser parked below.

"A Jussstice Department patrol car hasss been left abandoned, ssstill broadcassting a sssignal... no sssign of the occupantsss."

"Resssisstance?"

I instinctively glanced at Lox the moment the voice on the other end of the radio drifted across the roof. The strength of it was such that it was clearly audible over the background noise, and it had a different timbre to the greys' dry, sibilant hiss; this had a note of authority, an inflection of power, behind it. My sphincter muscle puckered just at the sound of that one word, and the implied menace that was tangible in the speaker. I could see from the expression on Lox's face that she felt the same way: that there was some unseen Big Bad far worse than we ever imagined.

"It'sss posssible," the Judge replied. "They may have ambussshed the unit. It wasss logged asss being called to assisssst a ninety-nine red a few hourss earlier, but that was further back up the interssstate. It hasss not reported back sssince then."

"Sssinnersss evidently ssstill are at work in the ruinsss," the disembodied voice intoned. It made my ears hurt to hear it. "Have you had any sssightingsss?"

"No visssual confirmation, sssir."

"I had hoped the rainssss would flusssh out the guilty from their hidey-holesss, and yet sssome ssstill remain. They are assss tenacioussss assss vermin." What sounded like wind whistling through the open doors of an ancient mausoleum emerged from the comm-device, and it took me a moment to realise that the speaker was sighing. "Complete a circuit of the perimeter fence; tell me if you ssspot any criminalssss at large. Any resssissstance mussst be nullified. The living *mussst* be extinguissshed."

"Very well, sssir."

Both greys turned as one and stalked back to the H-Wagon, disappearing back up the boarding ramp. Seconds later the craft trembled, the lifters began to whine even louder, and it started to rise.

"Get ready!" Loxley shouted. "Pull yourself back in as far as you can go." She spread-eagled herself like a starfish in the compartment that housed the landing gear just as they started to retract. I did the same, my nose a centimetre from the strut once it clunked into place.

"Have you done this before?" I yelled across to her, the wind now whipping across my face as I watched the roof drop away beneath me. Vertigo lurched in my stomach, and I couldn't stop feeling the sensation that I was about to fall any second.

"Once or twice," she admitted. "It gets easier with experience."

"Yeah, I'm not going to be making a habit of this."

"Just follow my lead. I'll need you to jump when I tell you. If you hesitate, you're dead."

The H-Wagon banked, and the landscape below us lurched; I wanted to close my eyes and imagine I was somewhere else, but the nausea intensified the moment I shut them as I lost all centre of balance. I focused instead on a broken church spire below and tried to clear my mind of anything but that, ignoring the throb of the engine behind me, the stink of oil and exhaust, and the air sluicing past in the vents. Despite my efforts, my gaze kept wandering to the rest of the wrecked town and, at this remove, the scale of the destruction was sobering. I kept seeing little details—a scrawled SOS on a banner strung between two trees in some family's backyard, pleading for help that never came; a flock of those vulture things feasting on the contents of an upturned car; a pylon that had crushed several static homes as it had come down on a trailer park—that personalised the tragedy, reinforced the number of innocent lives lost through the machinations of these maniacs. All those bodies that had once been loved and cherished husbands and wives, sons and daughters, reduced to nothing; a statistic. Unheard voices crying out, lost in the mass slaughter, raging at the injustice—you could imagine it seeping into the earth. The flesh might rot, the bones crumble, but the anger, the grief, would remain like an imprint, an indelible mark on this benighted land.

I saw the fence of the facility emerge from the corner of my viewpoint, and cast a glance at Lox. She nodded, as best she was able, and put her arm round the landing strut, shifting her position. The craft was doing a circuit of the perimeter, following the edge of the boundary; before us the main building was huge, and relatively untouched by the storm, its glass façade reflecting the wagon as it passed. It veered to the left and began a circle around the rear of the complex, from which many pipes and power outages sprouted. A fire escape ran between a pair of vast generators—Lox pointed, and pulled herself around so she was on the other side of the leg. I, trembling, did the same.

"Remember, go when I say so," she said. "Miss the opportunity and you'll splat against the side of building."

The fire escape swung parallel to us frighteningly fast, and I didn't have the time to steel myself before I heard Loxley shout and I leapt, the steel gantry rushing up to greet me. She landed on her feet and rolled, whereas I managed to collide with the handrail, rebounded and tumbled down half a dozen steps. A hand grabbed my shirt collar and stopped me going any further. The H-Wagon swept on, seemingly unaware two stowaways had disembarked mid-flight.

I groaned and held my side, what felt like a fire spreading across my chest.

"You okay?" Lox asked.

"Think... I bruised a rib at least," I said when I had my breath back. "Aw, man, that's sore." I looked at her. "How'd you get so graceful?"

"It's what I used to be paid for, back in the old days. There's a reason a lumbering ox like you isn't a professional cat burglar."

"Point."

"Come on," she said, gripping my left hand and pulling me up. "You'll manage the pain. That's what *you're* good at, right?"

"Has become a specialty, I'll admit. Plenty of goddamn practice."

She jogged down the stairs, me following more gingerly, every step sending an ache up my torso. She paused at one of the fire doors. "Try to open this from the outside and it'll more than likely set off an alarm."

"So how do we get in, then?"

"Oh, we still use it. We just disable the alarm first." She vaulted over the side of the fire escape and landed beside a localised power station housed in a small shed-like construction fronted by a pair of metal doors festooned with warning signs. She dug in her inside jacket pocket and produced a small case, from which she extracted a screwdriver and rammed it between the doors, forcing them open. Once she had access, she got to work, her hands playing over the circuit switches. "I'll probably trip something else too—lights or whatever—but hopefully we'll be in before anyone realises."

Moments later, she was back up the stairs. "I'll need your help here." She levered the screwdriver into the jamb, and indicated that I should yank the door back, which I did one-handed, bicep straining. I created enough of a gap for her to slide through, then once she was in she opened it from the inside.

We were in. Time to finish this.

CHAPTER TEN

There were Justice Department facilities like this all over the north state, although the CDR was one of the largest. I got to know about several civilian-staffed centres in the past through the Bushman's gossipy enforcers—because they were largely populated by non-Judicial personnel, it was relatively easy to make contacts and find an inside man willing to smuggle merchandise out, or so I was reliably informed. Contraband storage depots were the most lucrative, though tech-development labs often paid out in hardware; when it came to securing new territories, the latest weaponry in your hand was a useful tool in a turf war. Whitecoats could have their heads turned by a flash of cold hard creds with little trouble, and were more than willing to pass on dope, guns and intel for an extra bounce on the side. Government-funded set-ups like this notoriously didn't pay for shit, and their disgruntled workforce were ripe for exploitation.

Stender, as he'd been keen to point out on several occasions, wasn't HoJ, and clearly most of the researchers working here hadn't been either, up to the point of De'Ath's coup. Whether they'd refused to comply with the new regime, or were simply in the way, their bodies littered the corridors. It looked like most had simply been disposed of where they stood, though there was a variance in the state of the corpses: some had been shot—a trio sat with their backs to the wall, a triple explosion of crimson on the plaster behind them, suggesting they'd been lined up and executed—while others were bags of bones, rotted skeletons that had seemingly melted in their clothes. Jellified skulls grinned at me from behind desks, sunk back into shirt collars. I was at a loss as to what could've happened to them; doused in some chemical agent, possibly. Whatever the cause, it meant the place was rank with the smell of decay, the sterile antiseptic scent of a facility like this replaced by a grimy stench, like the air of a sealed tomb.

"You think anyone's been left alive?" Lox whispered, eyeing the remains.

"Past experience says no."

She nodded and popped her head around glass-partitioned offices, noting the carnage everywhere she looked. "Nothing useful here. Where should we head for?"

"This seems to be some kind of admin section. Let's check the floor-list at the next set of elevators."

Just as we reached the end of the corridor, Lox pulled me back. "Wait a second," she said. She cast a glance around the corner. "CCTV camera on the wall by the els. Hold on." She delved back into her jacket pocket and produced a slim device the size and shape of a credit card, which she held up and pressed the centre of. A red light blinked on its end; satisfied, she stuffed it away. "Okay, let's go."

"What was that?"

"Localised EMP pulse. It'll knock it out of action."

The guide on the wall stated that viral labs were a couple of storeys below us. She shook her head when I made towards the elevators, and instead took my arm and directed me towards the stairs, which we nimbly descended, the stairwell dark and silent apart from our footsteps tapping on the concrete. The building felt unnervingly dead while at the same time it was impossible to dispel the sensation that something very still and patient lurked in the shadows, waiting. I thought I could hear breathing coming from close by, but I realised that it was my own. I kept looking over my shoulder, convinced that multiple figures were following. The place was getting under my skin. Fatigue may have been playing a factor, but I couldn't shake the notion that it was because we were in the presence of an entity of an entirely different stripe to what we had encountered up to now. Between the walls, something presided over the chill emptiness, infecting the entire structure.

We reached a pair of double doors stencilled with biohazard signs that by the look of them were ordinarily only accessed by a keypad but had been forced open, a blackened scorch mark emanating from the lock. Loxley reached out and traced its outline with her fingers, brow furrowed. I unaccountably felt nervous watching her do that, and touched her arm; she pulled her hand away and straightened.

"You feel that?" I asked.

"What?"

"I don't know... I keep feeling there's something here. You not getting the bad vibes? There's like a toxic atmosphere."

"Been sensing bad vibes since you first turned up at my door, Jackson."

"No, this is different. There's a power here. I can't explain it." I lightly pushed open one of the doors. "Promise you'll stick close to me. I don't like what we're heading into."

"I can look after myself."

"I know, I know. But something's given me the wiggins like I've never felt before."

We slid into the lab which was mostly in darkness, lit by red emergency bulbs positioned on the walls. Rows upon rows of cooler units sat on either side of the room, each filled with shelves racked with vials similar to the kind Stender had on him when our paths first crossed. I walked over to the nearest one, but found it impossible to read anything in the gloom.

"You got a torch?"

"Yep." She fished a compact penlight out of her back pocket and handed it to me.

I ran it over the samples, but each was labelled with the same ten-digit serial numbers that were on Stender's vial-packs; I could glean nothing from them. "All Greek to me," I murmured. "Can't tell what any of this stuff is."

"Jays sure have been storing up on their bacterial warfare," she said, looking around with an expression of disdain on her face. "I'm betting this all predates the current assholes."

"Reckon they would've used any of this on us, if they'd had the chance?"

"Without question. It's only now in this little bastard Sidney that someone who's enough of a psychopath has come along and shown them how to do it."

"So what do we do?" I asked. "Without Stender we got no hope of finding Red Mosquito. I can't tell one of these test tubes from a damn hole in the ground."

"We bring down the whole place, like I said. Put a wrecking ball to it. It doesn't deserve to still be standing, all the fucking horrors it's created."

"You know how to do that?"

"I can jerryrig an explosive using the accelerant from a fire extinguisher. If we find one, I can fashion something that'll go boom. Hopefully, all this is flammable enough to go up like a firework."

"Place like this will have a sprinkler system, surely."

"Not if you knock out the localised circuit that controls the sensors."

"I thought you said you were a thief, not a saboteur. You were quite forceful on that topic, I recall."

She shrugged. "I've done corporate espionage gigs. I'm not proud."

"Every day's a marvel with you, Lox," I said. "Okay, let's get to it."

We moved cautiously further into the lab, and I played the torch over the floor and walls. We'd barely taken a few steps when the beam alighted on something. "You see that?" I murmured.

I readjusted the torch in my grip so it gave us a better view. It was the bodies of several Tek geeks, sprawled across their workbenches, and it seemed that their whitecoats was all that was left of them; their head and limbs had been reduced to a skeletal frame, a thin veneer of tissue still attached in places. Their mouths open, rictus grins locked in apparent terror, their bodies were contorted as if they'd writhed in pain at the point of their demise. Now they were glued to the surface and each other through a thick crust of liquidised matter.

"What the hell...?" I breathed. "This is like the others upstairs. It's as if they've been melted."

"Not melted," Loxley replied, crouching down and peering at the corpses. "Rotted. You smell that? The bodies have decomposed—damn quickly too. I wouldn't be surprised, judging by the way they've arched themselves, if it was done to them while they were still alive. That it was *that* which killed them."

"They decayed? What, at someone's command?"

"I'd say so."

"This is some Ming the Merciless shit right here."

Loxley tutted and stood. "You read anything other than comic books, McGill?"

She stepped past the bodies and continued down the aisle between the work surfaces before I could answer. I followed, beam flicking from wall to wall, reflecting back at me now and again as it alighted on a blank monitor screen or glass cabinet door. More dead eyes, peeled back in their sockets, tracked our progress from across the bloodily smeared tiled floor. A shiny red cylindrical object gleamed in a small alcove to my left, and I paused: fire extinguisher. I tapped Lox on the shoulder to point it out and she turned and held up a raised finger, her head cocked as if straining to listen. She arched her eyebrows to suggest I do the same. I concentrated, and caught the sounds of movement further down the lab, possibly voices, though they were too low to discern.

"We're not alone," she whispered.

"Then we get out of here; find somewhere else from which to knock this place out."

"If we want to make sure Red Mosquito is destroyed, it'd be better to do it down here."

"We don't know how many there are," I hissed urgently. "We know what they're capable of; we've seen it often enough. We don't want to be taking chances. We go back."

Loxley had a look on her face like she wasn't prepared to be dissuaded. "The fire has to start here if it wants any chance of wiping all this out. C'mon, they don't know we're here—we can take them by surprise."

"But we don't know the numbers—"

"I think there's only two. Three at the most." She started to crouch-run, weaving between the chairs and workstations. I groaned inwardly and lumbered after her, keeping my head down, snapping off the torch. The voices got louder as we approached. She stopped and peeked through some shelving, then dropped onto her haunches. "I was right. There's three of those grey pricks," she muttered. "They're shifting pallets of something. I reckon if we came at them from both sides, we could drop them before they had time to do anything."

"What are you thinking? Headshots? Blow their rancid skulls apart. They don't get up after that."

"Gunfire's going to bring the rest of their crew down here, Jackson."

"What else are you going to do? Hurl bad language at them?"

"We can't take the risk."

My eyes roved quickly over my surroundings and settled on a wrench-like contraption that was sitting with some other measuring equipment on a desk. It felt reassuringly heavy in my left hand when I picked it up.

"Let's try to keep this stealthy," she said. "No shots unless necessary."

"Once they're down, you rig the place to blow, and we're gone. I don't want to stay here any longer than we have to. I got the creeps something bad."

She nodded.

"Two minutes," I said, "then cause a distraction."

I tracked round to the left, keeping to the shadows, my back to the shelves. Like Lox had said, they were stacking crates, the contents of which weren't visible. They murmured amongst each other in some kind of language though it was more like the whispering rush of ancient trees communing; a kind of susurration known only to themselves. Christ knew what zombie cops talked about to each other, but these guys sounded like they were channelling dead spirits; maybe it was the hum of whatever spark of animus gave them life, ticking over as they were in standby mode.

Something rattled across the room as Lox did her thing, and as one they turned their heads to investigate. It never failed to raise the hairs on the back of my neck the way they all moved simultaneously, limbs jerkily kicking into life. The moment they started to shuffle towards Loxley's position, I detached myself from the dark edges of the lab and strode forward, instrument raised. I struck the nearest one cleanly on the back of the skull and caved it in almost instantly; fucking thing fell apart like a month-old pumpkin. It stood motionless, the rest of its head split asunder, while the other two did some kind of approximation of a surprised double-take, and I attempted to take out the next with a back-handed swing. It managed to flick out its daystick and block the strike, parrying the wrench to one side. Its mouth creased into a smile that remained in place long enough for me to drive my right fist through it.

I'd done it without thinking, an instinctive defensive jab, but as I removed my dripping, gore-soaked fist from the liquescent mulch where its jaw used to be I realised that I hadn't felt any pain. My strapped-up hand was completely numb, deadened to the point where it may as well have been prosthetic. The notion gave me a micro-second's pause for concern before I realised that I hadn't put the second Judge down, merely inconvenienced it, and it caught me a glancing blow on the temple with its daystick. I staggered back, seeing stars, and the grey thing advanced on me, seemingly oblivious to the fact that its lower face was now a grim black hole. It swung again and I used my right hand as a shield, where I barely felt the impact, then hit it in the ribs with the wrench. It made a solid cracking retort but didn't slow it down any; it got inside my reach and rammed the daystick lengthways against my throat with a two-handed thrust, which pinwheeled me back hard against the shelving. The supports wobbled and vials, microscopes and other breakables hit the floor with a smash.

White spots danced across my vision as I struggled for breath, my trachea slowly crushed millimetre by millimetre. Over my attacker's shoulder I saw the third Judge briefly talking into its radio just before Lox appeared with a computer monitor held above her head and slammed it down on the grey's skull, obliterating it. She didn't give it a backwards glance and ran over to help me, but the Judge holding me slapped her back just as she was about to place a hand on its shoulder; nevertheless it released the pressure enough for me to snatch some air, and manoeuvre enough room to headbutt the greasy freak into next week. More of its face was concaved, its eyes almost closed. I heard it emit the word 'Ssssinnner' like gas was escaping before Lox sprang back up and pistol-whipped it to the ground, pummelling the thing with her gun-butt while it made weak attempts to fend her off. She broke it apart with each blow, reducing it to a wide red circle on the floor.

"So much for stealth," she said between gasps as she sought to get her breath back.

I tried to answer but couldn't get any sounds out. I ran a hand over my throat, wincing at the skin's rawness, and struggled to swallow. Something felt jagged in there. I put a hand on her arm and looked into her eyes; she appeared confused for a moment, then realised I'd lost my voice. I motioned with my head, and she nodded, squeezing my bicep in sympathy. I turned away, caught movement in the corner of my eye, then immediately pushed her to one side just as a bullet ricocheted off a stanchion inches from where she'd been standing a second ago. She spun, following my gaze, and saw the half dozen greys marching up the lab, Lawgivers raised. The lead pusbag fired again and we scrambled out of the way, bullets tearing up the room around us, while I managed to pull my gun free and pumped the trigger blindly behind me as we ran. We threw ourselves over a desk, giving Lox enough time to free up her weapon, then return fire, blowing a chunk out of the midriff of the nearest Judge. The round ploughed through its body and exploded one of the pallets the other helmets had been stacking. A number of containers tumbled out, the lid of one popping off as it hit the ground. What looked like a human brain oozed free onto the cold hard floor.

"Jesus," Loxley exclaimed, revulsion momentarily giving her pause.

They didn't let up, pouring on the fire as they advanced, not bothering to seek cover, unconcerned about any injuries they sustained in the process. Wounds didn't seem to matter to them; they were beyond any human sensation. We both knew this was going to be a fight we weren't going to win, and I motioned that we should retreat. She agreed, and we scooted to our feet and ran back the way we'd come, heads low as the bullets smacked into the walls and furniture around us.

What did we believe we could achieve, coming here? I thought as I fled. How did we ever think we could fight this? It was always going to go one way.

Predestination, you stupid motherfucker. You should've guessed the future's immutable.

Lox grabbed my shoulder and pointed to something I hadn't paid attention to on the way in: there was a glass-fronted cabinet to one side of a storeroom, racked inside with compressed-air cylinders. Without hesitation she put her booted foot through it and hauled one out, toppling it onto its side then kicking it down back down the lab's aisle. As it rolled towards the greys, she sighted her gun and fired.

The explosion knocked us both onto our backs, the flash igniting the room in a ballooning fireball. Half the Judges went with it, incinerated where they stood; the others took a tumble, flames licking their uniforms even as it crawled up the ceiling. An alarm sounded and the sprinklers stuttered into life, raining on the conflagration.

"*Go!*" Lox said, and pushed me, slipping, back towards the lab entrance. We barrelled through it and made for the stairs just as the elevator pinged its arrival. Ordinarily, I should've simply kept going, but the sliding open doors caught my attention, my curiosity getting the better of me. That familiar tingling sense of dread returned. I slowed, transfixed by the darkness inside the cab, horribly fascinated by what could lie within.

Then it stepped out into the light, head turning this way and that, as if catching our scent. Its gaze finally settled on us, even though the large eye sockets were empty.

The badge on its chest said this was Mortis.

For a moment, my breath caught in my chest, my heart palpitated. Fear flooded through me like I'd never felt before. This creature was something new, something far beyond the monstrosities that we'd battled since it all went down; it exuded power, a presence. This was the source of the bad feeling I'd experienced upon entering, the creeping unease that had seeped into the very walls. It was a nightmare walking, one of the architects—if Stender was to be believed—of the doom of mankind. It wore an approximation of a Judge's uniform, but it was adorned with bones, the skeleton of some mammal attached to one shoulder. Its bare hands and feet were gnarled and clawed like an animal, and between its legs I could see the hint of a whip-like tail that emerged from its lower back. But it was the head that held the attention: a large sheep's skull, bleached of all flesh, regarded us impassively. There was nothing within that empty cranium save darkness yet it watched all the same. If, like the De'Ath character Hawkins had mentioned, Mortis had been human once, I couldn't comprehend what process had brought it to its current state.

"The interloperssss," it said, and I realised that had been the voice I'd heard on the greys' comms back in Rennick. The timbre was unmistakeable, a heavy rumble behind the dry hiss. "I'd been hoping I would catch you before you attempted to leave."

I glanced at Lox and she was as motionless as me, eyes wide with terror. Somehow the thought of flight seemed pointless, that we were now trapped within its field. Could we have turned and run? It's possible—the thing didn't seem equipped for sprinting. But the black energy that came off it in waves made us powerless. We were the condemned before the executioner's block, sapped of resistance.

And yet… my left hand, held down at my side, balled into a fist all the same.

"You lawbreakersss continually ssseek to evade jussstice," it said, stepping forward, making for Loxley. "Rather than accept your guilt, you do all you can to obssstruct and delay your dessserved punissshment." It reached out a taloned hand and ran its fingers through her hair; Lox gave out a snipped cry of alarm. "You ssshould be lambsss to the ssslaughter, ressssigned to your fate. Yet sssinnersss will not recognissse the very ssinss of which they are guilty."

"Guilty of what?" Lox rasped, some steel still in her eyes.

"The mossst heinousss crime of all, child," it replied. "Life." It curled a finger round a lock, and I saw the hair turn white instantly. "The Sisstersss sshowed us the way—that all crime is committed by the living, therefore exissstence itssself musssst be eradicated if we are to maintain order. We ssshucked off our mortal remainsss, partook the Dead Fluidsss, and embraced Death asss the one true ssstate of being." It removed its hand from her hair and spread its fingers wide as if to place it upon her face. "Peace, and remorssse for your crimesss, will only come if you do the sssame."

"Stop," I croaked. It had taken an effort of will to force the word out. "Stay away from her."

Mortis paused, its hand an inch from Lox's cheek, and turned its skull-head in my direction. "You expect forgivenessss? I cannot absssolve sssuch flagrant wrong-doing."

"I said stay the fuck away."

"McGill—" Loxley warned through a clenched jaw, shooting daggers at me.

I couldn't catch her eye but instead stepped forward, keeping my focus on the skull-headed asshole. It watched me approach, inscrutable.

...and in my head I'm back in the ring, coming out of my corner, blood up, heart pounding. My fists are like iron, my legs rock solid. The chants of the crowd are a white-noise background roar, faces lost in darkness beyond the ropes. There is only the canvas and my opponent, rushing out to meet me, and the anticipation, the release, is in awaiting that first contact, that aggression-fuelled jab, the satisfaction of flesh yielding to my glove, and the stings and blows that will greet me in return will only serve to drive me harder, pay back in kind twentyfold until one of us weakens and falls...

I lashed out my good left fist and caught Mortis on the cheekbone, snapping its head to the side. It made no sound and simply slowly, lazily, returned to study me, a hairline crack now in the bone. I pulled back and drove my fist again at the Judge-thing's ribs, but this time its hand flashed out and grabbed my wrist before it could make contact. It held it there between us, motionless, and I felt an ice-cold sensation creep into my wrist; I tore my eyes from Mortis's gaze and looked down to see the flesh dissolving where its claws encircled my skin. Pain started to resonate up my arm in waves as the atrophy spread.

Then it broke the contact. "Wait," it said, as if to itself. Its other hand lifted my right, the bandages rotting away instantly. It traced a wizened finger over my palm where I'd been bitten, the entire appendage a purpley-black. "Well, well. Little sssseedss have taken root..." It stepped away. "I think jussstice would be better ssserved if the sssinnerss faced up to their own ssssinss *together*, don't you?"

Shaking from the searing agony—the bone of my wrist was now visible amidst the meat and tendons—I suddenly found myself unaccountably turning away from Mortis and walking towards Lox. I had no control over my actions; my limbs were being directed by another power. Loxley looked at me in bewilderment, eyes moist, as I stepped up in front her, and found myself taking her hands in mine.

She let out a gasp, which turned into rapid breaths of pain. I could see I was spreading Mortis's fetid touch, and her arms were shaking as the skin sloughed from them with frightening speed. "No..." I whispered. "Don't make me do this..."

I couldn't pull away, however. The decay reached Lox's chest and neck, the flesh crumbling and turning to ashes, pieces of her curling up and dissipating into the air. "I'm sorry," I told her, our eyes locked as she was reduced to a skeletal frame in seconds. Her mouth remained open as her lips and gums shrivelled back, her hair withered and died. "You were... I always wanted to say..."

Then she was just bone, all light from her gone. She fell to dust at my feet, the last of her running through my fingers.

"How poetic," I heard Mortis say behind me as it came closer. "The guilty punissshed by a fellow sssinner." I couldn't move. I merely stared at my hands and the residue on them, and shuddered at the damage they had wrought. "Perhapsss I'll keep you around. Fate, it ssseemss, hass brought usss together, and you may prove usssefu1."

One of the grey Judges emerged from the wreckage the explosion had caused with a crate that we'd seen them stacking. Mortis turned to it. "Are they sssalvageable?"

"We've lossst one or two," it replied. "Mossst are ssstill intact."

"Excellent." Mortis returned its attention to me. "The Mossquito *will* fly, have no fear of that." It reached down and picked up a container in which the grey matter slopped around, looking at it with what appeared to be pride etched on its hideous skull-face.

"I've got my bessst mindssss working on it."

PART TWO

BONE WHITE SEEDS

CHAPTER ELEVEN

10 March

Mr Graham died yesterday. I can't say it wasn't unexpected—the guy was, like, three hundred years old, and the gangrene that had set in after Kez had tied off his stump was too severe for the mediocre meds that we've got at our disposal to treat, so it was always a waiting game—but even so, it hit us all hard. He was the first of our 'family' to pass, and I guess once the first one goes, it's a reminder that we're all living on borrowed time. He'd been so sprightly when I first met him, managing to keep his sense of humour in spite of all this crap that's raining down on us, and to see him diminished and suffering was heartbreaking. The funeral was short and perfunctory, done under the cover of night, and nobody felt much like talking, so by the time we'd all retreated to our sleeping bags, it was as if the old boy had never existed. All that was left was an absence—an empty corner in which his meagre belongings had been tidied up and folded away.

It struck me there was no one recording this, no one keeping track of these departed lives. Needless to say, the grave didn't have a marker, and he'd been buried deep enough that any disturbed earth wasn't visible from the air. I wondered how long it would be before we forgot Mr Graham was a part of our group. I mean, I can't remember now if he ever told me his first name—he was kind of a stickler for formality, despite our circumstances. Here we were, living nose to tail, nine of us in this one space, and he felt uncomfortable with me being too familiar! Ancient geezers can be like that, I guess, used to the proper way of doing things. Can't say it ever offended me—in fact, I found his determination to stick to his old-school protocol kind of admirable; too easy these days to lose sense of who we were before the world went down. But, like I say, the man I knew as Mr Graham was going to risk drifting from our minds if somebody didn't make a note that he was once here.

I found this journal amongst a bunch of old papers in an office upstairs. Looks like it was intended for book-keeping or something similar, but it was untouched and the damp hadn't got to it so I sequestered it for the purposes of this very diary you're reading (that is, if there's anyone left to read it—maybe it'll be discovered in years to come, who knows? Gotta have hope there's gonna be something left, or someone to come after). I haven't kept a diary since I was twelve, and even then I lost interest before the year was out 'cause not enough interesting stuff was happening for me to keep it up (I know! If I knew then what I know now, etc), but I reckon I've got a duty now to get all this down in writing. Routine's kinda important to keep your head together, so if I make a habit every evening before lights out of at least penning something, then I should stick with it. Doesn't have to be Shakespeare, right?

I'm sure Mr Graham wouldn't mind that I'm not the greatest wordsmith—it's the intention that's the main thing. He could forgive a lot when he was alive. He was always a little soft on us younger ones; would give us the benefit of the doubt, throw a few extra rations our way, let us off some of the chores if he was supervising that day. That didn't always go down well with some of the other 'dults if they caught wind he was giving us an easy ride—Kez is kinda hardcore about everyone pulling their weight regardless of age, and has been known to even bawl out little Bren if he kicks up a stink when it's his turn to clean out the latrine or whatever—but he didn't care. He'd tip us the wink that let us know there was more to life than this. Exactly what there is beyond our situation is pretty much up for debate. Clearly, Mr Graham didn't agree that day-to-day toil in miserable conditions simply for the benefit of a continued existence was any way to live your life. 'Course, being an old codger, he could afford to think like that; his best days were behind him, and every extra hour of breath was a tiny, precious gift. Then again, everyone's best days are behind them—even the kids'. No one's looking to the future, just dealing with the here and now.

The way he was around us, you'd assume he and Mrs Graham had a flock of children and grandchildren to dote on, but they never had any. I never asked him, but I guessed this wasn't through choice—he was too patient with, and comfortable around, youngsters to be ambivalent to them. I got the impression that they were everyone's favourite neighbourhood elderly couple—the honorary uncle and auntie that became part of the street's extended family. His wife was a retired schoolteacher, which would account for their natural affinity with kids, while he had something to do with importing machine parts. He did tell me, but I have to confess I zoned out a little bit at the time, which I'm embarrassed to admit I did on more than one occasion. Yeah, yeah, I feel bad for taking him for granted—he would yap away and I'd have one ear turned off, aware that I'd heard the anecdote umpteen times already. What can I say? I've got no excuses for my ingratitude other than my callow youth.

But now that he's gone, I want to do right by Mr Graham, 'cause he was always there for all of us, and as I look across at the mattress he'd slept on for the last six months, now propped up against the wall, all I can think of is things I wish I'd said to him, and how I should've listened without complaint, and enjoyed every minute of his company while I still had it. So this is my small tribute to him, and the life he left behind, and the people he touched, before the memory fades.

It was actually his motorhome that picked up several of us the night it all started to fall apart—it's kind of testament to his innate good nature that he stuck his neck out for a bunch of strangers he could've just as easily breezed past. Plenty of others did—I saw streets log-jammed with vehicles as people fled the city in panic, and those on the sidewalks were banging on car windows and hoods, pleading for a ride. Few, if any, were willing to open their doors and take on extra passengers. Mr Graham did—he saw us separating from the mob, saw the greys shooting at the crowd, must've seen Joel going down, and reckoned that we were going to be next. I can still remember looking back down at Joel sprawled on the tarmac, blood spreading around his head, fear propelling me forward, and then the red flare of the brake lights of the Winnebago a few metres ahead catching my attention. A door swung open just as I came level with it, and I didn't even think, just threw myself through it, aware of others piling in behind me, and then the vehicle lurching away, a couple of bullets smacking into the rear window. That was it—Mr Graham had saved my life, and the three others that had joined me: Riggs, Emily and her son Bren. He probably would've waited for more but had to get out of the line of fire. Emily told me later that it was her husband Tony that had shoved her and their boy aboard, but she never did find out what happened to him. I think we can all guess.

It was at least half an hour, once he'd negotiated his way out of the capital, before Mr Graham called out from the cab to check we were okay. We'd all been curled on the floor of the motorhome, listening to the screams and the explosions and the rattle of gunfire, too scared to raise our heads. I was clutching my knees, which I'd raised up to chin, eyes screwed shut, reverting back to my seven-year-old self under my eiderdown, believing that what you couldn't see couldn't hurt you. Bren was sobbing, his mother shushing him, offering words of comfort. Mr Graham's voice cut through our hysteria, to a degree. He said he was pulling over at the first opportunity, and would come back and check on us. Minutes later, we came to a halt. He appeared through the curtain separating the cab from the lounge area and introduced himself, offering us water from the fridge, coaxing us out of our shell-shocked states. He seemed remarkably calm, as if this was an everyday occurrence, even taking the time to fish out a chocolate bar from a kitchenette drawer for Bren that managed to dry his tears briefly. But he had another reason for parking up—he vanished into a bedroom, and returned in moments carrying a sheeted body in his arms, which he lifted down off the vehicle. I slid up onto a seat and watched through a window as he took the corpse into the scrubland lining the road. He returned a full fifteen minutes later, empty-handed, and climbed back into the driver's seat without a word.

It was, of course, Mrs Graham, I was to learn later; one of the first to be purged. On her way back from the corner store, she'd been shot in the side of the head as she'd run up the path to their front door and what she'd hoped was safety. Her husband had come out onto their front yard, concerned at the chaos he could hear, and found her bleeding out on the step. He told me he'd placed her body in a hollow tree, covered in bracken, where she could hopefully find some peace, far from the horror. He only referenced her intermittently in the weeks that followed, as if he was holding on to precious memories that he didn't want to spoil by voicing. What they'd had was locked inside his head and his heart, and he only gave us—me, really; he took a shine to me the most, I think—the briefest glimpses. He compensated by rabbiting on about everything else under the sun—including how to fuel and drive the RV, the one subject for which I was happy to be taken under his wing. I LOVED that! I'd been aching to get behind the wheel since I turned sixteen, and Mom and Dad, they… Well. I never got the chance, let's put it that way. As it turned out, I picked it up pretty easily.

Yeah, he was a good instructor, Mr Graham, and a friend I'm glad to have made amongst all this; one that was hurting a lot, I think, but kept it all internalised and covered it up with kindness and bonhomie. Maybe he was a surrogate parent (or grandparent) for me, I don't know. I probably sought his approval in the early days, 'cause I wanted him to know I was 'worth' saving that night. I had a lot of messed-up thoughts in the days after the Fall, along the lines of why I should've got to live when so many didn't. If the Lawgiver bullet had been a few inches over, then it would've been me hitting the slab, not Joel; if I'd tripped or been slower getting to the motorhome, then I would've been left behind. It was pure luck that I got to survive that night when so many others didn't, and the ramifications of that plagued my dreams: *what could've been*. I tried to talk it over with Mr Graham sometimes, these feelings of guilt and inadequacy, but I don't think he was well-equipped to give me the advice I needed. He listened and sympathised, but had the embarrassed air of a man who didn't know what was wanted of him, and didn't want to be put in that position. He was of a generation where you didn't speak about your problems quite so openly.

It was that same randomness that took him from us—or at least set in motion his decline. Three weeks ago he went out to collect gas from one of the abandoned stations along the interstate, and according to Riggs, who was riding shotgun, he ventured off the forecourt because he thought he heard someone crying for help. He stepped on an IED that the Resistance had laid to take out greys, and it destroyed his right leg just above the knee. Such a stupid thing to do: the cries were probably just a recording to lure in the deadwalkers, if they existed at all outside his head. I could well imagine him conjuring up the phantom pleas of those he couldn't help that night to torture himself; to beat himself up over the fact that he wasn't there to save his wife. I don't know, this is all supposition—he'd never reveal what he was really thinking, obvs. But there was definitely a sadness that you'd catch when he assumed you weren't looking, and it was buried deep, and it affected him more than he'd let on. Once he was bedbound after the injury, and when it became clear that we couldn't stem the infection, the smiles vanished and he retreated into his dark kernel, no longer able to deny it. Pain and delirium claimed him for the hours before his heart gave out.

So that was Mr Graham: a good man, who fell victim to what the world's become, like so many others. Soon he'll just be bones, lost amongst the rest, but I want to put it down on paper that there was a life lived once: an obituary for the first of us to be taken, that forces us to remember, and ensures he's accorded the proper respect. Sleep well, old pal.

Candle's getting low so I better call it a night. Will be up early (as usual!). :-(

11 March

Found myself surprisingly looking forward to writing in the diary tonight. Considered it a chore when I was younger and struggling to know what to write, but now it's like a release. I can pour everything onto the page that I can't express elsewhere. People are still acting reserved since Mr Graham passed, and no one's really talking—it's like this dam has been built through unspoken agreement, and everyone's maintaining it in case it breaks and the grief floods out. It can't be healthy to be shielding ourselves from our emotions like this—and I'm just as guilty, I'm tiptoeing around with the best of them—but I don't know how to get past this barrier we've somehow constructed. It becomes all about the work, all about the act of survival, and to be distracted from that is to allow weakness in. Maybe they all think Mr Graham was weak, and that's why he died—if they don't want to go the same way, then they need to be robust in how they deal with the loss of one of their own. More likely they're scared: Death's taint has reached our community, and few want to admit it.

Kez, for example, is as hard as nails, and probably sees the old geezer's passing on her watch as a personal slight, for which she hasn't forgiven him. She worked through the night to limit the damage to his leg—transfusing blood herself, tying off the stump, cauterising the wound (though the infection still spread)—and she's got minimal medical skills. She's a physiotherapist by trade, if I remember right. You can't help thinking that half her clients must've been scared stiff of her; she's kind of formidable and no-nonsense, and takes charge with little argument from anyone else. She's the ideal person to have around in a crisis, but it's fair to say empathy isn't her forte—or perhaps she hides it well. She assumed leadership of our group with no opposition and immediately started delegating tasks. We do it partly out of the need for it to be done, but mainly out of fear of disappointing her. Her temper is legendary.

Some of the others have whispered—a little bit unkindly, I reckon—that the day the zomboids took over was the best thing to ever happen to Kez; that she's kinda like one of those militia survivalist goons that praises God when war starts so they can shuck off their regular clothes and climb into their camo gear. That they don't have to hide any more, they can be their true selves. I suppose you could say that she's risen to the occasion, given the circumstances, but no one would ever be grateful for the mess we're in. She doesn't relish any of this, she doesn't enjoy it (or at least I'm pretty sure that she doesn't—she rarely smiles). She simply ploughs her energies into keeping us alive, because the alternative is too hideous to contemplate. We've all seen the body orchards where people lost the will to keep going—Kez is damned if she's going to let that happen to her. She's kinda inspiring in her obstinacy, and makes us all the more determined to not succumb to dark thoughts. But she is one hell of a hard taskmaster.

I tried to talk to her about Mr Graham at dinner, 'cause I knew how hard she fought to save him. She's not big on conversation, even less when she's eating, so I figured I'd have an uphill struggle. Turns out I was right. Meal was rice and beans (yuk!), so it wasn't like I wasn't distracting her from anything mouth-watering, but she just sat there on her bunk, pawing the contents of her bowl into her mouth, barely pausing to look up. I squatted next to her and asked how her arm was doing (still bandaged from where the transfusion had been). She grunted and pursed her lips and raised her eyebrows as if to say that she'd live.

"Thank you for doing all you could for him," I persevered, keen to get the old man's death into the open.

"Odds weren't good," she murmured, making a point of not looking me in the eye, and slung her now-empty bowl beside her onto the mattress.

"Even so," I said. "We're all going to miss him."

"He was a fool, who took an unnecessary risk. That kind of thing puts a strain on our resources."

I was a bit taken aback by that. "Is that all you remember him as?"

"Gotta think of the group." She stood up, looking at me for the first time. "Misha, we lose one, we consolidate. That's what this is. No time for tears, okay?"

She walked off towards the storeroom (probably to count supplies again). Thanks for the pep talk, pal! I'm not convinced it's not an act she's putting on, that she's denying stuff she doesn't want to deal with. Feel like this place is a pressure cooker at times, bubbling away just waiting to blow.

CHAPTER TWELVE

THERE WERE MANY things that Cafferly was struggling to get used to in the new set-up, but what the Hall of Injustice had become was possibly the most unsettling. The shift had happened virtually overnight, within hours of the regime change, and walking its corridors she found herself in a metamorphosed building, as if the structure had warped to better reflect the psyche of its current masters. Walls had darkened to a sickly green and were icy to the touch. Ceilings stretched and bowed impossibly, almost as tall as a cathedral in places, the material grown supple. A chill breeze blew in from somewhere, carrying with it the permanent stench of decay. How this had happened without her noticing at the time was decidedly unnerving, causing her to question her own perception and senses. This was, no doubt, the new normal now, but she hadn't anticipated how subtle the transformation would be. Within the space of an eye-blink, further mutations could ripple through the Hall as the powers that be secured their position.

Clearly, the new Chief was in league with dark forces. Cafferly had yet to meet them first-hand, but she detected their psi-presence all the time, like a background hum that once you tuned into it, you couldn't drown it out. Their malignancy was soaked into the very rockcrete. She knew they were watching, reporting back to Sidney, whispering in his ear, trying to influence his decisions, guiding his hand. The kid probably liked to think he was the architect of this new world, but *they* were the power behind the throne; they'd more than likely enabled him to seize the Grand Hall in the first place. *What* they were, she couldn't read—she gleaned aspects of their psignature (female, twin sisters, wholly black-hearted, like life itself was an anathema to them), but believed they were manifestations of a greater intelligence, and as such its defences were far too strong for her to probe further. Cafferly had to be careful: if she started putting her mind in places that weren't welcome, she would be more than likely hauled before the Chief and negated. It was one of the perils of being a Psi-Judge—you were always aware of the secrets swirling around the ether, but had to learn when to turn a deaf ear to what you're not supposed to hear, otherwise it could come back to bite you. Or at least you gave the impression you hadn't heard it. Whichever, Psi-Div operatives were regarded with suspicion and distrust regardless: nobody liked the idea that someone could comb through their heads on a whim.

It had been true enough before the Fall—then, it was the perps who had eyed her with fear and contempt as they had sat across from her in the interrogation cubes and she had divulged their guilt. They were minds that were easy to pick apart, built on base instincts and cowardly self-interest, and she had taken no small pleasure in drilling down into their unconscious and spilling out every thought and deed that had passed through their skulls. If they got antagonistic and resisted, she filled their brains with broken glass and re-awoke childhood traumas, then watched them squirm. They learned not to mess with her after that. As a telepath, there was little that could be hidden from her, and even the dead—if they were fresh enough—could be read from the latent images still ghosting in their slowly disintegrating cerebella, revealing up to the point of their demise their final moments and, if you were lucky, the identities of their killers.

It had been a curse since birth, and a talent that she'd

never been comfortable with. It started slowly—moments of startling precognition, the muted whisper of her parents' minds leaking into hers, which she at first thought was a sign of schizophrenia—but it was finally the age of five that brought with it a sharpening of her mental faculties, like someone had plugged her into the direct current. Suddenly, every voice in the neighbourhood was in her head, and she couldn't hide it any longer, couldn't control the rush of information that was flooding into her. It sent her over the edge. Her parents, who taught her how to control her abilities, submitted her to Justice Department without delay and she was made a ward of Psi-Division, enrolled as a cadet.

Cafferly underwent eight years of intensive training, and her mind, once a scattershot receiver, became a deftly wielded weapon. Her supervisor Burrell and the rest of her tutors instructed her how to channel her residual psi-power into a force she could deploy with the same level of skill as a Lawgiver or daystick. She was still occasionally at the mercy of random flashes—shards of the future interrupting her consciousness, bleed-through from disturbances in the veil between the dimensions—but these were part and parcel of being a Psi-Judge, and a useful asset at the HoJ's disposal. Glimpses of imminent gang conflicts, a predicted domestic murder, discovering the hideaways of pro-democratic seditionist cells: she turned her now-powerful mind to all of them, and as such ensured the perpetrators were brought to book. She'd been brought up to respect the Judges, and now that she was the eyes scanning the city, she had to admit she enjoyed the position of authority it gave her, stealing into creeps' heads with relish.

It was remarkable that, given the influence that Psi-Div held within the Grand Hall—and the number of operatives working for the department—no one saw the coup coming. That was in itself troubling. The entities that Sidney had fallen in with had managed to cloak themselves to such a degree that the pre-cogs and empaths had no knowledge or warning of their presence before they were upon them, inveigling their twisted creed in through the back door, as it were. De'Ath too should've raised some red flags before he showed his hand, the virulence of his anti-life agenda caught by telepaths such as herself, but his psychopathy was well-hidden among the rank and file uniforms already predisposed to extreme acts of brutality. The street Judges were not a stable bunch by and large, many hopped up on aggression-enhancing drugs: seeking out a deranged mind amongst that lot would've been no easy task. So it was that Sidney's ruthless rise to the top came as a surprise to them all, his youth by no means a handicap to his pervading desire to wipe out all criminality (and by extension every living thing capable of it). Together with his inner circle of lieutenants—themselves warped by their close exposure to the sisterly creatures—De'Ath had installed himself in Chief Drabbon's chair before anyone knew what was happening, or indeed could do much to stop it.

Some resisted—even the hardliners who'd previously advocated summary executions for pet-owners whose animals fouled the sked weren't prepared to be party to the wholesale genocide of humanity. But the fightback was easily quashed, the rebels battling a regime that couldn't be destroyed by conventional means. Many of their heads now adorned Sidney's office, a reminder of the fate of those that opposed him. Others, mainly auxiliaries and support staff, fled, taking their chances with the citizenry, merely delaying the inevitable. The majority in the Grand Hall, however, were given the ultimatum *adapt or die*, and they plumped for the former, drinking specially concocted fluids prepared by De'Ath's associates that transformed them into beings that went beyond normal mortality. Life was the enemy now, and Sidney's troops were no longer part of that hateful state; instead they were his zombified acolytes, carrying out the slaughter on his orders.

Cafferly didn't fight the regime change—she accepted without question the new state of affairs, and the demands of her new boss. Part of it was self-preservation, but mostly it was a way to protect her sanity. At the beginning of the purge, those with soft talents like hers were swamped by the psychic backlash of the mass murder taking place in the capital and beyond—Psi-Div experienced a near total whiteout in the first few hours, something that the department had never witnessed before. Operatives were entering catatonic states, third eyes effectively blinded by the nuclear blast of suffering reflecting back from the psychosphere. It reminded her of the burgeoning of her abilities as a teen: a sudden rush of energy and information that threatened to blow her mind like an overloaded circuit. Then, she'd needed Judicial training to teach her how to turn it on and off; now, she, and the rest of the division, required help by non-human means to shield them from the sharp end of De'Ath's designs. Sidney still had uses for Psi-Judges, wanting them to play a part in his global carnage, and so they were all instructed to partake of the Fluids, promised that they would be better attuned to what the world was becoming. Cafferly didn't argue—in truth, at the time she was incapable of argument, rational thought drowned out by the persistent screaming of the dying and the dead—and the change, when it came, was akin to the volume knob on a radio being turned mercifully low.

Physically, she was undoubtedly different—her skin became sallow, her hair thinned, her teeth rotted, and she found that she barely needed food and water any more—but the important thing was that her mental faculties were as keen as a blade. She even sensed something opening in her head when she concentrated, as if she was gaining insight through a higher power. A glance in a mirror showed light leaking through a sphincter-like orifice that was now at the centre of her papery-thin forehead, the origins of which she couldn't begin to fathom. However, after the initial shock, she accepted it as part of her new state of being: a badge to declare that she was loyal to the current authority. Sidney was very big on loyalty, on his lieutenants following his every lead, and those that weren't up to the task—or displeased him in some way; he was notoriously fickle—were purged mercilessly, their new lives beyond death cut short. It fed into a general air of paranoia that existed in the Grand Hall, worry of falling short of the Chief's demands and expectations; having seen what he was doing to the general population, no one under his command wanted to suffer the same fate. That was why Cafferly was keen not to antagonise the sisters that De'Ath was so beholden to at any point, or poke her nose into their doings. If they were casting an eye over her from afar, let them see she was a good little soldier for the cause.

Right now that's what she was, engaging in the task that occupied most of her waking hours (not that she slept much; the act felt alien these days): rooting out survivors. With her digital map up on her screen before her, and her mind racing along its channels, she was adept at zeroing in on the living, breathing guilty holed up in their rats' nests. Sometimes it was a particularly strong psignature that she locked on to; other times she picked up the notes of fear and distress in the ether, like a wine-taster divining the balance of ingredients in any given glass, and followed them back to their source. There was a certain amount of needle-in-a-haystack sifting to do considering the sheer volume of conflicting signals washing through the psychic plane, but she was nothing if not dedicated. It was a sacred calling to bring lawbreakers to justice.

For the last hour or so, she'd been tracing elements that had caught her attention in the upper north-east quadrant of the capital. She'd had to tease them out, sieve away some of the more distracting psi-chatter so she could focus on what they were and exactly where they were coming from. She peeled back layer after layer of white noise, the objects of her interest gleaming brighter in the dark like undersea jewels the harder she concentrated. They had the delicious psychic aroma of terror and hunger, both of which always gave off a unique scent, and she followed her nose, telepathically speaking. That combination was a surefire indication that one or more perpetrators had shut themselves away to escape Sidney's legions, and were now slowly starving to death as they ran low on supplies. It would be a dereliction of her duty not to hasten their demise by directing a couple of uniforms to their door.

"Any units in the vicinity of Bleeker Street," she said into her mic on her headset, "I have a strong indication that several justice-evaders have sought refuge at..." She furrowed her brow, sensing that her third eye was pulsating at the same time, and touched a finger to her temple. "...Two-nine-eight. That's an old furniture store, on the corner with Klein." Her other hand lightly brushed the map screen, and it zoomed in, buildings and thoroughfares lighting up. "It's a weak signal—suggests they're in the basement."

"Copy that, Control," a sibilant voice responded in her ear. "Maher and Venablesss ressponding. Prossseeding to location."

Cafferly could've ended the connection there and moved on to the next target, but curiosity and a certain sadistic voyeuristic interest—call it like it is, she told herself; there was no point denying her nature now—meant she lingered on Bleeker, keen to see justice being meted out. She'd been doing it more often recently, a little addicted, it had to be said, to the vicarious thrill that came with setting up the slaughter. De'Ath probably wouldn't approve, if he knew, having lectured previously on the importance of dispassionate genocide, of punishment without emotional attachment, but then again the guy could suck the fun out of everything. Anyway, she knew that he still got a tingle in his Department-issue jocks when a lawbreaker was ended by his hand.

She cast her mind out and found the pair of Judges arriving at the address, watching events unfold inside her head as if she were there, witnessing it in person. Bodies were strewn about the street, rotting where they lay, and the uniforms didn't even attempt to negotiate their Lawriders around them, simply ploughing through limbs and organs. It was just roadkill now: the guilty punished and discarded. They dismounted, and one tried the door handle. When it was evidently locked, he drew his gun and smashed the glass frontage with the butt, reaching inside and popping the latch. They entered, showing little concern for their entrance being advertised. Their new state of being gave them no reason to be afraid; they had partaken of the Fluids and gone beyond death. All that mattered to them was the execution of the criminals unlawfully clinging to life.

Cafferly zoomed her remote viewing into the store with the two greys. It was dark, but they had no need of light; indeed, it was likely that neither Maher nor Venables still had eyes to see with anyway. Their liquescent complexion suggested they were sloughing off all the vestiges of their bodies in life, and becoming nothing more than revenants adorned with a badge. They moved purposefully towards the back of the building, striding past plastic-sheeted three-piece suites and pine cabinets that belonged to a world that didn't exist any more, pausing momentarily before a maintenance door, heads turning to the side as if trying to catch a sound or a scent, though they no longer had the senses for either. They worked instead by some innate impulse. As one they shouldered the door, and descended the stairs that led to the basement, justice inexorable and remorseless.

The psi felt a pleasurable knot turn in her stomach. The anticipation was always the best part. Would the survivors accept judgement meekly and with grateful resignation?

They rarely did. Before the Judges had stepped off the last stair, one of the humans stepped out from behind a stack of pallets and levelled a shotgun at them. The report when he pulled the trigger was deafening, and Cafferly's mind's eye twitched in discomfort. The shell blew a hole clean through Maher, sticky black tendrils splattering the floor, but it barely slowed him. The Judges returned fire instantly, riddling the man with bullets, and continued their progress even as he hit the floor, as if he'd been nothing more than a minor inconvenience. Maher paused briefly and looked down at the wound torn in his sternum with something approaching curiosity, running a gloved finger around the glistening hole, before moving on. Cafferly sensed his mild confusion, some tiny vestige of his living brain remarking that this should've hurt, but the lack of functioning nerve endings meant he had felt nothing. The body was just an empty shell.

As they rounded the corner, Venables took a shot to the head, ricocheting off his helmet. It had hit with sufficient force to cleave the metal, exposing the grey-green skull beneath, but he simply pumped his trigger without breaking his stride, shredding the crates the young woman with the revolver was sheltering behind until she had to abandon her cover. He snapped off an SE round just as she fled towards the stairs and blew her jaw in two.

For a moment, there was stillness, smoke rising from their barrels, wooden shards pattering on the earthen floor. The two Judges stood side by side, scanning the darkness. Cafferly furrowed her brow, aware that there was more living here than just the two that had been despatched. She pushed, and got a response back.

"There," she whispered aloud to herself, and in her head Venables' gaze alighted on a section of the panelling around the bottom of the far wall. He stalked forward without hesitation, reached down and wrenched it free; several scared pairs of eyes looked out at him from the gloom, their owners lying horizontally in the crawlspace. A baby's whimper echoed in that split-second of quiet. Then Maher joined him, and they both levelled their Lawgivers.

Cafferly broke the connection and her mind shut down. It was only after she emerged out of the static fuzz that came from an abrupt viewing termination that she wondered why she'd turned it off. She'd done it without thinking, the psi version of a repulsed look away. She wasn't normally so squeamish. That was... unusual.

She sensed a figure standing at her shoulder, and glanced up to see Mortis's creature waiting for her attention. It was a sad, shambling thing, decayed and moulded by his master's touch.

"The Chief *wuh*-wants to *suh*-see you," it stammered, exposed teeth chattering.

Cafferly felt a weird sense of unease, but pushed it down so it wouldn't show. She nodded and stood up, shoving past the pathetic servant, keen to make it know it was beneath her and she wasn't concerned by its presence or its message. She stepped into the corridor, and headed for the stairs, hands trembling slightly on the guardrail as she climbed.

A directive to report to Sidney in person was not to be ignored, nor taken lightly.

CHAPTER THIRTEEN

14 March

Awoke from a bad dream this morning, which put me on edge for the rest of the day. Of course, some of us have bad dreams every night—Emily constantly suffers from night terrors, to the point where her mattress has been placed in an adjoining passage, where she can't disturb the others—and, frankly, no one wants to hear about them come sun-up. I can sympathise with that: enough horror in the waking world without adding to it by reeling off whatever surrealist nightmare plagued your head whilst you slept. Plus listening to someone describe their dream is, like, super-dull. The downside is that I'm left with no one to talk to about the images left coated on the inside of my skull that troubled me so; no one, that is, except you, dear diary, so you're going to have to take one for the team.

There was nothing literal about it, no sense of being chased by monsters or being trapped and unable to escape—surprising, considering that's our day-to-day life now. If I close my eyes, I can still see the crush of screaming faces on the day of the Fall, smell the blood and smoke, hear the blare of the sirens. Yet that rarely invades my dreams, as if I've unconsciously shuttered the most traumatic moments away and only call them up when I need to. My dreams are usually dark, formless things, the product of exhaustion. Last night was different: light, pin-sharp and painful, was shining through my skin. I was looking at my hands and studying the bones of my fingers, picked out in silhouette through the seemingly translucent flesh, dispassionately observing the light growing brighter until it started to tear through the papery epidermis. There was no panic, just cold dream-logic as I watched the rents pull wider and the light spilled through. The holes were now big enough to push a knuckle into and out the other side. I was in the bare bedroom of my childhood home, wooden floorboards beneath my feet, nothing on the walls save a mirror in an alcove on the opposite side of the chamber. Fascinated by the transformation taking place, I walked over and examined myself in the glass, touching my forehead and cheeks where the skin was starting to wither and retreat, spokes of light punching out. The gleam was such that my reflection became obscured and I was disappearing as the light consumed me: I was a skeleton haloed by fire.

I woke just as I lost sight of myself entirely, my eyes snapping open and my breath caught in mid-gasp. It took me a moment to get my bearings, the last of the blazing light still lingering on the back of my retina; once it dissipated, I realised where I was and became aware of the shadowed mounds around me that were the others, slumbering in the dark. A faint moan drifted across the room, which I put down to Emily, out there in the corridor, lost in her own private macabre loop from which she never seemed to escape. I lay back on my pillow—or rather the bundled-up clothes that serve as my pillow—and counted down from ten to slow my hammering heart. Eventually I drifted off back into a fitful sleep that lasted a couple of hours, but I was grateful to finally see the sun's rays slide across the floor via the small window at the top of the basement as dawn broke. Normally, I'm reluctant to leave the comfort of my sleeping bag, and have been known to get a less than gentle toeing in the side from Kez to ensure that I'm fully awake, but this morning I was up and boiling the water for everyone's breakfast before they'd even stirred.

But the dream clung to me. Every moment I had to myself I found my mind unconsciously returning to the images like a tongue repeatedly probing a painful tooth. The sight of my skin parting and the golden light pouring through was impossible to dispel, and no matter how much it unnerved me I couldn't look away, couldn't help calling it up again and again to unsettle me further. I couldn't affix any meaning to it; as far as I knew, it was nonsense farted out by my sleeping brain over which I had no control. That's all dreams were—random information broadcast behind your eyelids. Synaptic bursts of gobbledegook. I remember one I had back when I was a schoolkid of riding my bike through the water of a swimming pool, and marvelling at how bizarre it was, how it had taken two elements and misaligned them like a double-exposed photograph.

But it was precisely because I hadn't dreamed like that for a long time that last night's one left such an impression and why I struggled to just dismiss it as overheated brain-stew. It got to me. The pain of the light piercing my skin had been so intense it felt like iced water being pumped through my veins: the hurt was almost incandescent. Upon waking, I'd checked my arms, hands and face for any scratches because I was convinced that some physical harm had come to me, but inevitably there was nothing. Still the hairs on the back of my neck tingled every time I thought of the sensation, and I wondered if some psychosomatic condition was going on here: that through the sheer will of my imagination a wound would open on my body. That would've been enough to leave it alone, to push the dream back into the farthest recesses of my head, but of course I couldn't stop returning to it, like a song I couldn't stand on constant repeat to the point where it was actively driving me crazy.

It didn't go unnoticed—like I say, the dream put me in a pissy mood. Kez snapped at me for switching off and I'd barked back, telling her to get off my case. I was supposed to be helping her with the supply inventory (her favourite pastime—woman's obsessed with it!) and she'd caught me staring into space. It surprised her into silence, but I'll pay for it later: she'll corner me tomorrow and dress me down, put me on latrine duty for a week or something. I'll plead I had a headache and wasn't feeling myself—which is in part true—but I doubt it'll get me out of shit-detail. I was uncommunicative with the others too, and they picked up a 'don't mess' vibe, and duly gave me a wide berth, a frostiness which I'll probably have to go some way to repair at some point. They've no doubt got me marked down as having a snotty teenager moment (I'm on the last knockings of eighteen, I'm hardly a teen any more!), but my irritability and sullenness wasn't something I felt inclined to explain or apologise for—I was too preoccupied by the vividness of the dream, repeatedly beating against the inside of my skull. No matter how I employed my mind in whatever capacity—chores, sentry duty, reading (we found a pile of musty paperbacks stacked in a chest when we moved in, mostly cheap airport thrillers)—there it was, residing in a corner of my head and colouring my thoughts. I'd never had a nightmare linger like this, affect my whole mood. It was seemingly less like just a bad night's sleep and more a trauma that had scarred my waking hours.

I'm kinda nervous about going to bed in case it happens again: nothing I can control once I close my eyes. What if it's a persistent, recurring vision that I'm never going to be able to escape? What if I'm doomed to weeks and months of self-inflicted insomnia, and finally snap? Kez could give me serious grief if I'm strung out on no sleep and the possessor of a damaged brain. She wouldn't think twice about booting me down to menial duties (in fact, you could say she wouldn't lose sleep over it, ha ha); all it takes is a half-awake bozo not doing their job and the greys could get wise to us.

Oh God, now I'm stressing about sleeping. Gonna send me <u>mental</u> at this rate!

* * *

15 March

SUCCESS! A PEACEFUL slumber, with barely anything to remember that would hang around me like a fug. You can't imagine how relived I feel not to have had another nightly horrorshow projected on the inside of my skull. Sounds a bit melodramatic, but I felt almost like a new person once I rolled off the mattress this morning, rested and reasonably content that the previous night's dream had simply been a one-off, caused by factors unknown. I'd like to say that I'd prevented it by cutting out the cheese before bedtime, but it's been a good while since any of us tasted dairy (indeed, my preoccupation these days is now almost solely diary, arf!). No, simple fact is I got no idea why I was spared, but I'll take what small victories I can get.

I mean, I look at Emily when she rises come the dawn and realise how grateful I should be that my nights are—or have been up until now—for the most part uneventful. Poor E looks wrecked: dark circles under her eyes, washed out, grey hair encroaching at the temples. She's aged incredibly in the weeks we've been down here, adding a couple of decades to her appearance. She was a young mum when she and Bren first threw themselves onto Mr Graham's RV; she has a good eight years or so on me, but still when we first met, she was fresh-faced and kinda neat and composed. Night after night of her 'mares has destroyed that—she now looks more like her kid's mad old auntie than his parent. She won't talk about her dreams, should the unwritten rule of disinterest amongst the others be broken briefly and someone asks: she just shakes her head and refuses to be drawn on the subject. Everybody can see she's suffering—hell, everyone can hear her suffering every night, to the point where her mattress was moved for the sake of the group's sanity—but no-one can do anything about it. How do you stop the bad thoughts from entering a person's head?

I've often pondered what it is that haunts her so—is it guilt over the fact that she survived and her husband didn't? Did she see something prior to leaping aboard the vehicle that stayed with her? Is it a mother's natural instinct to protect her son, and she's wracked by 'what if' scenarios in which Bren is lost to the monsters? Whichever it is, or it's a combination of all three, it's playing havoc with her mental well-being. The way Bren looks at her, from his perspective he's losing <u>her</u> to the dark forces—she's fraught, frazzled, and lashes out at the smallest of infractions. He's only nine, so prone to belligerence and unco-operation at times, and she's been known to smack him upside of the head on occasion when he answers her back or won't do what he's told, and then she instantly regrets it, apologising in a flood of tears. The fear's slowly killing her. She can't carry on for much longer in this state of constant despair, sapped of strength, before the inevitable collapse.

It's equally unspoken that Emily's the weak link in the group, physically and emotionally: the one we can't necessarily rely on. It's rarely discussed (because that would be tantamount to admitting it, natch) but just naturally assumed that we'll cover for her. We figure we'll cut her some slack as the woman's clearly suffering. She's never posted on lookout, isn't taken on reconnaissance or supply missions, and is generally kept away from being outside—the view from the front yard... isn't good. She doesn't need to see it. Frankly, no one does, since it doesn't do anyone's well-being any favours (always reminds me of those medieval paintings from my art-history text books at school, whereby the apocalypse was imagined as the dead returning to shovel the living into back of carts) but, like I say, we're willing to keep that from her and divide the rota and extra work between us. I don't know if she's aware of that—that we're doing all this to save her additional mental strain—because she never comments on it, but I suspect that she's rarely with us in spirit at the best of times. So little sleep, I reckon her days are pretty much a blur, a fractured collage of random thoughts that only occasionally phase into the present. It must've been weeks since she last saw sunlight. I must remember to recommend to Kez that we pick up some Vitamin D for her, if we can, before she fades away completely. Got Bren to think about too, of course: God knows what it'd do to him if she was gone.

Our glorious leader has so far bit her tongue on the E issue, and been willing to accept that it's better she's kept out of the way when it comes to all the frontline stuff. You can tell Kez isn't happy about it—EVERYONE pulls their weight, no exceptions—but she's probably resigned to the fact now that putting Emily in a conflict situation she's just going to be a liability, and could end up risking the lives of others. It's that factor that makes me worry about E's continued place in the group; that Kez will use it as an excuse to have her exiled, stating that she threatens to compromise the safety of the community as a whole. Despite past form, I can't see the big K ever being that much of an asshole, but I guess it only needs a shortage of food, or a change of circumstances, before she starts making the hard choices. If she feels she needs to start cutting the dead wood, then Emily could be for the chop. What that would mean for her son, I don't know. Really hope it won't come to that, I really do, because it's the kind of decision that could come back to haunt us. Rip us apart, even.

This kind of thinking makes me shudder, to be honest, because it leads me down the inevitable road of what sort of future any of us can expect. Kez is doing all this so we survive, and reiterates that she's safeguarding the sanctity of this bolthole we've made for ourselves, but what's the endgame? Is this the life I've got to look forward to—writing these words by candlelight as I contemplate another day of foraging and hiding and watching and waiting, all for the continued benefit of breathing? What exactly is Emily's weakness going to threaten—the civilised way of life we've got going on here? I shit in a hole in the ground! I eat month-out-of-date beans from a tin that's been snatched from a looted supermarket's shelf! What the hell am I pushing towards?

I suppose at the back of all our heads there's the vague hope that someone's going to save us; that we've just got to bide our time and authority's going to come to our rescue and send these grey bastards packing. That's all it is, though: a vague hope. And not a very likely one. We all saw the system collapse on the night of the Fall, the jays overwhelmed by the forces loyal to the new Chief. We heard on the radio before it cut out completely that there'd been a regime change at the HoJ: some guy called Sidney installing himself in the big chair. I'm sure there're pockets of resistance out there—badges that are still human fighting a guerrilla war against the creatures—but somehow I imagine not enough to turn the tide. The new powers that be are too strong, their soldiers growing in number by the day, thanks to some kind of liquid drug that's getting passed around. Lance, who fled from the east side, said he saw it being dealt and injected on the street, causing physical abnormalities. He didn't go into details, but what he did describe—related with a certain degree of ghoulish relish, I have to say—was enough to give us all the heebie-jeebies. And the world itself is changing—the soil sickening, the animal life either dying off or adapting to strange new forms. Even the sky looks an odd colour now after we had that three-day downpour. It begs the question: even if we could reclaim it from the monsters, has it been spoiled beyond further use? Is the world too far gone to fix? Will there be anything left to save?

I said when I started writing this journal that I hoped someone would come after to read it—that you had to have some kind of belief that life would prevail in some shape further down the line, otherwise you were giving up on all humanity. It could be that this book is a future archaeological find, dug out of the earth decades, centuries, or aeons later and pored over. It gives me slim comfort that that might be the case—that life found a way, that its seed escaped complete extermination. If I'm feeling optimistic, then I'm convinced that this isn't the end: that we're too stubborn and resilient and tenacious as a species to be wiped out entirely. We've weathered worse storms than this, as Mr Graham might've said, and managed to cling on to existence.

But in my more practical moments, I can't see any way back for us. We scrabble to survive but, let's face it, this is our swan song. The world's dying before our eyes, and one by one we're falling into the dark from which there'll be no return.

Ugh. Black thoughts... and I'd been feeling so upbeat too after my dream-free sleep. Dunno where that all came from. Tired, I expect, and getting cranky. Depressed thinking about what Emily's going through. Last word before I blow out the flame:

I STILL BELIEVE IN YOU, FUTURE READER! YOU'RE OUT THERE, I KNOW IT! THIS WON'T BE THE END OF US!

CHAPTER FOURTEEN

If the transformed Grand Hall was an unnerving environment, then the Chief's office at its apex was the blackly beating heart of this new architectural construct. Or perhaps more pertinently, the still void, since life was most certainly not welcome here. Nothing with a pulse resided on the top floor—it was a dark, silent tomb, shrouded by a mist that swirled throughout the corridors several inches off the ground, and which swallowed the sound of any footfall. The walls were coated in moisture, green mould spreading across the ceiling too. As Cafferly emerged from the stairwell, the dank, oppressive atmosphere hit her like a fist, and her psi-senses deadened almost instantly, akin to a radio signal cutting out in a tunnel. There was something dreamlike about the way she had to carry herself forward, head full of cotton wool, an unknown pressure bearing down on her, mist barely moving as she waded through it. There was power here, but it wasn't entirely Sidney's; it was *them*, the creatures he was in league with. His sponsors. Their chill tendrils were behind everything.

She'd never been to De'Ath's office before; she'd had no cause to. To ascend to his domain was at his invitation or instruction only, and any trespassers would be dealt with before they'd even left the top step. She was in no doubt that her progress was being watched, and for the moment she was allowed to continue unimpeded. There was no sign of anyone else: he had no need of guards, for he was confident—arrogant, even—in his own abilities to deal with any threat that may come his way. He'd transcended mortality, and as such had little fear. His living body had simply been a chrysalis that he'd emerged from into his new higher state of being, and all that concerned him was laying waste to a planet so its inhabitants—all of them, every single one—felt too that blessed peace, put themselves beyond sin and wickedness and embraced judgement. Some would resist but they were like bugs that he casually swatted away, causing him the minimum of grief. They could not harm him—who could withstand Death, the Great Leveller? It was the most powerful, immutable force in the universe, and he was its personification. He was an anti-god, decimating all before him, nullifying where there has once been creation.

He had his lieutenants, of course, with whom he shared his crusade, and they too had sloughed off their humanity in line with their leader. On the surface, Sidney evidently entrusted them with overseeing various branches of his genocidal scheme, but Cafferly suspected that De'Ath was innately suspicious of everyone and loyalty extended only so far. Once the last bones of the last living creature were finally laid to rest, the psi wouldn't be at all surprised if the Chief didn't turn next on his own brothers and rend them from existence too so the global graveyard was his alone to enjoy. His subordinates may well be aware of this even as they continued to do his bidding—they were several degrees of inscrutable—but it clearly didn't diminish their fanaticism. They were as committed as he was.

As she approached Sidney's chamber, one of his seconds-in-command emerged from the shadows to her right, the pale white bone of his sheep's-skull-head breaching the gloom like a shark's fin. His hollow eye sockets regarded her, twin pits of soul-ravaging emptiness that could swallow sanity whole. No matter how much Cafferly had changed, she still instinctively trembled in the presence of a Dark Judge. His name was Mortis, and he was the futurist of Sidney's inner circle, the one most interested in the development of change, and how it could be brought about. He had initiated the weaponisation of cultures, of insects and natural elements, and sought to apply those to the extermination of mankind. He was, she supposed, the tek-spod of De'Ath's group. He'd had some success with mutations to the food chain, and was unquestionably behind the reprogramming of the cloud-farming drones that had led to the widespread flooding that had destroyed many of the communities outside the capital. The body count of that had been in the tens of thousands, which had been much celebrated. Mortis was often found tinkering in his labs, conjuring up more atrocities.

"Death hass sssent for you," he said, his jaw unmoving, his voice resounding within his skull. It was a statement, not a question.

She nodded, trying not to wince at the white-noise blast of psi-blindness that assailed her. Even if she'd been foolish enough to attempt to get inside the head of a being such as this, she would've hit a null-wall, a barrier of absolute emptiness that she'd never be able to penetrate. Mortis exuded anti-thought in waves, blanking out her senses while she was in his field. She'd never encountered such power in anything living before—but, of course, De'Ath and his cadre were no longer abiding by such rules. The more they divested themselves of their recognisable humanoid features, the more they became abstractions, driven by a single instinct: to negate all life. Morality, empathy, all base functions were abandoned, in favour of this single-minded pursuit of the end of all things. They wanted to render the world to nothing, and as such the psychic static that needled her as she stood before the Judge was a glimpse of what they wanted—a dead zone, bereft of light and breath.

She refused to cower, though; as hollow as Mortis was, she detected occasionally a certain preening aspect that she found contemptible. He enjoyed the reactions he instilled—there was a vanity there. Cafferly wouldn't indulge him, and hid the discomfort behind an unyielding mask, conscious that she wasn't going to cede dominance to the Dark Judge, even if technically he was her superior. She would be respectful but wouldn't give him an inch. She was not to be toyed with.

"I'll join you," he said, falling in alongside her and trailing a clawed finger against the wall, rot blackening wherever he touched. He had that ability, which she'd seen exhibited numerous times on various prisoners and resistance fighters that had passed through these walls: to lay his rancid hands upon an organism and bring instant decay. A person could be reduced to mere dust in a matter of seconds. It was a spectacle that was impossible to tear your eyes away from once you were confronted with it, so complete was the destruction of the victim. Another glorious gift of the Sisters, something they'd bestowed upon each of the anointed four—Sidney, Mortis and the other two henchmen he kept close at hand, Fear and Fire.

He jerkily stalked next to her with the hunched-over gait of a predatory animal learning to walk on its hind legs, and she reminded herself that the body he was occupying was no doubt long dead, its muscles having atrophied. He looked like a bag of bones that would be blown apart by a stiff wind, and while that was possibly true the spirit that animated it was very resilient indeed— indestructible, even. It paid not to underestimate him, as flimsy as he appeared.

De'Ath's door loomed before them, as tall and wide as a church's porch, a dense black that sucked in what little light there was, carved in ornate gothic pictograms. It unlatched itself before Cafferly could reach out to knock, and swung silently wide, the Psi-Judge crossing the threshold without waiting for word from the Chief, or offering Mortis the chance to go first. She had to put up a front, she told herself, that she was not to be intimidated or manipulated. The Grand Hall was dog-eat-dog now, an amoral environment in which you had to prove—or at least give a convincing impression—that you were on the right side. Every moment, Sidney and his skeletal comrade here—not to mention *them*, somewhere behind the scenes—would be testing her, seeking out weakness. She needed to be on her guard at all times, bullish and forthright.

Sidney's inner sanctum was gloomy to the point of impenetrable, thick folds of darkness layering each corner. The flames burning from the twin Baroque candelabra placed either side of his desk did little to dispel the murk, but Cafferly suspected they were simply for show anyway. The Chief embraced the shadows, sought succour from them, and in actuality had no real need of light; the eyes behind the helm were undoubtedly rotting away. Still, that gaze could paralyse you if you were caught within it, some power fixing you in its sights even if the organs themselves were no longer there.

De'Ath also seemed to like the dark for what it hid, and the Psi-Judge could sense other beings inside the room besides her and Mortis. They weren't visible—or at least they weren't allowing her to see them, which was more likely—but she could feel the pressure drops and the movement of the air as they slid past less than a hair's breadth from her face. If she surreptitiously pushed out a psychic feeler to gauge anything about them, she picked up enough to reel it back in PDQ. Unlike Mortis or Sidney, they'd *never* been human, and were almost certainly not of this world to begin with. They'd been brought here by the same witchery that had enabled De'Ath to transform into his undead state, and spearhead his quest for global annihilation—the same black arts that had always guided him up to now.

Its practitioners were the sisters—Phobia and Nausea—there at his shoulder, studying her as she entered as they might a strange, repulsive life form that they had never witnessed before, evoking pity and clinical curiosity as much as outright contempt. They loomed over Sidney, an ancient evil despite their teenage facades; she knew they were eons-old entities at their core. The Chief seemed mildly irritated by their proximity, and shrugged his shoulders to have them remove their hands from his uniform livery, expelling a tetchy hiss like an animal warning another to keep out of its personal space. Cafferly guessed that he was starting to tire of having these dank-haired witches around. He'd outgrown them—the worldwide genocide was *his* conception, *his* masterpiece, and he was damned if he was sharing it with anyone. The Sisters no doubt felt different.

De'Ath finally seemed aware of her presence in his room and ran his gaze up and down her for a moment before beckoning her forward with a single bony finger. She took a couple of steps but stopped short of the desk, which she couldn't help noticing was virtually bare: no paperwork, no personalised effects, no stationery. She glanced at the filing cabinets behind him that would've once housed arrest reports and personnel files when this had been the old chief's office, and realised for the first time since entering that their contents had been unceremoniously emptied, drawers still hanging open. Blackened scorch marks up the walls suggested much of it had been put to the torch. Her attention must've lingered a little too long for Sidney followed her line of sight and realised what was interesting her.

"They belonged to the old world," he declared, his voice as cold and dry and lifeless as sand rasping off a concrete surface; it chafed almost to listen to it. "Sssuch rulesss and regulationsss no longer concern usss now. There isss only oblivion and what we can do to hasssten it."

She nodded. "Is *no one* recording your work here, sir?"

"Who would be left to read it?" one of the Sisters snapped from De'Ath's shoulder, silenced from speaking further by a glare from the Chief. She looked from Cafferly to Sidney and retreated a little further into the gloom, a sour expression on her face before darkness swallowed it up.

"No, there will be no recordsss," he answered, turning back to the Psi-Judge. "The bonefieldsss will be my lasssting tessstament. Every criminal will have been sssentenced to death, and asss ssuch there isss no need for a record of their missdeedsss. Every living thing isss guilty, and all will receive the sssame punissshment, princcce or pauper. Sssuch purity of judgement makesss filesss and reportsss redundant, don't you agree?" He cocked his head to one side, inviting a response.

She cleared her throat. "Your planetary masterpiece will be your legacy, there's no doubt."

"You sssound... unconvinccced," he murmured after a moment's deliberation.

"Oh no," she replied quickly. "Quite the opposite. I mean, the work you're doing here, the mission, it's truly unprecedented. The scale of it, the commitment... it's the extermination of the guilty like no one has ever attempted before."

"No one *dared*," De'Ath interjected testily.

Cafferly nodded again, aware of how eager to please she was appearing but sensing that this was the best way to stroke the Chief's ego; it wasn't subtle and she found her toadying distasteful, but there was palpable tension in the room that was making her uneasy and it seemed he required mollifying. Sidney, for all his absolute authority, appeared insecure and seeking affirmation regarding his leadership. It wasn't quite what she was expecting of him: cold, yes, and ruthless, but right now the power at the top was coming across as self-obsessed, eager for praise and more than a little vain. She wondered just what kind of snakes' pit the office of the Chief had become for him to be so touchy of criticism. The visible antagonism Sidney was displaying towards the Sisters indicated that he was growing increasingly angry at being considered nothing more than their puppet creature, and wanted acknowledgement of what he'd achieved through his own actions. Of course, the Sisters had unquestionably enabled him in the first place, though she doubted anyone in his inner circle had the nerve to bring that up.

"Exactly," she answered. "It's a vision of a world absent of illegality that required utter dedication. Anything that comes after will be a footnote to your achievement."

"Nothing will come after. That'sss the point."

"Of course."

De'Ath rose and stepped out from behind the desk in an unsettlingly fluid motion as if a section of shadow had detached itself from the room. He was before her in a heartbeat, or what she could remember the space of a heartbeat being like. Even up close, details of his face beyond the visor were not distinct, just the wet glisten of the rotten parts: the eye sockets, mouth and nose. He wasn't an especially imposing figure—not taller than she was, and rake-thin; she'd seen footage of Sidney pre-mortem, and he was a snotty slip of a kid, not in the least bit physically imposing, but chilling to the marrow when you glimpsed something of what was going on inside his head—but nevertheless he exuded a malignancy that was startlingly potent. Here was the enemy of all that ever was. He was the cancer, the defiler, wrapped up in one slight humanoid form, and to have him studying you was to experience having your senses corrupted one atom at a time.

"You are fully onboard, then, yesss?" he enquired. "You have no qualmsss about what needsss to be done? No tracccesss of"—he had to spit the word out, like gristle lodged in his throat—"conssscienccce?"

Cafferly flashed back for a second to her remote-viewing of the survivors' execution, or rather the moments leading up to it before she cut the connection. She dismissed it, all the while maintaining her poker face. "None whatsoever, sir."

"Good. Becaussse we have further need of your particular talentsss, Pssi-Judge Cafferly."

"Oh?"

"Mortisss?" De'Ath hissed over her shoulder. "The floor isss yourssss."

The Dark Judge emerged from whatever corner he'd been silently occupying and joined them in the centre of the room. Cafferly turned to regard him, though she was never sure quite whereabouts she should make eye-contact with him, or indeed through what unholy magic he could see her that he could address her directly.

"We wisssh to ssstep up the purgesss," he said. "Psssi-

Divisssion'sss record for finding criminalsss that have ssso far evaded jussstice hasss been... haphazard at bessst."

"It's not an exact science, as I'm sure you're well aware," she replied. "Given the conditions and the scale of the task, I'd say our eighty per cent termination target is more than acceptable."

"*All* musssst *die!*" Mortis roared, his skeletal frame visibly shaking. Cafferly, despite herself, took an involuntary step back. "*All* mussst be *judged!* Eighty per cent, ninety per cent, isss not enough—only through *total* annihilation can we achieve our goal!"

"I assure you we're on the same page. But we're having to peel through an extraordinary amount of psychic residue to find the living. That's a lot of blind alleys to chase down—"

"Inefficient isss the word," Mortis interrupted. "The exterminations mussst be conducted in a more orderly fassshion, otherwissse too many will sssslip through the cracksss."

Cafferly bit down on her indignation. They were working twenty-four-seven as it was, solely committed to the cause; several of her fellow psi-operatives had burned themselves out, the empaths suffering the most from the torrential psychic backwash. Yet it wasn't enough, and clearly would *never* be enough, for Sidney and his lieutenants. As long as one living creature remained at large, then they were failing in their duty. "What do you propose?"

The Dark Judge turned towards the doorway. "Jacksssson?"

His minion schlepped into the room, presumably having been loitering outside waiting for its master's voice. She instinctively wrinkled her nose in disgust at once again being in the presence of this thing that Mortis kept around at his beck and call; his drones were one of his many special projects that he liked to experiment on, and this inside-out monstrosity was no different. Whoever it'd been in life, it was an entirely different entity now, with its bowels and stomach contents bundled on its side like a tumorous hump, its withered leg dragging behind it, and head dangling to one side upon an over-stretched neck. A portion of the scalp flapped free, where it looked like most of the brain had been removed.

It handed Mortis a skull-cap device. "Thisss," the Dark Judge said, turning it over in his hands, "may prove decisssive."

"What is it?"

"Ssssomething I've been developing. A variation of the psssi-amplifier." He fixed his hollow-eyed gaze on Cafferly. "And *you* will be the firssst to try it out."

CHAPTER FIFTEEN

22 March

My god… My god… I thought we were safe.

I…

Can't write, hand's shaking. Need to stop now.

It's just after nine, and things have quietened down a little. Inside of my head's still a screaming, fractured collage of insanity, but at least it's all in one place for the time being. Better that it's contained here, where it's just me that has to deal with it, than loose in the world. What this means, though, where we go from here… I don't know.

I've made a bit of a mess of the journal, so I hope you can read this. Ink's smudged in places, and my handwriting's gone to pot (felt like my fingers couldn't remember how to hold a pen, weirdly—went all numb and useless). The book's taken a bit of a battering too—it must've got bent in two when I grabbed it, and the pages have come a bit loose where the spine's cracked. Strange things that you catch yourself thinking: I saw the state of it and thought I'd get some sticky tape and patch it up. Then, of course, I correct myself: where the hell am I going to get tape from? It's just not something that's easily to hand any more, or you can pop to the corner store to buy some. Funny, after everything, after all these weeks, you still don't realise what's gone, what you did as routine without considering it a luxury.

Sticky tape a luxury. Christ, clean water is a fucking luxury these days.

As it was, I cut a strip of bandage adhesive from the med-kit when Kez wasn't looking and did a first-aid job on it (wasn't very much and not going to mean the difference between life and death for anyone that might need it). With its field-dressed cover and crumpled exterior, it looks like a proper refugee journal now that's fled a warzone, which is kinda fitting—makes me feel closer to it. Me and these words, they're surviving somehow, making it through by hook or by crook.

Sorry, I'm babbling. I think I'm trying to avoid thinking about—and therefore putting down on paper—what's happened. It's easier to skirt round the edges and ruminate on all manner of inconsequential tripe than get to grips with the heart of the matter. That would mean reliving it, deciphering the aforementioned collage. It's raw and terrible and I don't know where to start, what's the best way to transfer it from mind to script.

I'm digging the nails of my left hand into my palm as I scrawl this, my knuckles flaring white. The pain makes me angry, as does the despair. I want to rip my eyes from their sockets. I want to tear the pen through the page—

The beginning. Start at the beginning.

Like I said, I thought we were safe, which is a relative term these days, I know. We were safe if we played it careful. We—under Kez's admittedly wise if authoritarian direction—did nothing to draw attention to ourselves, used our common sense when it came to scouting, or foraging for supplies. There's nothing to prevent against plain bad luck but plenty you can do to ensure you don't make your own problems, and we were all about that from the start. Rule number one was don't give anything away. The farm was nondescript from the air, all signs of life carefully camouflaged, and deep below the ground, in the storm cellar, we carved out a frugal existence. The two RVs in the lean-to were draped in tarpaulins, next to a pile of discarded tractor parts. We did everything within our means to disappear from their radar. We were as safe as anyone could possibly be in the circumstances. Maybe we were kidding ourselves, and were just delaying the inevitable, but I thought—despite my moans and discomforts—we had a pretty robust system. It had been days since we'd last seen an H-wagon go overhead, and presumed that this area had been written off as uninhabited. No one was relaxed—we were all very much aware of becoming complacent—but we figured if we kept this up, then we had a good chance of staying off the grid.

We were wrong. I guess no set-up will withstand an enemy utterly committed to hunting you out, whose entire raison d'etre is to find and eliminate you. They will not give up, and even the strongest wall will crumple if battered enough times. There's always a weak spot, a crack, a thread to be unravelled.

Emily was ours. Kez had seen it, and knew something had to be done sooner or later for the sanctity of the group. Like I said before, everyone knew it even if they didn't like to admit it—yeah, including me—but reasoned that we still had enough humanity not to brook the idea of taking decisive action. That was our folly, and our safety—despite all our due care and attention—was fatally compromised.

The beginning. Put it down. Confront it.

It started on the night of the twenty-first. It was late, deep in the early hours of the morning (or that's what it felt like). Something roused me, and I'm still not sure if it was a sound or some part of my hind brain sending me a warning signal that I should awake. I just remember opening my eyes to the purple shadows of the basement, and unease was my first sensation. Then I became aware of movement and voices, and panic gave me that kickstart into full consciousness.

I stumbled to my feet, at the same time snatching up the torch that I kept next to my mattress, and flipping it on. The first thing that struck me was that there were several empty beds, the covers slung back and discarded. How long had people been up? If there was a crisis, how come I hadn't been awoken at the same time? As it turned out, only minutes had passed in the interim, but at the time I was stuck by an inescapable fear of being abandoned. I deduced the source of the consternation was coming from upstairs and followed, beam swinging this way and that in the darkness, and caught a couple of dazed-looking faces—the young Mellius sisters only just emerging from sleep too, squinting perplexedly at the light. I didn't stop but climbed the wooden steps at speed, the trapdoor wide open, sounds growing louder. That was when I first heard Emily's name being called.

Out of the basement and into the kitchen, which had long since been stripped of anything useful. Up-top was generally more of a dispiriting sight than the underground dorm we called home, the few remnants of what was—an old calendar tacked to the wall with birthdays written in biro, a broken eggcup sitting on a windowsill—a sharp reminder of what had been lost, and I for one no longer cared to linger within the rooms of the farmhouse. You felt like a ghost moving through the burned-out shell of someone else's memories. The torch played over the walls and windows—it was pitch-black outside—as I crossed to the back door, where four or five figures were standing just on the edge of the threshold, seemingly unwilling to go much further. I squeezed past and joined them.

"What's going on?" I said to the person next to me, who turned out to be Riggs, whom I've never especially warmed to. Weaselly guy only interested in his own survival, and always the first to bitch about not getting his fair share.

"It's Emily," he replied. "She's out there, on the boundary wall. She won't move, just staring up at the sky."

"Why? What's she want?"

"Christ knows. I think she's finally cracked."

"Well, why doesn't anyone bring her in—"

"She's got Bren."

I played the beam out across the courtyard, and in the stark spotlight I caught the both of them perched on the brick wall—not high, only four feet at most—that separated the house from the fields on the other side. Emily's face was turned upwards like she wanted to bathe her skin in the moonlight, though there was no moon visible, and her features were composed, serene; what made my bowels turn to water was that she had her arm around Bren's neck. It could've been construed as a motherly protective hug, but the fright in his eyes suggested he most certainly didn't want to be there. She was gripping him tightly, her bicep under his chin, refusing to allow him to wrest himself free. If she squeezed further, he'd struggle to breathe.

I realised that there was someone standing slightly ahead of the pack, looking like they were trying to inch forward in Emily's direction, and I didn't need my torch to confirm that it was Kez. In fact, in that moment she seemed to become aware that I was there and glanced over her shoulder and hissed at me to switch it off. I did so, reducing us all to silhouettes on a dark grey background.

"Emily, please," Kez whispered. "It's not safe out here, not for any of us. The longer we're in the open, the greater the chance we're spotted. Please come inside. You don't want to hurt Bren, do you? 'Cause you're scaring him right now."

Emily appeared not to hear the words, her head slightly motioning from side to side as if she were listening to music from somewhere. Her son's attention was on us, however, his panicky gaze never leaving our direction. Fear seemed to have silenced him. Kez chanced another couple of steps forward like she was playing a high-stakes version of a school playground game, but I didn't know what she intended to do should she get within reach of them.

"Emily said anything?" I murmured to Riggs.

"Nothing. First we know about it is when we heard the trapdoor opening, then by the time we get out here, she's already got Bren on the wall."

"Maybe she's sleepwalking."

"More likely having a psychotic episode." He looked up at the sky himself. "She's putting us all at risk. All it needs is one fly-by with their infrared scanners working and that's us screwed. Kez manages to get her inside, she's done—the kid might be able to stay, but she's gone."

"We can't abandon her—"

"The hell we can't," another chipped in to my left. It was Lionel, a sixty-year-old prissy, NIMBY type, who'd lost his partner in the floods before he'd stumbled upon the farmhouse. He had an unctuous air about him, and did everything Kez said without question. "Our lives are on the line because of that maniac. She has to go—she's gone full-blown whacko now."

"She's traumatised!" I snapped. "Show some freakin' compassion—"

"This isn't your decision to make, Mish," Riggs said. "Adults get to choose what's right for the group."

I was about to round on him and unleash what I thought of the adults in our particular community when Kez started imploring to Emily again. I'd never heard her so empathic; she sure could turn it on when she needed to. But it made no difference; the woman's mind was clearly in a different space and unaware of what was going on around her. The way she kept tilting her head to the heavens suggested she was receiving a message, as if listening to instructions or directions. And the way she was holding Bren… I became scared she was taking him somewhere, under orders from a voice that resounded only in her ears.

Maybe it was a waking dream, I mused, and she was far from logic or rational thought. She was trapped inside something that right now only made sense to her—in which case she needed to be stopped before she hurt herself or her son. But someone needed to act before it was too late.

I glanced at Kez, who was still trying to reach out, one eye scanning the horizon for any telltale lights. The others were nervously retreating, already uneasy about having spent so long outside without cover. None of them could be trusted not to suddenly shut and barricade the door behind us. In that second, I ran at Emily.

I heard Kez hiss a warning, but there was no tug on my arm to hold me back (I suspect I moved too fast for her to respond) and I launched myself in the woman's direction. The transformation was chillingly abrupt—Emily's space-cadet demeanour vanished in an instant and her eyes locked onto mine. Bren shook his head, his own expression pleading—"No, Mama," he cried, straining as hard he could to wrest himself free, "No, Mama, please, no"—before his mother tightened her arm around his neck and yanked his head to one side in one swift motion.

The snap of his young neck breaking still echoes inside my skull. The loudness of it. The shock. In the space of a moment I flashed back to that night when we all ran, the retort of the guns behind us, and then Joel falling beside me, and I looked back and the blood haloed his head where the skull had blown apart, and only the night before I'd been twirling my fingers through his hair as we'd watched TV together on the sofa in his apartment, his right cheek on my lap, legs stretched out on the cushions, when everything felt comfortable and secure and you didn't want to be anywhere else at that point but now... now it was gone, ripped from you with the finality of a door slamming shut on all the goodness in your life. A bang. A crack. The world splits open and everything you cherished is gone in a heartbeat.

I think I screamed, partly in rage, partly in fright—maybe in frustration too that I didn't get to him in time. It was purely instinctual, an animal howl of grief. Bren dropped to the ground just as I launched myself at Emily, and she made no attempt to defend herself when I clattered into her, throwing her off the wall. We landed in a heap on the other side, me on top, grabbing her by her jacket lapels and yanking her towards me, eyesight blurry from the tears, bawling in her face, asking her if she knew what she had done, what she'd just destroyed. Her own eyes were rolled back in their sockets, whites only visible between the lids, and she flopped back and forth in my hands like all the energy had deserted her. I got tired of shaking her and let her fall to the earth. A small smile creased her lips and the words "It ends" emerged from her throat like an exhalation. It didn't sound like Emily's voice; there was a dry, rustling quality to it, far beyond her years. It was ancient, bereft of life and humanity.

I stumbled to my feet and backed away from her, fear clawing at me. Then I heard Kez's shout. I turned and saw her pointing at the sky. I followed her gaze and there in the darkness were twin pinpoints of light rapidly growing bigger as they approached, a rumble filling the sky where once there'd been silence.

They'd found us.

A cry of panic ran through those still congregating at the doorway and they collided with each other in their haste to scurry back inside the house. Kez yelled at them to stop, that it was no longer safe, but her voice was being drowned out by the H-Wagon's lifters as it descended towards us, and the others were too scared to pay attention in any case, vanishing across the threshold in the vain hope that they hadn't been spotted. But the Judges knew we were here; that's what the whole pantomime with Emily had been in aid of. She'd been a beacon for them, or some kind of transmitter they could home in on. They'd been following her signal, one they'd probably caused her to broadcast. Our weak link—the one I really didn't want Kez to exile from the group despite the security risk she posed—would prove to be our undoing.

Her back towards me, our leader's shoulders slumped as she realised she wasn't getting through to them. Then she evidently noticed I was still there, and regained some of her composure.

"We have to leave," Kez snapped at me. "They know about this place—cowering in the basement and hope they don't find us any more isn't an option any more." She nodded in the direction of the farmhouse. "We have to convince the others to go."

"Go where?" I asked.

"Anywhere. If we stay, we die." She started to jog towards the doorway, and motioned at the same time to the RVs parked under the lean-to. "You know how to drive one of those, right? The old boy taught you."

"Yeah, but I'm still a beginner—"

"Doesn't matter. Right now that's our only way out." The wind began to pick up as the craft drew closer, violently whipping our hair about our faces. Kez looked back over her shoulder at it, a slab of shadow falling towards us. "Get it started. You know where the keys are?"

"In the RV's glovebox."

"Good. I'm gonna evacuate as many as I can. We got maybe a couple of minutes' grace before that thing lands."

"Jesus," I breathed. "All our stuff... There're kids down there too. Can we get them all out in time?"

She didn't answer, vanishing into the house at speed. I ran towards the vehicles, heart pounding, legs trembling. One of the RVs was more prone to stalling than the other—an older model scarred with rust that the Mellius family had arrived in, trailing exhaust smoke—and nowhere near as user-friendly as the one Mr Graham had taught me in, so I avoided that and went straight for what I knew. Just as I tugged off the tarpaulin I heard a skin-crawling caterwaul above the rumble of the H-Wagon's engines, and saw Emily crawling on hands and knees towards the body of her son. Lucidity had returned, and with it the awful realisation of what had happened. Did she know she was responsible? It was impossible to tell. I was convinced she hadn't been in control of her actions—that it was them, remote-controlling her—but she wouldn't understand that. Her keening as she pulled his thin frame to her lap was heartbreaking. Everything she'd done over the weeks since the Fall had been to keep him safe, and now she was the architect of her own failure.

As the H-Wagon landed in the field beyond, I leapt into the RV driver's seat, grabbing the keys and inserting them into the ignition. It took a couple of cranks, but the engine roared into life. I wrenched it into gear, stomped on the accelerator, and the RV lurched forward, scraping the bodywork of the other one as I struggled to get to grips with the steering. The back fishtailed and smacked the perimeter wall, but I kept it going.

Figures emerged from the Judge ship and headed in our direction. I braked and leaned out of the window, trying to warn Emily. She gave no indication she heard me, or was aware of the impending danger. I punched the horn, and the blare was enough to make her look up and around, her cheeks wet with tears. The greys—there were four of them, advancing in a line—were holding weapons of some kind, attached to tanks on their backs.

Flamethrowers, I realised at the very moment they let rip.

A blossom of orange flame erupted from the nozzles and Emily and Bren disappeared in the fiery blast. When the Judges pulled their fingers from the triggers, mother and son were nothing more than a dark centre in the midst of the roiling flames that lit up the night and sent flickering shadows across the courtyard. I squeezed the steering wheel in terror as the four uniforms walked past the burning bodies without a backward glance and came nearer.

At that moment, Kez came barrelling out of the doorway, shepherding half a dozen of our group, revolver in hand. She shot a grey as it brought its weapon to bear—the bullet passed through its midriff, causing it little concern—then bellowed at everyone to get on the RV. The people, some clutching holdalls but most empty-handed, tore towards the open door of the vehicle, and needed no further encouragement to climb aboard. Danny Mellius hesitated, and glanced across at his own motorhome. His wife, Katherine, tugged at him.

"There's not going to be enough room for everyone!" he shouted. "We need ours too!"

"There's no time," she pleaded.

"Get the girls on. I'll be right behind you." He headed off towards the remaining vehicle.

Kez pushed everyone onto the RV as another lance of flame shot past. "Is there anyone still left in the house?" I yelled as they tumbled past into the main living area, where once I too had thrown myself to escape the purge, saved by Mr Graham. "Kez!" I repeated when I got no reply. "Are you sure we haven't left anyone behind?"

"I rounded up all I could," she muttered, looking shellshocked.

Before I could stop myself, I jumped down and ran into the house, my brain screaming at me to get out, but I knew in all conscience I couldn't have handled the guilt if we'd abandoned anyone. I fell down the steps into the cellar, calling all the way, but receiving no reply. It looked deserted, though there was clothing and possessions strewn everywhere. That's when I saw you, dear diary, and I snatched you up and held you to my chest, beating a swift retreat. Was it you I was after all along, and couldn't admit it to myself? Couldn't I bear to lose my confidant?

Smoke was billowing into the kitchen as I fled, and I had to shoulder-barge a grey out of the way, who was standing by the doorway and unleashing his flamethrower at the house. The wooden frames were quickly catching and spreading across the façade. I slalomed between another two jays, who staggered back as Kez fired again from the door of the RV, and she pulled me in the driver's seat. The vehicle shuddered forward as I stepped on the gas and we bumped our way out of the gate and onto the road that led to the highway beyond.

I looked in the mirror and saw Danny Mellius's motorhome emerge from the lean-to. It started to pick up speed, then the gears crunched and the engine died. Katherine screamed her husband's name. The greys doused the stationary vehicle in fire, and the instant the tank caught, it blew out, an ear-splitting detonation of glass and metal.

I put my foot to the floor and accelerated away from the

inferno in my mirror, eyes staring straight ahead, not daring to look at the faces of the traumatised survivors beside me. I drove like that for a long time, my mind blank.

Kez told me later that she had to prise me out of the driver's seat when the fuel gauge finally hit zero and we spluttered to a stop. I hadn't even noticed.

THAT'S ENOUGH FOR now. Hand's cramping, head's hurting. Need to rest.

CHAPTER SIXTEEN

'IT ENDS...'

Cafferly removed the psi-amp helm and opened her eyes. It took a moment for the rush of the here and now to reassert itself, like she had to retune her perceptions. Colours settled, sounds stabilised; everything swam into focus. If she'd still breathed, she would've taken a gulp of air after feeling like she'd held it for the last two—three?—hours. As it was, despite her dormant pulse, the reorientation nevertheless brought a surge of... something. Fear? Excitement? It was enervating, and pronounced enough to take her aback. She was more than used to disappearing down the rabbit hole of her own mind, but the experience under the psi-amp had been something else entirely: the only way to describe it was if she'd slid outside herself and rode a narrow-cast beam of pure thought.

She looked down at the amp, turning it over her hands. Quite what Mortis had created here she didn't know, but she'd never felt so powerful. It had boosted her psi-projection to an extraordinary degree, channelled it from a soft, wide-ranging talent into hard, laser-like precision. She'd felt in control throughout, never lost and at the mercy of her head like she did when she'd had to corral her senses previously to find meaning in the jumbled imagery. This was absolute mastery.

She had to admit that she'd felt a certain degree of

apprehension when the Dark Judge had foisted the instrument upon her. She'd been in no position to refuse—certainly not in front of De'Ath, who in his paranoid frame of mind would no doubt consider it insubordination and relish any opportunity to have her purged from the ranks like so many others;—to show unwillingness to aid the hunt for survivors was to suggest you weren't fully committed. Nevertheless, she'd had her misgivings: Mortis's experiments were notorious, as much for their side effects as for what he actually produced. That walking abomination that served as his minion—Jackson, he'd been called in life, some victim spared the dignity of true obliteration—was a walking advertisement for the DJ's unusual predilection for testing the viability of new forms, and, it had to be said, throwing a certain scientific rigour out of the window. There was no need for the Jackson thing to exist other than it pleased Mortis to violate nature. Cafferly was under the impression that his brothers Fear, Fire and Sidney tolerated the meddling he got up to in his labs because of the results that sprang from it, but ultimately considered that when it resulted in entities like his servant, it merely seemed inefficient and unfathomable. Why play with life when you can simply exterminate it?

The psi-amp had had the potential to be another grand folly—she'd heard rumours of his early forays into dimensional jumps that had torn his human guinea pigs in two—that could've rendered her braindead, or overloaded her cerebellum to the point where she'd haemorrhaged. Mortis, unsurprisingly, cared little for the failures, and she would've been scooped into one of the burial pits with the rest of that day's harvest with no one to mourn her, while a mark-two version of the amp would be thrust upon the next Psi-Judge before Cafferly had even stopped twitching. It was a relief, therefore, that it appeared the DJ had got his schematics right, and so far she could feel no lasting damage.

It had been terrifying at first, when she turned it on, but also exhilarating. She'd almost been overwhelmed by the power. Her mind had flown like an arrow, straight and true, and initially she'd had to cling to it, not letting it get away from her, seeing where she was taken. Once accustomed to its tightly channelled direction, however, she'd soon clambered into the saddle and took up the reins, all the while marvelling at how the amp purified her telepathy, left her feeling like she was a blazing comet arcing across the ether. Mental faultlines all around her lit up like a circuit board, ripe for exploiting, and she'd zeroed in on one instantly; its fragility was virtually beckoning her, her psychic bullet eagerly seeking its bullseye.

Cafferly had slid past the lawbreaker's non-existent defences—Emily, her name had been, she'd noted on the way in—and found the woman's head a mass of fears and anxieties, buoyed by a lack of sleep. Info flooded her mind the moment she took residence—Emily's history, her son, the people she'd been surviving with and where they were—and it became relatively easy, thanks to the amp's augmentation of her psi-processes, to pick apart her brain like shellfish and plant her own seeds of suggestion into the fertile ground. Little white seeds, she liked to think of them as, the colour of bone, embedded deep in the grey matter, and from them roots and tendrils spread, taking over the host. Emily offered little in the way of resistance, and was probably only dimly aware that there was an invading presence in her head at all; her cracked psyche just let Cafferly steal in and go about doing the maximum damage. Indeed, she could've shut her down entirely, reduced her to nothing more than a puppet, but a criminal needs to know *why* they're being punished—see the consequences of their actions—so the Psi-Judge simply disconnected Emily for as long as was required, with the intention of giving her back what was left of her mind at the painful, traumatic last.

Oh, the pain her victim had suffered had been joyous to sample, bordering on the ecstatic. Cafferly's nerve endings had long since been deadened, so the pleasure hadn't been experienced physically—it was a psychic rush delivered direct to her frontal lobe. There was still sensory life there. She knew that De'Ath and his lieutenants enjoyed the same thrill that came from punishing criminals; they'd retained a vestige of their humanity, deep in their core, so they could appreciate the satisfaction that lay in lawful, just annihilation. They weren't mindless zombies—they didn't decimate the living unthinkingly, oblivious to the excitement it generated. All lawkeepers got *some* emotional charge from bringing retribution upon the guilty—it was their job, after all; the enforcement of justice brought an inevitable *frisson*—so she didn't believe she, or any of them, were traitors to the Chief's ideology by still having that spark in their otherwise cold, post-mortem bodies. She wouldn't feel any sense of shame at the way her brain had lit up as the woman's raw agony had blossomed in her head like a fireball; on the contrary, it signalled a job well done. Who wouldn't take gratification at the way this nest of perpetrators had screamed and bled as the law had landed upon them?

With the Emily marionette at her control, she was easy to direct as a psychic beacon, broadcasting her location back to the Grand Hall. The H-wagon was in the air within minutes, and she'd watched briefly through the woman's eyes as the flame-squad had set about burning the criminal cell to the ground. That many of them had escaped was unfortunate, but they wouldn't survive for long out in the open; the important thing was that they were driven from their bolthole, forced to run and discover that nowhere was safe. If they were made to confront the hopelessness of their situation, to realise that evading justice was simply delaying the inevitable, then they were more likely to welcome that ultimate sanction. De'Ath wasn't interested in those that repented or admitted their guilt—all would receive the same judgement—but if they came forward and offered themselves for execution, then it made the whole process a lot smoother, and sped things on considerably. The Chief genuinely couldn't understand why they weren't lining up to be judged, for they had to be aware that they reeked of sin; every breath, every heartbeat, was a criminal act. They were drowning in their own lawlessness. It had to have a cumulative effect, that they would *want* to seek purification before their moral turpitude overwhelmed them, but perps being perps, they just rolled in it like pigs and did everything they could to avoid facing up to the seriousness of their illegality. Consequently, every officer in the Hall of Injustice was strapped in for the long haul, aware that De'Ath's grand design was going to take some time to achieve. The guilty wouldn't submit to their authority willingly, and would continue to fight it. It was frustrating—if only they knew the peace of the grave, they'd rush towards it.

Cafferly wondered if Sidney ever contemplated the sheer scale of what he was attempting to do—of what he *would* do. She suspected he was never daunted by it; his kind of pure philosophy ensured that he wasn't intimidated by the scope of the task ahead. Rather, he relished the job at hand, the logistics it would require. When you had righteousness on your side—and the Chief's reasoning was impossible to argue against—then it became a calling, a project for which you were destined, and which you would devote your (undead) life to. With mortality no longer an issue, it became an ongoing work-in-progress of which he'd never tire. His sponsors—the Sisters, and the beings that they represented—would make sure that his zeal never wavered, and De'Ath in turn felt that he was guided by higher powers, pushed towards a purpose that transcended any earthly pursuits. He was remaking a world, and there couldn't be any holier mission than that—

No remorse.

(No

going back—)

Cafferly winced, instinctively holding her right hand up to her temple.

One law.

(Justice

for all—)

She'd never got any flashes from her previous life, but she had one now, and it startled her in its vividness. Thinking about Sidney's crusade brought to mind a general she'd seen on television when she was a child, interviewed about the war he was engaging in a foreign land—he was a ranking officer in Justice Department's military wing, leading an invasion (she couldn't remember the exact whys or wherefores, but it seemed like the opposing country had different political beliefs; there were quite a few similarly motivated interventions in those days, or so it felt). Her parents had insisted she watch it; she remembers them making her sit before the screen. The general's face filled Cafferly's mind as clearly as Emily's son had just moments before when he'd pleaded for his life; she could suddenly picture the craggy pores in the man's cheeks as the camera zoomed in, the jutting chin, the sun glinting on his silvery mirrored shades. She could visualise the yellowy, bleached scrub of the landscape behind him as he gave his press conference, radiating dust and heat, and she focused on the pulse in his jaw as he chewed gum while he spoke to the assembled journos. There was the soft clicking of photographers off-camera. This moment from thirty years ago was right there behind her eyes, unbidden, perfectly captured. The general looked at her, right out of the TV, and said in cold, deliberate tones that there would be no respite, no negotiation, no compromise, only total decimation. There was one law and it was absolute. He made it sound like the most reasonable course of action possible, for to disagree was to side with the enemy. It was that simple. It had struck her just how plainly his ruthless plan had been spelled out, the unwavering strength of will. Doubt or empathy would never enter his mind.

One law.

(Justice

for all—)

"Dammit," Cafferly murmured aloud, rubbing her head. An ache bloomed in her skull.

That moment, that general and his stony-faced adherence to absolute certainty, stayed with her for years. She wasn't sure at the time why that particular image lodged, splinter-like, in her brain, impossible to shake free; yet when she'd close her eyes at night, there it was, affixed to her retina. Not long afterwards, her parents entrusted her to Justice Department, and she began to wonder if the connection she'd felt with the man on the TV screen had been some kind of coded message from the future, reverse déjà vu that had significance for what was yet to come. Her nascent precognition was tweaking her, speaking to her before she fully understood the language.

(No remorse.)

A figure, standing in a bare room, haloed by fire. The punishment due.

All this has been seen before.

She shook her head to dispel a rush of images. Light flickering through holes in skin. She saw herself as a child, curled in the dark at the top of the stairs in her home—

(punishment)

This wasn't right. Post-mortem, much of her experiences from the time before had been wiped from her memory, a clean reboot so she could dedicate her powers to De'Ath's cause without distraction. The Sisters had made sure of that. Her history hadn't penetrated her thoughts like this since she'd consumed the Dead Fluids.

All this

(is due punishment—)

She realised she was still holding the psi-amp in her trembling left hand, and flung it down onto the stone floor, where it bounced with a dull *clang* and rolled next to her boots. She slouched forward in her chair, resting her elbows on her knees, panic gnawing at her. Was Mortis's contraption opening fractures in her own head? It had sharpened her soft talents, but could it have sliced the wielder at the same time? And what else was going to come bleeding through, presuming the damage was irreparable?

She angrily got to her feet, the chair scraping back, and kicked the device across the room, where it disappeared into a shadowy corner. She was in one of the small isolation chambers psi-operatives used for out-of-body operations, and as such it was little more than a gloomy cell—all the better to turn her concentration inwards. Now it felt claustrophobic, and she paced its circumference, trying to calm herself. As exhilarating as the use of the amp had been, she was regretting now ever allowing it access to her head—once doors were opened, they couldn't often be closed again. This kind of psychic fragility she knew all too well, and had exploited it often enough in the past. The mind of the woman, Emily, for instance, had been the equivalent of a rickety wooden gate, hanging off its broken hinges, requiring only the lightest of nudges to push it wide. She would never have been able to keep Cafferly out. But the Psi-Judge now recognised a similar precariousness in herself; what once was stable now seemed loose and floating. Her psyche had become unmoored. Whether she'd be able to tether it again, she didn't know.

(—pure justice—)

She screamed, hammering the heels of her hands against her temples, willing herself to clear her mind. Discipline, she told herself. Composure. After a moment, the chaos in her head faltered and faded. She was back in charge.

One thing was for sure, she thought: the amp was like bad acid—an experience not to be repeated. Additional exposure was undoubtedly only going to further loosen the bonds in her brain, and she had to keep it together. That the HoJ was such a bear-pit, where every thought and utterance could be used against her, was enough of a challenge; if she didn't approach it confident of her own mind, then her enemies were going to eat her... well, if not 'alive,' then the undead equivalent.

She stopped pacing and glanced suddenly towards the chamber's door. Paranoia crawled up her spine. Mortis had pointedly singled her out for flight-testing the prototype—what if he was aware of what it would do to her? What if Phobia and Nausea had pushed him towards it? But to what end—to weaken her, eventually destroy her? There were simpler ways of getting rid of her if they saw her as a rival or felt she was showing signs that her resolve was softening. They could probably atomise her with a word. An experiment to see what the amp's after-effects were? There were prisoners in Mortis's labs that would've been just as disposable. Nonetheless, the suspicion that this had been done to her deliberately clung, as if it was a smell she couldn't get out from under her nostrils.

She shook her head. The paranoia could just as well be another symptom of her mind's displacement. But what felt more likely was that it was magnifying what she already suspected; that there were forces at work of which she had to be wary. It had heightened her sensitivity. She would have to be careful she didn't betray her feelings to Sidney and the rest whenever she was in their vicinity. Better to maintain a straight face, let them assume there had been no change.

Cafferly walked over to where she'd kicked the device and plucked it back up, dusting it down. They couldn't know.

She wrenched open the door, and strode out into the corridor, where she found Mortis waiting for her, that smooth white head looming out of the dark like an undersea predator. She should've expected that he'd be there, but his abrupt, silent presence nevertheless forced her to bite down on a surprised reaction.

"Excccellent work," he hissed. "The ressponsse time was excceptional." He held out his hand, and she passed him the amp. He studied it with the care a child might devote to a pet. "How did you find it?"

"Powerful." He glanced at her, clearly expecting more. She was conscious her reticence was too obvious, so she attempted to elaborate. "I mean, it took me a few moments to control it. Once I did, though... it was like I was at the centre of everything."

That seemed to please him, and he returned to prodding his toy. "There will inevitably be sssome fine-tuning. I want to eventually roll them out to all psssi-unitssss. It would strengthen our forccce a thousssand-fold. You'd have no problem with that?"

She shook her head.

"Imagine," Mortis continued, "the ability to detect and eliminate every lawbreaker the world over. Nowhere would be sssafe. There'd be nowhere to hide. An entire psssi-amplified divisssion that could make the criminalsss desssstroy themsssselvesss, if their mindsss were put to it."

"It would streamline the process immeasurably."

"And you got no psssychic backwassssh?"

"Nothing I noticed."

The Dark Judge nodded, or gave the approximation of a nod. "I want you to have further ssesssions with it. Let me adjussst the levelssss, sssee if it can be further attuned to your pssignature."

Cafferly watched him retreat down the corridor. She had little doubt now they were using her—she had to find out why before they broke her head apart irrevocably.

CHAPTER SEVENTEEN

30 March

Been kinda lax in keeping up the journal. Frankly, I think it's a combination of fatigue and lack of motivation that's been preventing me from picking up the pen—figure depression's caught up with me. I don't know, I can't self-diagnose, and there's no one here that's got any kind of qualification in that department, but a few days ago I spent nearly twenty-four hours curled up at the back of the RV sleeping, or trying to (dreams have been weird again, which shouldn't really come as much surprise. Even so, they weren't graphic replays of the grey attack, but claustrophobic anxiety sequences involving small bare rooms and silhouettes burned onto walls). Had no appetite, no desire to converse with anyone, just felt sapped of energy. One of the others may have tried to talk to me, or get me to eat, but I've got no recollection of it, or whether I ever responded. When I finally emerged from under my blanket, I didn't feel any more rested—I simply felt numb. The thought of trying to write this down and make some kind of sense of the jumbled stew of emotions slurping around in my head was exhausting enough—actually doing it required some concerted willpower. I started a couple of times—there's a whole mess of torn out, scrunched-up pages over in the corner that are testament to my aborted beginnings—but nothing flowed, or made sense. I don't suppose it has to, in the end; it's looking increasingly like no one else but me will read it. Why should I care what these ravings amount to? But the truth is, the straighter I get it on the page, the better I feel. I've had to force myself to sit down and write this, and it's given me a certain amount of purpose.

Kez has let me have some space and pretty much tiptoed around me, which is wholly unlike her. I've noticed a change in her since we escaped from the farmhouse—she's still taking charge, but some of the resolve has gone, maybe. She was always tough—still is tough—but there's a fear in her eyes these days that wasn't there before. She thought she was keeping us all safe, and was doing a damn good job of it—but they got to us in the end. No matter how careful we were, they got to us. That realisation has destroyed a little part of her, I think. But, like I say, she's remained our leader and is keeping us alive from one day to the next. We're a diminished group now, the last remnants of our original community—just the seven of us, including me (Kez, Riggs, Lionel, Katherine and her daughters Meredith and Holly being the others)—crammed into Mr Graham's old motorhome, but she's doing her best to find us a new haven. The options are thin on the ground, and it feels like we're running in tighter and tighter circles, but we're all aware we don't have much choice. We flee and we hide, or we die.

Like I said, I completely ran the fuel tank dry hot-footing it from the farmhouse. It gave us some distance, but left us stranded. All credit to Kez, she was as traumatised as everyone else, but she had the wherewithal to organise a foraging party to rustle up some gas; plenty of abandoned vehicles on the highways (and the Judges don't seem concerned about moving them, just leaving them there on the road to rust), and she and Riggs were able to siphon enough to eventually get us off the main drag and into a stretch of woodland, where we were no longer visible from the air. Justice Department was still going to be looking for us, and were aware of what we were travelling in, so there was a lot of practical talk about ditching the RV, but in the meantime it was our base until something more secure came along. So far, that kind of bolthole has been in short supply—buildings are either wrecked, or in the hands of other survivors that don't take kindly to sharing. The fact that we're being driven to extinction you'd think would be a rallying cause, with a common enemy to band against, but no, cold hard human greed and self-preservation wins the day. We didn't realise how lucky we were in that farmhouse cellar, locked away in our own little bubble with enough sustenance and water to last us—although I suppose we would've been the same if a large group came cap in hand, seeking access to our larder (others had joined us in the past, but only as individuals, mostly). Now, we are on the outside, asking for sanctuary, and likewise no one's letting us come anywhere near their hideouts. Kez returns from her expeditions with tales of home-made signs strung on chainlink fences prohibiting further access, and unseen lookouts putting warning shots across her path. No one has the resources or the inclination to take on further mouths to feed, nor do they want the Judges led to their door (though that concern may be moot if our experience was any indication—they can find us wherever we go). So for now the RV is our halfway home from home.

Our circumstances are reduced, there's no question of that. Our meals are rationed out in meagre amounts, and restocks are proving difficult to find. Hunger is making people increasingly tetchy, though Kat is hardly eating at all, and acting worryingly distant with her daughters. Lionel, despite me thinking him a bit of a tool in the past, has actually been pretty sweet around the girls, and shouldered some of the parenting duties, not least sharing a good half of his dinner with them most nights. I have to admit, I've struggled to keep even basic foodstuffs down, and my digestion's shot to hell—can't remember when I last passed a solid...

Ha! TMI, Future Reader? Well, fuck you. This shit's important to me—literally. You think I want to die constipated?

3 April

UGH, REREAD THE last entry and I can't believe I'm making toilet jokes, as if what's happening around us is just a bad camping weekend—"OMG, had to totally piss in a bush yesterday," etc.—and not, like, the complete end of the fucking world. Maybe the crazies are setting in, and before I know it, I'll be daubing the walls with my excrement (should I have the good fortune to actually crap any). Would I even know if I was losing my mind? I seem to have enough self-awareness to feel guilt for cracking funnies when we're in the direst of straits, so I'm fairly confident I haven't gone ga-ga yet. Should I feel ashamed, anyway? It's looking like the chances of anyone reading this are practically nil.

A kind of despondency has settled over the group that we're not going to make it out of this alive. Food and water's really low, and we're all suffering forms of malnutrition. Riggs has picked up some kind of infection (I think something bit him out in the woods), and he's been vomiting, feverish. There's not much in the med supplies that can treat it, despite Kez's best efforts, and an ill smell now permeates the RV—of sickness, of human failing. The air's stale and sticky, and reeks of resignation. Should we stay and starve, or take our chances on the road, given what we know is out there hunting for us? I'm not even sure some of us are fit to move—the girls are becoming as reserved as their mom, the three of them sitting on the banquette together, Kat's arms around her gaunt-faced daughters, staring into space for hours. Kez gets some sips of water into them but not much else. If ever I wanted to witness at what point people give up, I'm seeing it now. Complete shutdown, minds and bodies traumatised to such an extent that they crawl into a corner of themselves like animals seeking a quiet place to die. I had a cat like that once when I was a kid—an old, ratty tom he was by the end, who knew in his bones that the end was coming and one day disappeared into a corner of the garden behind the apple-tree stump and curled up and went to sleep and didn't wake up. We found him a day or so later, head tucked between his paws, tail looped around him, taking the long dirt nap, looking just like a creature that had made its peace with the fact that it was its time to vacate the earth.

God, Bartleby—I haven't thought about him for years. Why has he suddenly popped into my head? Weird the stuff that occupies your mind when mortality's pressing down on it, as if life's not so much flashing before your eyes as replaying in slow motion in little highlighted bursts. My dreams the last few days have been like that too, bogged down with past significance. I keep picturing the top of the stairs in my asshole parents' house, the long corridor behind it leading to the bedrooms, the leaded window dominating the landing but allowing minimal light through. It was a place I was sent to as punishment, if I mouthed off or didn't do as I was told, and I grew to fear that dark corner, like it held bad memories that had impregnated the walls, indelibly stained the plaster and floorboards. I never knew why it gave off such a nightmarish vibe, and my dipshit mum and dad never intimated that there was any reason for it to be so, though it didn't stop them using it as discipline when they needed to, aware of just how uncomfortable I felt sitting on that top step in total silence, knees drawn up, listening to the building shift around me. I could be up there for a couple of hours, depending on the severity of my transgression. I never quite got over it, even in my mid teens when I escaped to college—reluctant return visits were always marked by a nervous glance up the staircase as if I half expected to meet someone descending. I put it down to some childhood brainfart that I couldn't quite dispel, and never gave it much of a thought away from the old place… but now the sensation I felt as a kid is back, oddly, as if I'm there again, hard wood beneath me, lengthening shadows crawling across the ceiling. I keep feeling in my half-sleep that I've been forced there, that my rule-breaking requires correction. In my dreams, I drift upwards towards the top step, fearful of what awaits me.

It leaves me breathless and trembling when I wake, old anxieties born anew. Can't understand why it's come back now, and to such a degree. It's as bad as when I first experienced it, and I'm, like, ten years older. Is it 'cause we're all being punished now, every one of us? We've all been declared guilty—seemingly for the crime of simply being alive—and it's only a matter of time before each of us receives the ultimate sanction. Having that hanging over your head could be responsible for these familial flashbacks, I suppose—the notion that we're all just errant, rule-breaking juveniles for whom the law must be strictly administered. I can see some similarities in the black-and-white thinking between these monstrous fucks that have taken over the HoJ and my authoritarian folks. Both slapped down their version of how it was going to be, and there was nothing in the way of compromise.

God, I can't believe my bloody parents are infiltrating my diary. I'd done my best to get away from them—hadn't even given them much thought since all this started; presumed at the back of my mind that they'd met a fate much like many caught in the suburbs, and dispatched on their doorstep with a bullet to their heads—and here they are, haunting the journal's pages. I can't grieve for them since by the last time I saw them, I barely had any feelings for them. They were people I recognised, nothing more—and a lot of people I knew have fallen in the days and weeks that followed the night it all changed, and I don't have the capacity to weep for every one of them. That seems harsh, reading it back, but so many have died you become punch-drunk on it.

Aargh, this is such bullshit. Eyes are pricking, cheeks feel like they're burning. I don't want to be thinking about this stuff, I really don't. It still hurts. I didn't realise how raw I feel inside. But a hot mess is being stirred up in my head, though, and I don't know if it's delayed trauma, or the hunger, or our impending inevitable demise, or what—but something's triggered it.

5 April

DAMN DREAMS ARE getting worse, and even more personal. Made me wake with a gasp in the early hours, and took a while to fade—it was my viewpoint, looking up at my mum and dad, and they were glaring down at me, not saying anything, just regarding me with complete distaste, like I was a bisected rodent that Bartleby had semi-digested and then brought into the house and left on the kitchen floor. I tried to say something to them, ask them what was wrong, but no words emerged, and my limbs felt heavy and unresponsive when I tried to reach out to them. Very claustrophobic and suffocating, like I was trapped under glass. The angle that they were looking down at me suggested I was prone on the ground—either that or very small—which made me wonder if it was some early memory thing.

But the expression on their faces... Parents wouldn't look at their young kid like that, would they, somewhere south of revulsion? Need to keep telling myself that this crap doesn't mean anything, that it's just random images fed by my misfiring brain, but it's all so vivid, so real—and so pointed. I can't help feeling there's a message in these dreams.

Couldn't get back to sleep, and felt dreadful all day. Haven't eaten for over twelve hours so pretty weak and wobbly too. Kez has now started rationing out rainwater she's catching in a disgusting old tarpaulin. No gas left to boil it, so I dread to think what bacteria we're ingesting.

* * *

9 April

RIGGS DIED. I should be sadder, but my first thought was that it was one less mouth to feed—kinda felt a little bit jealous too that he'd skipped out early. No more suffering, no more pain; just peace, dark and dreamless. Blissssss...

Whoa. Not going down that avenue. I don't have the death wish just yet.

Head's so fuzzy from disturbed sleep my waking hours feel like a succession of still photographs laced with déjà vu. I remember seeing Kez remove the body from the RV, but it was as if I was watching it on a television. She told me she'd buried him in a shallow grave several feet into the woods and I struggled to recall who she was talking about. Minutes (hours?) later, I'd apparently asked where Riggs was.

Don't know what's real any more.

(No remorse.)

A figure, standing in a bare room, haloed by fire. The punishment due.

All this has been seen before.

16 April

MOM. I'M SORRY. Please forgive me. I didn't mean to hurt you and Dad. I never wanted to disappoint you.

Please stop haunting me. I close my eyes and there you both are. Judging.

I can't eat, can't sleep. You're in my head, always. Whatever I do, you're there, disapproving.

I don't want to be punished any more. Are you listening? Can I talk to you through this diary?

Don't have the strength any more.

Enough.

(No remorse.)

A figure, standing in a bare room, haloed by fire. The punishment due.

All this has been seen before.

17 April

Enough. Please.

Please…

…take me with you.

I've had enough. Tak e me h o me

Darknessss callsssss…

All this
(is due punishment—)

18 April

if i knew the peace of the grave i'd rush towards it

25 April

Holy Christ. Holy fuck. What the hell was I tripping on?

I have no recollection of the last five days. Literal blank. I'm writing this on the RV, but everyone's gone—Kez, Lionel, the girls, all of them—and I've no idea where they are. Their stuff's mostly all here, though it looks like there was some kind of altercation, or they left in a hurry: furniture's overturned, a window's smashed. There's a bit of blood spray on the glass, which is freaking me out. If my handwriting looks like shit, it's 'cause I'm shivering like hell—shock, fear, I don't know which.

Where did they go? Did they run, or were they taken? Thing is, no one gets taken—you just get executed. But there're no bodies.

There's a Judge here. A human one, I mean, not a grey. She's sitting just across the way from me, keeping watch by the driver's seat (I don't know what time it is, maybe early morning). She found me in the woods, she says, and she brought me back here. Said I was lost, incoherent, blundering about, raving. I was going to give away our location to Justice Dept; a patrol was close to the treeline. She grabbed me, made sure they didn't hear me, and talked me down until I finally shut up. She didn't say what I was blabbering on about, but I get the impression she thought I was trying to get myself killed. She said I wasn't in a fit state of mind to be out there on my own.

Why was I out there on my own? Did I leave when everyone else did? Were we attacked, and we all fled in different directions? My memory's a void.

Hawkins is the Judge's name. She's been out there on her own since this started, by all accounts. Face is all fucked up, a knot of burnt tissue—God knows what happened to her, looks like she stuck her head in a furnace. She doesn't say much if she doesn't have to (obviously hurts her—mouth is partially fused, so she keeps conversations short and to the point), and I'm not entirely sure she's completely compos mentis—which is rich coming from me, right? Looking at my diary entries previous to this, talk about the balance of mind being disturbed. Hunger and stress must've sent me off the deep end. But she's given me some of her rations, which I managed to keep down—first thing I've eaten in days—and I feel a bit clearer in my head.

Still don't know where the others have gone, though, or how I ended up in the woods. Hawkins reckons that we can't stay here—greys are sweeping in apparently, going to be overrunning this area. When night falls, she's going to get us out. I don't want to abandon the others, if they're around, but I can't see I've got a choice. Got to keep moving, if I don't want to fragment; if I want to stay alive.

<u>If...</u>

No, I do. I do. I really do. Not going to give up now.

CHAPTER EIGHTEEN

SHE'D RARELY VENTURED beyond the walls of the HoJ in the days since the Fall, and frankly it was discouraged unless you were a street unit—for a psi-operative like her, her place was at her station. The belief was that there was no need for her to leave her post since anything outside the job in hand was simply a distraction. She—like so many of her colleagues in the new world order—was now in a state of being that should require next to no external stimuli; there was only the Chief's orders, and the actioning of the global cull. That was their world entire, their reason to exist. If you weren't putting Sidney's words into deeds, then your attention was elsewhere and your effectiveness was consequently diminished. As such, Cafferly encountered some static from the uniforms standing guard at the Grand Hall's entrance, and it was not lost on her that they were as stringent on who they allowed to *leave* the building as who they let enter. It seemed another manifestation of the man at the top's paranoid insecurity, and it kindled a brief flame of anger at her core that she and the rest of De'Ath's rank-and-file troops were as much under the threat of judgement as the living. They were prisoners; worse, slaves, enacting their master's will.

The badges on the door were weak-minded wormfood, however, and it didn't require much in the way of effort for her to slide into their heads and plant a suggestion that they let her pass. Their brains were mostly rancid fly-blown organs, capable of the barest motor functions, and she dipped out as quickly as possible, leaving them with a mild expression of confusion on their sallow faces as they stepped aside and she walked out into the twilit grim. It had been a while since she'd seen natural light, and the novelty took some getting used to—that and the sensation of a breeze upon her skin—though a tenebrous gloom seemed to have settled over the city, as deep and dark as a bruise. A thick bank of clouds hung heavy above the rooftops, allowing a meagre amount of light to filter through, and it cast the streets with a monochrome pall, deadening the world still further. There was the flicker of flames in the distance where Judge Fire and his incendiary squads had been busy—she'd heard that they were creating funeral pyres for the thousands already butchered as a form of wall around the capital's central sectors—but the shadows it threw on the buildings seemed oddly inanimate. There was no doubt the smoke was adding to the greasy quality in the air, particulates of ash and bone twisting in the gentle wind. It was indeed becoming a necropolis, a place fit only for those that had crawled from a grave.

She couldn't deny she felt no small amount of freedom, and wished that she had longer to drink it in; but she was doubtlessly being tracked. The reeks that she'd pside-swiped past had been one thing, but the Sisters were something else, their presence tangible throughout the Grand Hall. Nothing occurred within its environs that they weren't aware of, and they would've been alerted the moment she crossed the threshold. They distrusted her intensely already—now that she'd gone off-reservation, there were going to be convinced she was up to something. She couldn't dally; it was surely only a matter of time before they intervened, or they got Sidney to order her detained. She needed transport.

The bike pool beneath the HoJ was another level of complication she didn't want to deal with so she'd have to commandeer one from the streets. That proved easy enough, casting her mind out and psychically steering a deadbeat to her, muddying his perception so that he was under the impression he'd received new directives in the next district over before forcing him to head off on foot. She swung onto the Lawranger and peeled away, once again relishing the distance she put between her and the CJ's headquarters.

It was the first vehicle she'd handled post-mortem, but she hadn't forgotten how to ride it; indeed, the skill was instinctive, her gauntlets gripping the handlebars firmly, her weight in the saddle perfectly proportioned. She could've let the onboard computer do most of the piloting, but there was pleasure to be had in controlling it by her own means, and that in itself was unusual—feeling the emotion for something that benefited only her was a strange sensation. She should've outgrown such petty concerns, which belonged to a life pre-De'Ath. But it was inescapable, as she curled the bike through the choked, smouldering thoroughfares of the city, leaning into the turns and twisting the throttle on the straights—adrenaline of a sort was coursing through her, synapses thought long-withered-away firing at the exhilaration. Memories stirred like a seething cauldron of gumbo, nuggets of her past rising from the depths: recollections of her cadet days, registering in the top percentile of her class for Applied Lawranger proficiency, and being taken out onto the streets for the first time with her assessing senior Judge. The rush had been extraordinary back then, had penetrated her very marrow. She'd known nothing else like it.

Yet she shouldn't be able to remember any of this; this all should've been wiped from her mind by the raging fire of the Dead Fluids, scourging her of her past existence and birthing her anew. Nothing of the old days should trouble her. But here it was, seeping into her consciousness like water bubbling up through the earth from a cracked underground pipe, as if fragments had only ever been buried, not vaporised entirely. The psi-amplifier had done this, she was convinced—it had splintered her psyche, allowed her to access elements locked inside her head that she otherwise wouldn't have been able to open. She was feeling emotions, thinking independently, acting against the Chief's wishes; the psi-amp had caused a glitch in her programming.

There was unease at all this too, she had to admit. The sudden flow of images from her previous existence was unnerving—previously suppressed snapshots of her past flashing up unbidden in her head. Some she recognised, others she didn't, but she couldn't be certain that whatever the amp had done to her head hadn't in some way distorted them—was she seeing how things were, or a twisted version, corrupted by a fractured mind? She hoped, perversely, that for the most part it was the latter; that this was her history viewed through a funhouse mirror—strange and warped and bearing little relation to the reality. Otherwise, digging through the truth would be harder to process. For example, the concept of punishment kept rearing up at her, of receiving strict discipline for misdemeanours perpetrated as a child, and it brought a chill that was both at once familiar and weird. Somehow, she knew she used to be scared when she was younger (pre Justice Department?), that it played a big part of her early childhood, and yet, in her post-mortem state, she'd never been frightened by anything, despite the monsters she was now allied with. Fear had been an emotion that no longer troubled her. But suddenly here she was feeling it again, and it was unmistakable, like the musty scent of a favourite toy that had been clutched every night under the bedclothes. She knew it intimately. How much of these memories were real? Had she really used to feel like this? Who *was* she—or perhaps more pertinently, who did she *used* to be?

She had to find out before Mortis's contraption snapped her mind in two. There had to be a reason why she'd been chosen for the prototype—she was convinced that answers lay somewhere in the mental sludge that was being dredged from her brain. Corroboration was more than likely to be found in the old records of the Academy.

Cafferly skirted a vast pile of corpses that had been ladled on the side of the road, clearly awaiting Judge Fire's touch. The dead had been stacked without dignity, heads and limbs entangled, and countless filmy eyes regarded her accusingly as she passed. She instinctively turned away, refusing to meet their glassy gaze, prompting her to remember the execution she'd declined to watch the other day. She'd been curious about her squeamishness at the time, wondering the reason behind it. It was prior to her use of the amp, so the blame couldn't be laid on that in this instance. Evidently, some small change in her had occurred naturally... or as natural as anything could be in Sidney's blighted world. Maybe the Sisters had sensed that, ordered Mortis to line her up for the experiment—they wanted to know something, find something out about her, aware of what it could do to her.

She roared the Lawranger away from the bodies, furious. Fucking Phobia and Nausea! Everyone was just puppets to them, to be used and picked apart at their whim.

Crossing the sector at speed, she reached her destination without incident. The few units she saw were either conducting summary judgements or disposing of the aftermath. They paid her no mind. The capital was surprisingly quiet, much of the central districts having been purged of life entirely, and apart from the distant cries of some lawbreakers protesting at the sentences before being cut short by the retort of a Lawgiver muzzle, nothing stirred beyond flies feasting on grey flesh. De'Ath's forces were moving out, widening the coverage beyond the city limits and into the outlying areas. Work had already been done both environmentally and ecologically, to wipe out a lot of the mass population, and much of the task ahead for the Chief's goons was simply mopping up. Nevertheless, it was going to be a slow process. That suited Cafferly—it meant she was less likely to be disturbed.

She pulled up her bike at the foot of the building's grandiose steps and dismounted, climbing up to the shattered entrance, the façade wrecked by flame and gunfire. Tiny shards of glasseen crunched beneath the soles of her boots, and she had to duck her head under a beam that had torn loose from its housing before she could slide across the threshold.

The Academy of Law had certainly seen better days. On the night of the Fall it had been one of the first buildings targeted by forces loyal to Sidney, determined to wipe out all those within the department that might oppose him. By all accounts, it was the site of a ruthless massacre. A few cadets had pledged allegiance in a bid to escape execution, but most were too young to be any use to the cause, or too ingrained with the doctrine—either way, De'Ath ordered a scorched-earth policy and the juves had no chance, a pogrom made all the more chilling by the fact that the Chief wasn't that much older at the time than the cadets he ordered killed. Colleagues he would've eaten with, shared dormitories with, passed trials and examinations with, he butchered without a second thought.

It was empty of corpses now—in a nod to efficiency, the majority of the youngsters had been lined up in the exercise yards and shot—but you could still see the remnants of those final hours as Cafferly passed through the silent corridors. Bullet holes pockmarked the plaster, and blood spray had darkened to rust; rooms where last stands had been fought were blackened shells, blistered by multiple high-explosive discharges. She'd never seen a ghost, ironically, despite all that she'd witnessed in recent times and the feats her mind had performed, but she could imagine them haunting the rec areas and shooting galleries in here, the violence perpetrated within these walls absorbed into the rockcrete. She was aware that there was a rare psi-talent that enabled the operative to tap into the psyche of a structure, to read the echoes of life that reverberated through the building and soak in its past, but she figured any attempt on the Academy's ruins would be the equivalent of listening to one long, piercing scream. As it was, even without the talent, the timbre of the place was oppressive, like a persistent pressure on her skull. She really didn't want to linger any longer than possible.

She found her way to a set of stairs and descended, the well gloomy and thick with silence. Next to no power was still functioning, and she relied on the handrail to guide her. At the bottom, dust swirled as she disturbed it for the first time in weeks, and she drew her Lawgiver, using the torchlight mounted above the barrel as a means of getting her bearings. The records room was a vast warehouse-style open-plan area, lined by an endless number of shelves on which stood multiple storage boxes. They contained the details of every cadet that had passed over the threshold since the early days, even those that had dropped out. There was a computer system, of course, but that was redundant right now given the lack of electricity, and in any case it looked like someone had taken a daystick to several of the terminals. Frankly, she was surprised that this huge chamber of info relating to the old department had so far escaped Judge Fire's pyre; it was the kind of documentation that represented the former order, all mention of which Sidney was extinguishing. Cafferly didn't hold out any hope for it surviving much longer—once Fire had finished with the bodies, his attention would doubtless turn to buildings and their contents. All would be put to the flame until De'Ath presided over an empire of ash and bone.

Ordinarily, physically searching this mountain of paperwork without the aid of the digitised index or an auxiliary that knew their way around the filing would be a task she wouldn't attempt if she didn't want to be holed up here for days on end. But she was confident she could cast her mind out and alight on what she needed. It was a form of dowsing, and—holstering her gun—she laid one hand on the shelving struts as she tried to piece together a picture in her head of the young psi-cadet she once was. An image coalesced hazily, as if behind misted glass, but it was enough to tug her senses in a particular direction; she released her hold of the shelf and allowed herself to be led, trance-like, across the room. Signifiers lit up, her consciousness a motherboard that saw past and memory synching, and she followed the psi-trails that glowed golden behind her eyes. It was a path, a breadcrumb trail, and with each step the blurry face swam a little more into focus. There was the outline of a young girl, for the moment just a silhouette, but colour and detail were bleeding through, like a snapshot fading into clarity.

Cafferly stumbled through boxes, sending sheaves tumbling as she progressed, but paid no attention. Her mind knew where to go. She reached out and pulled a container from its housing, and emptied it contents on the floor, names and profiles of former cadets scattering before her: *Ferdinand, Jorn. Pace, Cecily. Fenrick, Bifford. Duke, Sasha.* She flashed through them, searching for that connection as the trails glowed brighter and the girl in her head gained resolution: brown eyes, dark complexion, mouth tight in a scowl, head shaven in a buzz cut. Was this her? Her hand trembled as it touched one manila cover, and a spark burned across her brain, threatening to white it out entirely—

(I STILL BELIEVE IN YOU, FUTURE READER)

Wait, what? She snapped out of her fugue state, disorientated, and snatched up the file, tearing it open.

"Ssssisssster Cafferly," a voice called behind her. She spun, admonishing herself that her senses had been so preoccupied that she hadn't been alerted to another's presence.

It was Nausea. She was in her human guise, though that couldn't hide the malevolence that was radiating from her, ancient and terrible, despite the young face that she was wearing. She danced across the space, bare feet nimbly edging around the upturned boxes and wrecked monitors, long auburn hair flailing behind her, a teenager to all appearances pirouetting to music only she could hear. The nonchalance with which she came towards the Psi-Judge was all the more disturbing, picking her way unhurriedly, eyes occasionally catching Cafferly's and a smile creasing her lips. As Nausea got closer, a gentle hum could be heard emanating from her akin to a simple nursery lullaby. It stopped when she finally came to standstill before the psi.

"What are you doing here, sssisster?" the witch asked. "Why aren't you at your possst?"

Cafferly figured a degree of honesty was the best policy; she could feel incremental nudges of pressure in her head where Nausea was probing her defences, teasing out the truth. In any case, there was nothing innocent about her questions: she was well aware of what the Judge was doing here. "I... was experiencing difficulties. My abilities were being interrupted."

"Interrupted?"

"Crossed signals. Random images. It happens sometimes."

"Doesss it?" Nausea tilted her head unnervingly, one eyebrow rising.

"Only sometimes. Par for the course with soft talents like mine. You get... well, sort of feedback, and it can lead to disconnection."

The witch nodded as if she sympathised, but there was nothing soothing in the gesture. Cafferly got the impression that Nausea was playing with her, which she didn't appreciate. Her grip hardened around the file she realised she was still holding, and she pushed back forcefully against the mental inveigling, sensing it retreat slightly.

Nausea glanced briefly at what Cafferly was holding before returning to meet her gaze. "Isss thisss ssssomething to do with Brother Mortisss's trial? The amplifier?"

"No, not entirely—"

"Because the intention wasss to increassse Psssi-Divisssion'sss efficiency. To greater aid ussss in our caussse. If there have been... ssside effectssss, then we need to know." She sidled closer. "What are you *doing* here, sssister?" she whispered in Cafferly's ear. "What brought you here? What are you *after?*" She reached out and laid her hand over the psi's clutching the file.

Cafferly snatched her hand away and involuntarily took a step back. "Don't come any fucking closer."

Any false bonhomie vanished from the witch's face in an instant. "Have a care, dead thing," she scowled. "You exissst only becaussse of ussss. You can be unmade jussst assss easssily."

The psi refused to back down, disregarding any notion of bowing to Nausea's authority. She felt a steely resolve growing, tired of being manipulated and lorded over by the witch and her sibling, of being a servant to Sidney's tyranny. The two locked stares, and Cafferly once again felt Nausea insistently probing her mind, trying to get past her mental wall.

"Are you *with* usss, ssssisster?" Nausea rasped. "Have you truly embraced what it isss to become one of Death's crusssadersssss?" Her brow twitched ever so slightly as if she'd just realised something. "Becaussse I don't think you are, are you? I don't think you're a hundred per cent committed."

"Why did Mortis choose me for the trial? It wasn't random, was it?"

"I think you know already. It ssseemsss it brought you here, to the Academy, for anssswersss."

"There was something in my past." She held up the file, and paper and photographs slid out, pooling at her feet. That sullen-faced girl looked up at her from the floor. "I keep getting flashes, sense-memories, like the amplifier unlocked them. You and Mortis, you knew that would happen, didn't you? That's why I was the subject. You wanted to see what the effect would be."

"You were an aberration, my dear."

"An aberration?"

"A rare inssstance where the Dead Fluidssss didn't remove the ssself. Your old wretched humanity wassss trying to reasssert itssself. You were caught between two ssstatesss."

Cafferly thought of her sudden attack of conscience watching the executions, and the mystery of where that had come from. At that moment, the person she'd been, pre-mortem, had briefly floated to the top. The idea that it had still been there, trapped in her dead shell, appalled her.

"Your mind wasss cleaved," Nausea continued. "The amplifier wasss a chance to sssee if it would correct it...

eventually." She shrugged. "Or at the very leassst, from a clinical point of view, witnessss what would happen to your sssanity. Brother Mortisss is collecting brainsss for a project of hissss own; yoursss would've been a worthy addition, once the requissssite work was done on it." She looked down and casually toed one of the Polaroids. "You were a ssspecial casse, right from the beginning. The girl with the unique mind, gifted to Jusstice Department by her parentsss." The witch glanced up at Cafferly with a dark expression and smiled. "You *alwaysss* belonged to ussss."

The psi dropped the file, and in one swift motion drew her Lawgiver, pointing the barrel directly between Nausea's eyes. The witch's mouth made an 'o' shape, and her eyebrows rose a fraction. She looked like she was waiting to see what Cafferly would do next.

She pulled the trigger.

CHAPTER NINETEEN

30 April

CATCHING A RARE moment's downtime—been travelling almost constantly for the last few days, and not had the opportunity to sit and write. Hawkins would sleep in the saddle if she could; she doesn't like to stay stationary for any longer than is necessary. Figures we make less of a target, or we have less chance of being discovered, if we're on the move. She's given me a rudimentary guide to piloting the Lawranger so she can catch some zees on the pillion, and I picked it up surprisingly quickly—even Hawkins seemed taken aback by my aptitude for it. Onboard computer does most of the work, to be honest, and she registered me with it so it would follow my instructions, but even so I had an affinity with the controls that was kinda disarming. Dunno where that's come from—had no dealings with the jays prior to That Night and I've never been near one of their bikes before. Mr Graham called me a natural when he taught me to drive the RV, so maybe I've found my calling; just a shame it's coincided with the end of the world.

It's testament to Hawkins' desire not to stick around that she's letting me near the throttle at all. I've caught her many times looking at me oddly, like she doesn't trust me or isn't convinced that I am who I say I am, or she's weighing up in her head what to believe. But she needs a co-driver—a wing-woman?—to take up the slack when she's too shattered to continue. I suspect she's only got one eye closed at any given time regardless, and I wouldn't at all be shocked to learn that the barrel of her Lawgiver was never far from the small of my back at any given moment. I don't take it personally. I'm pretty suspicious of myself these days, given what happened back on the mobile home, the events of which I'm still none the wiser about. How could Kez and the rest just disappear? What was I doing out in the woods—raving, according to Hawkins. Did I kill them all while the balance of my mind was disturbed? Something occurred during those memory gaps, and looking back at the scrawl in my journal, I was losing my grip on sanity. It was the dreams that had been tipping me over the edge; the crushing sense of judgement they contained, of punishment. They were at once both familiar, and like they belonged to someone else. Someone's bad vibes stealing into my sleep.

I like to think I'm not capable of that, that I could never murder. But what if I am? Emily was the gentlest soul, and they got inside her head and made her kill her own child. I could've been acting on those fuckers' behalf, just like her, tranced out, a puppet they directed to butcher all those around me. The fact that I could have blood on my hands and not know, to be responsible for something so horrendous... The sick feeling at the pit of my stomach is like acid, eating away at me. So, yeah, until my recall comes back and says different, I really don't blame Hawkins for giving me the stink-eye.

She's under no obligation to save me, to keep me from harm. Common sense would've told her to dump me by the side of the road and take her own chances. But when I asked her why she's brought me with her, she said she's on the side of life—that every beating heart is worth fighting for. To abandon me would make her no better than the forces of death that are hounding the planet to extinction. Funny to hear a jay talk like that, 'cause from what I can remember they were never big on human rights; but I guess maybe facing a greater evil can lead you revaluate what's important. Maybe Hawkins was that rare good cop, even before this all kicked off. She's certainly not short of guts—I asked about what happened to her face, and she reluctantly told me that she came under fire while allowing some cits she was escorting to escape. She drove through a ball of flame and managed to come out the other side.

She's convinced there's a resistance faction—Judges opposed to the new Chief, that escaped the slaughter at the Grand Hall—that she needs to regroup with. That's where we're heading, if we can find it; she listens constantly to her radio, desperately trying to pick up chatter amongst the dead channels. Sometimes she thinks she hears a faint trace, ghostly voices emerging from the ether, and tries to make contact, but they're beyond any broadcast ability. I'm sceptical those voices are even there, and suspect that Hawkins may be clinging to a vain hope, but I naturally keep this opinion to myself. She's been out here without support from her fellow uniforms for weeks, and I know what it is to hold on tightly to a belief—it gives you resolve in the face of insurmountable odds. It's probably kept her on the right side of madness too. I'll stick with her on her search—'cause where else am I going to go?—but I don't have her faith that this rebel enclave is out there. Maybe I'll be proved wrong. I hope I am.

THE BULLET PASSED through Nausea's forehead and exited from the back of her skull, though there was no accompanying gore; the skin simply rippled, as if a pebble had been dropped into a pond. She flew back and landed in a heap several feet away.

Cafferly stood motionless for a beat, looking down at her gun and then across at the body of the witch, the implications of what she'd just done spinning in her mind.

Oh, fuck.

She stumbled for the doorway, kicking aside crates and box files in her haste, and had made it to the foot of the stairs when she felt a magnetic tug from behind. She attempted to shrug it off and continue her ascent, but its grip grew more powerful, her legs more leaden with every step. Eventually, it grasped her like an invisible cord attached to her collar and flung her violently back into the records room, where she smashed into a metal stanchion. She heard brittle bones snap, but she felt nothing.

Cafferly uneasily got to her feet, a splintered pelvis struggling to support her. Joints and cartilage crackled, and she realised, glancing down, that her femur had torn through the thin, papery meat of the leg that had housed it; the shattered bone was black with decay. Although there was no pain, she was aware of the limitations entropy had put on her post-mortem physical body; she could just as easily be taken apart, even if death didn't hold any sting, and broken limbs would still impede her.

The air around her was swirling, thousands of files caught in a mini-tornado in the centre of the room, paper birds twisting in the eddies, and hovering at the base of it was Nausea, floating slowly in the Psi-Judge's direction. The wound in her forehead had vanished.

"That wasss a missstake, sssissster," she hissed as she drew nearer. "But I knew you'd ssshow your true coloursss eventually. I'd alwaysss ssusspected that you were not to be trusssted. I ssshould thank you for confirming it: it will make dissspossssing of you ssso much lesssss... perfunctory."

"What *are* you?" Cafferly asked, holding herself upright against a shelf. "You're not human at all, are you?"

"Once, perhapsssss," the witch replied. "The girl wassss asss young assss the face of hersss I wear today. She and her sssibling were practitionerssss of the dark artsss—they made contact acrossss the dimensionssss and opened their soulsss to ussss. We sssaw a meansss to an end—to create our four championssss, who will bring blessssed peace to thisss world, and hopefully more to come."

"Except Sidney's outgrowing you, isn't he? He's tired of being your dog, obeying your commands. He's shaping his *own* world."

Nausea narrowed her eyes, and looked aggrieved. "De'Ath is oursss, and oursss alone. We made him, like we made you all. When the final bonessss are laid to ressst, it will be *our* kingdom to rule over."

"Yeah? Try telling your protégé that. I can see the ambition in him—the desire for power, for recognition. He's your pet no longer." Cafferly gathered her strength and hobbled forward. "I'm surprised you and Phobia are so blind to that—that you've created something you can no longer control. He'll turn on you, and usurp your precious fucking kingdom."

Nausea flicked her eyes sideways and Cafferly's right arm wrenched itself out of its socket and went spiralling across the room, the Lawgiver still clutched in its hand. The Psi-Judge looked down at the dark, gaping wound below her shoulder and saw only fronds of rotten matter—no blood, no muscle, just desiccated sinew. Again, there was no physical sensation, but she experienced perhaps for the first time a disgust at what she'd become.

"You can't feel anything, can you, dead thing?" the witch murmured. "I could peel you apart limb by limb, organ by organ, and it would be like picking petalssss off a flower. Lesss commotion when there'ssss no pain, but it doesss remove ssssome of the pleasssure, it hasss to be sssaid."

Cafferly didn't answer. She could feel the power emanating from Nausea, building like an electrical storm. She was no match for the witch, this vessel for some other entity entirely.

"You're jussst a collection of partssss, given a new purpossse by usss. There is nothing of you that issss of any worth." She stopped to consider for a second. "Except, of courssse, your brain... Asss I sssaid, Brother Mortissss would be mossst interesssted. Yoursss would be invaluable to ssstudy—essspecially consssidering your... heritage."

"What did you mean, I was gifted to Justice Department?"

"Exactly that. Your parentsss were... championsss of Jussstice Department. Sssstaunch believerss. They could sssee from an early age that you were ssspecial, that you had powersss. They wanted Jussstice Department to make usssse of thossse. Ssso they hothoussed you."

"They...?"

"They moulded you for the Judgesss. Psssychologically. Physssically—

(the punishment due)

"—And you were given to the Hall of Injusssstice like an offering. A ssacrifice to the law."

"Why... why don't I remember...?"

"Because the Dead Fluidssss ssshould've sscoured it from you. There *wasss* no life before usss. Before our brotherssss. It all ssshould have been purged. But you... you were indeed unique. The Fluidsss didn't obliterate it all—your mind ssstarted to reassssert itssself, claw back your original identity. We had never sssseen that before."

"I get flashes... images..."

"Memoriesssss, buried in your cortex. They have proved remarkably resssilient to wiping."

Cafferly looked around her at the files scattered in every direction, the heaps of documents gathered in drifts, and recalled that spark that came the moment she picked up one. But it hadn't been one of her own memories, or a trace of her past—or at least, not hers personally. There was someone else—someone else's voice in her head.

"Misha," she whispered before she could stop herself.

Nausea wasn't slow to pick it up. "What'sss that?"

"It... it's nothing..."

"No, I can sssensse your mind consssolidating around that name. What doesss it mean ?"

The Psi-Judge felt her mental defences—what was left of them—bow under the witch's pressure. Evidently, this information was something Nausea wasn't aware of, and was intrigued to learn more. Cafferly tried to push back, but couldn't hold on to the name and repel the psychic advances at the same time; it kept slipping from her.

"What doesss thisss name mean to you?" Nausea persisted. *"Tell me."*

"I don't know..."

"You do. It'sss there in your head, hidden from usss. Let me in..."

"No, keep out... s-stay away..." But Cafferly was faltering, she could feel herself falling apart.

"You can't deny me," Nausea rasped angrily. "Let me

(in)

2 May

I THINK NOW that

Misha stopped in mid sentence, her pen paused above the page of her journal. Her hand was shaking as a chill suddenly swept through her.

"Sister," she murmured.

CHAPTER TWENTY

NAUSEA DID LOVE to dance. She suspected it was a hangover from the human form she'd adopted, a trace personality trait that hadn't been fully extinguished. They'd been young women, she and Phobia, when they'd made contact with the beings across the veil—little more than teenagers—so it was hardly surprising that youthful pursuits should still play a part in their lives, no matter how much they'd given over of themselves to the dark arts. For all the magic and power they wielded, they were still juveniles, occasionally susceptible to a certain immaturity—she and her sister had exhibited an unfortunate level of brattishness at the start, quick to show off and bicker childishly. The entity that was now Nausea would've expected to have fully assimilated all of what the girl had once been, shrugging on her physical body like an overcoat and absorbing her identity, but the desire to dance never entirely faded, as if it were the faint ghost of an imprint on what her blank soul had become. It had never been able to rid her of it entirely.

As such, she could see why unique cases like Cafferly emerged—the human spirit was remarkably stubborn. You could bleach it, burn it, blitz it and purge it, and still those echoes would prevail. Nausea's lingering character was like a scar she wore, or a limb that ached in winter that she'd had to grow accustomed to, but the Psi-Judge's mind had actively fought back against the Dead Fluids, reclaiming a lost past and slowly reinstating her old self. It was unheard of, a development that couldn't be allowed to continue. The toxicity of life meant that mankind *had* to be purified; there could be no elements of it left remaining. Cafferly needed studying to ensure the Fluids were working properly, that the human stain was sufficiently wiped clean.

She twirled down the corridor, jigging from foot to foot. She was barely conscious that she was doing it, if she was honest; the shade of the girl that once was sliding back into the driving seat when Nausea wasn't looking. She raised herself up on her bare toes and pirouetted, arms held out so her fingertips brushed the grime-encrusted walls, her smock flaring wide around her, then leaped from floor tile to floor tile like a ballerina, theatrically bowing with each landing for the benefit of an unseen audience. All the while she hummed discordantly, a tuneless melody that sounded half remembered, dredged from an earlier existence, and even though it was under her breath, such was the silence in the Hall that it carried in the stillness.

She was well aware that De'Ath didn't care for her eccentricities; he felt that too much of the teen had been retained, and she was too frivolous, too unpredictable. It was possible that he considered her and her sister touched by madness. She found herself caring little what he thought—though he was their champion of the apocalypse, their totaller of worlds, in whom they'd personally seen the potential to be elevated as the great leveller, he was a crashing bore. She and Phobia had been impressed initially by his zeal, his drive, his ruthlessness, but let loose upon this population he seemed to be all about the numbers. It was all work, work, work with him—he didn't seem to appreciate the beauty of the charnel pit even as he delivered body after body into it. She hated to admit it, but Cafferly had had a point—off the leash, their pet was turning against his mistresses, forgetting who made him, where he came from. He was increasingly insecure, believing all those around him were either conspirators or lacked his vision.

As the Psi-Judge had predicted, there may well come a reckoning, Nausea thought, spinning on one foot and pushing her shoulders back, arching her spine for a final flourish, and if there was a challenge to the hierarchy Sidney could soon discover that he was eminently replaceable. It was the witch-siblings that had created the Fluids, the post-mortem animus that was the font of all that had been created here, and that was where the power really lay: down here, in the bowels of the Grand Hall, as far from Sidney's lofty perch as you could imagine.

"Sssissster," she called, entering their chamber. "Have you made progressss?"

It was part laboratory, part workshop—the pair had relocated their magical devices from their woodland retreat into the Hall of Injustice once the authorities had been overthrown. In truth, they weren't fans of urban surroundings and slunk back here to this den at any given opportunity, content in each other's company and the business of spellcasting. An array of pipes and tubes fed multiple containers dotted around the space, beakers of ingredients lining the shelves, but central was the enormous cauldron that dominated the room, its flickering green light bathing the walls and ceiling in an emerald hue, a fire smouldering beneath. Phobia was standing over it, peering into its contents, her underlit features appearing goblin-esque. She glanced up at Nausea's entrance, eyes dark and menacing.

"The elementsss are in the right proportion. The invocationssss have been recited. The energy buildssss."

"Good." Nausea looked up. "And Judge Cafferly—are you ready to begin?"

The Psi's severed head didn't answer aloud, but her lower jaw ground slowly in a bovine manner, drool pooling from her bottom lip. The head was affixed above the apex of the cauldron by a pair of struts holding it in place, and the steam—sparks flashing and twisting within it—curled around it. What was emerging from the cauldron seemed to have a life of its own, teasing at the Judge's hair, vanishing into her nose and ears.

"I'll take that asss a yessss," the witch murmured. She placed her forearms on the lip of the cauldron, unconcerned by the heat from below, and gazed up, studying Cafferly's face. "You are a tough nut to crack, but make no missstake, we *will* sssspill your ssssecretsss."

"I don't know why thisss one fassscinatesss you ssso, sssissster," Phobia said. "It'ssss jussst another dead thing. Feed it to the crowsss."

"Oh, Judge Cafferly hasss much to give up. We can learn a great deal from her—not leassst her reaction to the Fluidssss. But even more intriguingly, there isss another. A sssibling, long sssince ssseparated, yet the two are connected."

Phobia glanced sharply at her twin, unable to disguise her sudden curiosity. "Oh, really? How do you know thissss?"

"Cafferly neuro-flipped with her—their mindssss and memoriesss merged. The pssssi-amp mussst've initiated it, forged the link that had previousssly been unknown to them."

"Ssshe didn't know of her sssisster?" Phobia asked, motioning towards the head above them, still dumbly grinding its jaw.

"No, the parentssss had her committed to the Academy while the other wasss sstill in the womb. Her powerssss were impresssive even then. But the sssecond daughter, when ssshe emerged, manifessssted no sssimilar talentsss—or sssso it was thought at the time."

"Interesssting..." Phobia rubbed her chin ruminatively. "But there mussst have been ssssome..."

"...Dormant, yessss, I believe ssso. At the very leassst, ssshe'sss a receiver. Sssshe may even have been remotely influenced by her sssisster during the flipssss."

"Huh. Well, that doessss make Cafferly rather more of value than ssssimple compossst."

"I thought you'd ssssee it that way, Phobia dear," Nausea said, smiling.

"Sssso you presssume to find this sssibling?"

"I'm sssmoking her out asss we ssspeak," Nausea remarked, pointing a bony finger at the strands of green steam that played in and around the Psi-Judge's skin, ears, eyes and mouth. "A living blood-relative could prove vital in developing the Fluidssss."

Phobia paused, then asked, "Have you told Mortisss of thisss yet?"

Nausea shrugged. "No. Let'ssss keep thisss between usss for the time being. No ssssensse ssshowing our hand unnecesssssarily. We may well need an advantage in the dayssss to come."

"Amen to that."

"Brother Mortissss can have what's left of Judge Cafferly'sss grey matter when I'm finissshed," Nausea whispered, closing her eyes and leaning forward to breathe in the clouds. "For now, sssshe and her ssisster are *mine*..."

For Thomas and Mary Cafferly, there was only the rule of law. Their home, their family, was governed like the city at large—with absolute iron authority—and woe betide anyone that chose not to accept that. The pair were passionate, party-donating believers in the Justice Department—anything else was chaos; liberal, communist anarchy—and the Judges were their gods, their strictures handed down and abided by without question. They instilled this in their first child Rachel from an early age, sitting her in front of TV footage of their uniformed overlords, and impressing upon her they were the icons to which she should bow. She imprinted upon the badge and the gun almost straight away, and that was around the first time she displayed signs of her soft talents.

When they discovered the level of power their daughter was capable of, Thomas and Mary were overjoyed. They had offspring that would join the Judges' fight against the pernicious, criminal society they hated, and to have your child joining the department's ranks was, in their eyes, like gifting your first-born to God. It was an opportunity they would not pass up. They moulded her abilities before she was five, encouraged her to expand her telepathic, projection and psychokinetic skills, prepared her for the day when they handed her over to the tutors at the Academy with glee etched on their faces. Punishments were severe if she neglected her exercises, the training brutal, but Thomas and Mary reasoned that it would get no easier once she was a cadet. If Rachel was to be an effective instrument for justice, she was to be as finely honed as any weapon, her mind a powerful force; and indeed by the time she did don the uniform, her head had been filled with enough propaganda that she was the model recruit—disciplined, dedicated, utterly committed to the law.

Mary Cafferly was already pregnant by the time they lost their first child to the Judges, and they fervently hoped the second would follow suit. But the programming wouldn't take, no matter how harsh the consequences and how extensive the brainwashing; Misha rebelled at every opportunity. She flirted with democracy, and went on anti-Department demos, seeming undeterred by what repercussions would await her at home. She'd be banished to the dark at the top of the stairs for hours on end, and still she persisted. They forcibly tried to enrol her at the Academy, but she didn't make it past induction. She also showed no signs of the psychic talents that her sister had displayed, proving to be resolutely and disappointingly ordinary in every respect, apart from her refusal to respect authority. She couldn't have been more different to her sibling, of whom there was no mention within the family, nor were there photos—Rachel had been born again into the Department, her parents believed, and she had no life outside the Judicial ranks, hence she no longer belonged to the Cafferlys. Misha grew up unaware that her sister had ever existed.

By the time Misha entered college in her mid teens, Thomas and Mary barely acknowledged they had any children at all. The punishments, rather than steeling her like they'd done to Rachel, simply alienated her. They'd failed. And yet, there seemed like moments, sometimes—when she was left on that shadowy landing for refusing to do as she was told, when she took another beating at the hands of her mother and father—that Misha seemed aware of what had come before; there was a resonance, a recognition in her eyes. It gave them some kind of hope.

There was the seed of Rachel in her younger sister.

5 May

THE ONE CONSTANT I always clung to, even as I watched the world circle the drain, was that I knew who I was, that my humanity was without doubt. It gave me assurance for what was worth fighting for, that we were nothing like these creatures that have pledged to wipe us all out—even if they too were once regular people before they drank the zombie juice. Their genocidal schemes are against all that is right and natural. Now, though... I don't know if I'm the same woman that I was two months ago. My mind hasn't been my own—it's been invaded, sluiced with thoughts from a sibling that I never knew existed, a sister that's allied herself to monsters. I haven't been myself, and I don't know if I can ever be myself again.

I mean, what is true any more? I thought I was a survivor—but I might actually be a killer, sharing a mind with someone who wants to hasten that very extinction. She embedded herself in my brain and sprouted foulness, and made me complicit in her monstrousness. Kez, Katherine and the rest—their fates are unknown, yet more disappearances in a world being butchered by the millions, but I am sure that I was responsible, and my sister Rachel Cafferly drove me to it.

I can hear the whispers when I close my eyes—the siren songs, the entreaties, the promises. The creatures want to find me, and are casting out their hooks, trying to pull me in. What they want me for I've yet to ascertain, but they must be aware of the familial connection, and clearly seek to exploit it. If Rachel's still there, I don't know—but I do know for sure that I never want to meet her.

I should tell Hawkins about all this, that I'm compromised, a danger to her and everyone we meet. But I can't bring myself to—I don't know if I'm scared she'll put a bullet in my head there and then and leave me on the side of the road, or that by vocalising what's been entirely within my head up to this point, I'll be making the nightmare real. We're living through horror on a daily basis, but we've never been the ones responsible. Now... now I can't say that any more.

No, I'll keep the secrets locked up inside me and face this alone. In the meantime, we'll keep going and attempt to put distance between us and those that mean us harm, keep moving in the hope of finding a haven, even as I'm aware I'm bringing the darkness with me, like the cigarette-stink of death attaching itself to my clothes.

And she'll be with me, of course. Always. Sistersss to the end.

PART THREE

GREY FLESH FLIES

CHAPTER TWENTY-ONE

THE WORLD WAS incrementally dying; there was no doubt of that now. Bit by bit it was dropping away into darkness, slowly and steadily. There hadn't been an atomic flash that had exterminated millions in an instant or a seismic shift in the tectonic plates that had cracked continents in half; instead, it was deteriorating in stages, like a once healthy organ being eaten from the inside out. You were aware of it in the sudden sharp scent of corruption brought by the wind, in every fluctuation in the miasmic light, and especially in how the plant-life was responding to its new environment, contorting horribly like it couldn't understand what was happening to it. It made your heart break to see it, Misha thought; the flora was adapting with no comprehension to what was going on around it, once verdant shoots twisted by a poisoned earth to the point where they, like everything else on the planet, could no longer survive.

She was standing on a ridge looking down at a copse, and the trees were virtually petrified, noticeable for their sickly calcified brittleness. Considering the season—she was fairly sure they were somewhere in the summer months, but it was increasingly difficult to discern the passing of the days, as a tombstone-grey cloud settled permanently over the sky—the branches should've been bursting with leaves, but instead they'd been reduced to skeletonised shadows of their former selves. They hunched together like terminally ill old men, bewildered by the malicious toxicity of their situation, and as they struggled to maintain that pulse of life, the cancerous new eco-system was ensuring their eventual downfall. She imagined it wouldn't be long before fissures appeared in the bark, the trunks would split asunder, and the trees would collapse as little more than ash. Misha and Hawkins could pass by this way again in a week, and the landscape as it was would simply be a memory. She didn't want to come back, though; partly because retracing their steps would be one more sign that they had nowhere to go, and partly because she had no desire to witness such grim inevitability. Better to leave it in the rear-view mirror, decaying out of her sight.

She glanced across at Hawkins, the Judge bringing her toolkit to bear on the Lawrider's gearbox and grunting in irritation as she wrestled with it. The ability to keep moving was so far a luxury they'd taken for granted, but they might not have transport for much longer if the bike gave up on them. It was showing increasing signs of strain, its suspension shot and the onboard computer displaying worrying eccentricities. Hawkins needed the communications unit fully functioning if she was going to intercept radio traffic to guide them to safety, and she couldn't afford the A.I. to go on the fritz. (Misha, for her part, was philosophical about the slim possibility of such a sanctuary existing, but kept her opinions to herself, aware of how important it was to the Judge. Let her have something to hold on to, at the very least.) The loss of a ride would be a most troubling development indeed—it didn't pay to linger in any one place for too long. They'd learnt that to their cost.

It wasn't just the threat of discovery by the greys, though that was challenging enough on its own; it was seeing, like this, the devilish details of the land's destruction. It did things to your head, watching the change being wrought upon the world, the new status quo being foisted upon it. While the global scale of it was at times simply too vast to comprehend—and she had to assume that what was happening here was being repeated in other countries: the climatic shock was too great not to be affecting their overseas neighbours—it was brought home when she gazed down on acres of grassy plains shrivelling away to nothing, or abandoned fields of blighted crops that had degenerated into an ugly hue and now gave off a fetid stench. With, so she'd heard, most germinating insects effectively wiped out, fertilisation was now impossible. Nothing would seed or sprout; there would just be tracts of barren, hostile ground. Having that laid out before you, you couldn't help but want to weep, the sheer wrongness of it proving difficult to process. There's something not right about this picture, she wanted to say. This is against the natural order of things.

But of course, that was exactly what it was: a perversion, a tilting of a fragile balance that served the interests of the new rulers' anti-life agenda, and there was seemingly nothing that could be done to stop it. If the planet had any kind of consciousness—a Gaia spirit, Misha had once heard it called—it was being viciously choked, and these swathes of crumbling, blackened vegetation were symptoms of its death throes. Small wonder that she didn't want to hang around for too long: to confront this was to test the limits of your endurance.

Put it behind you. Put it behind you, however futile that may be. Outrun the world's unravelling.

She turned and crossed over to Hawkins, whose brow was furrowing as she twisted something deep in the bike's chassis with a wrench. "How's it looking?" Misha asked.

The Judge shook her head. Her speech was limited by the knotted mess of scar tissue that was the lower half of her face, and she could evidently only open her mouth so far without it causing her significant pain. Her diet subsisted mainly of liquidised rations that she could suck through a straw. Misha had never fully gleaned the whole story of what had happened to her, but then again, she didn't really need to—they were all walking wounded now, some carrying more obvious injuries than others. If she was still alive, then she'd fought her battles against the common enemy and come out the other side still in one piece, more or less, which was some kind of small victory. But the legacy of those encounters was unmistakably writ large upon her flesh, and they told enough of their own tale that the actual details seemed superfluous.

Given the weeks Misha had now spent in Hawkins' company, it meant the pair had developed a rudimentary sign language that the Judge clearly found less exhausting than trying to formulate words. The younger woman was surprised at how adept she quickly became at picking up what Hawkins was communicating simply from raised eyebrows and a few hand gestures. They seemed to understand each other intuitively, often predicting the other's actions, or knowing what needed to be done without any kind of signal. They had a solid system, and it had stood them in good stead so far—but Misha couldn't escape the fact that she didn't know how far the Judge trusted her. Hawkins had encountered the girl when the balance of her mind was disturbed, and effectively saved her from herself. The rest of Misha's fellow survivors had eerily vanished in uncertain circumstances, their fates unknown, and the teen had been discovered raving, on the verge of losing her sanity entirely. Hawkins had sat with her and brought her down gently.

Misha—for whom that entire episode remained something of a blank spot in her memory—was still unclear on why the Judge persevered with her, committed herself to pulling the girl back from the brink and bringing her with her. Hawkins could be forgiven for simply looking out for herself as the world crumbled; plenty of others had done just that. Yet here the two of them were—partners, of a kind. It could be that the Judge simply appreciated her company, that ironically her *own* mental health was in a better state having another human being to interact with, even one as borderline crazy as Misha (potentially; she'd never had another episode since) was. Maybe Hawkins simply saw something of herself in the younger woman that she wanted to protect. The teen was well aware she'd lucked out tagging along with the law officer, as she'd never have made it on her own, and felt beholden to prove herself useful should the prospect of her getting ditched ever finally come up. She went overboard in demonstrating her reliability and capability, hoping that every chore performed without complaint, or extra watch duty taken, reinforced her place in Hawkins' confidence. It seemed to do the trick, but, nevertheless, paranoid niggles remained that the Judge was just waiting for her to make one wrong move... and Misha had good reason not to fully trust herself.

Hawkins slung the wrench back in the toolbox and motioned towards the bike with angry resignation. She stood, stretching weary limbs, and looked out across the landscape, markedly avoiding eye contact. She shook her head again, then started to pack the gear into a rear pannier compartment.

"How long have we got?" Misha asked.

The Judge shrugged, and held up a finger.

"A day?"

She gestured with her hand: <thereabouts>.

"Fuck," Misha breathed. Hawkins nodded her agreement. "So we need a new set of wheels sharpish."

The Judge leaned back against the Lawrider's handlebars and picked up the comms transmitter, signalling that she was listening to it. "Stay in contact," she intoned, the words forced out, raw and raspy.

Hawkins' obsession with finding other uniforms hadn't dimmed, despite the radio giving out nothing but static for weeks. "You mean we somehow lay our hands on another Justice Department vehicle?"

The older woman spread out her gauntleted palms: <no choice>.

"Which would mean diverting towards the capital." They'd deliberately skirted pockets of civilisation as much as possible, which were dense with grey teams, and kept to the country roads. They'd found less trouble that way, but it also meant supplies were sparser. Picking up a car or truck that still had fuel was one thing; stealing a Judge's bike was a whole other level of complication. But Misha knew that Hawkins wouldn't be dissuaded on this one—she had to know that the resistance was out there, and that she could rendezvous with it.

The Judge threw her arms wide, indicating the barren expanse. "Want to walk?" she growled, though Misha imagined she heard the faint outline of a smile behind it.

The teen shook her head and kicked the dust at her feet. "Fuck," she repeated.

THINGS GOT WORSE the closer you got to the capital, as if that was possible: the smell, the sights, the pervading sense of despair. The horror had seemingly rippled out from the Hall of Injustice at the epicentre like an earthquake. So many had tried to escape being caught in the shockwaves, but the sheer weight of numbers and the ruthlessness of the new Chief's forces meant that few within the city's boundaries had survived the initial purge. Misha had been one of the lucky ones, bundled to safety thanks to the random kindness of a complete stranger, but plenty of others had been left behind, gunned down in their hundreds.

Some of them were still here, decaying bodies propped behind the wheels of their cars, massacred in the ensuing chaotic gridlock, but there was evidence that there had been a systematic clearance of corpses since that night. Smouldering pyres of bones lined the roads, and in the distance dotted points of flame suggested there were several burning away. It turned Misha's stomach, and she wished they could go back, abandon this plan. Even though they were still some distance from the capital proper, you could feel the dread sense of emptiness, the void it had become, gnawing at your mind. She had argued further with Hawkins against this folly, believing it to be an unnecessary risk, but the more she protested, the more the Judge dug her heels in. She would motion to the bike, indicate the unhealthy noise that the engine was making, and remind her that it wouldn't be long before their ride gave up the ghost entirely. The fact was the Lawrider *was* truly screwed—Hawkins hadn't been wrong about the extent of its problems. It had got them over rough terrain in the past few weeks, but it was showing the strain now, kicking out oily black smoke as power outages kept rebooting the onboard computer. It would only be a matter of time before they were locked out of the weapons systems and/or something ignited close to the fuel tank. It said something of Misha's fear of the city that she was aware that they were astride a failing machine and still she'd rather take her chances with that than go near the capital.

Of course, the teenager had reasons of her own not to get too close to the HoJ beside the obvious possibility of capture or, more likely, execution, but she had to be careful not to arouse Hawkins' suspicions. She'd want to know why the girl had such a hard-on for staying well out of its area, and if Misha came clean, that would almost certainly be a prelude to a parting of the ways. At the same time, she was aware she was compromising both of their safeties. She just hoped they could circle the outskirts and quickly find what they needed without entering the city any more than they had to, and she'd made Hawkins promise as such, citing her own personal trauma as an excuse. The Judge didn't need to know what Misha could bring down on them if they dallied too long in the Grand Hall's shadow.

It had been like an itch at the back of her brain up until now, a pressure she found she could push back against. She'd evidently been previously well outside the Sisters' reach: they'd been a background presence, an electrical charge in the air you could feel in the hairs on your arms, but nothing materialised beyond that. They were looking for her, casting out their psychic hooks in the hope that they'd get a fix on her location, try to worm inside her mind and plant their seeds of corruption, but she'd blocked them. It had been relatively easy when the psignal was that weak, and they were clearly casting a wide net, but now she was getting nearer to their centre of operations, it was only going to get harder to keep them out. All it took was one lapse in concentration, a drop in her defences, and they'd be inside her head, rifling through her thoughts, grabbing what they needed to direct their undead goons to pick her up—or worse, take control of her and force her to do their bidding.

They wanted her alive, she felt sure of that; or at least some approximation of it. It probably wouldn't matter to them if she was delivered in pieces as long as her grey matter was still functioning. The thing about psychic broadcasts was that it worked both ways—while they actively sought her out, Misha at the same time could pick up the reasons behind it, their motives. Their intentions permeated their emanations, an unmistakable flavour running through them, and the Sisters' curiosity about the girl showed strongly through their probes. They knew about Rachel, her sibling that had allied herself with the new CJ's creatures, and the neuro-flipping that had been occurring between the pair; this kind of link was ripe for exploitation, and Misha's potential abilities were too powerful to go to waste. She was sure that if the Sisters got their hands on her, they'd peel her brain apart for their own arcane amusement.

Needless to say, she'd told Hawkins none of this. It was a betrayal, after a fashion, that she was keenly ashamed of; she was endangering the Judge's life through her own cowardly secretiveness and self-interest. But she reasoned they'd come too far now to imperil their partnership, and she deliberately chose to disclose nothing about the entities snapping at her heels.

Misha coughed as the wind swept smoke from the pyres in their direction, the smell sticking in the back of her throat. She tapped Hawkins on the shoulder, and signalled that this was close enough.

To go any further was to enter Hades itself. They were on one of the main arterial freeways that serviced the capital—once a never-ending flow of traffic, now a graveyard—and looking ahead, the road had seemingly been paved in bones. Layer upon layer of skeletal remains coated the ground, piling up in drifts; virtually impassable on two wheels. Hawkins slowed the Lawrider to a crawl, and weaved the vehicle between two burned-out cars to shield them from view when she saw greys patrolling the city's boundaries. Leaving the engine idling, the Judge turned in her seat and motioned to the vibrations coming from within the engine.

<Getting worse,> she signed. <Hasn't got much life left in it.>

Misha shrugged theatrically and looked around with arched eyebrows, indicating that they weren't exactly spoiled for choice. They'd seen no abandoned Lawriders on their journey here, seemingly suggesting either that those resisting De'Ath had succeeded in fleeing the area, or they'd been incinerated on the spot. Hawkins raised a finger: <wait>. She flipped some switches on the bike's control panel, and it emitted a low, regular beep.

Transponder, the Judge mouthed. *Will flag any other Lawriders in the vicinity using the same signal.*

"Won't that also alert anyone that's listening that we're here?" the younger woman whispered.

Hawkins nodded. <Risk we have to take,> she signed. <Keep it broadcasting very briefly.>

Misha looked around nervously. An H-wagon flying overhead at that moment would pick them up instantly on its radar, and their movements tracked. She didn't like advertising their presence so blatantly, used to travelling well off the grid. She closed her eyes and counted down the seconds before her companion deactivated the transponder—

The tone changed suddenly and Hawkins grabbed the girl's arm, shaking her to pay attention. <Pingback,> the Judge revealed. <Found one. There's a stationary bike less than a couple of miles from here.> The Lawrider chimed again, and then emitted a succession of urgent, clipped bleeps.

"What's that?" Misha asked.

<Emergency protocol tagged to the signal,> Hawkins signed, frowning, squinting at the bike's readout. <SOS. Help me.>

* * *

THEY'D BECOME ADEPT at avoiding the greys, but their misfiring Lawrider was starting to feel like it could draw attention, so they abandoned it in an alleyway a mile out from where the signal was hailing, concealing it beneath a discarded tarpaulin, and made the rest of the way on foot. Hawkins took a portable receiver unit to continue to follow the broadcast, and they quickly and quietly threaded their way through the back lanes of a deserted commuter area that lay sprawled in the foothills of the capital. Any living presence was long gone, but the signs that people had once existed here were readily evident: plastic toys lay scattered in gardens, and washing flapped on clotheslines, never to be reclaimed. Many of the doors to the properties stood open where the residents had upped and fled, and Misha would cast an eye as they passed to see what she could see; but the interiors for the most part were dark and still. Whole stories could be written about the former occupiers, she thought, catching sight of children's drawings tacked to refrigerators alongside family photographs, or a dog's chain disappearing into a kennel in a front yard. SUVs were parked on driveways, their trunks stuffed with belongings, where the owners hadn't managed to get away fast enough. Their final remains were captured in a frozen moment in time, indications of who once existed here before they were purged from the picture.

Hawkins gestured for the pair of them to halt, and they crouched beside a dilapidated fence. She pointed to a shuttered garage a few metres ahead, and told Misha that's where it was holed up.

"In a civilian population sector?" the girl whispered back.

The Judge shrugged. <Must've come here to hide,> she signed.

"This smells like a trap," Misha said. The door looked well maintained, and there were tyre tracks on the concrete before it. "Something to draw us in. I don't like it."

<As a sworn member of Justice Department,> Hawkins swiftly signed, <I'm obliged to answer a distress call from a fellow officer.>

"You're a long way from the Grand Hall now, and that badge doesn't mean a whole lot in the current climate. Fact is, we don't know *what's* in there."

<They're broadcasting the right signal, and using Lawrider tech to do it. Can't ignore that.>

Hawkins stood and edged towards the garage, sliding her Lawgiver from its holster in one fluid movement. "Keep me covered," she rasped over her shoulder, and Misha unhitched her own gun from the waistband of her pants, a small snubnosed semi-automatic that Hawkins had given her and taught her how to shoot reasonably accurately without injuring herself. She had a fractious relationship with the weapon: she liked the reassurance that it was there, but hated pulling the trigger the few times that she'd been obliged to. Nevertheless, she was now training it on her companion as the Judge examined the padlock on the shutter.

<Not locked,> Hawkins signed across. She looked around, making sure there was no one in the vicinity, then got both hands under the lip at the bottom. "Help me with this," she huffed.

Misha jogged over and awkwardly grabbed the shutter while still holding the gun in her right hand—it didn't seem prudent to put it away just yet—and they pushed up in tandem. She was expecting rusty resistance, but it slid on its runners remarkably smoothly. Someone had been making sure to oil it, she thought. As soon as the door cleared their heads they were inside, weapons at the ready, light from the outside spilling in and illuminating the headlights of a Justice Department bike that filled the majority of the space. Beyond it, towards the back, was shelving and a workstation, and it was there, to the right of the Lawrider, that Misha caught sight of the figure, a hunched silhouette squatting near the ground.

"Hawkins," she exclaimed, directing the Judge's attention to what she'd seen, motioning with the snubnose.

"My god," she croaked, stepping forward, Lawgiver raised. "That's—"

"Hello, Trace," the figure answered quietly.

CHAPTER TWENTY-TWO

"BLAKE."

The name emerged from Hawkins' throat as barely a croak—more a grunt of recognition than a genuine question. The Lawgiver wavered in her hand as if she was in two minds as to whether she still needed it, her gaze not leaving the figure on the floor.

Misha's gaze flittered between the pair of them, her own gun decidedly more steadfast. "You know him?" she asked.

Hawkins nodded and edged round the bike towards the man, finally lowering her weapon and holstering it. She glanced at Misha and nodded that she do the same, though Misha was a little more reluctant, dropping her gun to her side but not sliding it back into her waistband. She kept it tight against her thigh and remained stationary, warily watching the Judge approach. Hawkins crouched and fished out a penlight from her belt pouch, clicking it on: the daylight from the open doors hadn't reached the rear of the room. A couple of fluorescent bulbs hung from the ceiling, but it was safer to keep them off, if they indeed still worked, so as not to draw unwelcome attention. The yellowing newspaper glued to the two windows wouldn't stop light being visible from the outside. A thought seemed to occur to Hawkins and she turned slightly, gesturing to Misha to pull the doors to, deepening the darkness except for a sliver of light that penetrated the crack the girl had left.

The penlight picked out a lumpen character slouched against the wall, blankets wrapped around him. He squinted at the glare when she waved the beam over his face, taking in the fortnight's worth of growth on his chin and jawline, his skin lined with dirt. His expression turned to one of consternation when he saw Hawkins' own features; he tilted his head and gasped, the fingers of his right hand emerging from the blankets to reach out and lightly brush the scarred tissue of her lower face. She retracted slightly, and his hand dropped away.

"What the hell happened to you?" he asked.

She shook her head, motioned towards her mouth. "Explosion," was all she could mutter, sweeping one hand towards outside.

"She finds it hard to talk," Misha felt compelled to interject, still standing near the doors. "Don't try to get her to say too much, it's painful."

Blake fleetingly looked round Hawkins to study the teenager. "You are?"

"Just her travelling companion." She felt uneasy about giving him her name; no reason why he needed to know it. "You a Judge too, I assume?"

"Was. No law left to uphold now. Chief Sidney's walking pusbags have the Grand Hall—they're running the show."

"They're also killing everyone," Misha replied testily. "I figured that was still illegal."

"It's a coup, a hostile military takeover. Statutes, penalties and criminality don't apply anymore. It's gone beyond that now."

"Even when innocent civilians are being gunned down? Seems to me that this is as much a premeditated massacre as it is a power grab. People are being slaughtered in their thousands—so what are you doing hiding away in here?"

Hawkins shot Misha a glare that told her to wind it back,

and the younger woman nodded, conciliatory, and made a zipping motion across her lips.

"Dying is what I'm doing," Blake said when Hawkins had turned back to him. "Or at least I will if I don't get to see a doc." He lifted a blanket to show a stained, crudely wrapped bandage around his shoulder and chest. The Judge's uniform had been cut away to accommodate it, and what still remained of his garb was filthy. Hawkins lifted her arms to indicate their surroundings; Blake understood. "How did I get here? Took a bullet trying to get out of the capital. Was holed up with a bunch of cits for a time when it first went down, waiting for the right moment to make a break. Nowhere felt safe, and we were being starved out, the civvies dropping like flies once the food evaporated."

Misha winced, recognizing the bid for survival amongst the group she'd once been a part of—the demoralising rations, the weakness and disease. They'd all succumbed too, eventually.

"I couldn't wait much longer. I knew how to get into the local sector house bike pool, steal one of the Lawriders," he continued. "Picked the moment and took my shot, but screwed it up royally—the wheels I boosted only had half a tank. They spotted me trying to make it to the city limits, and I got clipped. Had enough wherewithal to find shelter here—been broadcasting an SOS ever since in the hope that another badge would pick me up."

"What happened to the people you were hiding out with originally?" Misha asked.

Blake frowned for a second. "Oh, the cits? They were too far gone, too frail."

"So you left them there while you ran."

"Hey, fuck you," he snarled, sitting forward suddenly. "They were dying, there was nothing I could've done for them. Staying would've just meant me joining them—" Hawkins laid a palm on his good shoulder and eased him back. She then pointed at the bike and opened out her hands. Blake shook his head and looked at the other woman. "What's she saying?"

"She's asking if that means your Lawrider's got no fuel at all," Misha explained.

"No, she's dry," he replied, sighing. "It's working fine otherwise. Battery could probably do with a recharge, but that's all."

Hawkins slumped a little, then glanced round at the teen. She nodded outside and mimed siphoning gas. Misha gave a thumbs-up in agreement, aware Blake was watching the pair communicating with a mixture of confusion and anger.

"Hey, you ain't taking my ride and leaving me here," he said, turning his attention to Hawkins. "C'mon, Trace, we got a code amongst uniforms, right? We stick by rank, whatever the situation. You answered my distress call, so you got an obligation, man."

"You two serve together, then?" Misha enquired.

"Operated under the same watch commander back when we were rookies," he answered, hissing with pain as he adjusted his position. "Busted a fair few heads on those pro-Dem rallies, eh?" Hawkins looked away, then down at her feet, not meeting his gaze. "Sent a good number to hospital; put more than a handful in the morgue. Raided drug factories together, blown open organ farms. So, yeah, we got history." He studied Misha. "What's your deal? She pull your fat out of the fire, is that it?"

"Yeah, something like that."

"And now you're best buds."

"We're surviving, if that's what you mean."

"Too right," he said with a thin smile. "The living gotta stick together. If we just abandon each other to fate, then we're no better than those deadfucks out there. No point fighting for something if we lose it along the way."

"We ain't monsters," Hawkins said, each word a buzzsaw but voiced with quiet conviction.

"Amen to that," Blake responded.

Hawkins rose and walked back to where Misha stood. <He needs medical attention,> she signed. <Wound's going to be infected. He'll die unless it's treated.>

<Where will we get him help like that?> the younger woman replied, keeping her hand movements down where Blake couldn't see them, in the unlikely event he could gauge their meaning. <There's not a doc in a million miles.>

<There's a hospital not far from here, out in>—she spelled out the name—<C-O-T-T-E-R-I-D-G-E. See what we can salvage there. I can bind his injury with fresh bandages, clean it some. Whether he makes it>—Hawkins raised her eyebrows—<we'll have done what we can, at least.>

<Will the Lawrider handle three?>

<It'll be a squeeze, but we'll make it work.> She looked over her shoulder at the blanketed figure. <I can't leave him here. He's a badge.>

<I thought he said he wasn't a Judge anymore.>

<You're always a Judge, no matter what.>

"Okay," Misha said aloud, catching Blake's attention. "Can you walk unaided? When we get out of here, are you going to be able to stand on your own two feet?"

"Don't worry about me." He shifted his back against the garage wall and pushed himself up, getting his legs beneath him. He did it in bursts, stopping to pant for breath each time, eyes screwed shut, until he was upright. The blankets fell away at his feet. He opened his eyes, teeth gritted in an approximation of a steely grin, and tried to regain some composure. "See?" He took a step forward away from the wall's support, his left knee buckled, and he slumped back onto his haunches with a groan.

<He's lost too much blood,> Hawkins signed. <He can't go anywhere on foot.>

<Here's what I'll do,> Misha answered. <I'll head back to the bike, siphon off the fuel and the reserve. We've got the tubing from last time stashed away. The jump-leads are in the pannier too, I'll bring those back—we can plug those in to a power supply, charge the battery once the engine's turning over. You stay here and make sure he doesn't nod out.>

<Think you can handle it?>

<Not like I haven't done it before—and I've had a good teacher.> Misha looked towards the work surface at the rear of the building. <Need at least a couple of canisters,> she signed. "Yo, Blake," she called, wandering towards the cupboards on the other side of the bike, farthest from the doors. "There any jerry-cans in here that you know of?"

"In the bottom corner. Sure I saw some."

The teen looked as directed and pulled out one large metal can intended for kerosene, and a couple of bulbous glass bottles with handles and rubber stoppers that could've once held moonshine. "Perfect," she murmured, and headed back towards the outside, the three containers clinking in her right hand.

"Be careful," Hawkins croaked.

Misha gave her an A-OK sign with her free left hand, patted the gun tucked into her waistband, then cautiously slipped out through the crack in the doors and took off at speed.

HAWKINS STOOD AT the threshold and watched Misha disappear down the alleyway.

"She's not short of courage, that one," Blake said behind her.

"She's as scared as anyone," Hawkins replied flatly. "She didn't want us to come near the city, tried to argue against it. I... overruled her." She paused, wincing at the pain of talking, "Our Lawrider was dying and we need to be able to stay in contact with the outside world. Only a matter of time before we find them."

"Who, the resistance?"

Hawkins nodded.

Blake sighed. "Don't want to rain on your parade, Trace, but I'm pretty sure they're a myth. The new Chief's forces are too strong, too widespread. I think any surviving uniforms are few and far between."

"We've made it. No reason others haven't."

"But they're scattered, if they're out there at all. There's no organised fightback, no rebel cells—just the remnants of the old Justice Department scrabbling amidst the ruins."

"I think... think you're wrong," Hawkins said, holding her throbbing jaw. She wasn't used to being so vocal—Misha had been her only companion for so long. "Someone's leading the response. Someone will have taken charge."

"Maybe. Good luck finding them."

Hawkins' head ached. "You got any water?" She headed to the storage units above the workstation. "Or painkillers? What you been living on since you've been hold up here, anyway—?"

She tugged open the biggest cabinet door and came face to face with a plastic-wrapped human skull staring back at her through empty sockets. The skin was grey and puckered, and had shrivelled away from the bone. Her mind had a fraction of a millisecond to process what she was looking at before Blake slammed into her from behind and bounced her off the countertop. She lost her balance and tumbled over, thumping her forehead on the edge of the workspace as she went down. Stars danced in her vision.

Despite the black edges of unconsciousness encroaching into her sight, she wasn't dazed enough not to be aware of hands around her throat. She fought back against the wave of pain and channelled her energy into resisting the figure holding her prone. The more she bucked, the greater her anger became, and she found she had further reserves to draw upon—she grabbed hold of his wrists and attempted to pull them away from her throat, giving herself a moment's reprieve.

Now that the stars had faded, her vision regained some clarity, and she found herself looking up into Blake's demented eyes, devoid of compassion or reason. His face was contorted, a rictus fury she'd seen before on the amphetamine-hopped perps that she used to bust back in the old days. But those were lowlife drug fiends, sanity scoured away by a lifetime of substance abuse—this was Harrison Blake, her former colleague with whom she'd served on numerous occasions. They'd stood shoulder to shoulder once upon a time pacifying riots and blitzing tenements, one covering the other like all good uniforms should. He'd earned the helmet, graduated in the top third of his class. He was meant to represent everything she was fighting to preserve. Yet here he was, crazed beyond rational thought, almost unrecognisable in his mania—that he'd been driven to this was unfathomable. Or perhaps once it would've been unfathomable, a practical voice inside her declared, commenting objectively; now it was all too believable. Maybe she was naïve for not expecting this.

He brought his head back with the intention of driving his forehead into the bridge of her nose, but the move was telegraphed; she knew what was coming and swiftly craned her own head to one side at the last moment. He missed, connecting with the concrete floor. The impact tore a grunt from him, and Hawkins found the weight shifted as he was momentarily stunned; she pressed home the advantage and drove several sharp jabs to his kidneys, at the same time lifting him off her. He rolled, mewling like an animal caught in a trap, and she was up and out, springing to her feet and not allowing him a chance to recover—she kicked out and caught him on the chin, sending him flying back against the cabinet doors, rattling as he collided with them.

Hawkins' hand flew to her Lawgiver and brought it to bear on Blake, fully intending to dispense with the warning and drill a bullet in his skull without hesitation, but he came at her with such speed and venom and a lack of fear that he'd knocked aside her gun-arm in a fraction of a second. A cut had opened on his temple where he'd glanced off the floor, and the blood that now seeped down his nose and cheeks, coating his face, gave him a mask of utter madness, making him resemble a creature clothed in human form. They tussled, each trying to gain dominance over the weapon, his right hand clasped around hers clutching the butt of the Lawgiver and forcing the barrel back towards her, intending to use her own finger on the trigger. Crazy as he was, he clearly hadn't forgotten about the palm-print reader on the gun and wasn't about to fall victim to it.

They tangoed back and forth, neither releasing the pressure, until she saw an opening and drove her boot directly into his unprotected groin. He buckled, and relaxed his grip on her hand enough for her to wrest the gun free and smash the cold metal body of the Lawgiver into his mouth, leaving him staggering for a handful of brief moments like a boxer catching a knockout blow and teetering on the ropes. Fresh blood drooled over his lips, and he spat shards of broken teeth. Then he promptly fell ass-first onto the ground but remained seated upright, swaying slightly with the inebriated stupor of someone who'd been punched into next week. His head bobbed listlessly.

Hawkins aimed her gun at the figure on the floor, then pulled back and stalked over to the workstation cupboards, yanking them all open to be greeted with the sight of a range of body parts in varying states of putrefaction. All had been diligently swaddled in clear plastic, which accounted for why she hadn't smelled them when they'd entered. A hand still bore the remnants of the Judge's gauntlet that had encased it, and a jumble of weapons pouches and badges were piled at the back. Hawkins' eyes roved over the grim display with a quiet fury, then returned to where the man still sat.

She crouched before him, gun hovering at his head. He contemplated it like a drunk trying to focus on a hovering bluebottle.

"How many?" she asked. "How many have you murdered?"

"Four or five," he muttered, lisping slightly from his ruined mouth. "One... was already injured when he answered my distress signal, so I count that as a mercy killing. He was never going to survive much longer. I was doing him a favour, in the end. Reckon... reckon he might've been the first, now I think about it—the one that gave me the idea."

Hawkins shook her head. "What have you become, Blake? You were Justice Department. You were uniform."

"Yeah. When you got nowhere left to run, when you're starving... that doesn't count for much."

"And that?" She nodded at the chest injury he carried. "That all part of the act?"

He smiled and winced, as if suddenly reminded of it. "No, that's real. One of the last guys managed to get off a shot. Was hoping you'd actually get me out of here and patch me up—or at least, if not you, then your little citizen pal."

"Regular fucking Sawney Bean, aren't you?"

Blake laughed and spat blood on the floor between them. "Whatever works."

Hawkins shot him in the face.

MISHA RETURNED AT a jog, laden, and was surprised to find Hawkins in the process of wheeling the Lawrider out of the garage's open doors.

"Help me with this," was all the Judge said when the younger woman finally came level with her. Hawkins barely acknowledged her, nor asked her how successful she'd been. Her eyes were downcast, her mind evidently preoccupied.

"What's... going on?" Misha asked, placing the jerry cans on the ground and removing a coil of cables from her shoulder.

"Just push."

The teen did as she was instructed without further enquiry and the two of them guided the bike clear of the building. Once it was some distance away, Hawkins snapped the kickstand into place and walked back, snatching up one of the bottles half filled with gasoline as she passed, then proceeded to toss the contents through the doors, liberally coating the interior. Once it was empty, she dropped it and drew her gun, sighting it on the centre of the garage.

Misha watched from where she stood beside the Lawrider. "Hawkins? Isn't there stuff we—?"

"Nothing in here of any worth," she murmured and pulled the trigger, the structure igniting in a ball of orange flame.

The fire spread quickly, and soon the garage was engulfed. She stood before it for a few moments, silhouetted against the inferno, then marched back to her companion.

"But Blake...?" Misha prodded.

"Gone," Hawkins replied. "He's long gone." She reached out a hand, attention fixed on the dwellings nearby rather than the other woman. <Give me that cabling. We'll use one of these empty houses for the recharge. Power still seems to be on.>

"Hawkins, what happened?"

"From now on we trust no one," she answered as if she hadn't heard her companion, taking hold of the bike's handlebars and easing it down one of the alleyways. "Understand?"

"Sure," Misha murmured and, casting one eye at the blaze, picked up what remained of the fuel and followed the Judge.

CHAPTER TWENTY-THREE

It was rare for the four of them to be together these days. In the beginning, when the Sisters had first gifted Sidney with his post-mortem transformation, he'd personally selected the lieutenants that would aid him in his great mission: the chosen were those closest to him amongst the ranks, the personnel that had most fervently shared his vision. He'd seen in each of them their commitment, and allowed them to slough off their hateful humanity and adopt the more suitable garbs of office, along with the judicial powers that came with them. The Dead Fluids had changed them into the forms that would go on to define them, and individual names—whatever they'd been in life; they were left behind with all the rest of the mortal trappings—were replaced with archetypes. *Fear. Fire. Mortis.* Together with De'Ath, they were the architects of the planet's doom, bringers of annihilation. The Dark Judges.

They had fought together, killed together. They had communed for weeks on end about the best plan for the utter destruction of every single being that breathed around the globe. They were as tight as mummified skin stretched over a boiled skull.

Back then, it was the four of them against the world, but it quickly dawned on Sidney and his henchmen that the logistics of planet-wide obliteration meant they'd require help. For them to slaughter billions themselves would take far too long. Hence they'd distributed the Fluids amongst the men and women of the Hall of Injustice and created their own undead puppet police force to tackle the blunt end of the population purge. With more bodies on the ground to command and control, an element of delegation was required, each of the four taking charge of those areas that best suited their skills. De'Ath remained in the chief's chair, of course, with the Sisters there to advise him as he oversaw his masterwork, while Mortis disappeared into a rabbit hole of tek research, conjuring up new abominations in his laboratories and proposing ever more efficient methods of increasing the harvest. Fire took to the streets and instigated his flame-squads, igniting pyres throughout the capital, while Fear concentrated on psychological warfare, reasoning that if he could drive entire swathes of the citizenry insane, they would be more likely to take their own lives and speed the whole process up. They were, each of them, busy little bees, united in purpose.

So for Sidney to insist upon a meeting like this was unusual—De'Ath knew that the crusade took precedence, and to call them away from it could only be for the most serious of matters. As they congregated on the Grand Hall, it occurred to Fear, Fire and Mortis that once the work was done, they would be the last entities standing and they would undoubtedly become a unit again—the four masters of their graveyard kingdom. It would be a day to cherish. But until that time, their genocidal efforts consumed them, the scale of what they were achieving so vast in its scope that it demanded all of their attention, and administrative chores such as this were a distraction.

Nonetheless, you ignored a summons from the Chief at your peril.

They arrived virtually simultaneously, as befitted creatures of one mind, and found De'Ath alone and pacing his tenebrous office. He paused when he saw them enter, and walked over to his desk and sat opposite his lieutenants, who remained standing. The three nodded a curt greeting, which wasn't returned.

"The processs issss taking too long," Sidney stated, never one to mince his words. "Too many elude usssss."

"Are we in danger of missssing a deadline, brother?" Fear asked. "I wassss unaware that there wasss a timeframe in which our undertaking had to be completed."

De'Ath waved the comment away with a flick of his hand. "Of courssse not," he replied irritably. "But my desssire for jussstice meansss I want to sssee total devassstation delivered sssooner rather than later. That there are ssssurvivorsss ssstill clinging to life is affront to the rule of law. I want them laid wassste to, reaped like wheat."

"Asss do we all," Fire chimed in.

"Then in what waysss can we further expedite the ssslaughter?" Sidney asked. He turned his attention to Mortis. "Your pssi-operativesss were meant to be increassssing their productivity—have you ssseen any posssitive developmentssss?"

"The introduction of the pssi-amplifiers *hasss* generated sssome interesssting ressultsss," Mortis answered. "The disssscovery of sssurvivor cellssss hasss increasssed sssignificantly with a boosssted range. But it'sss taking itsss toll on the ussserss. Their mindsss can only take ssso much before they… sssnap."

Sidney shrugged. "We can find more, sssurely? All grissst to the grand ssscheme."

"Psisss are not asss common asss you think. We mussst ussse them ssparingly in thisss initial round of winkling the law-breakersss out."

De'Ath gave the approximation of an exasperated grunt and pushed away from the desk. He stood and resumed his angry pacing. Mortis shared a glance with his colleagues once the Chief's back was turned.

"While one life remainsss, we are failing," Sidney murmured.

"To exterminate a world," Fire offered, "it'ssss not an undertaking done lightly. Or one completed easssily."

"You musssst have patience, brother," Fear added.

"Patienccce?" De'Ath roared, rounding on the trio. *"Patienccce?"* His raspy voice rose into a screech. "Don't tell me what I musssst have, brother! *I* am the architect of thissss genocide, *I* called it into being! That perpetratorsss are out there, flaunting their lack of ressspect for the law, isss a ssstain upon my leaderssssship. They live, therefore they mussst be punissshed, yet they clearly feel they can essscape jussstice, carrying on committing further illegal actssss. It diminissshesss usss, makessss a mockery of our credo." He began to stalk the room again, like a caged wolf. "No, that will not do. That will not do at all."

"What do you proposssse, then?" Fire asked.

De'Ath faced them. "There isss an expresssion regarding boiling a frog. While the heat isss increasssed sssslowly, the frog iss unaware that it isss being cooked... until it isss too late. Thisss world issss that crucible in which our ssssubjectsss exisssst—we have been changing the environment around them, poisssoning it, toxifying it, sssso it becomesss uninhabitable. It wasss done under their nosssess, ssset in motion while they were unaware and before they could sssstop it. But now we mussst turn up the heat further, ssscourge the world of all life entirely. The time for sssubtlety is gone—sssscorched earth isss the only way."

"You believe we've been too... ssssubtle?" Fear asked, sailing close to the wind again. He couldn't help himself; he manipulated everyone around him, even his own kind, poking their sensitive areas.

"We've been ssssyssstematic, ordered in our purgesssss," De'Ath replied, "or relied on nature to take itsss toll. But thisss has proved a time-conssssuming method. There mussst be more... blanket approachesss."

"We dissscussssed the nuclear option," Fire said.

"Yesss, yesss," De'Ath answered. "Before I ripped out the heart of that traitor Drabbon, he'd locked down the sssilosss. No accessss for anyone without the required keycodessss, and he took thosssse with him to hisss damn grave."

"I could ssssimply set them ablaze. The reactorsss too. The radiation would causssse untold damage, and the resssulting atomic fireball would be without quessstion a sssight to ssssee." Fire's crackling eye sockets veritably glittered in anticipation.

"You'd rissssk global rupture. The planet'ssss crussst could not weather sssuch damage."

"Issss that sssuch a bad thing?"

"We want the world to ssstand, not collapssse in on itsssself."

"You'd achieve your required body count, brother," Fear put in.

"The world *mussst* ssstand," De'Ath insisted, refusing to be goaded. "It *mussst* exissst as a monument, a blasssted ruin. A bone-ssstrewn offering."

"To whom?"

Sidney didn't reply. Instead he wandered, head down as if contemplating the dust at his feet, hands clasped at the small of his back, tapping softly together.

"The Sisstersss," Fear said after a moment's pause. "Or the beingsss they ssserve—that'ssss who it'ssss for, isssn't it?"

"Have a care with your tone, brother," Sidney responded.

"Well, isssn't it?" Fear persisted. "That'sss to whom we owe our anti-life exissstencesss, after all." Fear looked around the shadowy room. "But how to explain Nausssea and Phobia'ssss absssence now, given how rarely they leave your ssside... are they otherwissse occupied?"

"It'ssss no sssecret that they have projectsss of their own that require their attention."

"I'll warrant that it'sss *them* who are pussshing for thisss rapid turnaround in resultssss. Are you *disssappointing* them, Sssidney?" Fear's voice took on a sickly aspect, sing-song yet dripping with malicious intent. "Are you not the masssster of the apocalypssse that they believed you to be? Have they dessserted you in favour of a more *productive* ssservant?"

De'Ath flew across his office and squared up to the other Judge, the darkness in the room appearing to swell and shift as if excited by the exchange. There were more eyes watching them than they had perhaps realised. The air became heated, motes flickering in the purple blackness like miniature flashes of lightning as the pressure increased. Fire seemed to be reacting to the new atmospheric conditions, his orange halo fading to green and blue, and he held up a skeletal hand to watch the flames flare and spark before casting an enquiring look at Mortis. The other Dark Judge simply gave the smallest shake of the head, warning against further questions, and returned his attention to his warring brothers, who growled softly as they sized each other up. He watched for long moments, fascinated, having never seen an outburst like this before; there'd been plenty of violence meted out against the living since the start of the new regime, but it hadn't ever been turned inwards. Fear and the Chief were snapping and hissing at one another like predators over a carcass.

In Mortis's clinical mind, he idly wondered how such a fight would manifest itself, on what resources the two would draw to settle their differences, but it was only a fleeting fancy. Conflict between the two would achieve nothing. He stepped forward and raised a hand. "Enough, brotherssss," he said stridently. The low rumble of antagonism between the pair ceased as they turned to look at him, then stepped back, the tension broken. The shadows ceased their roiling.

"Sssuch petty sssquabbling ill befitsss thisss office and all it ssstandsss for," Mortis remarked. "We have a common enemy, don't you agree? Our energiessss are better placed in eradicating that enemy."

"Indeed," Sidney responded, drawing himself up as if trying to pull back some dignity. "We ssshould be directing our ire at the criminalsss, not allowing it to conssssume oursselves. Ssssuch passssion for jussstice ssssometimessss... sssseeksss an outlet."

"An outlet, aye," Fear muttered.

"Asss it happensss, I may have a ssssolution to the issssue of fasssster massss annihilation," Mortis continued. "The Red Mosssquito project."

"I thought that had foundered," Fire said, his flames now orange and red again as the ethereal spirits withdrew and the background pressure returned to normal.

"It'ssss true that I had encountered sssome difficultiessss. The enzyme I had ordered produced was too powerful; it burnt itsssself out even as it killed. Livesssstock it wassss introduced to through their food chain all collapsed and died in a matter of hourssss... but it wasssn't being passssed from animal to animal—the Mosssquito lossst power and dissipated."

"No one in your tek team could come up with a way to make it work?" De'Ath asked.

"No, every iteration, every experiment, every variation in the methodsss, all produced the sssame resssult. It wassss, esssentially, too good at what it did, and wasss coming apart in its eagernessss to kill cell growth. I had my lab ssstaff toiling day and night on the conundrum to no effect. It wasss unfortunate that one of my bessst mindsss chossse to run, and died before we could return him here."

"Sssstender," Fear hissed.

"Yess, Ssstender. But it wasss that very notion of intelligence assss an absstration—what the besssst sscientific headsss can achieve—that took me in a new direction."

"Go on," De'Ath prompted.

"The ssscientissstss in my tek-lab, all I needed from them wassss their mindsss. Their bodiesss and their physssical pressssence were of no interessst to me. Sssso I ssseparated the two, created a linked intelligence unit—I plugged their brainsss together—sssslaved to the technology I've been employing on the psssi-ampsss. It boossssted their calculating and cognitive power to a phenomenal degree."

"Brother Mortisss, kindly cut to the chassse," Sidney interjected, exasperation creeping into his voice. "How would thissss aid usss in our grand ssslaughter?"

"By broadcasssting *suggessstion*. Red Mosssquito wouldn't work asss a conventional virusss, but what if we ssseeded the *idea* in the headsss of the living sssurvivorsss that all their food wassss infected? That everything they ate, or wanted to eat, wasss not fit for consssumption. All wasss rotten. Dissseasssed." Mortis became more animated as he spoke; putrefaction was his favourite topic. "They would ssstarve themsselvessss, ssssucumb to madnesss assss they were driven by a hunger for food they believe they cannot touch."

"I like it," Fear remarked. It was right inside his wheelhouse. "They die through their own fearsss."

"Quite ssso," Mortis said. "The young, old and infirm would perisssh firssst. They would ssssimply wassste away."

"Interesssting," De'Ath muttered. "How long before we'd ssstart ssseeing resultsss?"

"A matter of daysss, I believe. Weeksss at the mossst. Humanity issss intrinsically weak when it comes to sssusstenance. Ssssome may turn to cannibalisssm, but the Mosssquito would taint that too. Of courssse, if they ssstart eating each other, the end resssult is the sssame."

"And you think you can get your..."

"Top mindsss," Mortis said.

"Top mindsss to influence sssso many of the wretched law-breakersss at once?"

"I believe ssso. They have lived and breathed the project for ssso long—ssstripped of their external ssstimuli, they will radiate nothing elssse. Hooked up to the amp, they will broadcassst relentlessssly, and the Mosssquito will fly as a meme, a repeated concept that will gain sssignificance in the targetsss' headsss, passssed from one to another ass an idea. An idea that becomesss real through their collective psyche: *Don't eat. Don't eat. Don't eat.*"

"An audaciousss plan," Fire said, nodding his head approvingly.

"Let the criminalssss face up to jussstice themssselvess," Fear agreed. "Let the hand of God sssmite them with a divine famine of their own making."

De'Ath's ego puffed up suddenly at the notion, warming to the idea. This was the sort of thing a vengeful god would do—plagues and natural disasters hadn't shifted them, so let starvation do the trick. Lay waste to them all. Let them lie down and cease to be.

"Pusssh the button, brother Mortis," Sidney said, relishing the drama of the moment. "Releassse the Mossquito."

PHOBIA AND NAUSEA knew he was coming, of course, many moments before he appeared at their doorway. Their psychic energies were such that they could be operating at several different levels at once: conducting spells and communing with their parent entities on the other side of the veil, and simultaneously intimately aware of what was going on in the Hall of Injustice. Their minds pervaded every room, every corridor, a constant roving eye that surveilled the building and its inhabitants with an unblinking glare. No one escaped their attention. As such, they felt Sidney's rare trips to the bowels of the building well in advance. If he was hoping to catch them unawares, then he sorely underestimated their powers; but such was his growing arrogance, the witches thought, he probably *did* believe he could move around within these walls at liberty, free from their sight. Perhaps he considered himself a blank spot, a null-figure, empty of emotion and conventional thought that they wouldn't be able to get a fix on him: dead, inside and out. But on the contrary, he radiated a psychopathic zeal for butchery that indelibly marked him out in their minds.

"Hello, brother," Nausea greeted him the instant his silhouette filled the doorway, her eyes barely leaving the contents of their cauldron. Green wisps curled around her head. "What bringssss you to our ssssanctum?"

"Sssisstersss," De'Ath acknowledged. "I trusssst you are keeping bussssy."

"Asss ever," Nausea replied, with a clandestine eye-roll for her sibling. "Thissss planet won't kill itssself." Sidney truly was an officious, humourless buffoon, she thought, micro-managing the end of the world. He sucked all the fun out of it. Once, his inventive cruelty and disregard for life as a child had made him an attractive proposition, and his blossoming into monstrousness as soon as he became a Judge marked him as a worthy candidate for being their harbinger of the apocalypse. It didn't take much for them to encourage him to seek them out so he could take the next step and go beyond mortality. But now... now he was becoming insufferable, egotistically driven to believe that the global genocide was of his design. Admittedly, they had to take some of the blame—it was them that had gifted him the pedestal that he was now hoisting himself upon—but neither twin had perhaps fully anticipated what a colossal prick Sidney truly was, or would turn into. Hence, they were increasingly preferring to remain down here in their private chambers when they could, where they could conjure, free of his interference and, frankly, his company.

"Isss that Cafferly?" he asked, pointing at the severed head positioned above the Sisters' receptacle. Its jaw was moving slightly, as if grinding its teeth, while emerald smoke entered its nose and mouth.

"Yesss, ssshe'sss helping usss with a ssspecial assssignment," Phobia replied dismissively. She had no desire to expound further; what they were using her for was for their eyes only. "Did you want sssomething, Sssidney?"

For a moment, the Great Leveller looked a little lost. "I know there hasss been... disssapointment from your sssponsssorsss at the lack of progressss. I've ssssenssed the pressssure to deliver better resssultsss."

Humility from De'Ath? Phobia exchanged a psi-glance with her sister, who responded in kind. This was a new one. Could it be the task had proved more challenging than he thought?

"We've become aware of a certain level of impatience," Nausea said.

The Judge nodded. "Let them know that the matter *isss* in hand. I will not fail them, you can be asssured of that."

"You have a new ssscheme in mind?"

"We do. Mortisss will be sssetting it in motion in due coursssse. If it goessss to plan, thisss could be the world'ssss breaking point."

"Hallelujah to that," Phobia answered.

De'Ath nodded again and looked around the witches' lair. "I will not fail," he repeated quietly, sounding as if he was convincing himself. "All life *will* be dessstroyed. This world *will* be a fit boneyard for your masssterss. You have my word."

CHAPTER TWENTY-FOUR

"*I TOLD YOU THIS WAS A DAMN FOOL DIRECTION TO TAKE!*" Misha screamed, then instantly regretted it. The instant she'd pulled down the scarf and opened her mouth, she felt hard, thrumming bodies hitting her tongue and teeth. Barbed feet clawed at the inside of her cheeks and gums, and she gagged, spitting the interlopers out, curling a finger inside to fish out a few that had dug in. Doing this while still clinging on to Hawkins as she cranked the Lawrider up to eighty miles an hour was no easy task; even more so when they were engulfed in a swarm. She hitched the scarf back up into place and admonished herself for her stupidity—the Judge wouldn't hear her anyway, over the roar of the engine and the squealing buzz of the thousands of insects swirling around their heads. Her anger had got the better of her, and now she had the oily taint of bug carapaces at the back of her throat. Just the thought made the bile rise again, and she made a concerted effort to swallow it back down; she didn't need to be spewing at this speed, and having it wash back into her face. That really would put a cap on the day.

Misha put her head down and screwed her eyes shut, praying it would be over soon, doing her best to tune out the bug-splat pelleting her helmet and the high-pitched whine that invaded her ears like white noise. For all the ire she reserved for herself, there was nevertheless some truth to the matter, and a certain level of self-justification: she *had* advised Hawkins against going this way. Once the bike they'd taken from Blake had been refuelled and recharged, the older woman had been keen to put as much distance from the capital as possible, tearing down the highways that bisected the scrub to the city's west. Whatever had passed between the two officers—and Hawkins refused to be drawn, so Misha had to surmise she'd taken him out in self-defence and decided not to push for details—it had left the Judge even more withdrawn and uncommunicative. When she did respond to the teen's queries, she merely muttered that looking for resistance cells in the metropolis was a waste of time, and that nothing living was to be found within its boundaries. The girl didn't argue with that; she was only too happy to be heading in the opposite direction to the Hall of Injustice and the shadow cast by the Sisters.

So instead they barrelled across the Badlands, and Misha felt the pressure lift from her skull, the psychic probing fade away to an irritating hum. That had brought something resembling relief. But the radio on the new wheels was no more successful in picking up chatter than its predecessor, and on the few occasions when they took breaks, parking way off from the edge of the road so as not to be visible, Hawkins would spend hours trying the full bandwidth, hoping to hear just the merest hint of a voice. Sometimes, she'd talk into the comms unit and have a conversation with the imaginary receiver, explaining their location and predicament. Misha would be lying some distance away, trying to catch a little sleep, listening and trying not to let the hopelessness subsume her. The Judge would always come away and intimate that she'd unearthed a hint of law-enforcement traffic on the airwaves, and Misha would smile and nod and look encouraging, but she knew they were chasing ghosts at this point. The broadcasts—if indeed they existed—were surely automatic, the senders long dead.

But it was her belief that she had the inside track on the source of a Judicial transmission that made Hawkins make one of her very rare bad calls. By and large, her decisions up to this point were usually sound, grounded either in pragmatism or a sense of duty , but Misha wondered if a certain degree of desperation was starting to colour her critical faculties. She couldn't blame her—they'd been searching for this fabled resistance for so long now, any straw to clutch was one she was going to grab with both hands, a reason to keep going, to live. So when she heard what sounded like very faint official code originating somewhere north-east of their current location, she insisted they head towards it.

"But that's farm-belt territory," the girl had protested. "You've heard the stories of what's up there."

<That was months ago. The area's dead, there's nothing left to feed on.>

"Precisely because of the mutant fucking locusts eating anything in their path."

<And they would've moved on. They're not going to stick around with no food source.>

"And your jay-friends *would?* If they *are* there, they're operating out of a decimated zone with no crops to harvest and no supplies to salvage. Plus you've got no date on when that message was broadcast—it could've been cycling since the Fall, for all you know. It's too risky, Hawkins."

The Judge had an expression that she pulled when she was not going to be dissuaded—her scar tissue hardened further before the girl's eyes, the facial equivalent of shutters being pulled down—and Misha saw it then, resolve deepening across her features in the space of a couple of seconds. She knew there was going to be no reasoning with the older woman, and it was either accompany her or go their separate ways.

<I can't afford to ignore it,> Hawkins signed. <There's too much potential to dismiss it and run scared. Gotta check it out.>

"What was it you said? Trust no one?"

The Judge shrugged. <You want to stay put, let me know where to drop you off.>

Of course Misha had gone with her—what the hell else was she going to do? But her unease had deepened as they'd cut through field after field of devastated farmland, the earth grey and sterile. The few buildings they encountered looked as if a succession of tornadoes had torn across the land: roofs were caved in, windows smashed. Even the doors to the storm cellars had been wrenched open or holes punched in them like a great fist had repeatedly pounded on the wood. It reminded the girl of the basement sanctuary she and a number of her fellow survivors had lived in for a spell before it too became compromised. Huge rusted pieces of machinery were toppled over, tractors lying on their sides with their massive tyres in the air like fallen beasts that hadn't been able to right themselves—dinosaurs in tar pits, Misha had thought. There was very little sign of human life apart from a handful of skeletons lying amidst the rubble, and one picked-clean bag of bones hanging disconcertingly from the branches of a tree, picked up and deposited there by the sheer force of the whirlwind that had powered through. It was a disaster area, but no one was coming to its aid.

She'd considered numerous times when to suggest to the Judge that this was a bust, that they were needlessly putting themselves in danger pursuing a dead signal (or, to Misha's mind, a fantasy), but she knew Hawkins was seeing all this. She wasn't blind to the terrain they were heading into, yet she kept to her course, constantly tuning and retuning the radio for a stronger or updated broadcast. When she suddenly hit a wall of static that rhythmically fluctuated, she became so excited she slew the bike to the side of the road the better to concentrate.

<You see?> she'd animatedly signed. <Must be close.>

Misha had wished she could've shared the Judge's enthusiasm as she looked around at the dark and silent thoroughfare they'd stopped on, eerily desolate and far from anything resembling shelter. She felt exposed and vulnerable. She had to admit, there was something emanating from the radio that sounded different to the usual monotone, but it wasn't enough to assuage her fears.

"What *is* that?" Hawkins had croaked, craning an ear to the speaker. "Is that... voices?"

"Can't hear anything that resembles words," the girl replied. "Just a drone, from what I can tell."

<It's pitching differently. More organic than a simple lost signal.>

"Well, where's it coming from?"

"It's near, very near..." the Judge whispered. "It's in this vicinity."

She gunned the engine and they proceeded at a slower pace, trundling forward while she kept her head cocked to the comms-unit, alive to any changes. It did seem to be getting louder with every few dozen feet they travelled, and finally in the distance they could discern two sets of red lights gleaming in the dusk. As they got closer, they saw it was the back end of an articulated lorry slanted at forty-five degrees, while the cab had planted itself in the ditch that ran alongside the tarmac, and wedged beneath the truck's undercarriage were the compacted remains of a station wagon that had virtually had its roof sliced off by the impact. Judging by the tyre marks on the highway, both vehicles must've been going at some speed at the point of collision and dragged each other off to one side. Hawkins pulled up alongside and dismounted, but made a point to leave the engine running.

"Just going to take a look," she muttered before accentuating with her hands: <Stay there.>

"Is this the source of the transmission?" Misha whispered.

<Looks like,> the Judge signed, then walked towards the crash site, flicking on her torch and playing it over the scene. Misha caught a nightmarish glimpse of what had happened to the occupants of the car before Hawkins' torch-beam flicked away and settled elsewhere as she headed towards the cab.

The teenager slouched back on the Lawrider's pillion and cast an eye at the vehicle. The truck was Justice Department-affiliated—one of the many contractors supplying farm produce. That might explain the Judicial code Hawkins had originally heard, since the driver would be instructed in their use. But there was nothing here that was going to help them. The presumably vegetative contents of the trailer were rotting to high heaven, and it was highly doubtful anyone aboard was still alive—

Misha suddenly realised that the Judge was returning to the bike at speed, the torch-beam bobbing before her. She sat up, concerned, aware that the drone-like rasp of the broadcast was playing again... before it struck her that the sound was coming from beyond the Lawrider's receiver and was actually a background hum that filled the air. Confused, she opened her mouth to fire a question at Hawkins just as she swung her leg back over the bike and twisted the throttle, but the older woman was in no mood to answer her.

"Bad idea," was all she said as the tyres screeched and they shot off, past the crashed vehicles, and barrelled down the empty stretch of highway. The drone was still there, and getting incrementally louder.

Hawkins took one hand off the handlebars momentarily and hitched up the neck of her uniform, covering what little of her face was visible below the helmet. "Wrap something around your mouth," she called over the roar of the engine, casting an eye over her shoulder at Misha.

"What is it?" the girl shouted back, then twisted around and saw for herself as a black cloud swirled from where the lorry had been lying and began to sweep after them. "Aw, crap." She fumbled in her jacket pocket and pulled out a scarf, which she quickly looped around her mouth and nose. The swarm was already outpacing them, and the first of the insects were ricocheting off the bike or pattering against her back.

"Truck driver's CB radio was still broadcasting to an open channel," Hawkins yelled. "He was long dead, of course. The static we were picking up, it was the locusts... feeding."

Anger had risen in Misha's gullet and she'd cut loose, unable to stop herself, and got a mouthful of chitinous winged bullets as a consequence.

It was already dark; now, as the pulsating swarm descended, it was like driving through a sandstorm: visibility was practically zero. She clung to Hawkins and hoped the Judge could maintain their course despite it being virtually impossible to see anything more than a few feet ahead. Claustrophobia gnawed at her, and her heart thudded madly. It felt like the locusts were sucking out all the oxygen, as the densely packed bodies crowded around her head; it was hard enough breathing through the scarf, but now she was gulping down panicky snatches of air as if she was drowning.

Her body was alive with a million crawling things, and it was all she could do not to scream and release her grip on Hawkins and swat away at the countless creatures that were invading every available inch. She knew the Judge was feeling it too—she sensed the older woman tremble and stiffen, and beneath her she could feel the Lawrider pick up speed as Hawkins' instinct to flee at all costs got the better of her. They were tearing along now, to all intents and purposes blind to what was in front of them, and the incessant buzzing meant they'd been lowered into a pit of white noise. All senses had been blunted—nothing but animalistic fear was guiding them. Misha, in some rational part of her brain, knew that they had to slow down, that they were travelling at high velocity into the unknown, but she just wanted them to break free of the swarm, to burst out of its clutches.

Hawkins didn't see the car wreck until they were mere moments away from hitting it; she had time to emit a strangled cry of shock as the bike's headlights illuminated it abandoned in the middle of the road. The computer flashed up a collision warning, but they were going at such a speed as to make avoiding it impossible. The Judge valiantly attempted to wrench the Lawrider's steering to one side, squeezing hard on the brakes, but they still clipped the vehicle's left wing. There was a tremendous screech of tearing metal, and the next thing

Misha knew they were being flipped into the air, weightless for a fraction of a second, before hitting the tarmac with a bone-jarring thump, skidding and rolling for a hundred more yards.

It took her a full half-minute to gather her bearings, ears ringing, head throbbing. She looked back down the road and saw the eviscerated remains of the bike spread across the thoroughfare, portions of it sprinkled liberally from one side to the other. The wreck they'd hit had been shunted off the highway entirely, its front end having done a full three-sixty so the skeletal driver was now grinning in her direction. Must've got a flat, Misha thought absently. Didn't make it, and was eaten where he sat at the wheel. Or he starved to death, unable to leave the confines of the car, which became his tomb.

Get up, girl, a rather more strident voice cut through her dazed musings. *Get up before you're stripped, flensed, and digested where you lie.*

She staggered to her feet and turned her attention to the other direction, where the seemingly unconscious form of Hawkins was sprawled several feet away. Cursing, Misha limped over towards her, acutely aware both of the sharp ache in her left leg that suggested something was torn, sprained or badly bruised, and also of the persistent buzzing now starting to filter through her regained senses. Hard flying bodies were pattering against her, and she yelped, panic coming to the fore. She reached the Judge and rolled her on to her back, the older woman still breathing but refusing to stir, no matter how loud the teen screamed in her face or shook her by the shoulders. Locusts crawled over her helmeted visage, and were getting in Misha's too, despite her best efforts to effectively swaddle it with her scarf. The swarm was descending.

"Oh, God, oh, God," she breathed, looking around frantically. There was no way she could carry the Judge, or even drag her; in any case where was she going to go? There was no immediate shelter to head towards, nowhere they could flee to in time. Then a shimmer on the tarmac caught her eye, which took a second for her to identify: gasoline from the

Lawrider's ruptured tanks. It had leaked across the road. She reached into Hawkins' boot holster and pulled the Lawgiver free, remembering what the Judge had told her about the palm-encoded security system—nobody but Hawkins would be able to fire it without it self-detonating—and forced it into the woman's gauntleted right hand, curling her finger into the trigger guard before aiming as best she could at the fuel spray and the bike's wreckage. She squeezed and a bullet ignited the gas, a spark travelling along the line of liquid back to the Lawrider and the whole thing went up, an orange fireball blossoming into the dark sky.

The insects swirled around the sudden explosion, clouds of them incinerated by the wall of heat. The inferno provided an instant relief, the swarm dispelled. Blackened bodies hit the ground like carbonised hail, powdering into sooty smears. Misha couldn't help but let out a victorious laugh as she watched the locusts shrivel up around her. She holstered the gun, and then got an arm under Hawkins', lifting her to her feet, eliciting a groan from the Judge.

"C'mon, you tough old bird," the girl muttered. "I need you to help me out, here. Fire's not going to keep them at bay for long. We gotta get under cover."

She took a few steps but near collapsed, Hawkins' weight pushing her to her knees as the pain in her leg made her gasp. She sobbed, got to her feet and grabbed the Judge's uniform with two hands and pulled, desperate now. "C'mon!" It was useless. She let go and sat, head bowed, resigned.

She didn't know how long she'd been sitting there—three minutes? ten?—when she heard the sound of engines. Looking up, she saw multiple bright white headlamps getting bigger as they headed in her direction. Without thinking, she reached out and clasped Hawkins' hand, gripping it tight, and waited for the newcomers' arrival.

CHAPTER TWENTY-FIVE

Colm had always figured that the best way for him and his boy to survive was to go it alone. He'd seen the long refugee trains flooding out of the cities, desperately attempting to escape the genocide, and made a conscious decision not to join their ranks, choosing instead for the pair of them to forge their own path. His son had thought differently at the time, and pleaded with his father to seek safety in numbers, but Colm was adamant that it was a bad idea. Big groups always factionalised and grew tense, he'd said, and inevitably things would fall apart. Then there were leadership squabbles and accusations of dishonesty or greed; contagions swept through camps as they shared cooking utensils or washing facilities; and there was always a difference of opinion on the easiest and quickest route to a destination no one could agree on. No, Colm knew all too well just what happens when you put a number of people—starving, scared people, fleeing for their lives—in a pressure-cooker environment such as that. Human beings naturally found comfort in their peers at times of stress, and mistakenly believed that by clinging to one another they made it harder for the enemy to pick them off. On the contrary—in Colm's experience, it just made it more convenient for the Judges to find you.

He had some history with waging war on Justice Department—

and as a consequence picking the most practical way to pass beneath their radar—since his juve days. He'd been a pro-democracy agitator for as long as he could hold a spray-can, and ran with different cells as he grew older, each more militant than the last. What started as anti-authoritarian troublemaking in his early teens with a gang of his schoolmates that never extended much beyond scrawling tags and obscenities on government property, Colm found himself graduating to protest and sabotage as he fell in with the direct-action crowd—Jensen, Gabriel, Struckers and the young Loxley—picking up a few scars from brutally applied Judges' batons when the marches got dispersed. He even did a two-month stretch for disorderly conduct. The jaybirds never deterred him, though, merely strengthened his resolve: the fascist system needed tearing down, there was no question of that.

It was inevitably a girl that drew him deeper into the democracy circle, and eventually to their paramilitary wing. He and Lara killed their first Judge together, and more than likely conceived the boy the same night, and their union felt like a new dawn, that something pure and genuine could arise out of the violent resistance. They were together for seven more years, drifting between the pro-dem outfits, never allying themselves with one for too long, for they knew that Justice Department was watching, and underground groups that got too big or established became complacent and sloppy, and were then infiltrated and raided. Every so often they saw their colleagues executed by televised firing squad. Colm and Lara were wanted felons, and they had their son to protect, so they kept acquaintances and ties to a minimum, the better to walk away at a moment's notice. During this time, they murdered a further dozen badges, becoming expert in the art of assassination—they even got their own serial-killer media handle, the 'Snuffkins,' on account of the cutesy icon Lara had devised, which they'd draw at the scene in the victim's blood. Her thinking was that it completely devalued the seriousness of the act, made the deaths a joke at the expense of the Grand

Hall, which would only enrage Chief Drabbon even more (on that score, by all accounts, it worked spectacularly well). They would have gone on and dispatched twice that number if their luck hadn't finally run out, and their latest target got off a rogue ricocheting Lawgiver round as he died that went straight through Lara's right eye. She hit the sked, half her skull missing.

Grief-stricken, a panicking Colm doubled down on their reclusiveness and took the boy as far off the grid as he could, reasoning there were few they could trust. In any case, Lara's face was splashed all over the news and the trashzines—one half of the Snuffkins, snuffed out—and any fellow dems would deny ever being affiliated with him, or knowing who he was, once the jays started following the trail. He shielded his son from it as well he could, impressed on him that Father knew best (Mom had landed a job overseas, he told him), and was looking into how they could smuggle themselves abroad (where they could 'meet up with her'), when the weird shit started going down. Some kind of coup at the top was what he heard, though the reports of half-dead Judges indiscriminately slaughtering the citizens made him shiver as he imagined the corpses of his and Lara's kills coming back to claim revenge. Whatever the truth behind what was going on, he and his kid had to get out of there.

So it was just the two of them, eschewing company and making their own way in this new world order. Some radical part of him acknowledged that this development showed that his and Lara's past bloody political action had been justified—that the Judges were only ever one step away from this kind of mass cull of the populace, and if anything the Snuffkins should've taken even more down when they had the chance—but mostly he was tired of the carnage. This was no future for anyone.

They were traipsing through thick woodland, and the boy was complaining he was hungry, which he did often. Their supplies were dwindling, and they'd have to hunt again, if they could find edible wildlife, but they still had some strips of dried rabbit meat in his backpack, which would do in the interim. He told his son to hold up, and he slung the rucksack off his shoulders, head buzzing all of a sudden and his throat scratchy—tiredness, he thought, and dehydration. He was about to reach in when what he saw inside made him exclaim aloud in disgust and sling the pack away from him into the foliage.

"Dad?" the boy enquired querulously, frightened at the expression that was now etched on his father's face.

"Rotten..." Colm intoned, eyes wide and turned towards his son. "It's all *rotten*..."

The backpack trembled where it lay, split open, and a cloud of black flies issued forth, filling his vision forever.

"SSSISSTER," NAUSEA MURMURED, face wreathed in the steam emerging from the cauldron. "I'm channelling sssomething... I've got a trace."

"Oh, yesss? Our errant ssssibling?"

"Aye, I think sssso. Ssshe'ssss panicking, in dissstressss... It'sss forced her to drop her guard."

"We mussst be quick, dear heart, before ssshe realisssesss. Can you pinpoint a location?"

"That'sss up to Cafferly," Nausea replied, casually motioning to the disembodied head suspended above the wide pot. Its eyes rolled in their sockets, and its jaw ground relentlessly as if it was chewing cud. "Ssshe'sss our tracker."

"What are you reading from the ssssubject?"

"Excesssive levelsss of adrenaline... heartbeat'sss raissssed... fear factor'sss ssspiking. Rapid pulssse is making her psssignature flasssh like a sssiren."

"You're sssure it'sss her?"

"Without quesssstion. The tassste is ssso familiar."

Phobia joined her sister at the cauldron, glancing up as she did so. "Cafferly ssseeemss more animated than usssual."

"Ssshe can't dissguissse familial recognition."

"I guesss not." Phobia laid her arms on the receptacle's lip and placed her chin upon them in a juvenile fashion, watching the strands of vapour curl in the air, colours morphing within them, like a child studiously fascinated by a soap bubble. "She'sss been sssoo hard to pin down up to now… I wonder what'sss got her goossssey-gander up."

"Fright'sss a primal inssstinct. It'sss impossssible to manage or control. If ssshe'sss in fear of her life, there'sss no way ssshe'd be able to ssstop usss tracing her thoughtssss. The barrierssss are down."

"Ssshe could be about to die. In which cassse we may well lossse her forever."

"There isss alwaysss that risssk, though death, of coursssse, is a sssomewhat moveable feassst thessse dayssss. The sssignal'sss weak ssso ssshe'sss not nearby. We'd have to mobilissse unitsss ssstraight away."

"Then work your magic, darling Rachel," Phobia sang, swaying and raising her arms above her head in Cafferly's direction. "Find your sssisster. Find Misssha. Direct usss to her sssso we may reunite the two of you!"

Templeton wasn't sure when his own larder started to creep him out, but the feeling was unmistakeable now. It was weird—like a creeping sense of unease, or déjà vu from a dream he could no longer remember, just trace impressions lingering in his mind. He would stand on the threshold and pause, reluctant to enter, hand hovering next to the light switch, convinced that something was lurking within, or there was an unexplained reason why he should avoid stepping inside. At first it was just a moment's hesitation—an instinctual glance round the door frame as if expecting a figure to be there, a second blink when a blur at the corner of his eye caught his attention—but the room would give nothing away, stubbornly prosaic. Now, though, the sensation that something was very askew was overwhelming, as if it was radiating maliciousness, and a sick gnawing dread clawed at his gut whenever he approached it.

It had been a full five days since he'd eaten anything substantial, such was his refusal to go near the chamber. He had some root vegetables sprouting in the patch round the back of the house that he'd tried to chew on, but they tasted rancid, as if the soil itself was poisoning them, their skin filigreed with black cankers. Boiling them, mashing them, it made no difference—the rot was deep in the fibre. The hunger might've been eating him alive, but it was the knowledge that he had canned produce at his fingertips that he could consume if he could only summon the courage to retrieve it was worse. All that stock he'd carefully hoarded, all those measures he'd taken the moment he'd seen the riots on TV, the districts on fire around the Grand Hall, and he was going to skeletonise right in the middle of it, waste away surrounded by so much. He felt like one of those ancient pharaohs he'd read about at school, buried with their fortune to aid them in the afterlife; or perhaps more pertinently, one of those misers that got locked inside their own vaults at the end of the story in a horror comic, doomed to suffocate within the golden walls of their own privilege and greed.

Could this be divine retribution, he wondered. It seemed personal, a fate precision-engineered just for him by a deity with an eye for the ironic. But he didn't feel he deserved this, that it was a worthy punishment. Being prepared, reading the runes accordingly and taking steps to make sure you had enough when the world fell down outside your door—that surely wasn't a crime. Yes, he'd had to turn away many looking for sanctuary—a mansion like Templeton's attracted more than a few hungry, exhausted refugees, who saw his estate as easy pickings, and were willing to negotiate the high walls and motion-activated garden defences in a bid to gain access to what they assumed (rightly, it had to be said) was a bulging kitchen. You didn't protect a house like this to the extent of hiding tripwires in the topiary if you didn't have something worth stealing. He'd watched them on the CCTV, ripping themselves on the barbed wire or blown sky-high by the landmines, and felt not an ounce of responsibility. If they'd done as he had—filled their basements or outhouses with the supplies needed to survive the apocalypse—then they'd have no need to take what wasn't theirs. But no, they'd ignored the warning signs, and so were reaping the consequences. That wasn't his problem. The few of them that managed to enter the inner grounds and made it almost to his front step he met with his shotgun and gave a short, uncomplicated directive. Few, if any, complied, and he had no hesitation in pulling the trigger, their bodies ending up heaped over by the compost bins. But wasn't he justified? Wasn't he within his rights to preserve what was his? Share, and you're left with nothing.

No, this felt a cruel, vindictive response to a perfectly reasonable belief in one's own private property. To be surrounded by the spoils of one's canny foresight and not be able to touch it—to starve mere feet away from sustenance—was simply... well, *evil*. Templeton had never believed much in a deity before, but if one did exist, this simply proved that it was a very capricious entity. To plant this seed in his head, to allow it to fester, were the actions of one that delighted in suffering. As he'd explained to the last raggedy urchin that had circumvented the armed turrets and razorgrass to rap on his parlour window, *he* was the real victim here.

"Don't you see?" he'd wailed, one hand clutching at his breast, the other pointing both barrels at the teen. "I'm *dying* here! I'm being tortured to death! I have no more than you do!"

The kid hadn't understood, of course, and dismissed his cries as the ravings of a madman; in fact, he'd tried to push past Templeton and sought access to the house, so the man had no choice but to blow him in two. He'd taken no pleasure in the act, but felt instead that he'd been forced to demonstrate just how desperate he was—the hell that he was living through, that he wouldn't want others, even his worst enemy, to experience.

He had no doubt that if the youngster had been in his shoes, he would've done the same. *Keep away,* he would've said. *Keep out. There's nothing for you here.*

Since that boy, there'd been no further survivors that had tried to scale his walls, which Templeton put down to the Judges' increased efficiency in wiping out stragglers. The uniforms had yet to knock on his door, but he had no doubt they'd turn up eventually. What they'd find, he didn't know—he suspected he wouldn't be around to welcome them. The hunger pangs were making him delirious, and he felt weak and sick, as if he was one fall away from never getting up again; all his strength was deserting him. Often his feet instinctively guided him back to the larder in the hope that he would finally overcome his anxieties and manage at last to eat something, but it was never successful—no matter how nauseous or shaky he felt, he couldn't take that step. He was *afraid* of what was in there, and it was going to kill him.

He reeled where he stood outside the kitchen, crying, starving and in pain, a man alone in his mansion, ravaged by starvation yet surrounded by opulence. He felt like he was shrinking, that the great house was consuming him; he was becoming insignificant, translucent. In yet another fit of frustration, he lurched towards the foodstuffs cupboard, knowing he wouldn't be able to touch anything but desperately needing the comfort of a full belly.

Turn away, turn away, the voice in his head said as he flittered in and out of consciousness. *This is not for you. It's all* ROTTEN—

Templeton yelled and tugged open the door, and a cloud of buzzing black flies emerged, stripping him of what remained of his sanity.

"How goessss it, Mortissss?"

The Dark Judge looked up from his deliberations and paused before answering. It was impossible to say if there was any sense of surprise in his expression, given the skull was as inscrutable as ever, but from his physical demeanour, he evidently wasn't expecting visitors. He looked back at his machine briefly, adjusted a few controls, then returned his baleful gaze to the new arrival.

Is he afraid of me, Nausea pondered. The notion should be beyond any of the apocalyptic horsemen she and her sister had helped usher into being—such emotional responses had long been burnt out of them by the Fluids. Yet there was certainly a hesitancy about him that she found deliciously intriguing.

"The network issss online and operational," Mortis answered.

"And issss it *working?*" the witch prompted, feeling like a schoolteacher extracting a response from an especially slow student.

"By all accountssss. Of courssse, you and your sssibling would have a better idea than me."

Touché, Nausea thought. Wasn't *he* the prickly customer? But he was right, naturally—she and Phobia could easily cast their minds out and pick up the distress flooding the ether, register the pain, fear and confusion that the Mosquito was causing. It was plain that Mortis's great project was achieving its function—she merely had to dip her toe in, psychically speaking, and she could feel the psychological wreckage that it was racking up. It was flying from receptive victim to receptive victim, spreading its disease.

"Yesss indeed," she said, smiling. "The devassstation it'sss wreaking isss mossst impressssive. What you've achieved here issss highly commendable." Nausea's smile hardened. "But my quessstion remainsss—*issss it working?* Are we ssseeing an acceleration in the numberssss judged?"

Mortis looked away again, tapped his taloned fingers against one of the receptacles housing the brains wired to the mainframe; it glowed from whatever sludge the Dark Judge had concocted for it to sit in and conduct its energy through. "In the long term, I think—"

"'Long term' doessssn't interesssst my masssterss. They want to ssssee resssultssss."

"The Red Mosssquito will kill millionssss, given the time and right application. Posssibly not right away, but the ssseedsss are in place—"

"And there'sss the rub," Nausea interrupted. "It'sss been live for closssse to a week. We expected to sssee a more... immediate essscalation."

"You have to give it the ssspace to perform—"

"The powersss are not willing to be ssso patient. They want a world picked clean, and they want it today, not yearsss down the line."

"They asssk the imposssssible—"

"Are you denying them?"

"...No."

"Then I sssugessst you turn up the heat, Brother Mortisss." She looked around at his set-up. "Get thessse minds working overtime. What do you sssay?"

"I will sssee what I can do, ssssister."

"That'sss the ssspirit."

...AND JESSICA PUT a flaming torch to the supply stores, holding back her protesting, weeping fellow survivors at gunpoint. "Don't you see?" she asked, watching the black flies spiral into the air to escape the blaze. "It's *rotten*... contaminated. We mustn't touch it."

Her stomach ached sympathetically as she watched the food burn, tears pricking her eyes. "We mustn't eat *any* of it."

CHAPTER TWENTY-SIX

Misha recalled little of how she came to end up in the compound. She remembered the lights emerging through the swarm, the high-powered beams of what turned out to be a pair of dune buggies dazzling her as they approached, and the fact that she couldn't get the ever-present drone of the locusts out of her head; it had been lodged there like tinnitus, a white-noise hum that echoed in her skull in the quietest of moments. But the events beyond that were decidedly hazy—she suspected she'd blacked out, though she couldn't say for certain that she hadn't been deliberately knocked unconscious. She ached like she'd done ten rounds in a ring with an enraged gorilla, that was for goddamn sure.

When she woke, she'd found herself lying on an honest to goodness bed, complete with sheets and a pillow. She hadn't lain on one since the night before the Fall, and it took her aback a little, like she wasn't sure if it was part of a dream she'd hadn't entirely disentangled herself from. She'd run her hand over the cool smoothness of the linen for several minutes, pushed her head back against the mattress's soft yield, listened to the creak of the springs as she shifted position, and—once she'd established that it was real and not a product of her mind—felt a raw pang for a simple luxury that she'd taken for granted back in her old life. The texture of it was so easy to succumb to. Briefly, she never wanted to be anywhere else, and curling up in the bed's embrace seemed as good a place as any to see out the end of days. But eventually curiosity overcame her torpor, and she rose, swinging her legs over the side, noting that someone had undressed her and robed her in a white shift. She looked around, but her clothes were nowhere to be seen.

Placing her bare feet on the wooden floorboards, she made an attempt at standing, then tried again several more times until she felt she could do it without the aid of the bedframe's support. Looking down, she realised that clean bandages had been strapped around her calf, and putting her weight on her limb made it feel tender and tight, though manageable. Whatever she'd done to it—a torn muscle or a sprain rather than a break, she suspected—it would take a while to feel back to normal. There was another bed on the other side of the Spartan room, upon which Hawkins was slumbering, and Misha limped across to her, suddenly aware of how fragile and old the Judge looked. Her breathing was shallow. She'd taken quite a beating from the crash, her face and arms a mosaic of bruises and lacerations, and surgical tape had been wound round her scalp. She too had lost her uniform, and perhaps most pertinently her gun. The young woman tentatively reached out to clasp her shoulder and see if she could rouse her, but decided against it, figuring she had plenty more healing to do. Of course, whether they had time to rest and recover was, as of this moment, unknown.

The chamber's only other features beyond a few sticks of furniture were a nearby window and a door, and Misha hobbled to the former, peering out at a street in what looked like a relatively untouched town. The room was evidently on the second or third storey, and it afforded her a decent view: she saw tall narrow houses lining a main thoroughfare , fronted with small, scraggly gardens, and at the end of a short side street was a grandiose civic building complete with Doric columns and large clock dominating its façade. None of it looked like it had suffered under the greys. What caught her eye in particular were the towering corrugated metal walls at the edges of the town, presumably encircling it entirely, with sentry posts at regular intervals. Somebody had turned this once small-town haven into a fortress, and had so far done a successful job at keeping genocidal forces at bay—or perhaps it had up to this point operated under the Grand Hall's radar.

It was quietly surreal, watching people go about their business—and there were a fair few regular folk conversing on the sidewalks, or sweeping their front steps or hanging out laundry—without any notion that they should be scrabbling for their lives. Misha's last few months had been purely about the need to survive, and anyone else she and Hawkins had met had equally been scared, starving refugees, fleeing systematic slaughter—but these people seemed to have been preserved in a bubble, unaffected by events beyond those high forbidding walls. They looked well fed, clean and serene, a snapshot of a Midwest community from years ago, well before the shit went down. If she didn't know better, Misha would've wondered if she'd gone back in time.

One detail that did stick out, however—and set alarm bells ringing—was the clothing: they were all, men, woman and children, wearing the exact same outfit (cream-coloured shirt and trousers, with workboots and wide-brimmed straw hat), which immediately screamed one word in the girl's head: *cult*. There was some enforced regulation or religion going on here, despite the seemingly civilised surface. It was a uniform, from what she could see, and it was unlikely that outsiders would be welcomed that didn't conform. That would no doubt explain why her and Hawkins' duds had been taken away.

She tried the door, but it was locked. Rattling the handle several times in vain, she knew there was nothing she could do but retreat to her bed and wait. As it happened, minutes later a key turned in the lock and a tall, handsome middle-aged Asian woman entered, clad like the others, bearing similar outfits in her arms. She smiled warmly when she saw Misha, closed the door behind her, and walked over, placing the folded shirt and trousers on the sheets beside where the teen was perched.

"Here," she said.

The girl glanced down at the clothes she'd been offered, then turned her attention back to the woman. "Where… where *are* we?"

"Libitina."

"Liberty…?"

The woman's smile grew broader and she shook her head. "Not quite, though we are blessed with an enviable level of freedom here. All are equal under God's eye. No, *Libitina*. We're about fifty miles south of Green River."

Misha tried to quickly navigate the mental geography, but got all turned around. Hawkins' wild-goose chase following the Justice Department signal had led them further into the northwest than she was familiar with, and she had no idea how far they'd been taken in the buggies that had come to their aid. In short, they could well be in the ass-end of anywhere.

"You rescued us… There were cars that came and picked us up…"

"Brother Peterson saw the flames, by all accounts, and went to investigate. It was opportune that he did—if he'd arrived any later, there wouldn't have been much left of you or your friend. You were right in the middle of a locust swarm."

Misha remembered pulling the trigger on Hawkins' gun and the wreck going up like a firework display. As it turned out, it had been a highly effective flare.

"He brought us here?"

"Mm-hmm. You were both in a bad shape—malnourished, exhausted, physically injured. We did our best to repair some of the damage, as you've no doubt seen, but you'll need significant recuperation." Seeing a plain wooden chair positioned near the door, she brought it over to Misha's bed before seating herself. "Can I ask something? That was bad territory you were in. That stretch of farm belt is notorious for the wildlife—most avoid it. How did you end up there?"

Misha laughed sardonically. "Chasing ghosts." When she saw the woman's quizzical expression, she clarified: "Hawkins," she said, nodding at the figure of the Judge on the other bed, "was following a signal she thought originated from a Justice Department cell. Turned out to be a bust."

"Ah."

"She's... obsessed with reuniting with those she thinks are still left alive from the Grand Hall coup. She's convinced that there's a resistance that she just needs to rendezvous with. But so far I've seen no evidence it exists."

"How long have you two been out there?"

"A few months, I think. I've lost track of the time. At least a couple of seasons have passed, I'm sure." Misha looked down at her hands. "Before she... saved me, I'm under the impression she'd been surviving this thing on her own since the Fall."

The woman glanced at Hawkins, then turned back to the girl, lowering her voice slightly. "You think she's afflicted?"

It struck Misha as a strange term, kind of antiquated. "Psychologically damaged, you mean?"

The woman nodded.

"Yes," she replied, feeling terrible for voicing what had been for so long unspoken, but at the same time relieved that it was no longer solely hers to bear. "I think a lot of what she's listening to are voices in her head. This squad of Judge rebels or whatever she thinks are out there... it's delusional. There's no underground, there's no one fighting back. Any jays still alive are fleeing to some imagined safe haven like everyone else." Misha raised her eyes to the rest of the room. "Somewhere like this, I guess. What is this—some kind of gated community?"

"Indeed. It started as a barricade... I'm sorry, I haven't introduced myself. Ashia." She extended a hand, which Misha shook. The woman's palm was dry and a little rough; it felt calloused by a lot of manual labour.

"Misha. Misha Cafferly."

"Pleasure to meet you, Misha. Yes, so, the founder, Father

Arnold, and a few others, they put up the barrier as a means to defend themselves against the ghouls, right at the beginning. That, and others seeking to take what wasn't theirs. Once they'd successfully repelled them, it started to develop as a town, as a way of life."

'Ghouls,' the teenager noted. Another odd expression, reducing the greys to creatures from some fairy story. It was almost as if Ashia was unaware of where they'd come from, what they were beyond mere agents of destruction. Perhaps she wasn't—maybe too little info had filtered this far from the capital. Someone like Sidney De'Ath, if she'd heard of him at all, was going to be nothing more than a devil figure, conducting his apocalypse from a throne of bones.

"You get no attacks?"

"Very rarely. Usually, it's more raiders trying their luck to storm the walls. But we have a rigorous defence system that disposes of them very efficiently."

"Nothing from the air?" Misha asked, thinking of the H-Wagons that she and her fellow survivors used to hide from regularly as they swooped across the land, searchlights scanning for signs of life.

"No," she answered as if she'd never considered it before. "Must be outside their flight pattern. I have to say," she added, "that we've never encountered any Judges either, so you would appear to be right about your friend's"—she nodded at Hawkins—"quest."

Misha nodded slowly. No shit, she thought. Just try to convince Hawkins of that. "So you get to live in peace here? The whole end-of-the-world thing seems to be passing you by."

"We're aware of our limited time on the mortal sphere. But we're trying to do it on our own terms. We're generally a pretty insular, self-regulating community. We don't accept new arrivals very often."

"I never said thank you," Misha remarked meekly. "For taking us in."

"Well," Ashia said, standing. "You have some healing to do first. I'll let you get some rest—I'll bring along food in a little while."

"Thank you," Misha said again. "Oh," she added, flipping with one hand through the clothes beside her, "what's with the get-up?"

"Arnold's idea," she replied, making her way to the door. "You'll meet him soon enough. I suggest putting them on before you catch cold. I took the trouble of measuring you while you were unconscious, so it should all fit." She twisted the handle and disappeared over the threshold without another word, locking it behind her.

Misha sat quietly on the bed, running her fingers over the coarse material of the shirt and trousers, when she heard a cough and a groan. She glanced over at Hawkins and saw her eyelids fluttering, so she jumped down and padded across the floor to her. The Judge's eyes rolled a little, then settled when she saw the younger girl's face.

"Misha..."

"I'm here."

"So you think I'm delusional, huh?"

THE BLOUSE AND pants combo were as itchy as all hell, although the irritation the straw boater brought to her scalp distracted her slightly. Maybe it was some kind of hair-shirt type deal, Misha wondered, a penance for sins committed during the congregation's lifetime. She'd mentioned her discomfort to Ashia and a few others that she'd managed to get on speaking terms with in the few days that they'd been here, but received only benign smiles and tepid platitudes in response. Clearly, she would have to get used to it, as there didn't seem to be much in the way of compromise on the fashion front—she guessed it was either this or exit through the front gate. You wanted a seat at the table, you had to become one of them. She presumed the prickliness would subside at some point as she became inured to it, like those monks, centuries ago, that used to kneel on bare flagstones for at least twelve hours a fucking day. The flesh was weak and fleeting, but the soul was eternal—wasn't that the deal? She remembered reading about these kind of penitent religious orders at school and the basic comforts they'd deny themselves to better serve whatever deity they happened to choose; she never thought she'd end up joining one just as the human race was staring into the mouth of annihilation.

She felt like a fraud, there was no question of that: an imposter donning fancy dress so as to better blend in with a group whose beliefs she couldn't in all sincerity adopt. They called themselves the Church of the Immortal Spirit, and from the little that Misha had gleaned from the services she'd reluctantly had to attend—she was never very good at concentrating whenever she'd had to listen to this kind of hocus-pocus word salad—it was a denomination big on the survival of the essence beyond mere earthly pursuits. No matter what your fate in the physical realm, that spark of life force that dwelt within would endure under His almighty eye. She could see it had a certain reassuring appeal, but nevertheless she couldn't count herself amongst the faithful; there didn't seem to be any room for doubt or questioning outside the doctrine. Despite that, she wanted to stay.

Hawkins, however, was even more cynical towards the group. Although still convalescing, she'd graduated from her sickbed to a wheelchair, which invariably Misha was tasked with pushing most of the time, and she could ease herself in and out of it with minimal support. The compound leaders had given them a small two-bedroom bungalow for accommodation while they recovered and pondered their next move, and the two women had spent several awkward evenings sitting in silence in the living space, sometimes listening to the singing from the hall the people of Libitina used as their church.

Hawkins would shake her head and sign: <Fools. Clap-happy fools praising their god as the world burns.>

<They saved our lives,> the younger woman signed back. <We would've been dead without their help.>

<Maybe we already are.> The Judge plucked at her outfit in distaste—she too had been forced into the regulation clothes, despite her injuries. <Maybe this is what Hell's like.>

<In all our time on the road, surviving on the barest of supplies, surrounded by horror, have you ever seen *anything* like this? This organised, this... together? They nurse us, feed us, give us a roof over our heads—what's your problem?>

<Perhaps it's because I've busted communes like this back in the day when I was a street jock. They always have their kinks.>

<They're a religious order, like Quakers or the Amish. They've found a way to process this shitstorm we're all living through. I can't see the harm.>

<And you call *me* delusional?> Hawkins snorted in derision. The atmosphere between the two had soured after the older woman had regained consciousness and it became clear that she'd heard most of what Misha had said to Ashia. The teen had tried to apologise, but Hawkins had waved it away—the words had evidently stung, not least because she'd probably recognised an element of truth to them that she didn't like to admit. She signed without looking at the girl, casting her eyes to the window and the dark street beyond: <Soon as I'm out of here, the better.>

<I want to stay.>

<What for? You're no prayer freak, and don't tell me the uniform's growing on you.>

<Because it's stable. We've been living on the back of your damn bike for so long, it's a relief to have a regular place to sleep for once. And because I'm tired of nearly getting killed while you chase radio signals for a resistance group that isn't there. Whether it was taking us into the capital or out into the farmbelt—under protest, I might add—we've both almost died. Now I've got the chance to say, okay, enough. I'm making this my home.>

Hawkins paused for a moment, lost in thought. Then she signed: <You think this place is going to save you? That the zombie fucks won't find you?>

<Seems as good a rock to hide under as any,> Misha responded.

There was a knock at the door. The two women exchanged curious looks before Misha jumped up and padded through to the hallway to answer it. Ashia was standing there, smiling broadly, clearly having just come from the service, the darkness behind her now quiet and still.

"Blessed evening," she said, laying a hand on Misha's arm. "Are the both of you getting your strength back?"

"Yeah. We're... doing okay."

"Good, because I bring exciting news. Our great founder Father Arnold wishes to speak with you. You *and* your friend."

"What, now?"

"Right now."

CHAPTER TWENTY-SEVEN

When Cafferly started making the high keening noise, it took even Phobia by surprise. Neither of the Sisters had heard much emerge from between the former Psi-Judge's lips since her severed head had been plugged into their black-arts surveillance system, and if they were honest, they were starting to lose faith in her effectiveness. It was true that a suspended state of post-dismemberment could very much blunt your psychic edge, and they'd been starting to wonder if they'd pushed Cafferly too far—she had originally been divested of her limbs and body as punishment for her disloyalty, and her head had been retained to help find the sibling she was psi-connected to, but so far she'd been a bust. Now, though, she was veritably singing for her supper, and no one was more taken off guard than the witches themselves.

"Lisssten to her," Phobia called to Nausea, who hurried to join her sister from an antechamber. "Ssshe mussst've made contact."

"Indeed. Let ussss sseee what ssshe'sss telling usss..."

There was nothing identifiable as words emerging from Cafferly's throat—it was a kind of shrill ululation—so Nausea slid inside the rancid mush of what remained of the psi's mind and tried to gain an understanding of what the head was remote-viewing. At first it was a shifting blur of colours, and the witch struggled to secure a foothold on what she was perceiving, but the more she established dominance over Cafferly's limited consciousness—effectively taking up residence inside her darkened brain and grabbing hold of the controls—the more something resembling a picture began to coalesce.

"Yessss..." Nausea whispered, fingers held to her temples, straining as she pushed her way to the front of Cafferly's cerebellum. "Sssshe'sss found her..."

"Misssha?" Phobia asked, watching her sister intently.

"The girl'sss let her guard down, enough for our tracker to essstablisssh a location."

"Where isss ssshe, then? What are you ssseeing?"

"Ssshe'sss to the north. Quite a dissstance from here... ssshe'ssss found a refuge in sssome kind of retreat. It'sss a walled town, well fortified..."

"A nessst of warmssss?"

"A real hotssspot. How we missssed thissss one is a myssstery. Neverthelessss, there they are, and Missha issss among them. Sssshe'sss in pain, limping... the injury hassss dulled her mental defencessss."

"Can you sssecure the co-ordinatessss?"

"Getting them now..." A smile creased Nausea's face. "Oh, Missssha, my dear, you have no idea how exssscited I am to get the chance to bring you back here," she murmured to herself. "The fun we will have with you, essspecially when we reunite you with your long-lossst ssssibling..."

Cafferly's head seemed to shriek louder, rocking impossibly on the stanchions that held it in place above the witches' formidable cauldron.

"Their combined psssychic energy would be mossst beneficial," Phobia said. "Of coursssse, I can't sssee her sssubmitting wilfully..."

"Oh, no," Nausea replied. "There will undoubtedly be a level of dissssection. At the very leassst, limb removal. It'sss taken sssso long to find her, we can't have her essscaping usss again."

The screams rose an octave. Nausea glanced up, grimacing as she placed the flat of her hands now against the sides of her head.

"What issss it?" Phobia enquired anxiously, stepping forward to lay a supporting palm on her sister's arm.

"Cafferly... ssshe's *resssisssting...*"

"Ssshe knowsss what we intend to do to the girl...?"

"Sssshe'sss fighting againssst me... I'm losssing the connection..."

There was a final screech and one of the rods holding the Psi's head in place gave way. Cafferly tumbled into the dank depths of the cauldron with a scarcely audible plop, the witches peering over the edge and at the ripples the psi left in her wake.

"How did ssshe...?" Phobia started.

"Never mind that," Nausea replied blithely. "We'll fisssh her out later. For now, we have her sssissster's location. Inform Ssssidney—we'll need reinforcementsssss."

"We're going to get her?"

"We're going in persssson. One way or another, Misssha is coming back with *usss.*"

DE'ATH SAT ALONE in his Grand Hall eyrie, silently contemplating the dust and darkness that surrounded him. Was *this* what he ultimately sought in the end—total isolation, accompanied by nothing more than the murdered remains of the planet? Did he actively rush towards his own company, forsaking the proximity and voices of others? He suspected so—despite the fine work of his lieutenants, despite him personally selecting them to aid him in his grand scheme of eliminating crime once and for all from every corner of the globe—he took a certain amount of pleasure when it was just him and the boneyard of his making. He enjoyed the serenity it brought; the lack of clamour and chaos, the knowledge that justice and order had truly been delivered. The quiet calmed him. He had no emotional attachment to Mortis, Fear and Fire—he'd transcended that nonsense long ago—but considered them useful comrades in the pursuit of his goal. Nevertheless, he felt increasingly like he had to pull rank; that they were forgetting to whose tune they were dancing, and wished to share his place on the world stage. It was a tiresome distraction. All in all, it came as something of a relief to just be left on his own with the pindrop silence of the judged, reflecting on everything he'd achieved.

He'd never been one for friends, even as a child. He'd come out of the womb that way, pretty much, no doubt warped from birth by his father's psychopathy. Familial relations meant nothing to him; his mother and sister were pitiful, future victims in all but name, and the less said about the dog, the better. The only one he kind of respected for his sheer pathological hatred for mankind was Papa. A dentist by trade, who believed his patients' heads were full of worms, the old man delighted in causing pain to others, and Sidney would remember with some degree of affection the times when he aided his father in his mobile surgery or helped dispose of the corpses. Equally, he hadn't shirked from his duty when he finally reported De'Ath Senior to the Judges and had opted to pull the switch on his dad's execution himself. There'd been unmistakable pride in his father's eyes just before the volts went coursing through his body.

He'd taken the badge by that point, but nothing had changed—he was still a lone wolf, content to be by himself, and to believe in his own philosophy. To be a cadet was usually to become subsumed into the Justice Department system—another cog in the machine, more meat for the grinder—and indoctrinated into their way of thinking. But Sidney had never truly fitted in that way: severe even by their standards, his ruthlessness took them by surprise, and his arguments for execution as the standard punishment for all crimes were groundbreaking. His tutors had never considered a blanket use for the ultimate sanction—indeed, they initially baulked at it, lily-livered cowards that they were—but they couldn't refute his claim that none of his arrests ever repeat-offended.

His record was so consistent across the board that they had to revise their way of doing things. *You can't shoot jaywalkers,* they'd gasped. On the contrary, he'd countered, show me a convicted felon of mine that would be tempted to do it again. *You can't gun down those for whom a death sentence didn't apply,* they'd weaselled. Show me a law and order advocate that didn't push for tougher punishments, he'd reply. *We're not death squads,* they'd exclaim in exasperation. Well, that's where you're going wrong, he'd calmly assert. Such was his stone-cold logic, utterly pure in its rationale, that none of his superiors could admonish him for his actions, and began to consider instead that he actually had a point. The odd kid out—the father-frying weirdo that challenged the orthodoxy—was to all intents and purposes reshaping the Judicial model from the inside. He was the new face of Justice Department, and it wasn't long before a substantial number of the rank and file fell in line behind him.

Drabbon never saw it coming, of course. The Chief presided over a largely corrupt and disorganised force: drug-taking was rife—even encouraged, in the case of aggression-enhancing narcotics—and a blind eye was turned to sexual liaisons between officers. Payoffs were commonplace. He operated a 'cripple or cube' policy, with most of his Judges leaning towards the former, which meant the arrest rate was in the toilet but hospitals were heaving with those that had felt the full weight of a Judge's spiked baton. It was a short-sighted initiative that merely fostered resentment—if the crims recovered, then they'd return to their old ways as soon as they hit the streets—and didn't address the root cause of all crime, which was that one hundred per cent of it was committed by the living. Remove that chance for them to come back at you, and you were by definition winning the war. Drabbon operated a seedy, small-minded Justice Department, whose only concern was that if you didn't want to end up in intensive care, start coughing up for the privilege. Sidney saw a much bigger picture.

De'Ath smiled when he remembered how he'd made the Chief squirm and beg before he'd permanently ended his reign. He'd been a weak fool. He'd betrayed his position as a lawmaker, too concerned with monetary gain and rule by intimidation, his vision limited to what he could get for himself, be it power or reward. Sidney, on the other hand, knew that to eradicate crime was to end humanity itself. It was that kind of undertaking—that belief in what he had to achieve—that separated him from those like Drabbon who had come before. It was a life's work, if you will, except he would go beyond mortality in a bid to see a world scourged of lawlessness, of every single guilty being brought to justice. He had pledged to himself—and to the entities the Sisters represented—that he would deliver on that promise, by hook or by crook.

Mortis's viral Red Mosquito psi-meme seemed to be doing the trick, by all accounts—De'Ath's eyes on the ground were reporting that cases of insanity and surrender amongst the lawbreakers had tripled since it went online. Those that couldn't face self-enforced starvation—the food, to their eyes, rotten and inedible, shrouded with flies—were throwing themselves at his Judicial forces, who had little to do but mop up. Resistance had dropped by a third. He had to hand it to his tech-minded second-in-command: the idea of driving the populace out of its mind was an inspired one.

You really couldn't overestimate the power of suggestion, Sidney mused, as a word or image could balloon in the victim's head in seconds to utter madness. From nothing would spring the seeds of their own demise. Like his father's obsession with brainworms was a delusion that would prove his undoing, consuming him to the point of mania, so the fertile ground of the population's consciousness was the ideal place to ferment their doom. He quite liked the irony of the guilty bringing about their own end—a global suicide—because it made them face their own culpability and understand the need for their execution. The crime was life, and they'd all had a hand in perpetuating it; let them fall upon their swords (or a well-placed Lawgiver bullet) so they can receive the punishment that was due to them.

The Mosquito's reach was being widened as Mortis came under pressure from the powers that be to improve on already impressive results, but it was putting a strain on the psi-network. Minds were at risk of burnout, under the effort required to shape and distort neural activity on such a vast scale. De'Ath himself had naturally never been shy of ambition, but sometimes the sheer size of what was being attempted here was brought home to him; could it run the risk of getting away from him, thundering out of his control like an avalanche? Would he be dwarfed by it, lost in the maelstrom? He felt like he had to maintain his hand on the tiller, even while others were demanding more, more, *more*. He had to exert his authority.

The shadows shifted around him, and he was aware that even if he actively sought the peace of his own company, he was never truly alone. The Sisters' sponsors were always there, watching, cogitating, judging—the global extinction couldn't come soon enough in their eyes. Sidney's lieutenants—especially malcontents like Fear—queried his desire to speed up the process, to render the world lifeless as quickly as possible, reasoning that as immortal beings they had no need to stick to a timetable. But they didn't understand the pressure De'Ath was under to mollify his patrons: he had to satisfy *their* need for total annihilation as much as his own. Nevertheless, he bristled at their ever-present intrusion, and angrily pondered just who was the true superior—the entities that used Sidney and his brothers to bring into being a sundered world, or Judge De'Ath himself? It was *he* who wore the robes of office, *he* who had the globe in his grip.

He could hear the voice of his father, a self-made man, who answered to no one: *Don't let the worm-riddled fools dictate your vision, son,* he'd said as he pushed another body out of his van and onto an already substantial pile of corpses. *YOU are the navigator of your own destiny.*

Sidney stood suddenly and upended his desk, sending it crashing to the floor in a cloud of dust. It was *he* that had initiated the cull!

He picked up his chair by one arm and threw it across the room, where it shattered. It was *he* that the living should bow down before and receive judgement from!

He tore shelves down from the walls. It was *he* who led and others followed! *He* who was the great reaper—

Sidney abruptly stopped and stood motionless for a moment, regarding the destruction. The fury that had visited him was gone as quickly as it had come. He shook his head, attributing it to the juvenile core that still lay within; he did, he had to admit, have trouble managing his temper. Daddy issues, maybe. But it was the suggestion that someone or something else was controlling the narrative that set him off. *He* was in charge, he told himself. *He was in charge.* It was imperative that he knew that.

There'd be time enough for quiet and reflection, he thought as he headed for the door, when the last bones were laid. He should be out there, asserting his position lest his authority was undermined and his retreat taken as a sign of weakness. The trappings of the Chief Judge had perhaps removed him too much from the front line.

It was time he got his hands dirty again.

ASHIA SAID NOTHING as she led Misha and Hawkins across town to the civic building, but the girl noticed the whole place seemed a little subdued after the service. Not that it had ever been exactly jumping, from what she'd seen of it; but there was a decided lack of activity tonight, as if everyone had had the same idea of retreating into their homes and shutting their doors. The teen stole a fleeting glance at the sentry points atop the compound walls, and caught a glimpse of the guards' motionless silhouettes, rifles slung over shoulders, as they silently contemplated the land beyond. They were too far away for her to pick out individual details, but they were the only signs of life that she was aware of on their brief journey. She considered saying something off-hand to the woman, but thought twice about it, the muted atmosphere invading her head and stilling her tongue.

There was fortunately a long, looping ramp alongside the stone steps to the hall's grand entrance, and Misha was able to push Hawkins in her wheelchair up to the door, where Ashia patiently waited before heading inside. It was the first time that Misha had visited the place, and her eyes were drawn to the ornately carved ceiling, suggesting a tangle of flowers in bloom, and the closed heavy double doors that dominated the foyer. But the woman didn't make for those, instead veering left and marching them down a short service corridor, where she stopped at a plain wooden office door and indicated that Misha knock. A male voice called out from the other side that they should enter.

"I'll wait out here," Ashia said, sweeping them across the threshold and closing the door behind them.

The room appeared to be some kind of admin office; not the environs Misha expected of a great leader. It boasted the thin carpet and boxfile-packed shelves that she was familiar with from every accommodation officer and department head's room from her time at university, back in the day. It was poky, functional and anonymous, and she was immediately curious as to why the group's founder would squirrel himself away in here, or use it to play host to newcomers.

The man she presumed was Arnold was perched on the arm of an easy chair to one side of the office, not behind the desk—that was stacked with more boxes of paper. He rose as they entered and regarded them with a mixed air of benevolence and disdain, which Misha took immediate exception to. He was a thin, balding man in his sixties—clad like the others, minus the hat—who could've been a retired economics professor or amateur gadgets inventor, exuding about an equal level of menace. He didn't proffer his hand to shake but cast an assessing eye over them. No, not much of a threat, Misha thought, but a bit of a socially inept asshole.

"This the nerve centre, then?" she asked, breaking the ice.

"This?" The man followed her gaze, taking in the files and staid surroundings. "This was all here when we co-opted the place. But you might well indeed consider this the heart of the community. Its importance is immeasurable. The documents have been left exactly as they were when we moved in."

"Why? What are they?"

"Environmental reports. Charts monitoring climate change. Impact warnings. They detail the deleterious effect the shift in habitat conditions has had on species population, and the downturn in crop production, amongst other things."

"How far back do they go?"

"Way before the Fall."

"So... we were fucked even *without* the zombie pricks gunning us down?"

The man didn't blanch at Misha's language. "It's a school of thought. Some believe that this De'Ath character that's taken charge is merely a symptom—a carrion feeder attracted to a dying planet, hastening its demise."

"That's cheery."

"Why have you kept them?" Hawkins piped up, her voice strained. "The files, the paperwork."

"Because they're sacred," Arnold replied matter of factly. "They tell the truth about our planet's fate. And we—my community of Libitina—are shepherds of that ultimate destiny."

"Shepherds?" Misha asked, feeling queasy.

"Extinction acceptance, my child. We worship the end of the world."

CHAPTER TWENTY-EIGHT

"WHAT DID I tell you?" Hawkins rasped, side-eyeing her companion. "There's always a kink."

"Extinction *acceptance?*" Misha said, ignoring the Judge and incredulously addressing the old fart in front of her, whom she now realised was seriously deranged.

"There's no point rebelling against the inevitable," Arnold replied calmly. "These documents were the key to my enlightenment, and to how I could preach my gospel—the world as we know it was always finite. Humanity was never going to last forever. The reports say that the planet had been irrevocably changing for decades, if not centuries, and our time upon it was going to finally come to an end. We should embrace extinction for the opportunity that it is."

"Goddamned doomsday cult," Hawkins spat derisively.

"The Church of the Immortal Spirit... what, you think there's a better world beyond this one?" Misha said. "Is that your doctrine? Get behind total wipeout, because it's the stepping stone for your soul to somewhere nicer?"

"All flesh falls away, all matter... crumbles," Arnold replied. "Our essences will transcend entropy and find a purer home."

"If you're that keen on going on to a better place, why don't you all just do yourselves in? Seriously, you'd find Paradise all the quicker, if you passed around the Kool-Aid."

"It's not just our lives that are coming to an end—it's the world's too," Arnold said, not rising to her bait. "Indeed, our existences are somewhat fleeting and insignificant, compared with that of the planet. We're like flies crawling on a cadaver that's rotting away beneath our feet—this is all we've known, and all we ever will, and the Church's faith celebrates the death of the entity that we call home. If we were to simply commit suicide, we would not be able to bear witness to the end of the world and sing the praises of its passing."

"This is seriously messed up," Misha murmured, shaking her head. "You're celebrating the end of everything?"

"For a journey to start, there has to be destruction. For every stage in life, there is trauma before there is rebirth. For mankind to throw off its shackles and seek a new beginning, first must come dissolution. Like I say, the razing of our world is an opportunity for the betterment of our spiritual well-being."

"So De'Ath and his pusbag pals are doing us a favour by massacring us all?"

"A farmer torches his fields so he might see new growth next season. That is what is happening to us as a species."

"Why are we listening to this crap?" Hawkins growled. She grabbed Misha's arm, hauling herself out of her wheelchair, making an uneasy stand on two feet. "Let's get the hell out of here."

Misha nodded. "Can you walk?"

"I'll manage. I've spent enough time in that damn chair."

The teen turned back to Arnold. "I don't understand—the sentry guards, the walls. You're protecting yourselves from a fate that you singularly *want* to happen."

"The defences aren't to save us from the architects of the planet's doom, they're to stop other factions of survivors storming in and taking what's ours. We want to be here to see the end."

"I don't think you're going to get the choice," Misha said. "When the forces of the Hall of Injustice find you, they'll put you in the ground right then and there. You're not going to get a ringside seat to the end of days. Your worship and your prayers and your hymns will amount to nothing because there's a big empty void at the heart of your religion. There's nothing to be gained from extinction, just dust and bones."

The girl turned, and with her arm around the Judge's shoulders, headed towards the exit. Behind them, Arnold called out Ashia's name, and she immediately opened the door, blocking their path. All smiley bonhomie had gone, replaced with a steely glare. Over her shoulder a pair of bruiser types lingered in the corridor as backup.

"I wanted to see you tonight to see if you'd assimilated into our community, if you were becoming true members of our Church," the old man said. "It's my judgement that I deem you still outsiders—you're not willing or able to embrace the faith."

"Then let us go," Misha answered. "Let us walk out the front gate and we'll be gone."

"You still have your uses, though. My flock can be understandably nervous faced with their final hours—their belief can take a wobble. It does them no harm to see occasionally that death is truly transformative, that redemption can spring from annihilation. That's where you two can shine before the congregation."

"Sacrifice," Hawkins muttered.

"It'll be a worthy end to your journey," Arnold replied, "or perhaps the beginning of a new one. The natural first stop of your pilgrimage."

Misha considered how quiet the compound had been on their way over, the people shutting themselves away. "This was your plan all along, wasn't it? This is what you'd told your followers you were going to do. We were never going to be accepted—there was only one fate intended for us, wasn't there?"

Arnold didn't respond.

"So why nurse us back to health in the first place?" she asked. "Why save us?"

"The lamb is fed and looked after until it's needed, is it not?" Ashia said. "Even when its time upon the earth is short."

"Madness," Misha said. "It's bad enough we've got creatures out there wanting to hunt us all down and exterminate us—but now we've got you death fanatics helping them along the way."

"It *cannot* be stopped," Arnold reiterated. "You have to understand that."

"That doesn't mean we roll over and accept it. We fight them, every inch of the way—"

"Save your breath," Hawkins said, cutting the girl short, switching to sign. <You can't reason with them.>

Misha looked at the Judge. "You're giving up too?"

"Not quite," she grunted, and promptly swung her fist directly into Ashia's face, catching her unawares. The woman crumpled, staggering backwards, hands to her nose, blood streaming between her fingers. "*Go!*" Hawkins urged, pushing Misha towards the door.

"No!" Arnold roared, seizing hold of Hawkins' shoulder, but the Judge ducked under his reach, spun round to face him, grabbed two fistfuls of his shirt, then planted a solid headbutt on him, which dropped him like a stone.

Hawkins turned to see Ashia look up from her cupped, crimson-streaked hands, eyes narrowed, and went to shoulder-barge the woman out of the way, but the cultist stepped back, smoothly drawing a knife. She slashed out and Hawkins was unable to avoid the blade's arc, the wicked edge slicing her bicep. The Judge hissed in pain, stumbling into the shelving and knocking piles of documents onto the floor. She put a hand to the wound, feeling the hot pulse of blood trickling down her arm.

She watched Misha tear open the door just as one of the knuckleheads outside made to reach for her, and the girl nimbly dropped to a crouch and shot out her right foot, which contacted savagely with the man's ankle. He yelped and keeled over, his leg taken out from under him, and she followed up with a heel strike to his temple that bounced his head off the floor as she leapt towards the exit.

The Judge turned back to face Ashia just as she stepped forward and thrust the blade towards the older woman's chest. Hawkins scrabbled behind her for a boxfile and brought it round as a shield, the tip of the knife wedging in the cardboard lid. Ashia angrily attempted to wrest it free while Hawkins' icily numb left arm reached up and secured another box from the shelf, swinging it as hard as she could into the side of the cultist's skull. The file exploded, sheaves of paper fountaining out, as Ashia dropped to her knees, a dark red bead running down from her hairline. She looked momentarily stunned. Hawkins didn't hesitate: she gripped the knife handle, yanked it out, then drove it deep into the other woman's throat. Ashia coughed up bloody sputum, her eyes rolled in their sockets and she fell sideways to the carpet.

Hawkins slid the blade from Ashia's neck and glanced up in time to see the second thug hoist Misha up against the corridor wall, meaty hands around her windpipe. She stumbled forward, feet slipping on the paper covering the floor, left arm slick with blood and throbbing intensely. She'd need to bind it before she passed out. The guard that the girl had hobbled was groaning and attempting to rise, so as she passed him, she aimed a swift kick to the jaw that silenced him permanently.

Misha's eyes locked on Hawkins' as the Judge stepped up behind the goon, unaware of her presence, and she cut the guy's trachea with ruthless efficiency. Blood spray caught the teenager in the face before the thug's hands went slack and dropped her, and it continued to spritz in a wide semi-circle as he staggered for a few seconds, the walls and ceiling painted crimson as if from a high-pressure hose. Then he hit the deck and was still.

"Jesus," Misha spluttered, running a hand over her eyes and mouth, blood caked in her hair. "Oh, Christ."

"We need to go," Hawkins said, offering the girl a hand to help her stand. "Right now."

"No shit." Misha pulled herself up with the Judge's support, coughing and rubbing her bruised neck. She looked round at the carnage. "What the *fuck*, Hawkins?"

"No choice. Them or us, you know that."

"What about the old man? Is he dead too?"

"Just out for the count, I think. Now, c'mon, let's go."

"Wait... your arm."

The older woman looked down at the blood-sodden sleeve and nodded reluctantly. "Get me something to wrap around this." The girl did as she was asked and divested one of the cultists of their shirts, ripping it in half to use it as bandage. When she pulled it tight around Hawkins' bicep, the Judge snarled in pain; one of the few times that the teenager had heard her vocalise discomfort. Nevertheless, she inspected it and nodded her thanks.

The Judge pushed Misha down the corridor back towards the entrance, the girl looking back to the older woman in concern. They returned to the deserted lobby; Misha glanced to one side at the tall, heavy doors they'd seen on the way in, and held up a hand to Hawkins. She jogged over, grasped a heavy handle and eased it open a crack, poking her head around the frame. Inside were row upon row of pews, stretching into the distance for a good fifty feet or so, but there was no icons, no paintings to accompany them—indeed, the room's original furniture (she made out a lot of maps and workstations) was still in the room, albeit shoved to one side. They were making their own church, she supposed. Then she saw at the front of the pews, where the altar would be, what looked like a pair of home-made wooden crosses with straps attached, at wrist and ankle height. They looked like something that had been dragged out of an S&M dungeon. She quickly retreated and pulled the door shut again.

"What's up?" Hawkins asked, reading her expression as the girl joined her once more. "What's in there?"

"Better you don't know," she replied, wondering how that mad old bastard Arnold had planned to execute them in front of his gathered followers. What had he said he wanted to do—put his people's minds at rest? Show them that the Great Journey was nothing to be fearful of? Funny how these death cults were a little less keen on dying themselves than they were about encouraging others to do so. "You were right about the kink, Hawkins."

The Judge grunted. <Be on the street long enough and you'll soon have pretty low expectations of the citizenry. I know for a fact I'm not delusional about that.> She limped ahead before Misha could protest and cracked open the doors that lead out onto the street. "Still quiet out there." <Couldn't face what their glorious leader had planned, you think?>

"Or they're polishing their boots, waiting to be called in to witness it."

<Creepy-assed ritualised fuckers. But on the other hand, let's not ignore this gift horse.>

Hawkins slipped out and descended the stone steps a touch clumsily, legs evidently weak, and the teen followed her onto the street. The Judge pointed eastwards, which was the nearest direction to a perimeter wall, and her companion silently nodded, before the two of them set off as fast as they could, half crouched as if expecting discovery at any moment, and looking furtively to either side with every step. They were soon within a hundred yards of the corrugated metal barrier that marked the town's boundary, and it looked intimidatingly impenetrable up close, rising up before them like a towering wave.

"How are we going to get past that?" Misha whispered.

"Ways and means, gotta be," Hawkins muttered. Then she pointed: "There."

The girl followed her gaze and saw that the Judge was indicating a tall, narrow iron ladder bolted to the wall that scaled its full height. "Aw, man."

"You got a problem with heights?"

"I got a problem with falling to my death. That thing does not look safe."

<I'm presuming that's how the guards get up and down from their posts. If they can manage it, so can we. I'm hoping we'll be able to follow the perimeter wall around until we reach a gate.>

"Are you in any fit state to be climbing ladders? You could barely handle stairs a minute ago. You're still recovering—"

<I'll let you know what I can and can't manage,> Hawkins answered bluntly. <Keep an eye out—I'll signal when it's safe to come up too.>

She stumble-ran, head down, for the foot of the ladder, staying within the shadow of the wall as soon as she was close enough. Once there, she cast a glance up, established there were no guards in view, and started to ascend. Watching, Misha winced as Hawkins' limbs failed her, feet slipping, fingers failing to find purchase when she lost her balance and she had to hug herself to the risers. The Judge would pause for a second to catch her breath before continuing, slower every time. Words of encouragement were on the tip of Misha's tongue, but she decided it'd be foolish to say anything aloud.

The older woman was over halfway when the girl heard the sound of angry consternation heading in their direction. Misha retreated into foliage and cast an eye back towards from where they'd come—Arnold, sporting a golf-ball-sized lump on his forehead, and a five-strong lynch mob were storming towards their position. She returned without further ado to the ladder and quickly began to follow the Judge up.

"What are you doing?" the Judge hissed when she saw Misha catching up with her, the rungs trembling both with the added weight and the girl's urgency. Rusty bolts screwed into the metal squealed under the strain. "This can't take the both of us—"

The teenager jabbed a thumb over her shoulder. "Trouble coming."

Hawkins looked past her and saw the group getting nearer. "Oh, shit," she murmured and scrambled towards the top, feet clumsily missing rungs and making the ladder sway alarmingly. There were some shouts from below, and suddenly searchlights stationed along the wall were cranked on, dazzling beams sweeping the pair's position.

A shot rang out, ricocheting off a nearby stanchion. Misha yelped, saw Arnold raising the revolver again as he stood at the foot of the ladder, and she practically flung herself upwards. "Keep your head down!" she shouted to the Judge, fixing her sights on the brow of the wall. "He's—"

But the rest of the sentence was drowned out by the gun's second report and her own scream as she saw blood spray across the corrugated metal where the slug had torn through Hawkins' midriff. The older woman lost her grip and tumbled down several feet, only to get her leg wrapped around the rungs, and she dangled momentarily, just above Misha. Their gazes locked for a second, and the girl thought she saw a small smile grace the Judge's heavily scarred features; then she fell again, plummeting past her to hit the ground with a dull thud, just a few yards from where Arnold stood. Misha stared down in shock as she saw Hawkins' left leg tremble and flex slightly, realising that she was still alive. The small crowd that had come after them gathered round her twitching form.

Meanwhile, a searchlight beam caught the girl in its glare and she froze, transfixed in the light. She heard words being bellowed at her from above, and followed the sound in a daze, peering up at a couple of silhouettes leaning over the parapet. They waved at her to continue ascending, and after once more glancing down at the body of her friend she complied, dumbly putting one foot above the other until she was within the figures' reach. She was roughly hauled over the side onto the top of the perimeter wall, where she lay, catching her breath.

End of the road.

Shock made time elastic, then. Misha abandoned any resistance. She remembered being pulled to her feet and marched along the wall, but couldn't piece together how long she'd been walking, or when she'd stopped, to be left standing on the lip of a platform jutting out over the blasted landscape beyond the compound. The wind blew past her, bringing with it the smell of corruption. In the distance she saw fires burning. She felt she'd been made to stand here for hours, though it surely could only have been minutes—either way, the strength was ebbing from her legs, and her head felt full of cotton wool.

"Kneel," a voice behind her said, and she dropped to the ground with some degree of relief. She hadn't been allowed to look around, or speak, so the first time she was aware of others being up there with her was when a couple of cultists entered her field of vision, holding Hawkins between them. The Judge was in a pitiful state—face bruised extensively, one hand bent like a claw as if her wrist was broken, uniform ripped and bloody—and she offered nothing but a low groan as if she wasn't entirely there either.

"So we commit another living soul to the earth." It could only be Arnold, somewhere to her right, out of sight. "As the spirit passes, it joins the multitude, moving to a better plane of existence. Listen: they're all around us, thronging to watch the world's demise. To those dead, we offer our respect and fealty. You are the exalted ones. You have achieved a pureness of being that we can only envy. One day we will all be with you, when the planet has breathed its last. But until that moment, accept our offering—to show that we too will ascend from this crude matter, for that is our purpose and destiny. In the name of the spirit."

"In the name of the spirit," echoed multiple voices, some of them as if from a distance. The congregation must be watching this from the ground, gathered at the foot of the wall.

Arnold walked into view—now wearing a blood-red full-length ceremonial robe—indicated that the two holding Hawkins should release her, then reached up and gently planted a kiss on the woman's forehead. She stood there, shaking slightly, meeting his gaze before he shoved her sharply backwards off the platform.

"*No!*" Misha screamed and scrambled forward on instinct, only to feel hands roughly grasp her shoulders and keep her in place. Arnold looked around at the interjection, catching her eye for a second, then beckoned with his finger. The teen was hoisted up and frogmarched to the spot where the Judge had stood mere moments before. Tears streaming down her cheeks, an uncontrollable trembling taking over her body, she peered over the lip of the parapet and saw below Hawkins' broken form, impaled on crude metal spikes that had been positioned along the perimeter. Judging by the skeletal remains scattered nearby, the Judge hadn't been the first to be thrown to her death.

"Hush, child," Arnold whispered in her ear, bending close. "It'll be over soon. A moment of trauma and then the greatest of transformations."

"Fuck you, maniac," she spat back between chattering teeth.

He smiled and straightened. "So we commit another living soul to the earth—" he started, voice raised, then faltered. He cocked his head to one side. The whine of engines could be heard in the distance, growing louder by the second. "What *is* that?" he muttered.

"All Father, look!" One of the cultists holding Misha's arm let go and pointed in the direction of the horizon. She followed his gaze and saw what he was indicating—half a dozen Justice Department H-Wagons were approaching the compound, coming in low and fast.

She closed her eyes in quiet despair. The forces of De'Ath had found them.

CHAPTER TWENTY-NINE

The first guy that got taken out decided he'd exit as a martyr. It was one of the numbskulls that had been holding her down, Misha realised; as soon as he saw the H-wagons approaching, he scrambled to the lip of the platform edge and flung his arms wide open as if to embrace the rush of the divine. A laser bolt from the lead ship blew him apart like a puff of wind through a dandelion clock.

Fuck that, the girl thought, shielding her head from the waft of atomised cultist. She got to her feet and ran around the edge of the town wall, looking for a way back to ground level and eventually finding a rickety set of wooden steps, which many others were scrambling down. Arnold was nowhere to be seen. No one attempted to stop her—or, indeed, seemed to notice she was there. They had more pressing concerns now. The craft roared overhead and everyone in her vicinity ducked instinctively, their faces etched with confusion and fear.

Wasn't this what they wanted, she wondered. Hadn't they resigned themselves to their own personal apocalypse? It seemed that despite worshipping—indeed, welcoming—the end of the world, to be actually confronted with oblivion was a whole other matter. Suddenly, shit had, as it were, got real, and they were as frightened as anyone else. Their secluded little fortress of Libitina, or whatever stupid name they'd given themselves, had been far from the epicentre of De'Ath's purges, had escaped the organised slaughter up—until now. For Arnold and his deluded followers, extinction became a romantic ideal; a rapturous end-of-days event in which their spirits transported to paradise. Now, though, cold hard reality had come crashing into their idyll, and it wasn't at all as swoonsome as they'd been led to believe.

The craft banked for a second pass and they let loose more laser fire, blowing apart several houses in thunderous explosions of brickwork and plaster fragments, before slowing to come in to hover. Clearing space to land, Misha realised. Three of them descended like this, while the fourth circled the compound repeatedly, tracing the outline of the perimeter wall. Suddenly that barrier around the town didn't seem so smart: rather than affording protection, it was hemming the people in like sheep in a pen.

Seemingly having nowhere to run to didn't stop the cultists scattering in panic. Some made for shelter in the buildings still standing, while others fled towards the main gate. She heard them shouting about getting it unlocked and using the compound's vehicles. Misha followed that group, remembering that she and Hawkins had been brought here by a pair of buggies—if she could steal a ride on one of those, she'd be free and clear in no time.

As she ran with a surging crowd, she flashbacked to the night of the Fall and realised she was doing much the same thing as that night, all these months later: fleeing De'Ath's footsoldiers amongst a terrified throng, people stumbling and tripping in their haste to escape. Then, it'd been on the choked streets of the capital, citizens screaming as confusion reigned as to what was going on—the Judges, indiscriminately firing upon anyone in their path, had initially been a mystery. She'd lost her boyfriend Joel that night; a snap of gunfire and he'd tumbled to the tarmac beside her, blood leaking from his head wound. It was only luck and the kindness of strangers that meant she hadn't met a similar fate. Now, on either side of her, townsfolk staggered and fell, but momentum carried her forward, not allowing her to stop even if she was so inclined. These people meant nothing to her. For all she knew, they would've happily watched Arnold sacrifice both her and Hawkins; she wasn't going to start feeling any sympathy for these end-of-the-world-loving bozos now they were getting a taste of their own medicine.

She looked back and saw the three H-wagons had touched down and were lowering their landing ramps, disgorging armed greys. They came out shooting, targeting without hesitation the scared masses running for their lives. The air was filled with the crackle of gunfire and the thump of carcasses hitting the ground.

It was pandemonium. The first wave of cultists dashing for the main gate smashed against it, finding it barred, struggling to move the bolts and swing it open with so many crowding in from behind. Cries went out for people to stop surging, to step back and allow space for the doors to be pulled apart, but of course few cooperated. From her position towards the back, Misha saw sentries on the wall either side of the gate frantically waving people back, but any attempts to drag the gate open were stymied by the weight of bodies pressing against it. The sentries would break off from attempting to direct the crowd and sight their rifles on the greys heading towards them, dropping individual Judges with remarkably efficient headshots, but the uniformed ghouls were too many, and the H-wagon still in the air had the advantage; Misha watched with horrible inevitability as the craft came swooping back and vaporised the gunmen on the wall with a few well-placed laser blasts. The people crushed up against the gate wailed and started to trample over each other, an animalistic, hysterical bid to escape taking hold.

She knew they were outgunned and overwhelmed—nobody was going out the main gate any time soon. Misha ducked down a side road and sought relief from the crowd, hoping to find shelter in a quieter area of the town that the greys hadn't yet swarmed over. Maybe those folk that had run for cover in the houses had had the right idea: look for a bolthole, stay out of sight. It seemed you were dead if you went out in the open; the screams and sounds of massacre behind her were testament to that. She spotted a narrow alley and squeezed herself between its walls, hurriedly edging sideways until she emerged into a deserted courtyard, onto which three different buildings faced. The stillness was almost as disconcerting as the chaos she'd just left behind.

Misha leant against the nearest wall and sunk down onto her haunches, putting her face in her palms. In the darkness behind her eyes, all she could see was Hawkins being shoved off that platform, her body disappearing over the lip of the wall, the look of final fury in her eyes as she realised she was going to have to relinquish her life to the asshole that killed her. The Judge had been through so much since the Fall, so much trauma—permanently scarred by something that happened before they even met, she'd put herself in the way of danger repeatedly; mostly to protect her young ward but also in the determination to find that resistance movement she was so convinced existed. Her bravery—which Misha too often equated with stubbornness—was without question. Funny: before the end of the world, the girl had been no champion of the Judges, had pretty much loathed everything they stood for; yet in the last dying gasps of the planet, she'd counted one as her friend and protector. Her partner in survival.

The teenager didn't know what she was going to do without Hawkins if she survived the next... what? Hour? Twelve hours? Was it worth it, to keeping fighting for every breath when you had no idea where that life you were so desperately trying to save was going to go? She suspected Hawkins would say yes: snatch every moment till the last drop. But then the older woman had been a natural fighter, a pragmatic soul undaunted by what the world threw at her. Misha thought of herself as one that sheltered under the strength of others—first Kez in their hideout in the farmhouse cellar, and then Hawkins, when she was lost and alone. She needed that assurance, she realised, that dominant figure that she could rely on. Like an older sibling, or a proxy for one; someone to fill the absence where one once was. Like her sister. Like...

...Rachel.

—Yessss—

Misha dropped her hands away from her face in an instant. The voice had sounded as clear as a bell in her head, yet hadn't originated from anywhere nearby. She looked around, her eyes roving the courtyard, but she could see nothing out of the ordinary; she was alone, as far as she could tell. She eased herself back up to full height, still cautiously checking her surroundings.

—Missshaaa—

She gasped, putting a hand to her temple. Those creatures that for a time had sought to invade her mind, that had been pushing at the tendrils of her consciousness in a bid to locate her... they'd found her. They knew she was there. Their background presence had faded away somewhat, as she and Hawkins had journeyed from the capital—and, by extension, the Hall of Injustice, which is where she believed they were based. She'd presumed they'd lost contact. This far north, they'd disappeared entirely. Yet unmistakeably that was them: the Sisters. As if the thought of Rachel had opened a door, or a channel, and they'd slipped through it.

—We've been looking for you, Missshaa—

She grunted in pain. Their voices sounded huge in her skull; there was no way of resisting them now. Her head throbbed with the echo of them, pulsed with the reverberation of every sibilant word. She stumbled forward, vision blurry like the onset of a migraine; it felt as if her mind wasn't big enough to contain these entities that had seeped inside, that they were curling around her brainpan, filling every nook and cranny with their malign presence, and it ached from the pressure. To make matters worse, it sounded as if there were two voices speaking simultaneously, one weaving in and out of the other.

"Get out!" she screamed, aware even as she did so that the order was futile. They had their hooks in and were immovable; she felt powerless to shift them. "Get out!"

—We're going nowhere, Missshaa... We've been looking for you for too long—

"No..."

—But we found you, thanksss to Rachel... Ssshe'sss been reaching out, trying to help usss connect—

"Rachel...?"

—Sssshe joined our caussse, wasss vital in the war againssst lawlesssnessss... A Pssssi-Judge, capable of rooting out the guilty... But sssshe rebelled, reasssserted her humanity... BETRAYED USSSSS—

Misha winced at the sudden screech, and felt wetness on her top lip. She touched it, and her fingers came away tipped with crimson—her nose was bleeding. She ran the back of her hand against it defiantly.

"So she fought back against you evil fucks. Good on her."

—Her genetic make-up overcame the Dead Fluidsss... the ssssemblance of the woman that once wasss emerged... We had never ssseen that before... The Fluidsss ssshould have wiped everything of who sssshe wassss, but her mind cracked thankssss to an exsssperiment we conducted on her, and her identity floated to the top... releasssed from itsss mooring—

The Sisters' voices seemed to be competing for dominance now, like two children eager to tell the same story and speaking over each other in their hurry to relate it.

—But through our invessstigationsss into how Rachel came to be... Our very thorough invessstigationssss... We learned of the exissstence of you, dear Missshaa... The long-lossst ssssibling, who ssstill held a psychic tether to her ssssisster... We need to know more about you, too, Missshaa... We need to know if you are asss unique assss Rachel... We need to pick your brainssss, dear heart... There issss ssso much we can learn from each other—

The voices in her skull dissolved into cackling laughter.

Misha shook her head, trying to dispel the noise before it split apart entirely.

—Come to ussss, Missshaa... It would ssssave ssssso much time if you ssssubmitted willingly—

"Fuck you," the girl snarled. "I'd rather die."

—We do not have to have you in one piece... Your sssstudy can be achieved posssst-mortem, if necessssary—

"Then you'll have to try to come get me. Or are you creatures only good for skulking in the Grand Hall, issuing threats?"

—Oh, you misssundersssstand, my dear... We're already here... We would not rissssk the chance of losssssing you again... We have travelled here in perssssson... Indeed, thissss whole assssault on thissss nessst of criminalssss wassss purely for your benefit... You let usss into your head and allowed usss to find you... And thissss conversssation—

Misha heard a commotion heading in her direction.

—hassss sssimply been a method by which to pinpoint your location—

"Oh, shit." The words escaped her lips as she saw a wormy grey Judge emerge from the same alleyway that she herself had squeezed down moments ago and fix its putrescent gaze upon her. Its Lawgiver was already drawn and it took aim just as Misha started moving—she took three long strides, then launched herself through the ground-floor window of one of the buildings that edged the courtyard. The glass shattered and the frame splintered as she bowled through it shoulder-first, her back and left forearm lacerated with several long cuts, and she hit the bare tiled floor of the room she'd dived into with a bone-jarring thud, knocking the wind from her. Agility wasn't her strong point, she thought, as she scrambled to her feet, keeping her head down as gunfire raked the outside of the building and tore through the wrecked window. She hurried over to the nearest interior door and tugged it open, throwing herself into the hallway beyond. It was one of the cultist's houses, she figured, eyeing the muted décor and knick-knacks adorning the shelves, and it appeared to be deserted.

A set of stairs led to a first floor, and ahead of her at the far end of the hall was what looked like the door to the front of the property. She balanced her options even as she heard a high-explosive round blow out the wall from the room she'd just left: go up, or take her chances on the street. She'd seen the kind of odds that were available to her out in the open so decided to dash for the stairs. She took them two at a time until she reached the landing, pausing to look over the bannister at the sounds of destruction below; the grey emerged into the hallway, rotten head turning this way and that as it tried to determine which direction his quarry had gone. A distant echo of dry laughter trailed in her mind, and she realised that while the Sisters had their claws in her, they could direct their soldiers to where she was; sure enough, the grey's face turned towards the stairs and began to climb, gun still held out in front of it. Misha frantically gauged her surroundings and headed for the nearest bedroom, its furnishings as typically Spartan as the ward she and Hawkins had awoken in, and grabbed a wooden chair, lifting it above her head and backing up against the wall.

For long seconds she listened to the trudge of the thing ascending and redoubled her sweaty grip on the chair's legs, waiting for it to take one step into the room before she struck. There was a moment's pause, during which she held her breath, then bullets punched through the plaster, the first missing her head by millimetres, the second tearing through her shoulder, and the third blowing out her right elbow; she screamed and the chair clattered to the floor as Misha slumped to her knees, blood pooling around her. Again that cackle sounded in her head, and she admonished herself for her stupidity—she couldn't have ambushed the grey while the Sisters were in residence; they'd told it exactly where to find her.

It came through the doorway and stood over her, smoking Lawgiver barrel trained on her as she sobbed and tried to readjust her position, her wounds afire. She met its gaze, trembling with pain and shock.

"I thought... your mistresses w-wanted me alive," Misha said between gulps of air.

"They can work with what they have," the Judge replied in raspy voice. "Life and death are sssomewhat fluid thessse daysss."

She sighed. "Sh-shoot me, then. Let's get this over with."

The grey shuffled forward and sighted its weapon between her eyes, its finger on the trigger, just as Misha kicked sharply out with her feet and sent the upturned chair lying between them into its shins, which gave a brittle crack. As it stumbled on fractured bones, she swept her leg under its feet, toppling it completely. The Lawgiver went flying, clattering into a corner. The grey lay on its back, momentarily bewildered, and the girl grabbed the back of the chair with her left hand and with a cry of fury slammed it down on the Judge's head, a leg penetrating the creature's eye and impaling it to the floorboard in a fountain of brown ichor. It twitched, then was still.

She groaned and pulled herself to her knees, weak with blood loss. Her right arm was useless, dangling at her side, and a growing numbness was spreading from just below her neck. Her head felt heavy, her thoughts sluggish. She knew if she blacked out, she'd likely not wake up again.

—You sssee what happenssss when you resssisst usss, Missssshaa—

"Fucking leave me alone," she sobbed, snot and tears thickening her voice.

—There issss nowhere you can go... Our forcessss ssswarm over your world... It issss dying, and there'ssss nothing you can do to ssstop that—

"Why? W-why are you doing this? Killing everyone?"

—It issss the law—

She didn't have the strength to argue, concentrating instead on pushing back against the deadness seeping into her limbs; she had to get up, get moving, or else she'd succumb to the exhaustion. She put one foot under her and pushed, forcing herself upright, left hand on the wall to keep her steady. She reached down and picked up the Lawgiver, slotting into her waistband, then she walked forward, out onto the landing and back down the stairs, each step measured carefully, pain and lethargy threatening to overbalance her at any moment.

"You... you said you're here," she said. "In person. Where?"

—You wisssh to deliver yourssself to usssss at lassst?—

"Where?"

—On one of the H-wagonssss—

"I'll come to you"—she hissed as sharp agony lanced through her—"if I can get there... unhindered." Misha reached the hallway and limped to the front door, pulling it open. On the other side, multiple grey squads were combing the streets, moving through thoroughfares littered with bodies. They all turned to look at her as she emerged. "Let me pass."

—Very well... You will not be touched—

The girl swallowed hard and stepped out into the aftermath of a massacre, the butchers responsible silently regarding her as she hesitantly walked among them. Doing her best to keep her head high, breathing deeply, Misha staggered a haphazard path towards her rendezvous with the Sisters.

CHAPTER THIRTY

Surrounded by so much death, Misha had never wanted to live more. As she stumbled through the streets of Libitina, back towards where the H-wagons were stationed, she knew that the last of her was bleeding out, that these final few moments were all she had left. Her wounds were too severe from which to recover, and she was under no illusions as to what the Sisters would do to her once she was within their reach, but rather than resignation, she felt a raging grief that this was the end. Tears pricked her eyes at the injustice, at all that was being taken from her, of what she wanted to cling to now slipping from her grasp.

"I don't want to go," she realised she was intoning under her breath, every syllable punctuated by a hitch in her throat, a stagger, a fresh stab of pain. "I don't want to go."

But each faltering footstep followed the last as she circumvented the summary executions taking place all around her. Some of the townsfolk she passed lived up to their religion, quoting scripture from mouths set in beaming smiles, embracing the bullet to the head that would start them on the path to transformation and spiritual ascension. If this bemused the greys conducting the massacre, more accustomed to scared victims begging for mercy, they showed no sign, and went ahead with their task with dispassionate efficiency;

it mattered not to them that the dead went willingly, only that they obeyed their masters' orders. The majority of the cultists stood shivering and crying, the comfort of their faith colliding with the cold hard reality of the apocalypse, as they waited for the undead creatures to enact judgement. Misha couldn't look them in the eye, her own fear too strong for her to contemplate herself, much less see it reflected in the faces of others.

"I don't want to go... I don't want to go..."

She was walking through rivulets of blood, tripping on limbs tangled on the path. Gunshots barked either side of her, and crimson sprays arced up the walls. All life was being ruthlessly purged, and she felt at that moment she was the sole keeper of something precious that others were trying to wrest away from her; even as she hugged it tighter to her breast, so they sought all the harder to steal it. With her energy dwindling, she could resist no longer.

Misha approached the H-wagons, and there, standing at the foot of the boarding ramp of the central ship, was a skeletal figure, its bony fingers around Arnold's throat, lifting him off his feet entirely. It was gazing at the cult leader's expression, helmeted head cocked to one side as if curiously examining a specimen it had discovered, and only when it became aware of the girl's presence did it turn its eyes in her direction. She felt herself gasping involuntarily, an instinctive reaction in the face of the figure's rictus grin, desiccated skin and dark, impenetrable visor. She didn't need to glance at the badge on its chest to know who this was.

It held her under its stare for several long moments, then looked back at Arnold, quietly choking in its grip. "Extinction isss not sssomething to be taken lightly," it said finally, once again studying its victim. Its voice was the sibilant whisper of dread; every terrifying moment of despair, every threat of violence, was imbued in the words that crept from its mouth. "I do not passss judgement purely for the thrill of it. It isss done for the good of the sssspeciesss. Only by exterminating all life can we eradicate criminality. Sssuch a Herculean tasssk has fallen to me to undertake, and I accepted it with due ssseriousssssnesss." It turned its attention back to her. "You understsstand that, don't you, Missshaa?"

"I... I don't know why so many innocents have to die," she replied, her tongue dry.

The figure gave the approximation of a laugh, sounding unhinged. "But there *are* no innocentsss. You are *all* guilty. That isss why we must be even-handed and sssyssstematic in our approach, why it mussst be conducted with absssolute dedication and adherence to the law. Thisss missscreant, though"—it shook Arnold, who emitted a gurgle—"sssought to pervert the processs of natural jussstice with his messsssianic nonsense, belittling it, turning it into a ssssidessshow. An *amateur*"—it spat the word out—"sssselling the end of the world assss a lifessstyle choice. I have no time for sssuch chancsssersssss."

"He thought we were all doomed anyway."

"Thusss you ssssinnerssss are denied the chance to come to termsss with your own guilt. Thissss fool embraced extinction because he thought he could leap into the grave without acknowledging hisss own culpability—"

If you knew the purity of the grave, you'd race towards it. A lingering imprint of Misha's psi-connection with her sister flashed through her head. Signifiers lit up, that all this had been pre-ordained, that she'd been receiving glimpses of her fate: pathways to the here and now.

"—but no one essscapesss justice, as it ssshould be delivered. By a Judge'ssss hand."

De'Ath's fingers disappeared into the meat of Arnold's throat, and the man's eyes rolled up in their sockets. Somehow, De'Ath managed to splay his hand beneath the jawline, and the next thing Misha knew the cult leader's body had dropped to the ground while his head remained gripped by the Judge, a gore-streaked hand puppet. De'Ath took one final look at it before slinging it to one side.

"I'm finding the flesssh of the guilty growsss more malleable asss our crusssade continuesss," he murmured, preoccupied with flexing his digits. "It'ssss like I am a sssword of righteousssnesss, cutting through the lawbreakerssss..." He turned his attention back to the girl. "I've been too long away from thissss. Delegating such tasssksss to otherssss, you forget the pleasssure there issss in bringing the guilty to account."

He walked towards her, and Misha felt her bowels loosen. The creature was a study in malevolence, both magnetically evil and too intimidating to even contemplate attacking. Could she try? Could she stop things if she dashed his skull open with a rock? Was he even *capable* of being killed? The idea of one last grand gesture floated across her mind... but then the moment was gone. He stopped a foot or so away and silently regarded her, as if tasting her sputtering life-spirit; then he glided past her. "The Ssssisssterss are waiting for you," he said without a backwards glance.

Misha staggered up the ramp and into the darkness of the craft. The background noise of butchery faded, and for the moment she could only hear the soft, shallow rasps of her own breath. Her legs felt heavy, and tiredness weighed upon her as the blood loss took its toll. She used the wall of the short corridor she was in to prop her up and guide her into the main cabin.

And then there they were, seated and expecting her. They wore the bodies of girls not of a dissimilar age to Misha herself, hair wild and unkempt, dressed in nothing more than shifts, barefoot... but she knew they were vastly older and more menacing than they initially appeared. They'd been in her head, and she'd gleaned something of their psyche in the process too—they were ancient beings, of enormous power and utterly alien in their disregard for any other living thing.

"Hello, Misssha," one said, smiling.

"Which one of you is which?" she asked.

"Which witch is which?" The girl to Misha's left shrieked with abrupt, maniacal laughter. "I'm Nausssea." She lazily proffered a hand that the young woman had no intention of shaking.

"Which I guessss makesss me Phobia," the other added, looking the teen up and down. "I can hear your heart sssslowing. You don't have long, do you?"

Misha shook her head, putting all her efforts into staying upright.

"You were quite the prize, my dear," Phobia continued. "Quite the catch. After what we dissscovered about your sssisster, and learning that there was another Cafferly out there... well, we jussst had to bring you in. But you've been very evasssive."

"Where's Rachel?"

The Sisters exchanged a glance. "She'sss helping usss with our work," Nausea said.

"Is she alive?"

"After a fassshion. Ssshe overcame the Dead Fluidsss, regained her sssensse of ssself—we'd never ssseen that before. We're not going to lossse our prime sssubject."

"To experiment on, in other words," Misha remarked, spots dancing before her eyes.

"Ssshe'sss invaluable, let'sss put it that way," Phobia said. "And you can be reunited with her. The sssibling you never knew you had."

Misha's gaze alighted on a section of the hull and she sidled towards it, making a play of stumbling. Phobia's and Nausea's eyes never left her. "What *are* you?" she asked them. "I mean, really."

"I guesss you'd call ussss representativessss, dear heart," Phobia said.

"Mediatorssss," Nausea added.

"For whom?"

"Thossse with... vessssted interessstsss. There are partiesss outsssside thissss world, whossse power issss beyond your imagining. When they contacted ussss—"

"—or *we* contacted *them*—"

"—or we contacted them. The back and forth between the veil *isss* sssomewhat fuzzy, isssn't it, Sissster? When contact wassss made, they gave usss the meansss to create a global mausssoleum in their honour. De'Ath wasss the firssst to transsssform and lead the crusade—the firssst of many."

"You were human yourselves once."

The witches glanced at each other and smiled. "Once, perhapsss. A long time ago."

"Do you feel nothing for the lives you're destroying?" Misha felt faint, light-headed. She leant against the wall, dizziness washing through her, her blood loss now taking its toll.

Nausea chuckled. "Ssssuch petty concernssss. Minissscule exissstencesss crussshed beneath our grand ssschemesss."

"No," Phobia said, "it doessss not bother usssss. Life isss a crime—there can be only one penalty."

"That's what I thought," Misha said, and pulled the Lawgiver from her waistband, levelling it at the pair.

The Sisters swapped amused looks before Phobia gestured towards the weapon. "What ussse isss that, girl? The gun issss palm-encoded."

"Oh, I know," Misha replied. "But the collateral damage should be enough."

She swung her arm down so the Lawgiver was next to the section of fuselage that she'd propped herself against, and pulled the trigger. The witches had watched the movement in confusion, only to see the gun resting against an ammo store—and realised a fraction of a second too late what she was intending to do. The moment the CPU in the gun failed to recognise that hand gripping it, it self-detonated, taking the teen's limb with it—and catching the volatile ammunition within.

The H-wagon shuddered as part of the hull blew out. Inside, the damage was more catastrophic; the ignited ammo blossomed within the confines of the cabin, filling it with a lethal hail of shrapnel. The Sisters shrieked and clutched at each other in a bid to shield themselves, but they couldn't escape it—their forms were shredded, their vulnerable human cloaks pureed. Equipment and screens inside the craft were also obliterated, the interior plunged into darkness as the systems were knocked out, and fires caught when the electrics blew. Within moments, the ship was aflame, listing over on one crumpled landing gear.

Misha scarcely had time to register the loss of her hand before taking the full force of the ammo going up. Her scorched, riddled form was thrown across the cabin.

The fire spread to the fuel tanks which detonated in turn, tearing the craft apart in an apocalyptic blast, spewing flaming debris in all directions, including onto the H-wagons on either side; they too were orange infernos not long after. Greys paused in their massacre to impassively watch the conflagration at the centre of the township; unchecked, the fires would eventually consume Libitina, eating the compound from the inside out.

EPILOGUE

One Month Later

THE THING THAT had once been Jackson McGill only had a vague approximation of a sense of self. Sometimes, it had thoughts, impressions, a hint of an identity, but these seemed like fragments of a dream it had once had, and could only recollect in a series of disconnected images. A word might trigger some spark of recognition—'box' held some undoubted significance, for some unknown reason, and it would study its hands for long moments, convinced that answers were wrapped up in them—or the sight of an object could resonate. But instances like these were not common, and they were fleeting; its mind was not sharp or nimble enough to often process just what it was that was engaging with its unconscious brain. It acted on instinct a lot of the time, reacting to external stimuli in much the same way a low-level organism might. It could remember faces and follow simple instructions, but no more so than a well-trained pet.

McGill the man was an outline, a loose sketch of an idea, and every so often a line was connected, a piece filled in, that fired a long-dormant synapse. But understanding lay frustratingly out of reach, and the shuffling, servile creature never got any closer to clarity. Nevertheless, it kept these memory jags to itself and didn't report them to Mortis or the Sisters; partly because it didn't know how to vocalise them, but mainly because they were without question forbidden, and could result in its dissolution.

It knew things, though—it knew that Mortis was its master, for example, and as such owed its existence to him. It knew that disobedience was an infraction punishable by dismemberment. And somehow it knew that it wanted to free the remains of the girls the Sisters had hooked up, deep in the bowels of the Grand Hall. It didn't know why it had this strong conviction to help them, but it had remained lodged in its simple mind ever since it had first seen them. Mortis's Red Mosquito psi-meme needed a signal boost to cover a wider area, and Phobia and Nausea had produced these battered heads, barely still functioning: one was Cafferly the Psi-Judge—it recognised her—and the other was a young woman, who didn't look entirely dissimilar. She was blackened and bruised, but somehow the witches had managed to coax some life into her.

The Sisters were impatient with the project, but their mood had been foul ever since they'd lost their human forms in the firefight up north. Their spirits would find new ones—hell, they could spin up fresh hosts just as easily as fashioning a dress—but for the time being it inconvenienced them that they were without their favourite cloaks of blood and bone. De'Ath came by once or twice, but seemed amused more than anything by the Sisters' consternation. He was spending more time outside the Hall of Injustice, claiming the politics were distracting him from enacting judgement.

Between Phobia, Nausea and Mortis, they'd been trying to draw more energy from the subjects, the witches clearly believing there was potential locked up in them, that each could augment the other. It felt a twinge, an unfathomable stab of regret, watching this, and knew it didn't want it to continue. Were Cafferly and her twin aware of each other? It thought so, and it got the impression they were tortured by their situation, wishing it would end.

The thing that had once been Jackson McGill stood before the two heads, plugged into Mortis's mainframe, and grasped the wires. Their eyes seemed to meet and urged it not to delay. It looked around furtively, making sure it was alone. It was taking what remained of its life in its hands, interfering with the Sisters' pet project like this. It was sabotage, insubordination. Punishment would be terrible and merciless. But it somehow knew it had to do this.

It felt like it was taking the fight to the right guy.

ABOUT THE AUTHOR

Matthew Smith was employed as a desk editor for Pan Macmillan book publishers for three years before joining *2000 AD* as assistant editor in July 2000 to work on a comic he had read religiously since 1985. He became editor of the Galaxy's Greatest in December 2001, and then editor-in-chief of the *2000 AD* titles in January 2006. He lives in Oxford.

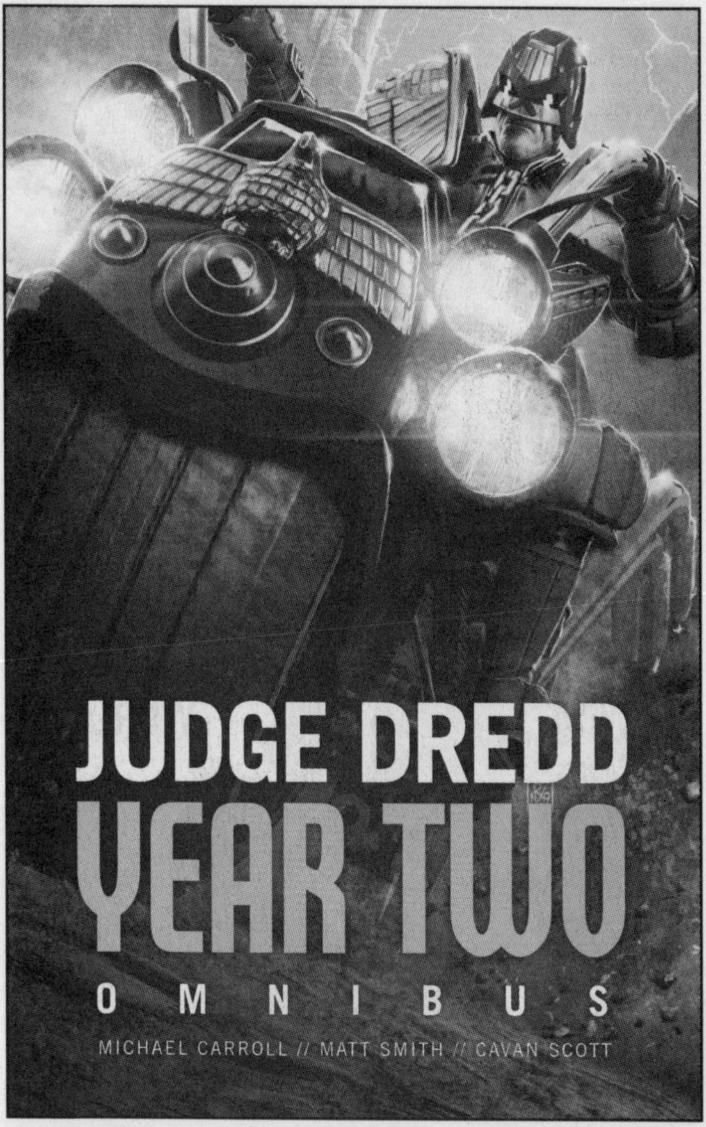
JUDGE DREDD
YEAR TWO
OMNIBUS
MICHAEL CARROLL // MATT SMITH // CAVAN SCOTT

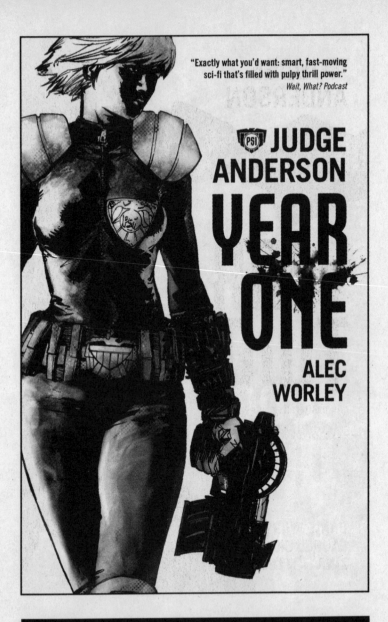

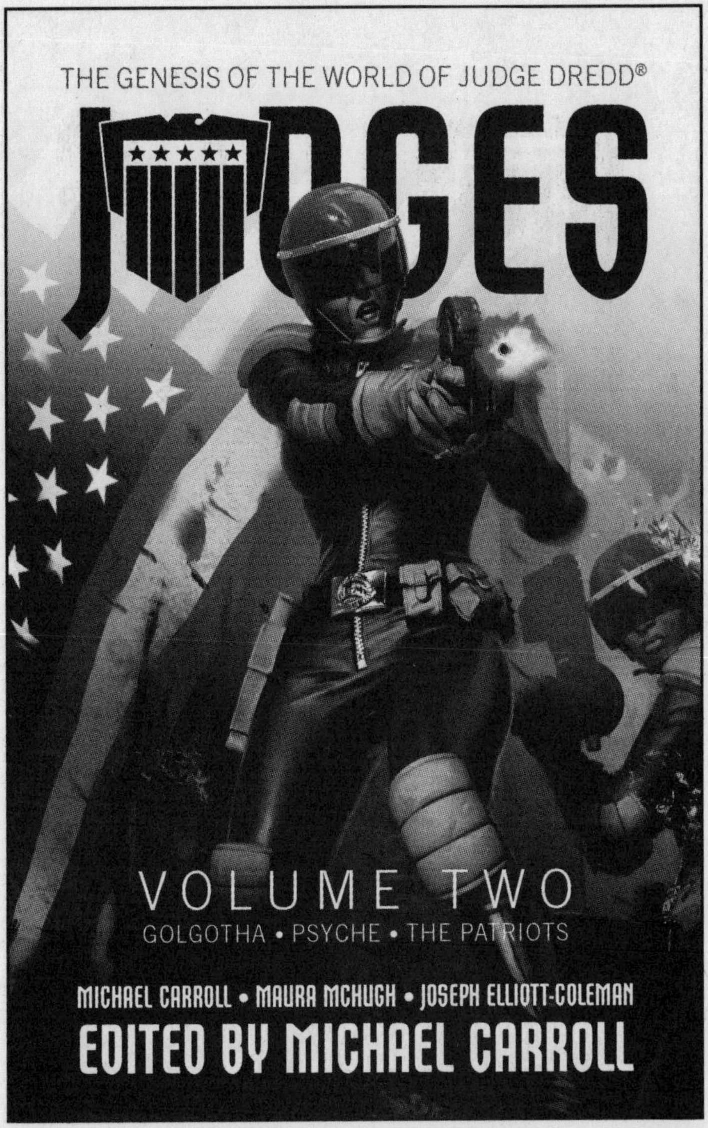
THE GENESIS OF THE WORLD OF JUDGE DREDD®
JUDGES
VOLUME TWO
GOLGOTHA • PSYCHE • THE PATRIOTS
MICHAEL CARROLL • MAURA MCHUGH • JOSEPH ELLIOTT-COLEMAN
EDITED BY MICHAEL CARROLL